In memory of Valerie Anne Ridgeway,
Mother, mentor, and cherished protector,
lovingly remembered through her selfless
desire to see her sons Tim, Jem & Mark
raised to become gentlemen.

Acknowledgements

In his travel book 'The Romancing of Rhodesia', A.S. Wadia talks of his enduring romance with Kashmir as 'that of a long-lost past and a decaying present', whereas he talks about; Rhodesia's as 'a pulsating present instinct with the promise of a glowing future.' The book was written in 1944 when paper shortages during the war had resulted in the book only being published in first edition in 1947. Wadia could not have known in those days during great human suffering, that his words would be of such significance sixty years later; a mere millionth of a second on the time scale of that grand vision etched into the African landscape, 'Victoria Falls'. His words would echo the suffering of a young nation intent on that bright future, but hamstrung by a litany of greed and self-aggrandisement. Never in the fragile history of such an infant nation had such infinitesimal injustices been borne by so eager a nationhood.

The failings of its leaders over those remarkably short sixty years had led to the promise being snuffed out by an ill wind, and all the 'abiding faith and unclouded vision' would be required all over again, to lift this chivalrous endeavour from the chronicles of a pitiful legacy and into the annals of unwritten history.

Those paper shortages, which had delayed the publishing of his tale of Romance, may well have been a harbinger of the crisis to follow. If Wadia had intended to defy the odds, traveling during a time when the world seemed intent on self-destruction; this haven of Utopia which had stood a billion years, unsullied by the ravages of a shifting world, but untainted by the human failings of recent times past, would have been no different. This was the Rhodesia of the early settlers, where man had been given the promise of a thousand years, but squandered it on the guarantee of an imminent future, short-lived and parochial. Thus, they had never given themselves a chance of this heralded vision of conquest and knightly pursuit, having failed to understand that the sacrifice of ancient crusaders was etched into history by not only their legends, but by subsequent authors with a penchant for the dramatic. Never has a Knight's Tale been written of those men that had failed in pursuit of their 'Holy Grail' and yet these men had taken this promise and paraded it as if it belonged to them alone; and the heritage of a bountiful land was worthlessly lost on human enterprise, that left nothing for its inheritors.

Somewhere in the mists of that savage continent, and from the clouds that hung over its ancient ramparts, on the edge of a chasm of infinite hope, was the makings of a history that would inspire subsequent authors to write. To write of these tales of crusaders and conquistadors, settlers and Voortrekkers, and just, maybe just, the promise of a tale of Courtney Selous, Alfred Beit and the subsequent pioneers. Call them what you might, colonizers, or conquistadors. The romance of that enduring legacy is stamped into the memories of an endearing nation, sacrificed in their blood on a largely forgotten land. It is of these pioneers in spirit that this novel has been written, in an attempt to write their contribution into a sadly misguided historical lunacy, that has seen the inherent injustices of that early nationhood, caste into the boiling pot of historical insignificance.

All this in a vain attempt to re-write those tales of fortitude and daring, as though they had been nothing more than a precursor to the main event, which a self-indulgent ruling class had deemed to be more important. Try as they might to claim sole ownership of their sovereign nation Zimbabwe, the historical facts stood as testimony to a savage continent, with even greater savage leaders. By erasing the road signs and place names of an infant nation, Mugabe did more to etch those names into the hearts and minds of a hopeful people, merely intent on eking out their own passage in the chapter of a history, in the final edition of a millennium old manuscript. Rhodesia had been the romantic castle, in a barbaric war of attrition, where self-effacement was not the objective, nor had been subsequently. Each of those who had come before, or after, had made the same mistakes, and to write some out of its brief history, was to fail to understand the journey it must travel.

So, like the 'thousand miles of pristine forbidding forests interspersed with grassy stretches of the open veldt', which had welcomed Wadia on his journey of enlightenment to the Dark Continent of 'Livingstonia'; this novel romances the one impalpable aspect of that expedition. What has driven men, from the ancient tribes who had hewn the rock edifice of the Zimbabwean ruins from the local granite formations, to the resting place of Cecil John Rhodes, whose burial site was engraved into those same granite rocks? The history of Zimbabwe had and must come full circle. Ignoring those contributions was tantamount to the defacing of a national treasure, and as with the Taliban in Afghanistan, who had erased the historical importance of the ancient Buddhists temples and rock carvings of several millennia; Mugabe and his henchmen were as guilty.

The leaders of the Great Zimbabwe would do well to remember the past, in order to heal themselves for the future. No amount of denial, from the eradication of street names, to the disempowerment of white politicians was going to serve any purpose. Mugabe would ultimately fail to write-off the past, as this undeniable travesty of injustice, would seem to foretell the history that would ultimately be written of him and his legacy.

All Zimbabweans would do well to recall what the 'Immigration Department of Southern Rhodesia' had told Wadia, before his epic travels; 'no restrictions would be placed and no distinctions made.' It was to this forbidding continent that he had travelled, and it is to this beacon of 'insurmountable divergences' that many a traveller should still; to Zimbabwe where 'lifelong convictions of common humanity and social equality,' can still be 'trampled upon by racial prejudices and colour distinctions.' This is a continent of forbidding injustices and grand ideals. No mere mortal would change the past, but a handful of those who cared, could with the same ambition that had brought their forefathers to the continent of Africa; change the outlook of a dismal past into the beacon of a bright future. It is to these pioneers of hope that I write, and to their courage and conviction to soldier on with the goal of a new frontier their common objective; which I petition.

Simon Paul

Foreword

Here's a novel that seeks to bring back to life the Africa of old: the old, dark continent, full of its mysteries, dangers and wonders. But not just a look at the past: a blending of past and present as the novel moves seamlessly from Zimbabwe to a stately home in England and from there to South Africa. Kenya, Malawi and the Congo are all traversed along paths known to the hunters of yore.

At the heart of the book, though, is Africa, which straddles no borders but spreads itself endless across savannah and jungle. And then there are the animals: the magnificent herds of matriarch-led elephants, the roar of lion and the puny adventures of humans as they strive to bend the wild to their own wills.

Here is Aubrey Pennington, the heir to a stately home and a title he doesn't want; here is the enigmatic butler (and so much more) Highpot; a former philosophy professor at King's College, Dingle, who is just a bit more than a retired academic who is more than he appears to be, and, of course, the babes who pop up everywhere.

You'll need a strong seatbelt to follow the intertwined plots and a geographic sense of where the novel plays out its stories, for they range far and wide and, of course, wild. A perfect book for armchair travellers and those who dream of Africa.

Jenny Crwys-Williams

Contents

Chapter 1

The Home coming

The gut-wrenching, rutted mud track ran through the forest with seemingly no end in sight. No sooner had they escaped the canopy of low hanging strangler fig branches at the crest of one rise; they were then met by the inevitable drop into the humid rain forest, and another series of bowel contorting twists and turns. The rains had lef7t the track knee deep in sludge, and in places the old Land Rover caught two wheels in the deeper ruts, and threatened to catapult its occupants into the dense vegetation. Built for hardy endurance marathons, she keeled over, the engine racing and the exhaust note becoming garbled as the exhaust sank below the pockets of liquefied mud. No sooner had it seemed that they were to be over-turned and lost in the undergrowth, then just as suddenly Angelo would wrestle the old three spoke steering wheel back on course. Each time, in concert with the roar of the diesel engine, the Landy was thrown back in line with the dark brown paths of mud, offering another chance for escape.

Aubrey and Angelo, jaws set in determination, were hurtling through the forest, their very lives dependant on that raging engine, cloaked by the dank water of a forgotten world. The tyres bit into the mosquito infested, primordial soup, throwing Aubrey against the raw metal door. He clung to the ragged edge of the door frame and with his right hand slipped under the seat frame he tried desperately to meet each jolt, by cushioning the muscles in his abdomen and breathing in as they escaped the quagmire, then sharply expelling his breath as they dived into the next rut.

Behind them they could hear the clatter of a distant AK47, as it emptied its magazine furtively into the canopy above them. Their pursuers were firing indiscriminately into the thick cover of the forest each time they reached a rise, but the sound of the gun fire began to weaken as Angelo raced along that ancient path, snapping branches that hung from a tangle of trees, untouched in generations. Generations of the lives of its original occupants; in that dark and mysterious realm! Inhabitants of that long forgotten world, whose wealth hung from those low-lying branches, in bunches of fruit and lush waxy leaves, that until now had remained the preserve of the Elephant!

Just as the great Airbus dipped its wing for the final approach to Gatwick, Aubrey was brought back to reality with a start. He had been dozing in his immense business class seat. The ravages of a twenty-hour journey, now taking its toll. He was now 44, but it had been some twenty years since he had seen his family home. He thought about that estate in Finsbury and how the years had not dimmed his memories. Of the grand entrance and the swooping marble staircase that had ascended like a renaissance rendition of the biblical Jacob's ladder. Aubrey had been born in that massive stately home, the product of his mothers' perseverance and his fathers' indifference. A midwife took care of his birth in the master bedroom, and his father, who had been out hunting duck when the momentous occasion occurred, had never been able to sleep in that bed again.

That world of ten servants and a menagerie of hounds and parakeets, had been electrified into sudden, cataclysmic chaos. Father who was titled and entitled by his enviable birth right, remained indifferent. Mother, had dealt with the birth and having secured the inheritance, became the care giver she had always desired to be. In so doing, it had left an indelible mark on the relationship Lord Pennington had with his only child. Aubrey had been born to a mother who was already in her forties and a father whose age would remain a mystery, until the funeral and subsequent reading of the will.

'God!' He thought. 'Was it really twenty years since he had seen his family home?'

What state of decay would he encounter? Would the impressive gates, that came into view after a two-mile hike down a quiet country lane, be the only things left standing after his absence in the heart of Africa? This had been his last view of the Estate as he left to pursue his travels, and it reminded him somewhat of the dirt tracks in Juba, Southern Sudan which had been his last port of call in the African hinterland. This was going to be some homecoming! Not a word had been said after his abrupt departure from his family solicitors' office in the City five years before. He had boarded a plane for the Congo two hours later, and would have only an annual account from the Pennington Trust Fund which was all that remained of his inheritance. It was to remain his only form of communication with the world he had left so hastily.

Aubrey Reginald Pennington, the only son of a callous and misogynistic father, and a quietly devout mother, was coming home to the very place his father had driven him from, and his only thoughts were; 'I wonder if the old gates are still standing?'

'Hell,' he thought, 'what would it matter if they weren't?' There was only one way they could have fallen and that was if an unlikely and direct cyclone or earthquake hit on the south of England, which is what it would take to shear the great stone towers from their footing.

'Mind you!' He mused. 'A cyclone might not be a far cry from reality, and given current weather patterns, who knew!' Aubrey smiled inwardly, but a clandestine turn of the upper lip, gave way to a chuckle.

'But would it be possible to have a generous hurricane or even one of those twister things touch down in West Sussex?' He chuckled to himself, with mirth at the workings of his own mind.

As he did so he looked up consciously, as his chuckle was now audible. He noticed that bloody awful chap sitting opposite him, who had taken off his shoes and socks earlier into the flight from Dubai.

'Hugh' had introduced himself after revealing his in-grown toenails. This gave Aubrey pause to think about those great dirty feet scratching in the earth, like some scruffy chicken in a remote Congo village in Yangambi Province. His thought transcended time and place despite the attentions of Hugh. He, like Aubrey had been upgraded from economy class to business.

'Why they had chosen him, he could not imagine.' Aubrey chuckled to himself again. It had been a lovely Emirate lass working behind the check-in counter at Dubai, who had offered him an upgrade. He had smiled devilishly at her with his flashing teeth, as he had caught the connecting flight from Kinshasa. Her eyes had creased up, averting them in an acknowledging and bashful manner, as she could not resist a forbidden smile behind her fashionable Hijab.

'He was some U.N. grave digger who was on his way back from a Congo faction fight in the East,' Aubrey reflected.

This fellow clearly had been there to count the skeletal remains of the genocide somewhere in Rwanda, and this was his employer's way of rewarding him for a job no one else could, nor would think of doing. Hugh was likely to be one of the statisticians from central office, and the leather pouch he had carefully secreted under his seat, filled with gruesome records, to justify some elaborate budget.

In the Southern Sudan on his last foray, Aubrey had witnessed the plight of those Elephant in the Garamba Province. There had been a long tradition of domesticating African Elephant in the Congo, and this pre-dated anything in the tourism trade by a hundred years. Aubrey had been shocked to see the condition of those Elephant, in contrast to his own operation up in Zimbabwe. They had been trained by the Belgian's in an effort to utilize their services in the rubber plantations of the Belgian Congo, and only a handful of Elephant remained, after several generations of these Elephant had died in the harsh conditions that was, and still is Central Africa. The UN was powerless to do anything about their plight, and it was only thanks to the help of certain animal rights organizations in the United States, that the issue was raised. But they were dismissed as irrelevant in a society intent on the destruction of all its resources for economic gain.

'The W.H.O. clearly wanted to be the do-gooders, bringing civilization to the 'great unwashed masses', as a way of purging themselves of all their Westernised collective guilt.' Aubrey reflected on his travels. But they had allowed the needless suffering of these animals because of humanitarian priorities. In Aubrey's opinion, there were already too many people on this earth! Helping save a few thousand more, would only proliferate the suffering of its animals.

'This', in his opinion, 'was as a result of handing over a continent to a largely ignorant people who had no idea of how to run a democracy, let alone an economy; let alone a continent!'

Aubrey stopped himself in mid-thought. He had to keep his bitterness towards the post suffrage franchise, with their sycophantic idealism in check. The U.N. had brought untold misery to Africa, despite their high ideals, and in the process endorsed a sybaritic social order amongst the political elite, driven by nepotism.

'The apple had not fallen far from the tree', he thought wryly. This was precisely what his father would have said. 'The heathens should have been left to butcher themselves!'

But despite his provocative thoughts, he had just spent the last ten years in a war-ravaged society, trying desperately to empower those less fortunate than the ruling tribe.

'No, this was no way of purging his contempt for that Kleptocracy! What would have happened if the United Nations had been disbanded back in '63 when the communists and the US had been at each other's throats?'

'A lot of ugly killings; so, what's new?' The Congo had become the graveyard of millions, through two African wars and copious billions of U.N. aid, whilst the political powers of Africa had jockeyed for position to profit themselves. Mugabe had played an integral part in that legalized war of attrition, as the rest of the worlds' focus was on another disaster of its own making. Whilst America and Europe focused on a cold war, communism and a subsequent rise in religious fanaticism, this had shielded the likes of Mugabe from being held accountable, for the injustices borne by their African populations. The Congo had been a veritable war zone over the last forty years and Aubrey, was only too aware of it.

He had played his part, albeit from a colloquial perspective. Aubrey would likewise need to purge himself of any guilt. Perhaps it was that his conscience was eating away at him again! This trip was critical to Aubrey's healing. This was his home coming thought! But would it be a 'home coming'?

This distraction had kept his mind pre-occupied when suddenly there was a jolt. He turned to see the tarmac appear out to the left, from his window seat, followed by yellow streaks passing under the fuselage and a wire mesh security fence washing past his view. Shaken back to the present, Aubrey gathered his thoughts and his belongings, and as soon as the Airbus ground to a juddering halt at the terminal, he was up and gone; that was, before he would have to make any small talk with Hugh.

A man stood at the exit to customs with a card with Aubrey's name on it. He hardly recognized the gentleman, but as he closed the several feet between them, he realized that the upright old gentleman, with bowler hat and bowtie, was none other than Mr. Highpot. Aubrey had as a child, endearingly referred to him as 'Highpot'. He was the estates' regal butler, driver and general gofer. He was a welcome sight indeed.

Aubrey took his outstretched hand - it was still firm, a little sinewy now, but still firm! It did not pretend to be assertive, but the duration and ambient temperature of this handshake, was the handshake of a man who held no societal pretences. Aubrey had studied body posture all his life. It was inherent in him like an electronic scanning device one uses to read a barcode. He was almost always; well at least 99% right and Aubrey had used this 'sixth sense' over the years to sum up friend or foe, in a matter of milliseconds. The angle of the proffered hand was upright, but not too assertive, firm but not arrogant. It just was! Aubrey briefly reflected on all those wet slippery handshakes of the man-servants he had used in his various abodes in Africa. The hand was always supine, placid, and almost suppliant. This was because their culture dictated a hierarchy based on paternalism. One was expected to show humility to the Chief always. Maybe that's why the people of Zimbabwe could not 'shake off' the repressive regime of Robert Mugabe. They were brought up to be submissive and to respect their elders. This had been of historical significance since the Great Zimbabwe, and tales that had been written of Alan Quattermain and King Solomon's

Mines. They had eulogized the relationships between King's and their subjects.

'It was their Achilles heel', thought Aubrey. 'They are doomed to be repressed, whether by the colonialists or by those raging megalomaniacs, who always die in office, fearing they will be shot, stabbed of poisoned if they relinquish power democratically. This was because a thousand years had taught them to apply the 'Brutus Strategy'. It is a 'kill or be killed philosophy!'

Aubrey was brought back to the present again as Highpot withdrew his hand and reached down to take Aubrey's hand luggage from him.

"Good morning Mr. Pennington. How was the flight?" always cordial and correct.

Realizing his bad manners, Aubrey smiled and placed his hand on Highpot's shoulder reassuringly giving it a brief squeeze saying.

"Fine, Mr. Highpot. But a little too long, as always! How have you been?"

"Well, thank you Sir." He was lying! Aubrey sensed the pain fifty years of service had scarred him with. 'Yes, fifty years', thought Aubrey. 'Now that's a long time!'

"What's the plan for today?" Aubrey asked, briskly getting on with the day's agenda. He was not sure what this trip had in store for him!

"We plan to take you back to Finsbury Sir!" replied Highpot, his left eyebrow arching as he said it.
Aubrey withdrew his hand. He was confused. How could they be staying at the Estate? Even his grasp of the financial statements of the Estate had led him to assume the place would have been abandoned!

"Why Sir, had you other plans?" Highpot enquired. But realizing he was prying, he corrected himself, "Perhaps Mr. Pennington would like to see some of the countryside?"

"No, no," interjected Aubrey, "It's just that I did not realize the Estate was habitable."

"Goodness. Yes, Sir," offered Highpot, "the Estate is as you left it Sir!"

Now it was Aubrey's turn to raise his eyebrow. "What, the place is still fit for human habitation?" I would not have mattered if it wasn't.

"Most certainly Sir, we have kept it in excellent condition and your personal items have been moved to the Master bedroom!"

A vision quickly shot across Aubrey's subconscious. It was that recollection of his father's verbal and physical tirade the day he had ventured into the master bedroom. Aubrey was lying in bed hugging his mother who was feeling very ill, or as his father put it more to the point, 'Drunk as a skunk again'. Far from being drunk, it was 10am and Aubrey's mother was admittedly nursing a hangover from the red wine of the night before. Something she did most nights. But these symptoms were rather more emotional than physical, as Aubrey's mother was suffering none other than a broken heart. Something his father refused to acknowledge. Seeing Aubrey lying in the great master bed with her had sent his father into an abusive rant. This sent the dogs scurrying out, the servants ducking into the pantry and cellar, and Aubrey diving under the silken quilt. He had been afraid of his father; that is until he became a grown man. Avoiding the projectiles being launched at him, from the welsh dresser and bookshelf in the room had somewhat jaded his view of his father. Despite this he had still sought his approval!

"You're kidding me?" Aubrey had almost assumed that Finsbury Hall would have been derelict and overgrown with weeds. The last time he had seen it was the morning before setting off on his travels twenty-two years before. The accounts he had been receiving had not painted a positive picture, and he imagined the weeds covering those once elegant lawns, and creepers growing through the oak sash windows.

"No not at all!" Highpot, himself was now confused. He was not to know that the accounts had been sent to Aubrey, but they had only contained his father's inheritance.

Aubrey did not venture anything further. This he had to see! He recalled his last memory of that room. It had been opulent, with tall southern facing Bay windows surrounded by large drapes, hung in a fashion that was contemporary Edwardian, but with a modern flair. He had remembered how the light had filtered through to the old four-poster, catching the gilt-edged tassels that hung from the canopy.

Aubrey had never again ventured into that room, especially when his father had been around, but had dared to peek into his father's dressing room when there had been a family tragedy sometime later. His mother and father had been called urgently to London one summer evening. He had never been given any details about that, and years later, as a teenager arriving back from boarding school, he had quizzed his mother on it. She had dismissed it out of hand. His interest had been piqued, although he could never get it out of her.

As they walked quickly to the exit, Aubrey's mind wandered again. Getting back to his vision of the master bedroom, Aubrey wondered how his father had managed to always look clean and tidy while sleeping in the guest suite of the eastern annex, with his clothes kept in the dressing room of the master bedroom. Had this, as he suspected all been a rouse?

When as a young man about to embark on his journey of adulthood to the esteemed Kings College, he had quizzed his mother on the finer details of his parentage. She had denied there being anything out of the ordinary. She had remained steadfast to her only love and for appearance-sake had defended Lord Pennington to the end. Only the servants of course knew the tawdry details of his fathers' nocturnal visits to the servants' quarters; and they were sworn to secrecy by their blind loyalty to 'Ma'am'.

His father had been guilty of this misdemeanour since the early years, but by then Aubrey, the only child was to become the heir apparent to the Estate. Everyone knew that the Lord and master of the Estate had not been terribly forthcoming with his 'marital duties', but that did not concern anyone other than Lady Pennington. Her unfailing love had been her downfall. She had taken to drinking in excess to deal with her broken heart, and as in any dysfunctional family the details were kept to themselves, at the expense of their sanity. Aubrey was to be born into a very wealthy family, and a title to which his mother had aspired, was assured due to the good old English tradition of 'keeping up appearances'. But his true heritage would remain unknown. This was as a consequence of his father's impropriety, and his mothers' singular indiscretion, brought about by jealousy and a few too many glasses of wine. She had fallen pregnant immediately, an over-abundance of hormones and undeniable good luck; or bad luck depending on which perspective one held. Aubrey was thus not terribly close to his father. There was not to be any other children, as the 'new' Lady Pennington would never be so indiscreet again, and Aubrey was to become an only child.

As they reached the end of the arrivals hall ramp, a gold coloured Phantom Rolls Royce came into view. This was the same family car Aubrey had been chauffeured back and forth in as a child, whilst later attending Kings College. She looked in fine fettle and Aubrey was amazed to see the white wall tyres and paintwork looking brand new. A young man seated behind the wheel, cap and tunic, erupted from the driver's side and darted for the rear of the vehicle to open the large boot, greeting Aubrey as they approached.

"Good morning Sir. May I take that Mr. Highpot?" he asked in an eloquent accent that was not 'Kings' but could have been mistaken for one of the lesser Colleges. Aubrey was by now quite bemused. Who was this second man, and why all the hoopla for such a singularly unimportant event? He had never imagined that he would be here, being ushered into a car he had long considered to be somewhere in a scrap heap. In fact, he had not even thought about it; these were unimportant trivialities in his world. A dented and thorn tree scratched '54 Landy had sufficed as his transport for the last five years.

"Please Sir," proffered Mr. Highpot opening the large rear door, while the new man quickly dispensed with the luggage and eased the boot lid closed without slamming it.

Aubrey gave Mr. Highpot a quizzical look, waiting for an introduction, but none was forthcoming. He figured sometime he would be obliged with an explanation, so slipped gently into the plush red leather interior of the graceful old beauty. He could smell the leather as if it were newly upholstered. The smell evoked childhood memories of his excitement at taking trips to the country fairs with Highpot, or to the local Finsbury village to fetch the double thick crème the local dairy had become famous for. Home for tea and English scones – not just any scones mind you - as the light pastry texture crumbled in the hand and melted on the tongue! Nothing beat those scones served with over sweet strawberry jam, and topped with the pure non-pasteurised double thick Finsbury decadence.

The door closed behind him and Aubrey reclined into the gracious armchair of the rear seat. The front doors opened and Highpot and the new man climbed in, without a word and off they went. The grand old lady on the bonnet guided them down the exit lane to the motorway. What had changed? Perhaps it was Aubrey, but there was a malleable sense of expectation in the air, as if the lack of introduction to this new man was not hard enough to reconcile, the furtive look between the two front seat occupants was secretive; almost ridiculous. Aubrey was not a man prone to drama and this was fast becoming a game. Like the 'I spy with my little eye' games long forgotten but never the less hugely entertaining, that Aubrey and Highpot had played when setting off on those excursions to the village. Disregarding the rigid formality of it all, Aubrey sat forward in the spacious seat and gripping the back of the palatial front seats as he had done as a child, he asked.

"So Highpot, who's the new man?"

Another furtive look between them, and then a sense of ease settled in.

"My apologies Mr. Pennington," returned Highpot. "This is Mr. Shaun, my son!"
"Good Lord, Highpot," exclaimed Aubrey. "When did this all happen? You old dog, you've been sneaking around behind our backs all these years?" Aubrey found himself openly expressing, and then realizing his gaff, he quickly corrected his bad form.

There was a further furtive glance, and had Aubrey not been so intrigued, he would have been exasperated by the conspiratorial air. Highpot was a man nearing his eighties in age, and he had certainly never given Aubrey, or anyone else for that matter, any indication of this earth-shattering event!

"The truth Sir is that Mr. Shaun is adopted, but he has been living with me as my son for twenty years." This was unexpected news.

"What! I never knew this."

Another exasperated look between father and son! They did not look at all similar. Despite Highpot being a slightly less impressive 5'11, although somewhat bent over now, he used to stand 6'1. The new man - sorry, Shaun, was a less-imposing 5'8, but had an uncanny resemblance to someone Aubrey knew, but could not place for now. So, if Shaun was his Christian name, his surname would then be Highpot then? Aubrey surmised.

Realising that he was quickly making a few too many gaffs Aubrey offered.

"I mean, really Highpot that's wonderful. You never mentioned anything about a son before!" Aubrey was secretly envious. He had considered Highpot more than a confident.

Silence was followed by an awkward cough from Highpot. Shaun fixed his gaze firmly on the road ahead, not venturing any comment.

Aubrey realised that he had somehow overstepped the boundary of good manners, and quickly and nonchalantly dismissed it all by adding, "I have several children all over the world, Highpot, there's no shame in having at least one!"

This did not help either. Highpot's silence was evidence enough that Aubrey's gaff was more than just a no-go area it was now becoming extremely uncomfortable.

"No worry sir, Dad has only had a while to get used to the idea," the moment had been saved by a crisp interjection from Shaun. Succinct and enunciated with clear authority of the spoken language.
"Ahh! I see," responded Aubrey, a furrow appearing between two full brows, but thankful for the release it had provided. He sat back in the comfort of that great leather interior, and the feeling of being cocooned, embraced him in his fond childhood memories again. Before too long he had escaped the silence and was washed away in his own thoughts.

The motorway gave way to a slip road to the country, which they manoeuvred onto; 'ironic that,' he thought as they trundled away from the traffic, 'this ring road, is supposed to be the lifeblood for London and the southeast, and is actually strangling its road occupants to death. 'The cholesterol that is hardening and blocking the source of its life-giving veins!'

They found the regional road that went through West Sussex, past Dunsfold and onto the sleepy village just outside Alfold. Soon the oak trees alongside the Estate's thousand yard newly gravel-strewn driveway, whooshed past the rear window. The newly shone tyres scrunched happily across the gravel before reaching the grand entrance of those imposing gates of Finsbury Estate.

Amazing, how they never ceased to impress him. Aubrey sat in the back as the gates opened electronically, almost as dramatic as a slow drawbridge to some mythical castle! One thing was for sure, this place was a myth unto itself. How had the family's sordid past escaped him for so long? As a young man growing up within the surrounds of this very place, he had scorned the treachery and deceit that epitomized everything the Estate stood for!

Aubrey had wandered through the first twenty years of his existence, unaware of all the intrigues and rumours floating around. His distant childhood memories soon gave way to a familiar knot in his stomach, which represented the distaste he had developed for those stately lawns and its grandiose water features - aspiring to be a mini Versailles in the heart of England. All the memories of chasing headlong into the duck ponds and hanging perilously off the algae stained statuettes, all the while furtively checking to ensure his father was in proximity, so as to catch his eye or impress him with his antics. Long forgotten in the haze of childhood naivety and giving way to a sense of unrequited love, Aubrey had languished for too long hoping to be the apple of his father's eye. Eventually all he had was a need to escape the hurtful indifference that came to characterize this relationship. His father had succumbed to arrogant disdain. Sometimes he was sure his father looked at him in a supercilious manner, with that knowingly smug demeanour. Today Aubrey considered such a look as one of disdain, but he had never understood what it meant coming from his father, at the time.

There was no doubting Aubrey looked nothing like his father. The hair was thick, darker than his father's and his chin somewhat jauntier than his father's weaker jaw line. Sometimes he would catch his father looking at him in profile and the exchange was always an uncomfortable one. He would be looking at his mother across the vast Rhodesian teak dining table, and in the framed mirror that stretched the length of the room, he would see his father assessing him. Aubrey, as a younger man, always returned his father's gaze, but this gave way to discomfort in later years, as he realised that his father was pretending not to be paying any attention to him.

As the Roller entered the gates with their bold repousse metalwork, Aubrey had an epiphany. The hymn he sang as a child in the cathedral came to mind; 'I will enter his gates with thanks giving in my heart; I will enter his gates with praise.' This was an unfamiliar thought, and Aubrey was amazed he could remember the words so readily. Perhaps this epiphany was a spiritual blessing. He had come to understand his heightened sense of spirituality in recent years. This was brought on by his health problems, and a deepened sense of communing with nature, during those long summers in the interior of the African jungle. Interesting! He mused, 'Maybe his mother was trying to connect with him again?'

As they began the final approach to the Manor house, Aubrey could see that the place had not changed at all. In fact, the neatly manicured lawns were exactly as they had been all those years ago, and the Ponds and fountains welcomed his return with a silvery brilliance reflecting the early morning sun. This was completely contrary to what Aubrey had imagined would be the case. He had been expecting a dilapidated stone brick ruin with overgrown weed infested lawns. What greeted his return was the splendour and grace of a timeless fairy tale. The fountains were in full cry, trumpeting his arrival into the air. The ponds beyond were sparkling blue and the wild fowl were in full residence, gracefully conducting their choreographed performances like figure skaters gliding on ice. They swept first this way, then that, foraging for titbits that floated unseen on the surface of the ponds. The Manor came into view over the brow of the hill, emerging as elegantly as the granite cliffs of Ngorogoro gorge, when one ascends from the forest canopy and into the African sun. The structure was still impressive, the

Edwardian parapet still glowing in bold yellow stone, reflecting the early sun, accentuating its luminous tinge. The sight almost caught Aubrey off guard. He was slightly breathless. This was one familiar sight he had never expected.

He bolted forward from his cushioned repose, as this stately home crowned in such magnificence was stunning to behold. Not even the granite cliffs of the Zambezi Gorge, cleaved by millions of years of erosion, were quite as shockingly beautiful as this. As he did this, Highpot and Shaun gave each other a look, which could only have been a knowing affirmation. Aubrey felt like a child again. As if this was one of his regular homecomings from all those years ago, his excitement was palpable, and he sat on the edge of the seat waiting to alight. The two in front allowed themselves a knowing smile and Highpot half-chuckled for the second time this morning. "Welcome home Mr. Pennington," he quipped.

'Well this was a pleasant surprise', he thought. Funny, it did feel like home despite all his previous misgivings. There was no way he could, nor would have imagined his feelings at this moment. He certainly would never have allowed himself to feel this way. He had not been home in twenty-two years, but he felt as though in a dream, he would have remembered it just as this.

The Roller slowed and came to a gentle halt in front of the monolithic columns caste from the great Zimbabwean granite of the Matopos hills. Years before, the ancestors of Pennington had dragged these massive stones from the virgin hills of the Matopos, in a province called Matabeleland. These vast golden columns were in fact hewn out of the very stone, that the great colonialist Rhodes had been buried in. The resting place of colonial power; the one great export Britain had given the world in pre-Edwardian times. The columns were impressive and had such a lustre that caught the rays of the early morning sun. Aubrey could imagine the huge outcrops of the stone rising out of the African bushveld, its shimmering stonework a testament to the erosion of millennia. Ironic, he thought, 'that the great Zimbabwe, which had super-ceded the Rhodesian era of subjugation of the Matabele and Shona tribes, had itself become a system of terror and repression.' This was the very reason he had chosen not to live in Zimbabwe. The pain of witnessing the insidious decline of a country his great grandfather had helped to drag out of the Stone Age.

Well quite literally, this stone had been dragged out of Zimbabwe, and was the only remnant of the Pennington footprint on the African hinterland. The columns stood as a witness to the arrogance of colonialism. To think that Britain thought they could pull that heathen nation from their ancient way of life in a mere century! The possibility existed, that a fair and honest dispensation could, in time eradicate the turmoil that had been left behind in a trail of wanton destruction. In the case of Zimbabwe, which was currently being ransacked for its raw material, the jovial hard working labourers were the only people who could salvage anything. It was their nation which was now being further raped in the lust for metal and minerals, which the Chinese desperately need for the expansion of their own massive economy.

It was the rise and fall of civilizations, while generation after generation, failed to learn from the former. This was Mugabe's legacy, and in it, he was determined to erase recent history, in a vain attempt to cut off the life-blood of what had been created by the white settlers. The land was what it all came down to. Mugabe wore that banner as a vestige of historical significance, attempting to reverse the injustices of the past by holding onto power! Wars, and skirmishes against the Shona tribes had removed the local inhabitants from the best farming land. But they had not learnt the mistakes of that recent past. No injustice, however marked, could be revised by further injustices! 'Just consider, he thought, Zimbabwe without a Robert Mugabe?'

'It would not have mattered,' he concluded to himself. 'One dictator or another; they were all the same. If the population had not the will or desire to fight for their own hard won democracy, they would never break the shackles of repression. They would simply exchange one dictatorship for another, in whichever guise it presented itself. It was all about the money in the end. Cynical? Well yes, he knew he was – but he knew that this was realistically the basis for all wars. And the next one was still to be fought.'

Aubrey was dragged back to the present, by the door being prized open. The smell of roses and something else wafted through his senses; followed by a more pungent smell that attacked his senses.

'What was that?' The scent was emanating from the gardens on the cusp of the gravel driveway. There was an odour that Aubrey remembered. 'Was it from his childhood? No this was definitely more recent!'

He climbed out of the Roller, and stretched. As he breathed in the fresh morning air, it hit him again. This was the smell of Africa welcoming him home. On closer inspection of the garden, he saw the culprit. It was the Flame Lily, which also grew on the great outcrops of granite that dotted the Zimbabwean landscape. The red and yellow petals emblazoned with its familiar motif, giving it its colloquial name. 'Funny that! This flower was a protected species in Zimbabwe; what was it doing growing in this climate? This was unusual for a savannah species of plant - hardy and drought resistant, and yet it seemed to be thriving in the heartland of England.'

Aubrey stooped to look at the flower growing up against the grand portals that towered above him; 'This was going to be another interesting journey indeed!'

The lily was the very essence of Zimbabwe, rarely seen anywhere other than the vast grasslands of the African savannah. The plant was a loner like Aubrey; it grew in the shallow soil of the rocky outcrops, defying the odds as it erupted from the earth like an allegorical flame, spouting forth to rekindle the dying flames of a lost nationhood.

'Maybe the Flame Lily could once more become the symbol of a proud national heartbeat. Strange, that the very marketing campaign of the seventies, to instil a sense of pride into that dying nation should have been named after this singular flower!' Aubrey could see how this flower had become a national treasure. It was a pity though, that while the flower survived, the flame of the resistance movement, had not. This simple flower had been the pre-cursor to the demise of the Old Rhodesia and with it that symbolism had pre-empted the rise of a tyrant. Tyranny was fleeting though, and that nation had seen many who had attempted to subjugate the people and its' land for their own benefit; but that simple flower had grown out from the cracks in the lee of those great granite out-crops, as if in defiance of the odds.

Maybe by eradicating the natural beauty of the nation, and destroying all symbols of its colonial heritage, Mugabe could continue to cling desperately to his fantastical sense of power. Even the Zimbabwe Ruins, itself, stood as a classical reminder of how the breadbasket of Southern Africa had become its', basket case. Those ancient ramparts built to an earlier civilization that had roamed the plains in search of gold and ivory.

How had a nation, able to build such a splendid structure, with it conical towers and vast inner walkways with towering granite walls, become so ruined? That was, if they had indeed built it? Perhaps the powers that be, that renamed it 'Zimbabwe', should have given thought to how this would be seen in the context of a national disaster. The name translated in a dialect called ChiKaranga, 'the great or big house built of stone boulders', was literally 'ziimba remabwe'. The ruins were still standing though, despite Mugabe's best efforts!

Aubrey could not but feel a great sense of homecoming as he ventured through the great entrance hall and on into the vast panelled reception room. He was indeed, home at last!

Chapter 2

Day dreaming

Aubrey had slipped up to the Master bedroom on the south-eastern wing of the Manor house. Highpot had suggested a nap before lunch was served, and Aubrey had gratefully accepted. Twenty-four hours of travelling had exacted its toll and he was finished.

Before climbing into the voluminous bed, which he could remember only too well, he removed his sneakers and trousers, donned a clean T-shirt from the hand luggage and clambered into that stately bed. The linen smelt of crisp daffodil filled fields, soaked in a tapestry of sensual aromas melting into his senses and evoking an immediate slumber.

Aubrey was floating on that wafted breeze, cart-wheeling through a summer of un-requited love. The fields awash with those daffodils calmed his breathing and softened the crease lines, scoured into the folds of sun-soaked skin around his eyes. He was totally relaxed and the arduous past two weeks began to slip away. Oblivion approached and his last conscious thought was his Mom.

She was standing at his bedside. He was six years old and she had stroked the sweat off his brow, one more time and calmed his ragged breath. The night sweats had been accompanied by an irrational fear, which always provoked them. He was falling, spinning uncontrollably into a darkened crevasse. There was no sense of the bottom, just an endless free-fall, spiralling to infinity. In his mind's eye, Aubrey knew he could control that fall, but it seemed dark and threatening. He was conscious, each time he had that dream that his mother was always with him. She was always at his bedside, but he could not prevent the dream. It had begun at the age of six and continued for two years. He could not quantify how many times it had occurred, but knew the fear was real. Each time it occurred, his breathing quickened, his head thrashed from side to side, and an overwhelming sense of evil permeated his core. Aubrey could not understand why his thoughts were provoked with this over-whelming sense of trepidation. Then one night, as he lay shaking from the cold-sweat, and his mother had retired to her bed, exhausted from her midnight vigil, Aubrey had an unequivocal epiphany. He climbed out of bed, conscious of a fear that something lay in wait below his bed, and grasping his palms together as he had seen done by the devout old ladies in the parish pews, he began to pray.

It was un-solicited and felt entirely natural. He held his palms together, wringing his hands as if to squeeze that evil from his very being, and he prayed.

"Dear God," he had vocalised. "Help me to fight the bad man who is hurting me." He knew that somewhere there was a bad man, he did not know where or why, but his immature brain had sensed this as the source of his pain.

"Make me strong and able to beat the bad man," he had persisted. There was solace in that mantra and in repeating those words he drew courage from the sense that he was not alone in his fight. Aubrey continued to pray those words, well into his teens, and in the knowledge, that he would always defeat the sinister powers that crept up on him in the late hours of the night, he could gain the sleep he had sorely coveted.

The bed-wetting had ceased and his midnight forays of sleep-walking subsided. In his embrace of a supernatural champion, he had defended himself from a force he now recognised as his own irrational sense of isolation. Aubrey would attend boarding school, without the added angst of having his nocturnal apparitions become a source of humiliation. He did, however, have to defend his right to pray at his bedside, a constant reminder to him, that he was somehow different to the other boys.

Aubrey, now fast asleep, in that comforting king size bed, began to dream of another home.

The morning sun had risen behind the dark and brooding Kopje. The camp had been set up away from the ridge, so as to ensure no prowling Leopard would venture towards the hastily erected bivouac. Whenever they had followed the elephant herd, he and his guide, had often had to make temporary shelters. To stave off exhaustion and hunger, they set up their camp, wherever they could, without disturbing the herds.

In the early morning mist that settled over the savannah Aubrey had sensed an air of tranquillity. The acacia mangrove had offered shelter to the herd and Aubrey and Wellington had been careful to camp down wind, so as not to startle the matriarch and her brood. She was a savvy old gal, whom Aubrey had assessed from her thick-set tusks an age of between fifty and sixty. She had led the herd from the dried-up watering hole, on the fringes of the national reserve, all the way along the now infamous Caprivi Strip, skirting the old Elephant paths and avoiding human settlements. Aubrey had made his notes each night, and plotted their progress on his fold-out map. She was as wise as King Solomon.

The ancient paths had crossed the border with Zambia and the old gook trails that had been rendered no-go areas by the planting of land mines. She had almost willingly skirted the rim of the northern Caprivi and as they had reached each ancient path, she had ventured just far enough North so as to test her senses to the limit. Whenever the herd came across the old desiccated bones of their own ancestors, she would stop at the grave site and inspect each set of bones. The Elephant had a sense of smell twenty thousand times more powerful than humans. Lifting the sun-bleached bones in her trunk, she would gently hold each piece reverently towards the herd, as they sniffed and inspected each. The way she turned each set of bones was not unlike that of an archaeologist coming across a sarcophagus in an ancient temple. She would delicately turn each remnant of that animal as if the very life blood still coursed through those bones.

Aubrey always kept a good distance as a mark of respect, but was fascinated by this reverence she had for one of her own. He could almost recognise in her, the human characteristics of an old-school Ma'am relaying the wisdom of the ages. The young ventured close, raising their trunks, and sniffing cautiously at the wizened old bones. Sun, wind and what rain had fallen, not to mention scavenger's teeth and claw marks had rendered the ancient relics unrecognisable. But she lifted each, as though the essence of each of her ancestors lay within those brittle bones and holding them aloft, it reminded Aubrey of the Gravediggers speech from the Shakespearean rendition of Hamlet, he had taken part in whilst at Eton.

"Alas, poor Yorick! I knew him, Horatio."

The words came back to Aubrey as though he were reciting them just the other day. The irony would have been more palpable had Aubrey not seen the humour in that brevity with which Shakespeare dealt with death. It required something similar within humanity to understand that the cultural icon of Yorick's skull being held aloft was ingrained in society. But to these Elephant, that moment of recognition to one of their own, was not so dissimilar as to make it truly human.

Had there been any humour to lessen the tragedy of that moment, Aubrey would have grabbed it with both hands; but alas, there was only a sense of the callousness of man and the brooding acceptance of that Matriarch. She knew only too well, the source of that wanton destruction and for now she kept the herd well away from it.

Aubrey and Wellington had watched in silence as she had taught the lessons of time, so that even the frolicking calves stood still for a moment to pay their respects. Aubrey sat, taking notes and attempting to capture his reflections of that moment. There was a lesson that mankind could learn, but Aubrey knew that therein lay the rub. Without the opportunity for each human on this earth to physically capture that moment for themselves, the senselessness of wanton greed and destruction held no sway. The world was too over-populated with humans and each decade that passed, secured the demise of these Elephant. The chances that mankind, a misnomer; could ever find a way of balancing their existence with these vastly intelligent animals, was highly unlikely.

Aubrey dreamed of the vast flowing Zambezi, into which the herd would have plunged, had it not been for the wisdom of that matriarch. She had scouted the southern bank of the river and led them towards the backwaters of the Chobe, where the river widened and lost its brute force. Here Aubrey and Wellington would have to leave them, as they crossed the calming eddies of the main tributary and swam despite their bulk, with the efficiency of a bull elephant seal. Time and circumstance would take the family away from him for this season, but next year Aubrey would be back and take off a few more weeks to learn from that growing clan.

Wellington would sit and impart all the knowledge he had gained from his fifty odd years, in the bush. Aubrey soaked up that wisdom and knew it would come in use sometime in the future. The size, shape of the ears; length of the trunk and each scoured marking on their tough old hides, were a constant source of wonderment. Wellington could recognise each of the herd by their silhouette and Aubrey would come to learn as much in time about how to identify the young males by the enlarged protrusion on their foreheads; decipher each left-handed or right-handed of the herd by the way they lifted their trunks to their mouths. This was the knowledge Aubrey relished and following that herd for ten years, he came to learn their secrets and each season they had become closer. He had gleaned a huge knowledge of the Elephant; but he still could not fathom mankind.

As he lay dreaming, Aubrey had a recollection of the day he had followed the herd in a thick area of dense brush. They had been watching the matriarch as she had lead the young females with their calves, directly into a gulley, through which the herd had meandered. Grazing on the rich supple bark off the baobab trees, the herd had found a plantation of these trees, their thick round boughs, almost impervious to the gouging tusks of the herd. They roughly peeled the bark as they sauntered through the deep gulley, and Aubrey and Wellington had a great view of the youngsters as they waited patiently for the elder females to show them how to strip the smooth bark.

Aubrey noted how they were almost pedantic in the way they chose their favourite tree. The bark offered a rich source of calcium and the sinewy crushed residue, provided good roughage to complement the early morning feast they had dined on the acacia mangrove. Aubrey sat on a large granite rock, overlooking the gulley, in the shade of an Acacia which offered what little shade there was during the sweltering heat of mid-day in the Zambezi Valley. As Wellington pointed out the youngster's antics, Aubrey took notes of which of the younger males fraternized with one another, and how the females almost sedately, brushed off their over-exuberance. The great trunks swished through the air, momentarily testing the air for danger, then gorging once more on the bark, then stripping more bark and stuffing it into their prehistoric looking mouths. They ground away on the mouthful and continued their carefree foraging.

It was as they watched the last of the young females rounding up the stragglers and swatting them lazily with a prompt of the trunk that Wellington placed a reassuring hand on Aubrey's knee and motioned to be silent, with a finger to his lips. Aubrey turned slowly to follow his gaze.

He was searching the brush off to his left, through the dense thicket on the verge of the gulley. Aubrey was almost about to ask, when he saw a slight movement of grey against the darker black of granite. There, almost a stone's throw from their position he spied an eye, watching them. The large round eye, unblinkingly regarded them from the camouflage of a dense thicket. Only the subtle movement of ears, fanning through the humid air of the summer haze, had given up her position. Wellington whispered into Aubrey's ear.

"She has been watching us for fifteen minutes."

Aubrey turned his head to look at Wellington. His smile showed his complete and utter respect for that old lady of the bush. She had doubled back on them, having reached the far side of the gulley, and leaving the herd to continue to forage, she had circled their position to investigate. The pursued was pursuing. She was there to gauge the danger and having sensed none, she had cautiously remained to observe them.

Aubrey and Wellington silently and with little fuss rose and retreated from the relative luxury of their position. They clambered quickly over the next rise and slipped soundlessly off to give her some space.

"Did you know she was watching us?" Aubrey had asked breathlessly, as they found some higher ground.

"Yes." Wellington had offered nonchalantly.

"She came to greet us." He smiled again, his large white teeth, exuding the confidence of his knowledge.

"We were being observed as we were observing the herd." His matter-of-fact comment had sunk in. Aubrey realised that these majestic beasts of Southern Africa, were not the victims any longer. They had gauged the relevance of man's intrusion into their world, and concluded where danger was not apparent, that they could selflessly cohabitate their world. The Matriarch had spent her adult years avoiding human settlements, but was not immune to curiosity. Those herds that stayed away from the mealie fields of the local tribes and resisted the trampling of the harvest, out of hunger would survive this onslaught from the invaders that coveted their land.

Aubrey would learn the nuances of that breed of creatures, willing to gain from their experience and admire the maternal instinct of the Matriarch. It was this dream that formulated his desire to know himself more. It was that vision that now haunted him.

Tossing in that large opulent bed, Aubrey now reflected on his relationship with his mother. She had stood by him through thick and thin, and unable to choose between her love for him and the loyalty she demanded of herself, for an uncaring husband; she had forced the one person she adored, to flee the family home. Aubrey knew that he had harboured that guilt for far too long. He had been unable to recognise that his choices had driven a further rift between himself and his mother. He had involuntarily forced her to choose between him and his prodigal father. But it was he who now felt like the prodigal son, returning home to make peace with the ghost of his mother. She had died of a broken heart and her soul was all that he now recognised. The large portraits in the entrance hall, and the reminders scattered all around the master bedroom, now filled his sub-conscious mind.

From somewhere in the darkness of his mind, Aubrey now heard the call of her spirit. Mother was with him in his unbridled desire to make amends. Aubrey could now make peace with her ghost, firm in the knowledge that it was her love he had coveted and her unflinching love for him that he now treasured. All the trappings of the life she had desired for him had meant nothing. It was always her wish to have the title of Lady, and the respect of her peers, that had been paramount in the lifestyle she had sought through marriage. To Aubrey, it had meant nothing.

Alone in the darkness of that world, through which he now visited, he saw his mother urging him forward. Her smile was all-embracing and in that greeting, he sensed her acknowledgement of why they had drifted apart. It was not that he did not love her any less, it was that he could not countenance the manner in which her social aspirations had been manipulated by the one man Aubrey had no tolerance of. In his adulthood, Aubrey had come to realise that the unrequited love he had desired of his father, was the ultimate knowledge that it was that unreturned affection which his father had used as a weapon.

Now alone in that unconsummated marital bed, Aubrey realised why he had no affiliation with his father. He had known this intrinsically, but it had always remained deep within the darkest regions of his formative mind. He had not consciously verbalised this, but knew somehow, that the divisions that had provoked his fleeing of the family estate, were in part due to the subconscious knowledge that now haunted him. Mother smiled and willed him on.

Aubrey was ascending into a world he neither recognised nor understood. All about him were the grandiose trappings of a material world for which he cared nothing. The rich tapestries that lined the walls and the plush carpets that softened his footfalls were no contest to the lush brooding vegetation of the Zambezi Valley. The dark wooden framed portraits that ascended alongside the grand imposing staircase, pleaded no contest to the deep crevasses of the Zambezi Gorge, as they reached upwards to the sky and the light of an African sunset, resplendent in the hues of a mesmerising western horizon.

Aubrey followed dutifully, his mother urging him ever upwards. But in that venture he rebelled, even her desires. He lagged behind, dragging his heels across that forbidden threshold, unwilling to commit himself. Somewhere in the distance he could hear the cascading river as it descended through cataracts and spiralling eddies. The haunting call of his mother whispering to him, seemed to be drowned by the similarly haunting tune of an eagle somewhere off in the distance.

The sounds and smells of the valley, with its abundance of vegetation, filled his senses with the diversity of its creation. Nowhere could mankind hope to imitate the grandness of nature and the complexity of her being. Every fibre in his body cried out for a return to nature and in the distance, he caught a glimpse of his mother slipping into a void, he could not quite determine nor follow. She was gone, and with that his mind was filled with the call of the wild. Aubrey knew intuitively, this was to be his home; but only for the interim.

Somewhere in the distance a clarion call alerted him to the present. The sound drowned out the call of the fish eagle and phased out the rushing of the waters of the grand old mother of Africa. Her rapids and echoes of the past million years, snubbed out by a deep, metallic sound, invasive and unwelcome.

Aubrey, roused from his slumber, opened his eyes. His ears were assaulted by the invasion of that foreign clamour, but his sight was met by the filtered light of the great bay windows, shielded by the lace curtains.

He swivelled, throwing his legs off the raised bed and with his stocking bound feet, he padded to the window. Off to the left, he saw the back of a large truck, its reverse lights on and the unfamiliar sound of a warning signal, Aubrey could only guess was emanating from within. He heard the muffled voices of men ushering the driver back, then caught a glimpse of Highpot.

The men approached the back of the now silent truck and swinging open the large metallic doors, they began to off-load furniture. Aubrey watched them as them swooped on the contents and manfully removed them from the truck. He would have a shower and then venture downstairs to see what all the fuss was about. For now, his sweaty pits and unshaved beard were his only concern.

Chapter 3

Familiarisation

Aubrey had spent several days exploring the grounds of Finsbury Hall, getting to know the ground staff, and re-familiarising himself with the extensive gardens. It had been on one such expedition, that he had run into a friendly fellow called Goodness.

Goodness was his name and certainly so was his nature. He had been employed by the Estate for two years and had come to England in search of work, having left a little village on the northern border of Matabeleland, close to Victoria Falls. He had been a tour guide on the canoe trips down the Zambezi River, along the jigsaw puzzle of borders that merge Zimbabwe, Zambia, Botswana and Namibia. The Caprivi Strip, a point at which all four countries share a common boundary, was dissected by the colonial masters of the late eighteenth century, in order for all four countries to have access to the fantastic riches of the Zambezi River.

Aubrey and Goodness had wondered through the gardens, Goodness showing him all the different sub-tropical plants that had taken up residence in the carefully sculptured flower beds. Both reminisced over the great expanse of water that they had navigated, like early Livingstonian explorers, whilst in Africa. It was heavenly meandering through the hidden islands that dotted the approach to the great falls. The Victoria Falls were the only living remnant of British rule that had not been renamed by the Mugabe regime. How cynical was politics, that for the convenience of the great American Dollar, the name of Victoria Falls had not been changed, so as to ensure the continuation of a steady stream of foreign tourism to this magnificent natural wonder of the world.

When Goodness spoke of the great river that flattens out on its approach to the wide chasm, forming a natural cleft in the earth, there was almost reverence in his voice. The ancient tribes that had made the area their home had called it 'Mosi 'O Tunia', or the 'Smoke that Thunders'. Aubrey had admired the simplicity of how only the ancient people whose very existence had depended on it, could have formulated such a name. They had wondered the land, managing their vast herds of cattle. These cattle were their only form of property. Slashing and burning the bush, they systematically denuded the land, before moving on to the next fertile piece. Never re-cultivating it, this was how they survived in their continuous use of shifting cultivation.

The burning had created a natural extermination of the dreaded Tsetse fly that had ravaged the land and these hardy people who were not immune to the malaria and the summer infestation of mosquitoes, had their population held in check by nature. That is until the early colonial explorers arrived, and brought Quinine with them.

Goodness and Aubrey also spoke about all the trips they had done on the great continent, Aubrey sharing his experience of getting too close to a pod of hippos, Africa's great killers of the waterways. Goodness had shared a story:

"Whilst canoeing a group of tourists around a pod of Hippo, I did not know that a mother and her calf had ventured up onto a dry bank during the late afternoon lull in activity."

Having been warned about the dangers of getting between the nursing mother, and the water, they had disturbed her when one of the ladies on the boat, had knocked her paddle against the fibre-glass side of the canoe, sending a loud clap through the silent afternoon air. This was met by a rush of noise akin to a rumbling freight train, and before they could take evasive action the mother and calf had launched themselves from the high bank above the water, over the top of the canoe, sending a tidal wave that nearly upended the tourist and Goodness, whose spectacular boatmanship, had saved the day.

It was amazing, the risks that were taken to please the tourist industry. Goodness had chuckled with mirth, when relating the story to Aubrey, his innate sense of humour a natural wonder, and his broad smile, like many of his brethren, a blessing. This was the only reason the country had survived the torments of 'Mugabeism' and thirty years of his dictatorship.

"My older brother died of cerebral malaria when I was sixteen, so I left home to work with the company he had been with." Goodness had told him.

"I am sorry to hear that," Aubrey had commiserated.

"No, don't be sorry," Goodness had flashed back. "This gave me the opportunity to meet many people. It is why I am here in England."

"Ah, I suppose you have a point!" Aubrey was conscious of how the savagery of the African continent was so often stereotyped by Westerners, whose logic had the benefit of several hundred years of industrialisation.

mechanisation and progress gave the European a perspective that Africans found unfathomable.

"My brother was a great man and he had taught me about the tourists." Goodness flashed his trademark smile.

Aubrey and Goodness shared their political ideals, in frank conversation. This was a welcome change to the stuffiness of the English staff who now served at Aubrey's pleasure. Of course, if such a massive estate could have been run without all the staff, Aubrey would have found some way of doing it. However, the place owed its' existence to the nurturing of Highpot and his ample staff, so Aubrey had not interfered.

The discussions with Goodness were an escape from the daily meetings Aubrey had with Highpot. Now that the newly titled Lord Pennington had returned to his land and his inheritance, these meetings were a necessity. Aubrey had been briefed on protocol and the finances of the estate. This was boring to Aubrey, who could not wait to take his daily walks in the gardens with Goodness. But attending these meetings was paramount, as Aubrey was beginning to get to grips with the full extent of his wealth.

Whilst in Africa, and after his father's death, Aubrey had been sent annual accounts of the family estate. These documents had seemed lengthy and unintelligible to Aubrey, whose three-year degree in Political Science at Kings had not given him much grasp of the financial world. It was not important to Aubrey, as he had always managed to make ends meet, moving from one career in tourism, to another in the mining industry. These jobs had taken him from one country to another and one continent to another. This was a consequence of his own unwillingness to embrace the conservative nature of a regulated lifestyle in Accountancy, which was what his father had demanded.

But he had resisted to the point that his father had said no to his studies at Cambridge, preferring Aubrey to attend Oxford as he and his grandfather had done. No! Aubrey was a free spirit, but more so a free thinker and it was this thinking that had steered him towards the Arts. Consequently, his mother had funded his degree and had severed the only remaining string of decorum that had remained between his parents. The result of which for appearance sakes, was to say the least; 'frosty'. He had never relied on any funding from his father after his mother's untimely passing, and had made his way adequately through life. So, when these accounts began arriving at the mine in Kabinda Province, Aubrey had attempted to understand them, but subsequently discarded them in favour of other pressing objectives. He had no interest in them, as his world was filled with the daily requirements of building a civil society at the expense of what was to be his own health. Aubrey's world was about to be turned upside down, and it was his own pride that would ultimately cost him one true value he held above all else. Aubrey was to come to realize that the further he had run, in securing his bohemian lifestyle, the more he would be drawn back. Like the elastic bonds of the Bungee cord on the Vic Falls Bridge he would be catapulted back into this world of high stakes finance and intrigue.

The meetings usually lasted all morning, so Aubrey found solace in his afternoon walks, skipping lunch and the opportunity to bond with streams of solicitors and investment bankers who arrived dutifully each day. He preferred to spend the afternoon in his pursuit of the humble bumble bee and the friendly banter of Goodness.

It was during one of these meetings, on the fifth day of his arrival that a bombshell landed in his lap. Aubrey approached the large wooden panelled study, having taken his breakfast on the stone veranda outside the dining hall. He had seen the large Bentley arrive whilst in the midst of his daily routine of abluting, showering and changing into a comfortable pair of khakis and hiking boots. Old habits were hard to break, and had he been allowed he would have worn his veldskoens and shorts too. However, protocol dictated he be suitably dressed to receive these pin striped fellows.

"Good morning Lord Pennington," the solicitor who had overseen his father's estate, greeted him

The other gentlemen were introduced as Mr. Price and a Mr. Rawlings. They had not impressed, their stiff and awkward personae the hallmark of a financial advisor. Aubrey had never been one to assess an individual without first looking them square in the eye, giving a good firm handshake and allowing them to make the first chit chat. Price was a little too generous with the handshake, reaching forward with a surprisingly strong grip for a man of his fragile stature, and slightly off-balancing Aubrey as he pulled him towards himself. The grip was over assertive, as Aubrey liked to put it, attempting to turn Aubrey's hand over with a dominant twist of his wrist, which Aubrey easily corrected by gripping, and turning his wrist back to an upright neutral position. This interplay went unnoticed by the others, but Price got the message discreetly. Aubrey then turned to Rawlings, who had remained back and to the side, only venturing forward when Aubrey took a step towards him and proffered his hand. Rawlings was a little too withdrawn, and Aubrey only managed to grip the end of his fingers as he held his ground. Not a very satisfactory greeting, which left Aubrey with a sense of unease. "Bad news was sure to follow," he thought to himself.

"Good morning Lord Pennington," they had both parroted, unaware of his unease with his new title.

Aubrey greeted them both in return. He was now familiar with Gordon Donald, a very rotund but hawkish looking man in his fifties. They all waited, bouncing on their toes in expectation.

Aubrey just nodded, then pulling the antique chair to the side of its matching walnut desk, he scraped the cabriole ball and claw feet across the carpeted floor and sat unceremoniously.

They each pulled a chair, now having to angle it towards the light streaming through the large sash windows. Aubrey was now silhouetted.

"Lord Pennington, we have come to discuss your mother's estate," ventured Price. Aubrey could now clearly see beads of perspiration on his brow. It was only nine in the morning, but the sun streamed through the large window, throwing a lattice of shadows against the far wall.

Nods all around from Rawlings and Gordon!

"Yes, we are to present to you the financial affairs of your late mother, Lady Pennington, which has been held in trust for your return." Price had taken the liberty of pulling a large dossier from his brief-case, his discomfort all the more apparent now that he was staring directly into the sun.

Aubrey ignored his squinting demeanour and ventured a nod in return.

"Thank you for agreeing to see us," Rawlings squirmed in the stiff-backed Queen Anne, which seemed to accentuate the formality of this incursion.

"I don't follow", queried Aubrey. He reached for the chair and sat. "What does my mother's financial position have to do with the Estates' affairs?" Aubrey was confused.

"Well, you see Lord Pennington," answered Price, "Your mother left a Will and Testament, which was only to be opened after the late Lord Pennington passed away."

'Very proper', thought Aubrey, just nodding but saying nothing. There were looks all around; Price looking at Gordon for affirmation that he could continue.

"Yes, you see," continued Price, "your mother had a sizeable estate of her own, which had been set aside until your return to Finsbury. This required the passing of the title to you."

He almost choked on the last sentence, which left him coughing. Donald offered him a glass of water. It was accepted gratefully.

Aubrey could not 'see' his point. His mother had never discussed an estate of her own with him, but he wondered what had this had to do with his father's death? What were these buffoons doing here, and why all the subterfuge?

"Lord Pennington, we have a Will and Testament here, that was held in trust by our Executors to your mother's estate, and held over until now," continued Price, not looking at Aubrey whilst he spoke.

Donald just nodded. His gaze was on Price, who was now up to speed. Aubrey was still not following the gist of the conversation.

"Well you see", laboured Price," your mother kept her estate a secret from everyone, including your father. She never wanted anyone to know until you returned and took up your title as Lord of Finsbury.

Donald nodded again in agreement. A little too hastily thought Aubrey. 'This was starting to make sense,' thought Aubrey, but he allowed Price to continue talking.

"When your father passed away, your mother's estate, which is sizeable to say the least, automatically vested to you. The assets were held in trust by her Executors at Williams, Price and Telby. Lord Pennington, your mother had us prepare a final Will and Testament, in the knowledge that should you, have been disinherited by your father, or your title had been withdrawn, we were to present this Will to you."

"Not even Mr. Gordon here was to know," interjected Rawlings from the other side of the table. Aubrey was dumb founded.

'His crafty old mom! Aubrey thought. But why would she have been concerned about Aubrey being disinherited?'

Price continued, pausing to give Rawlings a curt glance and after clearing his throat, he said,

"Lady Pennington had decided to keep this matter under her hat, so to speak, until there was ample reason to present this Will." Again, he looked a little too sheepish, or was Aubrey misreading the body language?

"Your inheritance is a matter which the Executors have asked me to present to you as an addendum to your titled inheritance your Lordship," proposed Donald

"As your solicitor, I felt it incumbent on me to present this document as part of the continuation of your affairs. Williams, Price and Telby have agreed to waive their rights as Executors on Lady Pennington's estate to allow me to present to you an overview of the situation." He cleared his throat.

"This is highly irregular Your Lordship, but I must insist for the sake of clarity, that this matter be put to bed, 'so to speak'" said Donald unwittingly.

Aubrey could not help but smile to himself as Donald used the 'inverted commas' sign popular among those to whom the affairs of legal matters forced them to be exact, so as not to be quoted directly. Hence his use of the double fingered, double handed, double speak, which Aubrey found cumbersome.

His embarrassment and the way Price and Rawlings shifted in their seats left Aubrey feeling a sense of foreboding himself. Aubrey waited as the pregnant pause continued, and until eventually Donald turned to his fellow conspirators and said, "May I continue."

"Yes, yes! Please do," replied Price, a little too enthusiastically.

Price leapt from his seat, and handed Donald a portfolio folder, with various folder sleeves crammed full of paperwork. Taking the folder and opening the front cover, a document came into view, which Aubrey could see was the Will, the italicized lettering in black ink a little too big, and the name of his late mother, 'Lady Daphne Charlotte Louise Pennington' came into focus. The manuscript preceded twenty-five other schedules, each with an accompanying array of papers.

The meeting took one and a half hours, with not one member of the room pausing to break for tea, or stopping to stretch or even glance out the window. It was a beautiful day outside, but time had stood still in that cloistered room. Not even Aubrey, who had not sat still for that length of time since writing his GCE exams, was willing to get up. Donald continued matter-of-factly throughout the entire meeting, flipping from one portfolio page to the next. By the time it was completed, Donald was almost breathless. Price was silent, trapped in his own thoughts and Rawlings with a smug twitch to his upper lip sat almost bewitched, almost lip synching every word spoken by Donald. He had obviously prepared the file, and being the senior man had an infinite knowledge of its contents. Price had ventured nothing through the meeting, allowing Donald his moment as agreed. While, every page was dramatically turned, Rawlings had almost got up and turned the page for him. As they finished and sat back in their chairs, Donald closed the file and looked up at Aubrey.

"Your Lordship, I hereby present the last Will and Testament of your mother, Lady Pennington," proffering the file towards Aubrey who did not even flinch.

Aubrey had remained silent throughout the reading and clearly out of his depth, had said nothing. He could not believe what he had just heard. The world he had known all his forty-six years had just collapsed before him.

'So, my mother's maiden name was Beattie,' he thought. 'Not very auspicious; but then mom had obviously married for the chance of a society name.' Strangely, he was sure, she had become disillusioned with the marriage, and all the society nonsense. Despite her best intentions for him, he believed his mom had done all this so as the family fortune would have an enduring legacy. Little did he know, to what extent.

The Will had contained details Aubrey had never heard mention of whilst a child living at home. It was as if someone had read him his life story, but he could not recognize it for what it was. The detail regarding his mother's fortune, inherited in part due to his Uncle Billy's death in 1969, was the most extraordinary. He could hardly remember his Uncle Billy, but could recall a funeral which he had attended without his father; his mother having taken him to the North Country, to a little village. As a six-year-old, he had remembered the ducks in the pond outside a small chapel in a quaint cul-de-sac. This is where his obsession with water fowl had started.

'Incredible,' he thought, 'that was a happy memory for such a sombre affair.'

Realising the enormity of what had just transpired; Donald remained quiet after passing the document folder across to Aubrey. Sitting to the left of the desk, Aubrey suddenly felt as an intruder might. He was uncomfortable with the idea of being the head of this vast household but, he had been catapulted into this position a mere five days before, and now was being released like a giant arrow on some medieval crossbow. He could feel the sense of relief, in a way that had always given him freedom to move from one contract to another. This was a privilege he had enjoyed whilst living in Africa, or the Far East, for that matter.

Aubrey had always avoided responsibilities, and it was the very reason he had escaped to Africa, when, five years prior to this he had received the key to the estate, after his father's death. Fearing the responsibilities it entailed, he had run, not as a coward, but because he had felt no innate sense of duty. Now five years on, the weight of this responsibility melted from his shoulders, like a giant robe of some ancient Greek mythological god. The feeling was electric, and being impulsive Aubrey instantly grasped the enormity of the moment. He had been the Lord of this vast estate only five days, and now he had just seen it slip from him. He was realistically, no longer Lord Pennington.

Aubrey, sat, smiled to himself, and leaned back in his chair. This was great. Not only was he not the real heir to the Title, but he was finally freed of the burden of being his father's son. Aubrey was a bastard, well not figuratively, although he had been called one, once or twice in his life. But literally, he no longer had a father, as there was no mention in the Will, of who it might possibly be. This was, he concluded, his mother's way of setting a task for him that she somehow knew he would pursue.

'That saucy devil,' he imagined the glee that his mother would have had in preparing this document. Knowing that his 'so-called' father might disinherit Aubrey, if the truth had come out, his mother had purposely withheld this fact until his fathers' death. Having a great sense of adventure, his mom had set about covering up the truth, not for the sake of conformity, but as a way of ensuring her progeny would be guaranteed success. She had wanted Aubrey to succeed, always ensuring the best education, the best social contacts, and of course the insurance of a title.

"So, the truth of the matter is that Lord Pennington had married a commoner, but a wealthy one at that." Aubrey addressed them.

"To not only ensure the succession of this title, but also the estate, your father had married into money," offered Donald.
"Being a titled land owner, did not guarantee his property would be secure, so Lord Pennington had married your mom, who was the daughter of a very

wealthy industrialist from the north." Donald continued. He had made his fortune in kitchen apparel. A respectable and honest trade, but none the less not very esteemed amongst the landed gentry.

Aubrey now realised that he was born into the family, not through the matrimonial bed, but to another father whose identity was not as yet known. Because Lord Pennington had married his mother, the security of the estate had been ensured through an ante nuptial contract, but Lord Pennington had gone off to pursue the veritable sowing of his wild oats.

His Mom, not being one to sit back idly, having achieved her goal to be a 'Lady', thus set about ensuring there would be an heir to this Title. She had been discrete, but with another man and her husband being cuckolded, never again ventured into the matrimonial bed.

The irony being that Aubrey had never wanted this title even from a young age. It had been forced upon him; and his father who had strived to ensure the continuance of the family estate was to be undone by the very scandal of his own making. It was not enough that the Pennington's should be made land holders on an estate that had been in the previous family for several centuries. But now having been graced with this title, Lord Oscar Pennington, his great grandfather had received this land in return for favours to Queen Victoria. She had reigned supreme as a monarch during the Empires' expansion into Africa, and it was her, that Oscar Pennington had returned in 1885 with enough ivory and gold, to ensure his family fortune and the start of the demise of a once mighty population of African Elephant. The irony was palpable.

Had the mere fact been, that Oscar Pennington made his fortune from any other source, other than ivory, Aubrey may have been able to withstand the humiliation.

No, it was too much to bear. Aubrey could not believe that this title stood for everything that he had strived to remedy in that vast continent for the last fifteen years. Life had an uncanny way of repeating itself, but Aubrey felt now, more than at any other time in his life, that it was time to put all these things right. If his title, and the land too which he had returned was the product of ill-gotten gain, then he was no better than Mugabe and his cronies.

Aubrey had not the will, nor the ambition to take this title. He was relieved to be set free from this burden now. But it was not as simple as that. In years gone by, he may have simply run away. Now was the time he would need to stand up and take stock of his situation and deal with the scourge of his great-grandfather's sins.

But if every sin ever committed in the name of progress, were to be undone, humankind would never have made any leap forward from their ancestral brethren, who had lived in caves.

He could not help but think of the study material he had soaked up as a student all those years ago. William Golding's, 'The Inheritors' had been an abject lesson in just how easily humans can fall from grace.

Yet how often can mankind honestly claim to be any better for having achieved these lofty goals, and yet having sinned through the very objectives they had set out to achieve, they push us one step further up the evolutionary ladder. Perhaps it was time for the process to be halted; or could it? The process was inextricably linked to our survival as a species. Each creature on this earth had evolved and would continue to evolve to take advantage of its environment; so, to, would mankind. But not at the expense of other creatures! For every Elephant shot to satiate the greed of one human, a counter ailment would befall human kind. Aubrey sat contemplating the enormity of his position.

So, it was that Zimbabwe was paying the price of their forefather's sins and this would continue until the balance was restored.

Fearing Aubrey's silence was a sign of his dissatisfaction, Price interjected.

"Ugh hem, your Lordship." He pronounced, finally acknowledging Aubrey's title, which had seconds ago, been dispelled, "Can I suggest that we revisit the Will in summary, and give you a synopsis, of ..."

Aubrey's raised hand silently cut short the interruption.

"No. That won't be necessary, Mr. Price," Aubrey returned, "I think I understand the gist of it."

Aubrey was inwardly pleased, but his mind was racing to get to grips with the moment. His old lecturer in Philosophy at King's had once said, "If you haven't anything of value to add to the debate Pennington, button your lip young man."
This was one such moment for Aubrey to contain his thoughts. Having been unofficially stripped of his title, through his lost birth right, he now needed to contend with the enormity of its long-term effect. Aubrey knew from his

time at Kings, that a title was the means to a future of lavish, wanton indulgence; Aubrey had not wanted it, but now that he could see the title being figuratively stripped from him, he needed to understand the nuances of what may happen.

"Mr. Gordon," Aubrey continued, to the collective in breath of his audience, "What would this mean to the estate should word of this get out?" He was now thinking like Lord Pennington.

"Well your Lordship…," Donald seemed to tail off the personification of the 'P'.

"If the offering of a title is handed down through the ceremonial passing of the rights and obligations of land, to the descendant of the title, well then there is a natural succession of title." He paused.

"In your case, this was guaranteed in the transfer of Lord Pennington's estate. When you inherited this estate from him as the only living relative, your title was secured."

Aubrey's father had ensured the title succession, fearing that the scandal, if it had become knowledge, would have destroyed four generations of Pennington titleship. The late Lord Pennington, being a pragmatist had erred on the side of realism. The title of Lord Pennington was his for the taking, but did he want it?

Many a wealthy businessman had forsaken all to earn a title, to be handed down by the Queen or King of England. Many a commoner had sought fame and favour, just to be allowed to gain access to the privileges of this society, and Aubrey could not have wanted it less.

'Funny that,' he considered. That ghastly man Al Fayed, who owned Harrods, desperately coveted the very favour, Aubrey was about to throw away. Well how could he be so nonchalant about it?'

"Mr. Gordon! It is essential that this matter be dealt with discreetly. I will expect that no mention of this document be made outside this room, and there is to be no mention of titles or inheritances to anyone else. Is that understood?" Aubrey asserted himself.

Aubrey now assumed the role of Lord and master with relative ease. Surprising himself, he had simply reverted to the very mannerism that his 'father', Lord Pennington would have, and which had in fact driven Aubrey away from the estate in the first place.

The time was right, he concluded, to take control of the situation, for the moment. He was used to taking a leading role, but usually it was as a principle that the role was assumed after consultation with the staff and the mine workers he was used to leading.

Aubrey had always sat his pit crew down before embarking on a new project, and in the great African tradition, he had initiated an 'Indaba'. It was a meeting which took the form of a debate, in which all the members of the pit crew were given an opportunity to discuss the project. This inevitably resulted in the crew taking ownership of the project by inclusion in the planning process. This was a cultural aspect of Africa that had led to many a colonial master, past and present, complaining about 'African Time'. It was a euphemism given to this elaborate and timely process.

It had been said that in early colonial days, a migrant worker would sit by the side of the road, anywhere in Africa waiting for a bus, or truck, which could take days to arrive. This was the only effective way of commuting to the mining towns that littered the continent. These mining towns sprang up wherever any potential resources could be found. Africa was akin to the 'Wild West' and every opportunist was there for the rich pickings it offered.

Aubrey often pondered the way a mine worker might simply discard a coke can in the veldt, having just emptied its contents into his thirsty mouth. He could not come up with a satisfactory answer for why this occurred, other than that his environment was not a consequence to someone when his primary objective was to feed himself. Until the poorer black people have property titleship they were not really going to care for their environment.

Africa was a relatively undeveloped landmass rich in resources, and a vast population. The paternal culture of looking after one's family members first, so firmly etched into the local cultural values, meant that no local official would be motivated to make a difference, because once elected, he had a job for life.

'Sad, thought Aubrey 'that a continent so rich in natural assets, would become dependent on hand outs from the international community, forty years after the installation of a western styled liberal democracy.'

But if those same countries continued through multinationals, to make grotesque profits at the expense of the local populations, then the problem would ensue for ever. It was simple in its simplicity, almost ridiculous in its ridicule. It was the very process by which corporate clothing and shoe manufacturers were forced to stop using child labour in Asia. Their indiscretions needed to be advertised, and if by this process of 'naming and shaming' they could not find a solution to Africa's poverty, then they deserved to go out of business.

All that was a distant distraction now that Aubrey had to deal with the matter at hand. What was he to do? He knew that he could keep word of his mother's indiscretion from becoming public knowledge. But how was he to deal with this himself?

Aubrey had not indulged himself ever, and this was a most difficult moment. His thoughts raced through all the potential options, but frankly, 'did he care what might be said'.

'Especially in the hallowed halls of Cambridge!'

'No', was the answer.

But he still had to contend with the unwelcome paperwork, and loathing all that red tape, he had to find an alternative. Would any value come of his discarding his title, and what would become of the estate?

'It would be sold to some American movie star or Saudi Prince with an itching for turning the family estate into a theme park! Or worse still, they might have tours of the Manor house, with little Chinese tourists, flocking through his mothers' bedroom, touching all the family heirlooms.

'No that would not do! The only course of action would be to ensure the estate remained free of outside influence, no matter what.'

Aubrey needed a solution.

Chapter 4

Matriarchs and saints

Aubrey breezed through the gardens looking for Goodness. He had not seen him earlier that morning whilst on his usual tour of the gardens. The summer had been a hot one and Aubrey looked for some shade under a large oak. The mid-day heat had transformed the previous evenings shower from glistening dew on the early morning lawn, into a stiflingly humid afternoon haze. The lawn smelt of cut grass, manicured and spotlessly swept. The smell reminded him of the damp hay troughs that stood in the Boma of the elephant paddock. This gently reminder of his failed sortie into the commercial world of nature conservation had tugged at his heart and filled him with a sense of doom. Aubrey was not one to dwell on his failings, but the stagnant afternoon odour of dank grass cuttings had an effect akin to a slap in the face.

Aubrey sat down on the bench below the canopy of that elegant oak, and the shade offered some respite from the un-seasonally debilitating heat. He sat for a while eager to sound out his new-found confidant. But Goodness was nowhere to be seen. Aubrey found himself dozing with his chin on his chest and his shoulders slumped forward in an exhausted submission. His mind wandered and his chest heaved in a singular sigh, before he fell into a heat-induced catnap.

The herd had embarked on the winter migration from the parched savannah scrubland of the Hwange Reserve. Aubrey had met Wellington as usual, a few days before the matriarch had trumpeted her intentions. The water holes had turned to dry, mud-caked troughs, and the Matriarch had led them from each water hole to the next, slowly moving northwards. The park fences, destroyed by the poachers and given no maintenance by the Parks Board, had offered them no contest. Aubrey had arrived several nights before and had packed his ruck-sack in anticipation of an early migration. The drought had dried out the land unexpectedly, weeks before they usually would have expected the herd to move on. Aubrey had dropped everything and raced south from the Falls at Wellington's behest.

The matriarch was uneasy and the two young additions to the herd were still suckling and rather unsteady on their ridiculously large feet. Aubrey had watched them the previous evening, over a dust laden sunset, mirrored off the brown earth. The herd had appeared restless and Wellington correctly predicted the migration for early the next morning. The matriarch, aware of a marauding lion pride, had corralled the youngsters into a laager with the older females and the adolescent males standing sentry. During the night, the constant source of prowling Hyena and Jackal had left the herd moving fractiously with every creak from the trees and each gust of wind had doused them in dust. Aubrey had hardly slept, but eventually past midnight and exhausted, he had fallen into a fitful state of semi-comatose slumber. But in the dim glow of the eastern horizon, Wellington had seen the herd beginning to stage their getaway.

Packed and ready to go, Wellington had roused Aubrey and they set off in pursuit. The herd moved surprisingly quickly. The youngsters kept up for as long as the females could endure their prodding and the tiny calves could hold onto their mother's fray-ended tails. By the time the sun had reached its scorching zenith, the matriarch had pulled them into a clump of withering acacia and rested their weary bulks. The foliage sufficed for what little sustenance they could get. They needed to get to a watering hole by sunset. Moving on as quickly as the herd could, she led them towards the only source of water there was.

Wellington had sensed the urgency in her direction and knew that this would end badly. The herd was being lead towards the settlement of Mawonezi, a small village on the northern perimeter of the park. It was known to be a haven for the poachers, who having caught a stricken bull in a snare made from the barbed wire fences that had formally ringed the western boundary of the park, had taken a bull elephant as bounty and had used machetes and hacked the large tusks from the dying elephant. He had submitted without a fight; his hunger and thirst having weakened and disabled him. Now the herd with young, unable to defend themselves were headed for the only place within reach, which had water.

Wellington and Aubrey, unable to divert their objective had followed helpless and fretful.

As they surmounted the hill overlooking the village, the Matriarch had paused to test the air. Then without any hesitation, the herd had descended the lee of the hill, heading straight for the stream that fed the fields on the southern bank.

By the time Aubrey and Wellington had caught up with the last of the herd, they had stampeded towards the water well that fed the stream. They both let out a cry of relief. The village was deserted.

They both stood on the hill and looked down towards the Elephants. The small village, with its twenty of so huts, built on the edge of the stream, seemed quiet and lifeless. The rondavels with their threadbare thatched roofs looked desolate and unkempt. Wellington looked bewildered.

"What has happened to the villagers?" Aubrey had asked.

Wellington had looked quizzically at him and shrugged his shoulders. The Elephant herd was quenching their thirst and enjoying the fresh spring water. The tiny babble of water formed a small temporary pond and the youngsters now oblivious to any anticipated danger, frolicked in the water unabashedly.

Wellington skirted the southern ridge and with Aubrey in tow, they descended to the village under cover of the buttressed walls of the hill. There were several huts with their spotlessly maintained quadrangle, perched on a plateau above the main kraal. The huts deserted, showed signs of the inhabitant's struggle. Here and there the pots were overturned, a cooking fire with its embers still smouldering, had been kicked through in what looked like a skirmish. The huts each had their contents ransacked and it looked like everyone had left in a hurry.

Wellington led Aubrey towards the river, conscious not to unsettle the herd from their contented guzzling. Their thirst was obvious and the largest male adolescents were soaking up gallon after gallon. The trunks dipped frequently into the now muddied water and they sucked and sprayed the contents gratefully into their upturned mouths. Aubrey watched, still hesitant to let down his guard.

Wellington had scouted around the remaining huts and when he returned he had a haunted look on his face.

"What is it?" Aubrey whispered looking on with mounting concern. The look in his eyes told Aubrey that Wellington had just witnessed or seen something that was to change their lives forever.

"There are shallow graves beyond the kraal that are very recent." He was in a state of heightened anxiety.

"How many?" Aubrey was once again focused on the villagers, no longer able to be distracted by the antics of the youngsters in the herd.

"All of them!" Aubrey could see from Wellington's dilated pupils, an abyss, as though he were staring into his very soul.

"The whole village?" Aubrey whispered back fiercely. He was shaking. The stories he had heard of Gukurahundi and the operations of Mugabe's Fifth Brigade began to filter through his mind.

"Yes, all of them." Wellington looked at him for the first time since they had met and what Aubrey saw was fear. Ancestral worship played a vital role in the daily spirituality of the Ndebele and Wellington looked as though he had just seen a ghost.

Superstition or not, Aubrey now needed to take control of the situation. Wellington would be of no use to him, if he was a gibbering wreck looking over his shoulder constantly for the next month. They required living off their wits and the land and if Wellington was seeing ghosts he needed to snap him out of it.

Aubrey stood up from his position near the edge of a brown mud walled rondavel and conscious not to disturb the watering elephants, he grabbed Wellington by the strap of his rucksack and headed up and away from the village. The Elephant were safe for now, but they would need to get away from the village before nightfall. There was no telling when the perpetrators of this massacre would return. Today, even more so than back in the early eighties, when the Fifth Brigade were running amok in Matabeleland, there was need to remain out of sight of the authorities. Rogue Generals were running their own details, oblivious of Mugabe and his autocratic rule. The country was rudderless, heading for an economic meltdown and the Generals were forming their own profit centres. This would have been the work of just such a detail. They were probably in cahoots with the poachers, who were in fact simple villagers, doing what their ancestors had done for centuries before, and living off their land.

But Aubrey knew that the Elephant would not have been their primary focus, but with the demand for ivory still huge in the Asian countries, they were easy prey and a source of a quick profit. What these villagers would have earned from the sale of those tusks, however large, would have been a pittance. Probably enough to buy the staple mealie meal and some other provisions for a week, but not enough to sustain the village for longer! The middleman who purchased those tusks would then sell them for thousands of dollars, a veritable fortune in this fast-declining economy, but it was the Chinese buyers who would turn the huge profits that sustained their growing economy. They suffered no sense of conscience and were so far removed from the brutality of this moment they could have cared less for the deaths of these villagers.

Aubrey knew that to the buyers of that ivory on the open market in Shanghai, the source of whence it had been derived was unimportant. It was a tradition going back to the days of the Ming dynasties and the ancient traders a thousand years ago. But then when they had traded, it had been sustainable economics that had dictated the loss of a few elephants. Now, it was pure greed that drove the demand and the prices. The Elephant would continue to be the victim of man's greed, until the purchasers of that ivory could be educated.

Aubrey slipped an arm into the crook of Wellingtons elbow and led him away up the hill and to the safety of the ridge. From there they would look down onto the village and wait for the Elephant to move on. As they skirted the dried-out mealie patch which had offered the villagers a welcome source of sustenance, Aubrey could see the baked earth, yielding nothing other than some withered kernels and the broken stalks of a few mealie plants. The desperation of a tribe, taken to the brink of existence, was evident in the lack of adequate provision of a crop to feed the families that lived in that community. The able-bodied men, still capable of earning a living, had left for the city of Bulawayo and ultimately the mecca of Johannesburg. Leaving behind the old men and the women folk, they had only returned for one week a year and that was when they could slip back across the border with South Africa without being rounded up and deported back. The families were broken up and the elderly left to fend for themselves.

They were victims of the brutal repression of the Mugabe regime. The ultimate sacrifice for their efforts to rid themselves of the colonialists had brought them face to face with the Devil himself. Mugabe was intent on holding onto power at all costs and the innocent victims were the simple peasants who had once supported the Liberation struggle. It was no wonder that the average Zimbabwean hankered after a past, which although repressive, was nowhere near as bad as the current regime. Aubrey was not advocating a return to those years, but any alternative to the present dispensation had to be better.

As they had clambered up over the rough boulders on the cusp of the ridge, Aubrey looked back down onto the relative tranquillity of the valley below. The Elephant seemed to sense the peacefulness of the deserted village and their boisterousness was evidence that they somehow recognised the return of their watering hole. The village would become a gravesite before long and the mud huts, crumbling and deserted would eventually return to the soil. But the ancestors would remain to watch over subsequent herds and without the invasion of man, they would return to their faithful migration paths.

Aubrey realised that the tenure of mankind on that land was fleeting and in time he recognised that despite the worst efforts of that failed incursion, the Elephants would remember.

Chapter 5

A breath of fresh air

Aubrey could feel the wind whipping in his face, as he took control of the Roller. It was the first opportunity he had of driving this behemoth through the winding country roads of West Sussex, on those quaint little English country roads. The 400 horses of the mighty Rolls Royce engine pulled him through the countryside like some medieval knight on a great stallion. As the old girl roared into the corners the suspension would react like the landing gear on a mighty Jumbo Jet. From the front seat the feeling was electric, as Aubrey had never travelled quite so fast through these narrow, Cranberry lined lanes before. He knew his way instinctively, but his adrenalin rushed through his veins as the Roller was swept through the dipping blind corners, urging him onward evermore, until eventually he started to get tunnel vision. He had thrown caution to the wind, to experience the one challenge that had eluded him all these forty years, and it felt stimulating. He felt aroused.

The only experience similar had been the one occasion that he and his cohort in his Congo adventure had been chased by a group of bandits in the Landy, whilst carrying a consignment of contraband that Aubrey had no intention of sharing with them. That experience had left him breathless, but this somehow was different. Exhilarating, but certainly not life threatening. He had never felt his life was at risk for one second as the 'Grand Old Lady' bore him on relentlessly, the engine not faltering once. Hurtling through those country lanes, the window open, and a 2.5-ton Phantom Roller, sweeping from corner to corner slewing through each corner, oblivious to the danger, testing the apex of those narrow-tarred lanes to the full.

Aubrey had very seldom seen any other traffic on this lane, as it had only one destination, the village of Finsbury. The car swerved assuredly through the downhill sweeps as Aubrey powered into the next bend, his line of sight obscured by the bramble lining the road. But twenty years of driving Landies through sub-tropical forests had honed his driving skills. He was having a thrilling time. The adrenaline pumped through him, as he took the next turn, oblivious to the reality of his surroundings and revelling in the feel of the wind in his face. The freedom to do what he finally wanted without fear of rebuke or favour was an aphrodisiac. Charging on inexorably, Aubrey was alive, as his senses were drawn towards the next sweep, the verge seemingly closer than ever. No limits were possible, or probable in his quest for immortality. Then suddenly, as quickly as he had started, he slammed on the brakes, the car slewing into the side hedge, scraping the window, and he came to his senses, yielding for a truck that met him headlong on a narrow bridge. The moment was gone. This had been a fantastical flight of fancy, but the harsh reality of his surrounds returned. He needed to be a little more cautious.

Of course, Highpot had complained bitterly that Aubrey should not go out in the car without Shaun, but Aubrey had summarily dismissed his objections. If he could not drive his own car, then what the hell was he doing as the Lord of the Manor? The fact that at 46, he still did not possess a valid driver's license did not matter.

Yes, he had a drivers' license from Zimbabwe, which he had dutifully converted to an International Drivers' License at the local AA office in Harare. But none of which had been procured as the result of a test. The way business was done in Africa was simple. The power of the dollar. Or as Aubrey liked to contend; 'keeping the currency flowing through affirmative employment'.

He had parted with ten dollars, and some lowly paid official had obliged him with the paperwork. It had helped to put food on one family's dining table for at least one evening. Favours offered and rewarded were the African way.

Why the dollar had become the currency of choice, when the pound had always been the stronger currency had baffled him. But it was not as tradable a commodity on the black market. By trading the dollars back to the currency dealers for ten times what the official exchange rate dictated, a bribe became a means of generating a profit of a hundred-fold, and making a tidy income. This in truth had resulted in the inflation rate climbing, and once it had reached the dizzying heights of one thousand percent, it was all downhill from there. Zimbabwe had never realistically stood a chance and each protagonist was equally to blame.

Aubrey allowed his mind to wander as he eased the Roller more sedately along the 'A' road into the tiny hamlet of Finsbury. He knew that as a direct result of the strength of corruption in these economies, their futures were never secure. He was equally to blame and it now all made sense. Bribery, corruption and nepotism had been there since the beginning. But it had been always swept under the carpet for convenience sake. Even with the arrival of the Peace Corp, in Africa in the early fifties, the process of the unravelling of the colonial administration had begun. Rumour had it that they were sent by the emerging CIA, during the heady days of communism, under the guise of the religious right, in the US. They were supposedly Christian evangelists, but Aubrey had met a few of those that had stayed on after their stints, choosing to become Malawian citizens, and they certainly did not give him the impression that they had Jesus on their side.

He remembered the time they had been sitting at the Mount Souche Hotel in Blantyre, Malawi. A great big fellow from Arkansas who had been drinking with them in the hotel bar had gotten himself into some trouble with the authorities. When Butch had needed more cash for their drinks, he had gone to the bedroom to get some cash from his suitcase. He had walked into the room while the cleaning man was busy. 'Old' Hastings Kamuzu Banda, who was then in his eighties and still President, had moral codes of behaviour. Woman could not wear skirts above the knee or be employed in menial tasks and men had to wear long pants at all times. So only men were employed to clean the rooms, and this was a prime example of what had ensured the country remained firmly in the back-waters of African politics.

Well, according to Butch, there was the cleaning guy, his hand firmly in Butch's suitcase, rummaging around for the cash. Butch had erupted, and being a six foot something defensive line backer for his college football team, he had charged the fellow, lifted his slight five foot eight frame off the ground, and thrown him head long through the plate glass window from the first-floor room, hurling him into the hotel swimming pool below. From the bar, they had heard the crash and looked up in time to see the cleaner pirouetting through the air. The poor guy nearly died. Despite his serious injuries, he could not swim and had to be hauled out of the pool with a cleaning net on the end of a ten-foot pole. He would have to think long and hard before trying it again.

From that day forward, Aubrey always referred to his local friends, affectionately, as 'non-swimmers'. Aubrey had left shortly afterwards, choosing to take the path of least resistance when the police had arrived to investigate. It was fascinating to watch as Butch and his fellow émigrés had continued to drink whilst the police had done their investigation. The policy of zero tolerance for theft or crime only extended to the impoverished masses. Whilst Banda himself; a wanton capitalist, with an eye for every business opportunity that existed in his dominion, stole indiscriminately. Banda and his cronies would quite literally put anyone out of business or expatriate them if he so desired, when someone stood between him and a potential profit. A case of 'Do as I say, and not as I do'. So strangely despite his criminal intent, the cleaner had claimed his innocence and Butch had been requested, politely, to leave the country. Aubrey chuckled mirthfully. He had good memories of that trip!

Arriving at the T-junction, that took him left into the village, Aubrey gunned the motor and within a minute he was at the outskirts of the quaint old town of Finsbury. Strangely, unlike its namesake in central London, this town had been spared the ravages of time and politics, and nestling in the South Downs, it had been the same ever since Aubrey could remember. The only difference now was 12 years of 'Blairism', and Labour red tape, had changed the idiosyncratic nature of the country village. The local Post Office, which had been the source of all local gatherings in the past, had now become an internet café. The locals had embraced it despite their initial reservations. Not known for their ability to accept change, rural England was coming to terms with Labour politics with the same relish as a Norman invasion.

'The Professor' had charmed the local ladies with his great humour and his devilish good looks, and the villagers had finally accepted it as an inevitable part of their new existence. The twenty first century had at last been thrust upon them. The Professor had kept in touch with Aubrey over the years and more recently, had been communicating with him from this internet café via email. He had even set up a Wi-Fi portal which allowed all those local inhabitants with computers and a modem at home, to link up to his system at no expense. A cup of good English tea packaged and marketed by those colonialists who still held their ground, high up on the slopes of Mount Kenya.

Wireless mouse bandying students, who would take up residence during summer vacations, were very happy to frequent the café in the knowledge that they had found a tutor, more than willing to impart the knowledge of forty years of university scholarship. They were from the vast number of colleges surrounding Finsbury and as far afield as Brighton. The old ladies sat side by side with students typing away on their thesis for the next semester. The town's gossip surrounded them as the latest talking point erupted with the arrival of the Rolls Royce outside. Honing the art of 'chin-wagging', to a level hitherto unheard.

It was to this reception that Aubrey, who was now the brunt of many a conversation since the news of his return home, had entered. His confident stride had all the occupants of the café a gawk with renewed vigour. The old ladies who fondly remembered him from his childhood days, could not believe that this confidant figure, was indeed little Aubrey. The students who had arrived on their bicycles from neighbouring towns, ceased working on their dissertations, and looked up as Aubrey walked in. Every set of eyes was inevitably on him.

Professor Dingle, who was behind the coffee bar serving a customer, looked up from his Victorian cash register as the little bell on the door chimed, and Aubrey entered. He immediately put down the bill in hand, and rushed through the seated restaurant holding out his arms, in a gesture of greeting unfamiliar to Aubrey. In Zimbabwe, when two friends, or acquaintances met they usually kept their greeting verbal, and the intricate handshake was the only sign of familiarity shown. Aubrey had learnt this custom, but it was an expression that only they were adept at. The hand clasping, monkey grip, finger snapping greeting was complex and personal. Aubrey had performed it only with those he knew more intimately; the rest were demoted to a more distant head nod and clapping of the hands. But here was Old Dingle, swooping through the very busy restaurant with every set of eyes in the place following him to where Aubrey now stood, a little awkwardly. Aubrey smiled as he was swept up in a genuine hug and very vocal greeting.

"Aubrey, you little devil, I immediately recognized you," ventured Dingle.

"You haven't changed a bit; well a bit bigger and a little puffier around the eyes! But you haven't changed a bit," he repeated.

"Well thank you," returned Aubrey, a little self-consciously, leaning back from the embrace. Body language was his strength, but this was verging on something more. Aubrey sensed, rather than looked as the room eyed them.

Aubrey, now released immediately assessed Dingle's stepping back to get a clearer picture.

"Hey Prof, you haven't changed at all yourself. Except for the little goatee and a little less hair!" He jokingly prodded Dingle with a finger, and gestured at the crowd, still watching.

"Wow, what an audience," he smiled and the room smiled back.

"Enough of the pleasantries," Dingle announced, more aware of the embarrassment he was causing Aubrey, "let's go to my office."

Aubrey followed Dingle through the crowded Cafe, smiling at one or two ladies he vaguely recognized, but whose names he could not remember. Because Aubrey had been at Eton for the bulk of his adolescent years, he had stayed well away from religion when returning each holiday, and rather than attend the local chapel with his mother every Sunday morning, had discovered his zest for adventure in the grounds of Finsbury Manor. Although not attending worship at the local village Anglican chapel, he had remembered some of the little old ladies from way back when he was a boy, rummaging through the local bookshop or antique store.

"Good God", he thought, "they must be in their nineties by now! Longevity had made its way to the heart of the English countryside."

"Two coffees please Emma," The Professor, motioned to the door. Aubrey followed.

Aubrey was pleased to escape the scrutiny, and on entering Dingle's office noticed that the large ornate framed mirror on the wall behind the cash desk was in fact a one-way glass mirror. Dingle could obviously keep an eye on his patrons while he sat in the office working on his own research. There was a very smart, modern 17" plasma screen, desk, but no sign of the computer box. Everything was very neatly placed, and a large wooden filing cabinet covered the entire far wall. Through the glass panelled cupboard doors Aubrey could see all the books and plastic spines of the theses. The office gave Aubrey a sense of unease.

"Please sit," gestured Dingle pulling out a chair for Aubrey.

He had been one of Dingle's erstwhile students at King's College; but so too had his entire faculty of fellow Philosophers. The Professor had a way with his students that immediately put them at ease, and which Aubrey could see had followed him from the auspicious halls of King's to this somewhat inauspicious coffee shop in Finsbury.

"How have you been?" asked Dingle as Aubrey sat in the leather Eastman, his back to the gossiping audience. The Professor looked intently at Aubrey, a probing inquisitive look. Aubrey again became self-conscious. He had always sought Dingle's advice while at college, but now having done the same via email, he was a little taken aback by the sincerity of Dingle's gaze. Aubrey could sense that natural empathy.

"Happy to be back," was Aubrey's reply.

Five years of working with his Afrikaans mine manager and work colleagues, had given him a brutal insight of reality. Aubrey had become friendly with some of the pit bosses, but the language barrier had always kept him just out of the inner circle of the rough neck, often coarse talking mineworkers. They kept the mines running with that brute power, often cruelly beating the offending mine labourer with clenched fists, if they were found idling or stealing. It was no world for the faint of heart, but was now being administered by the very governments whose fight for freedom from colonial domination, now enacted the same cycle of harsh treatment.

That was a far cry from his new reality. Sitting here with Dingle, Aubrey was reminded of the sense of calm that had been evident on his return some two weeks before. 'No wonder those old ladies lived so long,' he thought, 'stress free living, and don't forget the 'pot 'o tea.'

"So, what have you been up to for the last fortnight young man," insisted Dingle, his enquiring look, a gesture of his concern.

"Have you been so busy that you could not contact your old chum Dingle?"

"No, not at all," replied Aubrey.

"I just have not had access to a computer since getting back, and these confounded meetings for the Estate have kept me somewhat occupied."

"Sorry!" he apologized.

"No, don't apologise Aubrey," responded Dingle, "you clearly have had your hands full."

"What was the outcome?" Dingle dispensed the small talk and came right to the point.

"Well a lot more lucrative than I originally thought," replied Aubrey. "My mother had left her entire estate to me in a Trust, in perpetuity as an insurance against my father squandering his fortune, and then my mother's."

"What! You mean the place isn't entirely bankrupt then?" remarked Dingle, a satisfied grin on his face.

"So, you knew something?" Aubrey was troubled. The Professor smiled apologetically.

"Well, it was a bit of a surprise to me," responded Aubrey, not knowing just how much Dingle knew, and not wanting to venture too much.

"Good Lord," added Dingle, "it's been common knowledge for a while."

"What has," questioned Aubrey somewhat defensively. Dingle raised an eyebrow.

"That your estate was in good hands young man. Why, what did you think I meant?" queried Dingle.

"No, nothing that I can mention now," replied Aubrey, "but I will let you know sometime."

"Come on Aubrey, you can confide in 'Old Dingleberry'. His interest piqued.

"What is going on?"

"Everything, and nothing," replied Aubrey nonchalantly. He did not want to be drawn on the issue too much.

"I'll let you know soon enough." He turned in his chair, peering through the plate glass into the restaurant.

There was a polite rap on the door and Emma entered, two steaming mugs of coffee in hand. Slipping them onto the desk, she discreetly withdrew.

"So, what's all this about?" Aubrey swept his hand around the room, thankful for the interruption and adeptly changing the subject.

Professor Dingle had spent the best part of his working career as a Philosophy Professor at King's College. Having studied there and subsequently passed his major, he had stayed on as a Tutor and then eventually become a full-time lecturer after gaining his doctorate.

"I like to keep an eye on my loyal subjects," he grinned sheepishly.

"Nothing perverse," he offered. "It is a means for me to observe people undetected. I love watching people and making assumptions before I meet them"

"It's a bit creepy," ventured Aubrey.

"Not at all," the Prof brushed aside the remark.

"If we are truly to know each other, we must observe and learn. Nobody thinks of it being creepy when Naturalists venture into the jungles to watch Gorillas!"

Aubrey thought about that for a moment.

"So, what do you derive from watching people?" His interest piqued.

"Everything! We are social creatures and it is always in our social contact that the true nature of mankind is observed." That same passion boiled beneath a set of sanguine green eyes.

"Yes. I can relate to that." Aubrey understood him completely.

The Professor was an extremely principled man, and had never allowed his personal life to encroach on his ultimate passion. This was a career he had become married to, having never taken a wife, or any other full time commitment. He had never known any other form of obligation other than to his studies. It had become his obsession, with every working hour dedicated to his students and ultimately the pursuit of an answer to the biggest question of all:

'How did we get here and what is our place in the Universe?'

"So, have you solved the meaning of life?" Aubrey gestured to the vast library of work behind them.

"I fear we will never have an answer, because the question is forever evolving. But despite this, we must never relinquish our search!"

Professor Dingle had argued in favour of this eternal pursuit all his time as a Professor at Kings College. He hoped his students would strive for happier, healthier and more fulfilling lives, through the study of Philosophy.

"The universe is a swirling, expanding mass of gas and matter, which drives and derives its energy from the original, 'Big Bang', or Creation. Or whatever it was; there was existence." The Professor looked earnest.

"Why can't we not just accept that and get on with the joy of living?" After forty-six years of striving for this answer, it had somehow eluded Aubrey, and he'd have to be content with his less-than-conclusive conclusions.

"Because, once we have reached that conclusion, we have nothing left to pursue!" The Professor winked at Aubrey.

The Professor had retired into the country with his meagre pension, but not without a following, borne of years of indisputable hard work and caring. This was where he now found himself, and it was a blissful existence. The Professor could not have asked for more. He was indeed happy.

"Aubrey, if man were to be born with all his needs taken care of, from day one. Would he ever need to find the pursuit of existence, or the pursuit of excellence, for that matter?" He had asked this question of himself and his students, semester after semester.

Aubrey realized he could not answer the question.

"Each individual is unique and so no one answer could cater for all, I suppose!"

"It is all subjective, and it invariably will take a lifetime of pursuit, to gain self-understanding." The Professor reflected on his own question.

Aubrey realised that the Professor had made it his mission to assist those in the pursuit of greater self-understanding, through, life, history, self and the ultimate understanding. This was why he had continued to teach, albeit from this rural coffee shop.

"Hell!" he exclaimed, "if the disciples had evangelised from meal tables, who am I to deny those intent on learning from attending my Mass"

Aubrey realised he, like the Prof, had one life, and this was to be lived to the full. At seventy years strong, and an intellect clearly honed to the sharpness of a Shangaan's stabbing spear, he used his tongue as his intellectual rapier, and his lucid brain as his intellectual shield, to fend off any barbarians.

"This set up is quite impressive," Aubrey complimented. "I would not have taken you for an entrepreneur! How did you become familiar with retail?"

"I had some help." The Professor offered. His life's rationale was generally very well thought out, but this one had been a whim.

"I was visiting the countryside on a quiet vacation, and was staying some five miles away at Cranberry." It was on one of his usual holiday rambles, on a lazy summer afternoon three years before, when he had quite unexpectedly discovered the village of Finsbury.

The Professor was an avid rambler and having been as fit as a fiddle, had walked further than anticipated on this outing, with the butterflies and the larks as his only companions. It was as he reached the fence which formed the boundary between the common ground and the Estate that the Professor had been forced to take a diversion to the left and had found himself in the village, a million miles from that world he had known.

Serendipity and an unconscious desire to assess his surroundings had led to him stumble upon the Estate, not knowing to whom it belonged. The local village lady at the post office had then informed him of who had set up the fence on the ramblers' path, and it was then that he realized the estate belonged to the Pennington's. Ordinarily, the right of usufruct of land that lay within the rambler's path had been sacrosanct. It was only Lord Pennington's intercession at the highest levels that had made it possible to put up the fence. He had always cast dispersions on the commoners who chose the rambling paths to commune with nature. Aubrey could not have known this, as his world was always confined to the space on the other side of the fence.

"Funny that!" He now told the Professor. "I had never considered that having been always free to roam the estate, but I had never gone beyond its boundaries as a child."

The Professor nodded. "Yes. We are always confined to our world, until somehow we can be given an opportunity to look beyond it."

"Well we will have to remedy that!" Instinctively Aubrey knew he would take down that fence and allow the rambler's access. The Professor smiled.

This was the reaction he somehow knew he would receive. Aubrey was not constrained by the conservative nature of his father, and could now choose of his free will, to change the things that had always made the late Lord Pennington an outsider to his community. Within these walls, he and Aubrey could change their world. 'But to what extent, could Aubrey change his?' Aubrey would have to think this one through carefully.

"When I discovered that the Finsbury Post Office was closing due to Labour Government's cost reductions, I figured there was an opportunity amongst the chaos." The Professor had hatched a plan to take over the place and employ the postmaster, in his coffee shop.

It was in fact, this synchronicity that had lead Aubrey home. Despite the fears, he had of becoming embroiled in the financial affairs of the Estate, he knew this was something he had to face. Diligently, he had avoided the Estate after it had become bequeathed to him by his father. He had become Lord Pennington by default of inheritance and not from choice.

The Annual Reports that had been couriered to him every year for the last five years had been left largely unopened, as Aubrey resisted his inherited position. But although having moved continents to get away from this, he was finding that he could not escape his obligations any further.

They discussed the need for Aubrey to try to maintain good health through a regimen of long country walks and a well-balanced diet. They were also surprisingly able to find some common ground on what had been a relatively minor disagreement over the reason for Aubrey not finishing his degree at Kings'. Aubrey had left during the last semester of his final year, and the Professor had sought him out at the boat race the following summer.

Aubrey was there, not just to support the Cambridge team, but because of a fundamental distraction that had piqued his interest of late. The girls had been acquaintances of Aubrey's since childhood, and now at twenty-two, Aubrey was considered somewhat of a 'catch' among the society belles. However, he was clearly interested in only one.

Her name was Tracey and she was a quiet, shy slip of a girl. She somehow reminded him of a young Julie Andrews, with the wholesome qualities that Aubrey saw in his mother.

He had shown off a little for the ladies, to win her affections, but he had already had too many scotches; all this had done was to show up his immaturity and his own insecurities. Aubrey had been somewhat dismissive of Dingle in front of them, leaving the Professor embarrassed. The Professor left immediately, and Aubrey was shunned by Tracey. This was to be his first and last lesson in the abject stupidity of social decorum. He was a failure and took to drinking heavily, all the more.

When they had resumed communication, Aubrey apologised to the Professor promising that he would explain the entire sordid affair sometime. Well, this was that time, and Aubrey now sat in the Professors' office and spilt the beans.

It was a culmination of years of psychological bullying by his father. Aubrey explained to the Professor how for several years after he had left Eton, the relationship he had with his father then deteriorated even further. As Aubrey grew into manhood his father became ever more resentful of him. He had become a strapping six-footer after A' Levels and caught the eyes of the girls in a way that his father envied. Because Lord Pennington had been only five foot nine, the obvious was becoming an unavoidable fact. Aubrey, who had sought his father's attention for much of his formative years, now sub-consciously realised he was an outsider. Interestingly, his father had always remained distant and his mother avoided the subject. Aubrey had read in a scientific journal, that babies, when born, resembled their paternal ancestor for the duration of their infancy. In nature, they had proved that the reason was due to a survival protectionist gene. This ensured that the similarities between father and child, whether male or female was determined by obvious physical features. If that were true, then it was unsurprising that the relationship had always been so tenuous.

"Who then was my father?"

"Well that might prove to be a little more difficult to assess," the Professor had commented. "If we don't have any precise history of a dalliance that occurred in the early days of their marriage, it might prove a bit difficult!"

"Well there are all the letters of correspondence my mother had kept locked away. They were delivered in a metal Kist when the rest of my mother's personal effects were handed over."

"Yes, that's it." The Professor was animated. "Your mother was fastidious about letter writing. She wrote me often whilst you were at Cambridge. She was very interested in your progress."

"That is news to me," Aubrey was quite taken aback.

"Yes. She would write every term, asking me for an opinion on your development. She had been worried that you had become quite insular, and that she worried about your friendships."

"Whatever for?" Aubrey was probably a little defensive.

The Professor continued despite Aubrey's peculiar outburst, "When she wrote to me, the month that you had dropped out of university, she had asked me to attend the boat race."

"Oh. So, you were not there at the invitation of Lord Salisbury?" Aubrey had considered it odd that the Professor should have been there as a guest of the old man. They had been invited to his marquee, and maybe that was why he had assumed so.

"No. I had been accompanied by your mother, but she had not wanted you to suspect that it was she that had arranged the rendezvous." The Professor was apologetic.

"No worry," Aubrey continued. "My mom had always been a bit of an interferer. She could not help it, but for appearance sakes, she had always made out that it was my father who organised and paid for everything."

"Well, you see, your mom wanted me to ask you to reconsider finishing your degree. She was devastated when you had dropped out, and felt it was her fault that you had not represented Cambridge in the Race."

Aubrey had 'gone out' for the rowing team and had nearly made the 'eights' and the annual inter varsity regatta on the Thames, but his failure to make the team was the result of his heavy drinking.

Lord Pennington had derided him for this and it was the start of what became his father's way of controlling him. The pain it caused him was immense, but this was not the first time he had felt his father's psychological bullying. Not wanting to draw his mother into the fray, Aubrey had let it slip, but knowing what he now knew; Aubrey would never have approached his father in the first instance. Aubrey had never wanted to become beholden to anyone. He now knew that it was his mother that in fact held the purse strings, and it was this fact that had emasculated his father? The fact that Aubrey's father had never been able to pay for anything because the funds were coming from his mother, had never been raised as a topic of conversation, and was certainly not common knowledge. No. The Pennington's had kept this secret under wraps very effectively to the point that not even Aubrey knew.

In hindsight, it was probably not his father's fault entirely, but it was a combination of the lack of communication that had become a part of the family politics. With both parents trying to retain control, it was easy to see how the family became dysfunctional. Aubrey's efforts to get the family name into the hallowed annals of history, and the first Pennington to be included onto the famous boat house wall at Henley had led to his ultimate alienation from his father and mother. Aubrey had been devastated, and blamed himself.

All this scheming had led to Aubrey's disenchantment with his family, and he now realised this was the reason he had packed his bags the moment an opportunity presented itself, jumping on a freighter bound for Durban.

Chapter 6

The Great Escape

It was 1984. The ship had been in port only three days, when Aubrey had been ordered back to the freighter in the harbour at Durban's main terminal. This was the end of the road for him as one of the crew of the Misu Tong. The captain had been given word by the Port authorities that a young man fitting Aubrey's description was wanted by the South African Police. The captain, an Englishman from Liverpool, had taken a liking to Aubrey on the three-week voyage from Southampton, and now he was going to have to protect him from his own high spiritedness. The master of the ship was obliged to look after his crew, with a fatherly indulgence, and they in return were to keep themselves from misconduct and embarrassment to the ships company. Aubrey had joined the crew in Southampton for the journey to Singapore as one of the crew and soon found himself completely accepted amongst the rest. He learnt the ropes quickly and found himself at home amongst the rough crew.

The captain had been introduced to Aubrey at the first meeting when he was selecting his crew. He had realized that the young man sitting before him was of high breeding but had admired how the then twenty-two-year-old Aubrey had understated his education, to get onto the ship's crew. Aubrey had wanted to make his journey to the Far East a working trip for two reasons. Firstly, he wanted to learn and never be an unnecessary burden to anyone, and secondly, he was in fact penniless. Aubrey had decided to make this trip spontaneously. It had all happened whilst on a pub crawl with the lads in Southampton one evening.

Aubrey had met with several of his mates after they had been on an end of semester jaunt. Aubrey knew that they had all just graduated, and he would not go on to complete his honours with them but was in a mood to celebrate their success. He had opted out of Kings because of his own pride, but had more of the spirit of adventure coursing through his veins than he cared to admit. He was a Pennington, surprisingly in more ways than not. It may have been a quirk of immaturity, but to him he was about to embark on his way through life. As thousands of his fellow compatriots had done for centuries Aubrey was to start his grand adventure. He was no apologist for the spirit of British colonialism, despite his differences with the establishment. Always keen for a good binge he had been picked up from the estate on a balmy summer's day that would change his life forever. Aubrey could not resist a bit of a lark and subsequently joined them on their binge.

They found themselves at a pub in the docklands. The drinking took on a whole new meaning, however, when they hit the third pub, and the stakes were raised. So here they were in a pub, and they had decided to challenge for rounds. Aubrey would get to arm wrestle for a beer which was a challenge which he invariably won. Aubrey had discovered a great way to defeat his arm wrestling opponents, purely by chance. Provided he picked his victim well, and by that it meant that the guy had to be well on his way to inebriation and his senses not all that focused. Aubrey would pick on a guy who was invariably bigger than himself, but who by age was probably not as fit. Having challenged him to the arm wrestle, Aubrey would position himself at the end of the bar so that his body and full weight was on the left-hand side facing his opponent. Being right handed and providing his opponent was also right handed, Aubrey invariably had the advantage. No matter how strong the guy was, he still had to use all his strength against the natural balance advantage that Aubrey maintained. Customarily Aubrey won with the luckless victim having to buy a round of drinks for the group.

When Hilton was on form and he usually was, he would be able to down a pint of ale in less than 4 seconds, and his lager from a bottle, in 6 seconds. He used a technique where he expertly blew into the bottle before downing it to equalize the internal air pressure of the bottle making it easier for the beer to flow out. This was a great party trick and had the effect of leaving him inebriated and retching like a dog in the alley.

Then there was Dale; he had been involved in an unfortunate train accident at the age of twelve which had resulted in both his left foot and right ankle being severed. It was an awful accident, which occurred while crawling under a train, after finding himself on the wrong platform. The accident had left Dale with two prosthetics which were attached to the knee and formed the equivalent of two rather sturdy and impenetrable boots. Despite this disability, Dale had never allowed himself a moment's self-pity. He had become commendably proficient in martial arts, and was a third Dan black belt. Needless to say, he was a pretty handy chap to have around during a bar brawl. However, Dale's party trick was to get the intended victim to witness his karate chop of a bar stool leg, and then having done so, with spectacular results, Dale would proceed to challenge the guy by breaking a beer bottle over his leg. The poor guy mesmerized by the broken bar stool would end up paying for a round of drinks. This stint inevitably ended up with the whole lot of them being turfed out onto the street. Dale was a remarkable lad, and Aubrey had loved their wild nights on the town.

By the time they'd made it to the fourth pub on the street, they found themselves amidst a group of robust-looking merchant navy sailors. Aubrey found himself talking to a midshipman, who happened to know there was a freighter leaving for Durban and Hong Kong the next morning. Aubrey decided there and then to join them, and said farewell to his chums. After falling asleep in the door way of a terraced house on Blighty Road and not so much as a call to his beleaguered mother, he had set off for the Docks early the next morning, to meet the Captain of the Misu Tong.

It was how Aubrey had found himself in Durban, the last great bastion of the British Empire, but not exactly where he had wanted to be. The oppressiveness of an autocratic government, and at the height of the Apartheid era in the eighties had not left much of an impression on Aubrey. Having gotten into a bar fight over the closing times at regulation hour, Aubrey was now a marked man. He was fast becoming a loose cannon and realized that he would soon have to go somewhere that the long fist of the law, had not reached.

The Old British Colonies were an obvious area to be avoided at all costs. There was a sense of the all-seeing eye, even in the days before computer assisted tracking devices. Aubrey, although no hardened criminal, could feel the sense that all was not well with the world of Big Business driven autocracies. He was largely broke, and had just spent the majority of his seaman's wage, on three wild evenings on the town.

Luckily, the Captain had recognised his high spiritedness for what it was. He had kept back some wages and with eighty quid, he had directed him to a local ship bound for the port of Beira and summarily dismissed Aubrey.

So, it was that Aubrey now found himself on a Catamaran headed for the port of Beira, via the island of Bazaruto. Several months as a deck hand and some worthwhile scuba diving experience, Aubrey found himself shipping everything from frozen calamari to gold ingots. The gold had been pried from the hands of Zimbabwean villagers, a legacy of the vast gold reserves hidden from the Zimbabwean authorities and smuggled out through the Eastern Highlands across the narrow strip of land to the recently democratised Mozambiquean coast. The plunder was sold to the network of Black-Market pirates who plied their trade along the East African coast. The bounty a fraction of its true market value, but it was a living and there was always an eager seller. The villagers' only failing in life was their inability to make an honest living from trading with the Triads that pretty much controlled the movement of this gold. So, with little opportunity other than their wits and indomitable spirits, these villagers had forged a living from stealing from those that had already stolen from others. This was a lesson Aubrey would take to heart, and one day it would come in handy. Having seen enough action on the High seas, Aubrey decided he would need some shore leave.

This was how he came to be at Chembe, a tiny fishing village on the Cape Maclear peninsula, and a considerable world away from the stifling realities of the First world. The beach spanned the length of the northern peninsular, a billion years of surge and flow had packed the golden beach sand into a double crescent that rivalled the beaches of Rio, and the fresh water lake trapped into a deep gash in the earth's crust, lapped gently onto the lake shore. Everywhere the waters sparkled with a clarity that would catch Aubrey's breath. Then the sun would set across the waters, emblazoning her mark from the western stretch of the Nangangoda mountains bordering the lake, standing sentry over the tiny settlement of Chipoka. Each evening brought with it those sunsets, mesmerizing the eye and warming the heart.

They lived off the Chambo, a local delicacy, speared directly off Otter Point, in water so clear, his visibility was as though looking into and through an aquarium. So, it became known as such, and the tiny Cichlads that hid amongst the rocky outcrops multiplied in numbers, inter-breeding with each branch of its species, until they now numbered in the hundreds. Aubrey began to categorise each remarkable fish, with colours that hinted of a future world; diverse but unfathomable.

He rented a bungalow on the beach on a stretch of undeniable paradise, called Golden Sands. It was here that he delighted in the hospitality of the Chembe villagers, who would share his attention, starved as they were of any sense of education. It was after a drinking bout with Solomon, a sturdy man of great humour and little nonsense, that Aubrey had met a young man called David Cohen, a fellow traveller and an amateur scuba diver. He had come to the Cape Maclear to discover the emerging tourism mecca and wonder of the tropical reefs of the peninsular. Newly arrived from Israel and escaping the military service so many of his compatriots were being forced into, he chose the spirit of adventure rather than the shackles of patriotism. It was shekels he was after and he was no apologist for it. Being an idealist like Aubrey, with no desire to prop up a system doomed to failure, he had chosen to follow the Diaspora.

Idealism set aside, David was from the free-thinking city of Tel Aviv, a city born of new money, and independent of the more fundamentalist society that the State of Israel had birthed. He was a good-looking chap who found easy favour with the local tourist backpacking women, but he had a habit of talking his mind too freely, which made for some interesting discussions.

He had taken Aubrey out on an old wooden plank boat, which was the only long boat with a motor. Dave had secured the boat from a local fisherman as old as the seas, but only too willing to trade his lifestyle and the fish that he had caught for the local market, in return for a few hundred dollars, and an opportunity to work as a guide for the infant scuba diving industry. Lovemore had known all the reefs in the island chains and was an invaluable source of dive sites and information for Dave and Aubrey.

This was how Aubrey ended up, fortuitously, as a dive master on the peninsular and became known by a loyal following of Australian and American women as the Studebaker stud. Aubrey had been six months working with Dave on their fledgling business and after a successful period had managed to save a tidy 300 dollars for himself, a small fortune at the time. He set off for Blantyre for a weekend, with his earnings and the respectable Mount Souche Hotel, two days later had found himself in a card game with an old timer whom Aubrey had befriended. He learnt the game quickly, and in a stroke of luck, seldom seen before, he had beaten the table, and more importantly the old timer. When the old boy was down and out and could not stay at the table, he offered to sell his car to stay in the game, believing he could win it back.

Aubrey accepted, and buying what he thought was an old banger, he parted with three hundred dollars. In fact, the old timer lost the next three rounds and was soon out of cash. Instead of being a sore loser, and a fight ensuing, he had handed over the keys to Aubrey and they had parted ways. When Aubrey left, he saw the 59' Studebaker for the first time, and immediately fell in love. Aubrey drove the Studebaker the 200 miles back to the Cape Maclear peninsular. This was a far cry from the open country roads of Michigan where it had been built, but it was just as much at home on the long winding, strip tarmac roads. He took the powerful V8 motored machine along the coastal highway, enjoying the thrill of its power, and the balmy tropical air cascading into his face as he drove. Aubrey was in his element.

When he arrived back in Chembe, he would be swamped by the local village kids, who had grown to love Aubrey. The old Studebaker had done quarter of a million miles since new, and the compression ratio on the big old engine, was as the day it had been churned out of that Detroit factory. The rust was setting in, but Aubrey would spend days at a time in the off-season lovingly restoring her, but there was no alternative to the big block power of an American V8. Yet even this thinking was as tenuous as any discussion, they had during their tenure on the peninsular. Dave would counter Aubrey's monologues with the American tourists, whose love of Malawi only extended so far, but could not usurp their patriotic belief in the American way.

Whereas, Dave believed the opposite having witnessed first-hand the corrupting influence of Big Business on his own infant country. No amount of convincing would change his mind. One evening, sitting around the fire, a burly American with a wife half his age asked Dave;

"When the Israeli's have defeated the Palestinian terrorists, will you go back to Israel?"

Dave thought about this for a moment, and answered.

"Israel exists only for the duration of its usefulness to the American Government. When the oil in the Middle East is no longer available, or the onset of alternative fuels, renders it unprofitable, American Big Business won't need the stabilising effect of Israel's' Nuclear threat to the region. When that happens, and there is no necessity for selling military hardware to Israel, then I believe the Arabs will seek their opportunity to reclaim their lost lands."
He believed that no amount of convincing would deter Palestinians from what they consider their birth right.

"They blame the Americans for supporting Israel unequivocally, and Britain for interfering in 1948. They will continue to fight until they have achieved nationhood, whether that includes an Israeli State, or not!"

"This is a war of attrition and ideology aside, the Palestinians and the Jews have been fighting over the land for several millennia." The American listened.

"So, you believe peace efforts are futile?" The American had interjected.

"Of course, if Israel continues to allow the expansion of settlements directly alongside the partition! Imagine if Germany had managed to stop the advancing Russians on the border between Poland and East Germany. Then sued for peace, intending to keep those territories; the Allies would never have accepted that at the time, even if it had saved lives. So too, will the Palestinians not accept anything less than the withdrawal of Israel out of Palestine. If I were an Israeli Politician, I would be starting a dialogue with the Palestinians before they have outlived their usefulness, because without the might of the American's backing them, Israeli's will find themselves out numbered, and incapable of defending themselves against an historical adversary. Apartheid Israel will have to be more accommodating to the Palestinians', otherwise the alternative is not worth thinking about."

"You mean Israel will not survive if the Americans pull out of the Middle East?" The American had intently awaited his reply.

"Yes. I mean that once there is no need for Israel to act as an influence against Arab self-determination and the liberation of land usurped during the Six Day War, the Americans will desert them." Aaron quietly lucid, argued as a matter-of-fact.

"The oligarchies that control the Middle East have dictated for too long, and enjoyed the profits of an industry which is run like a cartel; once that system is replaced by more representative democracies, then Israel will have outlived its usefulness, and the West will turn their back on the Jews, as they had done in Africa." He was adamant.

The group had fallen silent. This was something neither Aubrey nor the others had even considered. Dave could not have known how accurate his prediction would be, or how ironic the analogy between the two states would become. Had he been a politician, he may have had a more direct influence on the outcome; but maybe not.

Aubrey and Dave were slowly carving out a name for themselves and it was not long before other operators were trying to get in on the tourist scuba action. The beach at Golden Sands was becoming synonymous with great dives as it was ideal for the loading and ferrying of divers out to the islands. Unlike the unpredictable oceans, Lake Malawi, was a fresh water lake, with a history that only Doctor David Livingston could have envisioned and pioneers like Aubrey could fabricate into a legacy. As he had stood on the shores of Cape Maclear, named after his erstwhile colleague in the Cape colony thousands of miles to the south; he had announced that the sun shone off the lake, "as a Lake of Stars". The sun rose spectacularly off the eastern shores with Mozambique, and unlike any other setting on the lake, allowed the sunsets, from the sanctuary of that peninsular, to kindle the western waters with a myriad of glistening reflections, off its mirrored surface.

Chapter 7

Reality check

Aubrey remembered so well, those shallow sandy beaches, which at low tide had stretched as far as the hand capped eyes could see. The moored boats, waiting patiently for the return of the moon's gravitational pull, and the odd howling of the village mutts, whose function in village life was to clean up the scraps that fell from the fish drying beds, strung out along the village shoreline and lofted high enough out of reach. But more fundamental to this, was the moon's influence on the major source of sustenance to the Chembe village and up and down the coast of Lake Nyasa, as it had been affectionately known.

The fishing village of Chembe had been in existence since the time of Dr. Livingstone, in 1859. This was where he had set up his first missionary station, believing God would help him bring civilisation to the local heathens. Negotiating with the Arab slave traders, Livingstone had helped to bring an end to this evil scourge.

But it was short-lived, because on his return some four years later, the entire village had been wiped out by Malaria. All his ideals were set aside for God's wrath on those pitiful fishermen, and nothing had changed in the interceding one hundred and fifty years.

This was Africa's reality. The lure of fish for hungry tummies, was as strong as the moon's influence on the fishing process. Late at night, as the moon rose above the pristine waters of Lake Nyasa, the fishermen would stoke their lanterns and head out into deeper waters. Here the silver bait, or Usipa drawn upwards towards the light, and tricked into believing the lanterns were the source of millions of years of a habituated instinct, were lured into the fisherman's nets, and unceremoniously hauled on board the waiting boats.

This was the staple diet for millions of Malawians, and yet the tiny Usipa contained more than just protein and vital sustenance. The lake, having been fished sparingly for a millennia, was now in the throes of a man-made crisis. Here where Livingstone had begun his ministry, was a population on the rise. Fifteen thousand strong after several generations of quinine and medical care, albeit limited, the population of Chembe was growing, as was the demand for fish. The pollution of first world packaging was already evident, and with it the toxic waste of a world out of synch.

But critically, Chembe Village, was the source of a growing tourism trade, that brought with it, a desire to have what those westerners had in abundance. The lure of the 'green-back' the currency of choice in Africa. This was the conundrum that awaited all societies, drawn towards a desire for amenities and luxuries, unknown to their ancestors, and the village of Chembe was in that un-envious paradox between a quaint fishing community from a by-gone era, which lured the tourists; and a demand by the locals to have what the emerging guest houses and lodges offered their dollar paying customers.

It was Aubrey's desire to see an improvement in the facilities that the villagers hungered for. But the obvious question arose from how to fund these much-needed conveniences. The Government of Kamuzu Banda was not interested in Chembe, tucked away on that isolated peninsular, so it would be up to Aubrey and like-minded humanitarians to help. This was the start of a love affair, with the people of Chembe, that would last a lifetime.

The valuing of human life, integrity and good old fashioned honesty, had unfortunately become such devalued commodities. A world that now seems to run on oil fumes and the incessant and growing greed and selfishness of a group of elitists who were drunk on greed and power. This was the World that Aubrey was witness to and which he could reshape, albeit a margin at a time.

Aubrey was back in real time. Back in the present, and he was driving on the motorway. Just driving. But as he had been day dreaming, he had found himself a short distance from the M4. With no meetings to attend to that afternoon, Aubrey had left Finsbury and spontaneously headed for the motorway on which he was now heading west. Only too happy to put his foot down, and feel the power of the Roller under him, the two, inseparable and incorrigible. It was like riding some great chariot to the Roman Coliseum, as Emperors of antiquity would have done. Aubrey was somewhere near Reading before he realized that he had been travelling at 100 miles an hour.

He immediately took his foot off the accelerator and began slowing down. He ducked off the M4, through a spaghetti-junction and was taking an A' road heading for the City. Aubrey opened his window slightly, to breath in some fresh air and as he did so there was a sudden noise like the wailing of the AIDS orphans he had witnessed in a clinic in Brazzaville. The sound assailed his senses. He had been focused on the roar of his engine and cocooned inside the Roller, had been oblivious to any external noise.

Assaulted by the sound of a siren, ear-splitting and insistent, he was literally shocked back to reality. Since he'd slowed down enough to look over his shoulder, Aubrey did so. Sighting the motorway patrol car with its blue flashing light, just behind him and to his left, his heart skipped a beat. He had not seen it come up behind him, some two miles back, winding its way through the traffic. The roar of the six litre V8 motor drowning out all external noise, he had been oblivious of his circumstances.

Like those new born children screaming for attention, the patrol vehicle suddenly filled his review mirror. The driver, in official-looking police uniform, with epaulets and black tie, broadcast his instruction through a loudhailer to take the next off ramp. Aubrey, who had never been pulled over by a traffic cop, in his life, was not sure if he should slow down even more as he was in the inside fast lane? Should he speed up, and get in front of the car blocking the middle lane, or slow down and allow the patrol vehicle to guide him off the motorway? Instinctively, he hammered the accelerator down to clear the Volvo to his left. As he did this he left the patrol car in his wake, and once clear he began to slow down again.

Before realizing his folly, what happened next was worthy of a James Bond movie special effect. Leaving the middle lane, Aubrey eased the car off the highway onto the shoulder to take the Reading inner-city exit. This had caused the patrolman in his brightly regaled Ford, to accelerate in anticipation of Aubrey's escape, only to realize that Aubrey had slowed again. The patrolman furiously hit the brakes to avoid hitting the Volvo as it had slowed to avoid Aubrey. But it was too late; the patrol car slewed sideways in its haste to follow Aubrey, and the two collided. The Volvo then slammed into the side of another vehicle, and they all ended up pirouetting harmlessly to a halt on the off ramp.

Aubrey glanced back in the large rear-view mirror to see this sheer chaos. Catching his breath, he recognised a welcome sign and turning left and doubling back, he made directly for the entrance to the University grounds. Along Whiteknights Road and right, into the main campus grounds he ducked. He could lose himself on the campus and drove south looking for the library. He soon found it deep in the heart of The Whiteknights Campus, he found the parking area and a welcome rendezvous with a restroom.

He could go back to check that the three drivers were uninjured, or relieve himself as quickly as possible. Even if he had gone back, he surmised, there would be unprecedented publicity, and an unwelcome incarceration for him at the local constabulary. If he ventured on, there may be even more recriminations, but having lived in frontier societies for the last twenty years it was a risk he was willing to tackle. Deniability was his master stroke, he argued with his growing conscience, but something the Professor had said triggered a sudden and irrevocable curiosity. He felt no real compunction of responsibility, so continued up the large concrete stairway to the entrance of the Main library.

The building was singularly uninspiring, with its contemporary structure, large plate glass windows allowing as much natural light into the building as the English weather permitted. He made for the reception desk, signed the visitors register as I.P Knightly, and headed for the café and the welcome sign of the 'men's room'.

Completing his ablutions with an involuntary shake, Aubrey wandered into the main foyer and looked through the glass doors. He had come to know his intuition and ventured inside. He needed somewhere quiet to reflect and what better place than a Library. He had felt this guidance so many times, that it had encouraged his interests and study in the esoteric field. Somehow, he knew it was some force of nature that was always protecting him. He knew he was only a passenger on these voyages and knew better than to question this impulse. He could not explain what was happening, when driven in this way. It was as if he were on a mission.

Aubrey recalled the great library on King's campus, which exuded an air of civility and learned scholarship. This library was an abject lesson in functionality for the masses and no sense of history or drama. The students were engrossed in their reading matter and studies, and as Aubrey entered one of the study rooms none of them even noticed his arrival. They were in various states of posture, as if they had spent too many long hours amongst those library walls. Some, with their backs glued to plastic chairs, bent from the weight of weary study, and others slouched across the broad rectangular tables, form meeting function. They focused intently on their books, with pencil and pen slowly twirling 'twixt hand and mouth as if to evoke deep thoughts of profundity. Whilst there were still others hunched up close to the tables, furiously writing notes.

He was not sure what he was looking for, but he knew he would need to have access to the main library shelves. What he needed was a recent study which had appeared in a journal of science. Aubrey made for the second floor, two steps at a time and the science section. He browsed through the rows of stacked books with a military precision, following the titles one after the other, from top to bottom, as he worked his way through an unending array. Although some felt they deserved more of his attention, he kept his eyes and his thoughts focused, on what he was meant to find. His head askew, to make reading of the subject labels easier. This evoked a thought as to why on earth titles were printed sideways. His thoughts a quiet criticism of this soulless pursuit of knowledge! The ancient Egyptians had formulated their Hieroglyphic text in just such a manner; but mankind would never learn from the past, so was doomed to continue making the same mistakes into the future.

He knew that he could have gone to the reception desk, and asked for help, but he did not feel like entering a conversation with what may become a notoriously inquisitive Librarian. Aubrey could spend the entire afternoon searching, but was now concerned about time. There seemed to be almost no subject matter that scientists had not pondered at or over, in their short tenure on this Earth. A tenure which barely amounted to one trillionth of the age of our universe. However, they had left almost no stone unturned, in the search for ultimate knowledge, but had neglected the one inevitable truth. Aubrey sensed that science and spirituality would ultimately end up as two locomotives, driven forward incessantly on a collision course. Somewhere, in his past studies, he recalled what Tesla had stated, "The day science begins to study non-physical phenomena, it will make more progress in one decade than in all the previous centuries of its existence."

Aubrey was spurred on by this insatiable appetite, and no discussion with a librarian would bring the knowledge to him any sooner. Surveying that vast array of scholarly works, he reminisced about his time at King's when as a student he had lost his sense of decorum in a bold and profound manner that only students could. His mind wandered as he recalled the events of that steamy tryst all those years ago. It aroused him and piqued his sexuality in a way that surprised and shocked him.

The King's College Library had been built in the neo-Gothic architecture of the early half of the nineteenth century. Built many years after the famous Chapel, it still evoked haunting visions of historical portent. The large ornate book shelves stood as sentinels to the group of students. They dominated the vast interior in neat rows, testament to the accumulation of centuries of works of literature. Their sombre quiet presence lent an air of earnest studiousness to the arcane atmosphere. Natural light arced through the large arched windows falling as if 'magically' across the works of some of the greatest minds of the last millennia. Through the Gothic inspired portals, a glow of gilded superiority was created from the opaque, lead-framed glass. The yellowish tinges of light softened and warmed the room, giving the library a tranquillity which inspired the mind. It threw shadows across the elaborate ceilings, with their lavish mouldings. It was an atmosphere, inviting, comfortable and alive.

It was enough to stimulate the mind and arouse the senses. Then as now, Aubrey had sifted through titles with names that beggared belief. The search for immortality was stacked above and beyond him amongst those learned columns of reading material. He knew the name of that inherent condition that somehow filled his mind and aroused his manhood. It was a condition known as **literarianism.**

Aubrey now recalled how he had looked up to see the girl from his study desk peering around the corner of the book shelf. She had obviously followed him when he had entered the library. He involuntarily smiled, and taking this as a come on, she approached him directly and without so much as a "hello", she kissed him full on the lips. This may have been unsolicited, but Aubrey felt his heart racing like the first time he had been seduced at the tender age of 16, by an older woman whilst on a school tour to Spain. Aubrey responded with the same intensity as he had then.

He returned the kiss with the full passion this spontaneous action required, and although she must have been no more than 19 or 20 years old, she was exceptionally confident and in full control of the moment. She smelt of lavender and a hint of a perfume which aroused him even more. He thought briefly about his mother, before kissing her again, even more passionately this time. Now he found himself reaching around her with both arms, placing the dictionary in his grasp, on the edge of the shelf just above them.

Pulling her towards him strongly she melted into his embrace. His mouth covered hers as she whimpered with a guttural intensity that told Aubrey she was ready. 'But here in the library? Why not', he had thought.

This was the moment he had long fantasized about during those long boring days at lectures and there was no mistaking her willingness. But how was he going to have her in there, with all the other student's mere meters away? He still had not had any conversation with her and decided to at least institute an introduction before proceeding any further.

She solved the problem in his mind, by going directly to her haunches, her bare thighs exposed as her skirt lifted from the knee, and in one deft movement she had unzipped him and reaching into his pants with one hand, she had released his burgeoning manhood with the other. Her mouth was on him in an instant and she was devouring him in a frenzy of lust.

'So much for English prudishness', he had thought. She was unhesitant and clearly enjoying herself as much as he was. The thought of someone peering around the corner intensified the moment of passion as Aubrey had leaned against the book shelf, his seducer performing fellatio on him with wild abandon. The thought of being exposed further excited him.

Ironically, he could not have been more aroused. This brought on a moment of sheer ecstasy which simply heightened his pleasure, and he knew he could ejaculate in a moment. Before this could happen, they were both brought down to earth by a thunder clap of a noise that erupted right next to them and echoed throughout the whole library. Looking around dazed and with his member still exposed, he saw the culprit.

The dictionary had been dislodged from the shelf by their wild antics and had hit the floor with a crash. This had nearly caused severe damage, had he not instantly reacted and withdrawn from her mouth. She had reacted by grabbing his hand and dragging him further into an annex, away from the main library hall, down two steps and into an open arena which was packed with old editions from one side to the other. As they reached the nearest rack, she had swung Aubrey back towards her, his momentum taking him back towards the shelf and back into her embrace. She continued kissing him, but now he could taste his own essence in her mouth, and it was strangely erotic. He had tried performing fellatio on himself as a young boy at Eton, when his class mates had dared him to, but had not enjoyed the taste. It was a taste he could not discern: nor recall.

His distracted mind was directed back to the moment, as the girl had once again, reached for his provoked manhood, placing a hand over it and drawing it further from his pants with a twist of her wrist. Simultaneously she expertly lifted her left leg, exposing her skirt as it hitched up to her waist, and with a lunge had raised herself onto her toes and literally skewered herself onto him. She was not wearing any panties and Aubrey could feel and smell the intensity of her heat, as the aroma hit him with a rush of pheromone. He took his queue and lifting her thigh, he wrapped her legs around his waist and without hesitation he had penetrated her with the passion that she had evoked in him. Aubrey was very close to release and could not hold himself back for much longer. With his mouth pressed against hers he suddenly felt the most powerful orgasm he had ever had overwhelm every fibre of his core. As the intensity of that moment had subsided, he had opened his eyes, his head appearing above the lower book shelf, and found himself looking back through the archway towards the row where they had been moments before.

The librarian was stooped over the dictionary laying on the floor, and with a quizzical look she had picked it up with both hands, peering left and right while she held it to her breast. Aubrey could see her between the stack of books, but she could clearly not see him. As he had watched her she placed the dictionary in her left hand and with one more, stern glance around the room, disappeared back along the aisle to her desk.

The memory of that moment came flooding back to him as he now stood in the central annex of that passionless building in Reading. The onset of education for the majority had ensured the evidence of such sterile academia. It was all geared to maximum facilitation and mass instruction. Computers, improved secondary education and vast Government budgets which bankrupted the country, now stood as testament to the progression of the social integration of the class wars in Britain. It had been going on since William the Conqueror had first built his castle on that Cambridge hill one thousand years before, and now continued with student riots. It would never cease until everyone was equal. But the sad truth was that the poor were getting poorer and the social welfare system was bankrupt, financially and morally.

Aubrey was not sure if he was supposed to be looking for a title, a word, a subject, something incorporated in the text, and perhaps not overtly visible. Aubrey knew in his mind's eye what he was looking for, but consciously could not fathom the word. The name was tantalisingly close, but for the fact that his thoughts were blocked by carnal images. What he needed to visualize, was the spelling of it; he would have to adopt one of his favourite studying techniques. Aubrey would recount the alphabet and slowly work his way down, starting with A and visually capturing every word and idea that came to him, as he did. This had helped him memorise large tracts of content for exams, and had also proven effective when trying to remember names of associates and colleagues.

But this was not a name he was familiar with and it was not a written word he had ever seen before, but a word he had heard mention of on television. The Professor would have known. He needed a mobile phone right now! Strange, over a billion cell phones were in operation but he had never been one of those billion who felt the urge to get one. He had always felt that if he was really needed, he could always be reached on a landline in his office. Nothing else was so urgent that it couldn't wait.

The world had created too much instant gratification for Aubrey's likes anyway. All his colleagues carried cell phones, and he was secretly incensed when they rang inappropriately during meetings. Knowing what he knew now, having escaped the Congo and not a moment too soon, Aubrey was decidedly anti-cell phone.

Aubrey decided that if he was to speed up his search he needed to get to a computer to browse the internet, or better still needed to make use of a... "Of course," why hadn't he thought of it sooner!

He turned around and walked back from the central annex where the floor space of the library was optimised to offer all the Sciences and Medical journals he needed. It would take him too long. He needed a computer and someone to log him on.

Amongst the students there would surely be someone willing to assist him amongst all these medical students.

He strolled to the study rooms once more, trying not to draw attention to himself. This was not a possibility because he was conscious of being twice the average age of all the occupants of the library. But he need not have worried as all the students had their heads down in their studies, and seemed not to notice his presence. As Aubrey reached the middle room, a young, very attractive brunette, with a pair of rimless reading spectacles, looked up from her computer console. She gave Aubrey a definite smile before abruptly catching herself, demurely averting her gaze so as not to encourage him further. He noticed that as she did so, she fidgeted uncomfortably in her seat.

He paused as he rounded the room and reached her side. He stood over her shoulder, the natural fall of thick curls gathered in a sensible ponytail. So as to not heighten her awkwardness, he sat on the table to her right. She peeked up at him again through those tiny spectacles that seemed to accentuate her green eyes; a fleeting turn of the corner of her full mouth and just a hint of lip gloss but no lipstick. She was clearly a studious type. Certainly, not the typical hussy Aubrey had become used to in the ladies' bars and members' clubs of the mining communities in Africa. She was exquisitely good-looking with a peaches and cream complexion which soon turned ruddy as she became conscious of his gaze. She squirmed in her seat lifting her head. Aubrey, who was now focused on the screen, turned and smiled once more into her eyes.

She smiled back, and knowing that he was using the computer as a pretext to strike up a conversation, she quickly closed the page she had been perusing, and pushed her chair back to get a better look at Aubrey.

Aubrey responded immediately, gauging the situation, he apologised for interrupting and whispered.

"Hello, I don't mean to interrupt, but I may need your help!"

She smiled back, and catching the gist of his subterfuge replied in a hushed but husky retort:
"And what makes you think that I could help you?"

"You have an access code to the computer!" He smiled. It was obvious.

"Ohhh!" She went scarlet again. She averted her gaze from his and looked back at the blank screen.

"I really am sorry for imposing. But I do need your help!" Aubrey was enjoying her discomfort, but only enough to provoke her conscience. She was less than half his age.

Casually he pulled an empty chair closer, and gesturing to sit, he smiled again.

"Yes, please do!" Intuitively she saw this as a welcome distraction.

"Thank you," taking the invitation, he sat.

"My name is Aubrey," he ventured.

He acknowledged her smile, keeping her gaze until the last second.

'Was she flirting with him?' Aubrey felt she was, and could sense a real wave of pheromones releasing into the stuffy afternoon air.

"Natasha." She returned his gaze. She was reading something in his soul. He cocked his head to one side, inquisitively.

Natasha averted her eyes.

"How can I help you, Aubrey?" But she already knew the answer.

"I was wondering if you could look up something on the internet." He was playing with her now.

"Yes certainly. Is it a condition or a treatment?" He suspected she knew that too.

"It is a word which I heard on a TV channel, while they were discussing treatment for liver cancer." Leaving the 'C' word hanging.

"Oh! What is the word?" Turning back instinctively to the keyboard, a welcome intervention to the proximity of their bodies.
He was silent. "That's the problem. I am not sure of the name, but it is one of those fancy medical jargons." He apologised.

"That's okay," she turned back to him. "Do you know what letter it starts with?"

His blank expression was evidence not.

"That's okay," Natasha now turned back to the computer. She keyed in "Liver Cancer / latest treatment / FDA approval.

'Bang!' There it was in a series of paragraphs, headed with a keynote in bold text.

'So much easier than browsing through medical journals and dictionaries in alphabetical order,' he thought, scooting in closer as her body heat became even more evident. He was instantly aroused.

She read through the text, clicked on the link and they silently read.

Aubrey could not help himself and kept looking between Natasha and the screen until it became patently obvious he was staring. She looked away from the screen again to acknowledge his gaze, and fidgeted again. It was like electricity.

He recalled the scene in the Library all those years ago. Her mouth had tasted of mint and something else he could not recall until now;

'That's it,' he remembered, 'Almond! That's what it had tasted like. 'Salted almonds!'

He could feel the waves flooding the room. Aubrey smiled again and quietly said. "Thank you."

Chapter 8

Cape Maclear 1989

Aubrey, had now been living at Cape Maclear for five years. The golden sands made so famous by Doctor Livingstone. The beaches and the sub-tropical vegetation had an air of mysticism about it. There were baobab and stinkwood, giant red flowered plants of an unknown Latin name, whilst the sultry vegetation seemed to encroach right into his room, there was a gentle expectancy of the cool breeze wafting across the languid blue waters, upon which the stars of sunlit reflection twinkled like the myriad of a night sky.

David Livingstone had stood on that very beach, looking out onto the waters and proclaimed them "as a myriad of winking galaxies glittering from the crystal facets of water," and then Lake Nyasa was born. He had set up his first Christian Mission on that very shore, claiming the land for Christ and his love of this land and its people, worthy of God's evangelical home. Sadly, the Mission had not contended with that one enemy of man, whom Satan himself had seemed to manifest through ever screen and gauze covering available to man; the mosquito.

On his return three years after the Mission had been built, he discovered that God himself had not made provision for the malaria virus, and a devastated Livingstone had relented to greater powers, and relocated that Mission to the aptly named Livingstonia, in the cooler climes of the southern mountain region. Aubrey could sense an almost tangible irony, upon which the legacy of Livingstone and his efforts to subdue the heathen, and eradicate the slave trade, had rested on so imperceptible a critter. On those star-speckled waters of the Lake Nyasa, his spiritual guide by his side, Aubrey was about to get a history lesson he would not forget.

Dave was as likeable and gregarious as any mate Aubrey had known. But unlike his friends at home, there was something shifty about the way he could not hold Aubrey's gaze, when pitching his latest grand scheme. Aubrey intuitively knew that this was how sales people made their fortunes, by pummelling the hapless public into buying something they need not have purchased, but with Dave it was contagious. He was ten years Aubrey's senior, and had a knack of getting Aubrey to agree, against his better judgement.

Aubrey put this down to his infectious good looks, and an ability to charm the young girls whose island trips invariably ended with his romantic exploits. From Dave's point of view, it was always a holiday romance. These sordid affairs invariably ended in broken hearts as backpackers, with wild abandon had thrown themselves at him. Aubrey, although finding these exploits extremely amusing, was always unsettled by Dave's proclivity of finding the most vulnerable young women. He would woo them, deflower them, and then dispose of them as soon as another nubile young tourist came along. It would have been all the more amusing, had it not been for the discomfort Aubrey felt every time he sent them on their way, initiated but smitten.

Then it became Aubrey's duty to pack them off to their respective lodge, with only a promise to give Dave their hastily prepared address so he would write them. If it were not so disconcerting, it would have made for interesting fire side stories. But Aubrey never forwarded the addresses because they may have ended in that fire anyway. To his credit, he never spoke of his exploits but kept his conquests a well-guarded secret. Aubrey, however was becoming aware of a lot more that he kept to himself.

Aubrey merely chose to err on the side of caution. He preferred the company of the local women whose breeding, and whose culture lessened the demands of Aubrey's time, outside of the boudoir. It was a hedonistic world of sun, sea and sex. The three combined would leave them exhausted, but the contagion of their circumstances somehow gave them the stamina to continue. Aubrey had not yet dabbled in the delights of the lovelorn lasses that literally threw themselves at the two sun-bronzed Adonis's. Yet it was inevitable.

So it was that the two of them had settled into a routine, with Dave expanding the business interests, and Aubrey containing the public relations issues. Scuba was their life, and the categorization of all the fish species became Aubrey's vocation. All the latest gadgets, and gizmos had to be acquired, and it became Aubrey's job to procure them. The business was expanding dramatically and they were making a name for themselves. Malawi was an inevitable paradise and the tourists flocked.

One fiery summer evening, whilst seated around the beach camp, caught in the flickering light of the bewitching, bloodstained sunset over Golden Sands, Dave became intoxicated by the sight and a little too much rum. This was the story he told of his father.

"My Grandfather was a Jewish immigrant to England. He escaped from the Bolsheviks in Saint Petersburg, just in time to avoid the purges. He had managed to buy his family train tickets out of Russia by bribing a border official on the Finnish border in the spring of 1917. It was in those days that the British had made the Balfour Declaration part of their attempt to garner the support of the Jewish community in London. This had a large influence on civil society, and the cash strapped Government. The Zionist movement had seen the shift of power moving towards the Allies in the Great War, so they saw their opportunity and with the League of Nations mandating the breakup of the Ottoman Empire, they lobbied for a Jewish Homeland."

Aubrey was unsure why Dave had suddenly begun divulging his family history; suffice it to say that he had never spoken of his family before. He was beginning to reach out to Aubrey, who was happy to share in his new-found sense of camaraderie. It certainly was uncharacteristic. He continued.

"The Zionist Foundation in London then paid for my Grand Parents and their twelve children to have their passage paid from Helsinki to London. It was only after the outset of the Second World War that my father, who was too old to join the army, and too young to sit around doing nothing, then embarked on a clandestine trip to Palestine, with funding from the Zionists."

Drunk from the punch they had been drinking, Aubrey sensed he was probably more intoxicated by his own success, and the splendour of the setting and thought this an opportune moment to share his family's history.

"In Palestine, he had heard rumours from the Jews who had managed to escape Hitler's Germany, about the concentration camps. This spurred him on to greater heights, and he eventually became a Captain in the newly formed Zionist resistance." Aubrey could imagine their sense of historic reverence.

"A return to the Biblical story of Joshua?" Aubrey had asked.

"In a manner of speaking!" Dave was impressed that Aubrey had a grasp of the history of Palestine.

"Anyway, he travelled from Palestine to Hungary and the old Czech Republic to help escaping Jews, and that was when he was wounded in an attempt to get a family out of Prague." He was naturally proud of his father's exploits, albeit, so distant a concept to his own philosophy.

"What he did not tell me until years later, was that he was not shot by the Germans, but by an angry Gypsy, with whose daughter my father had slept!" The smile acknowledged an irony.

"He had agreed to take them out of Prague when the persecution of his family had resulted in his two sons being sent to Auschwitz. His daughter was a beautiful woman who my father had agreed to take to safety. But when the time came to arrange the journey, my father reneged on his agreement. The Gypsy's were not to be double crossed, so they pursued him all the way to the border with Albania, to avenge his daughter's honour. The Gypsy sacrificed his own life to get my father. Fortunately for my dad, a German patrol heard the gun shots, and finding the Gypsy's they shot them, thinking they were trying to escape. My father managed to slip away. He never went back, but vowed thereafter to build a Jewish home for our family to ensure that these tragic events never happened again." Aaron was quiet. Aubrey did not move, nor make the effort to comment. The irony was palpable, in more ways than one.

Aubrey was not able to comprehend just how deep a scar these events must have left on Aaron's self-esteem. To imagine that he was here to enjoy the pleasures of this magical world of self-indulgence, but for the bad timing of an assassination attempt, and a German's bullet! Years later Aubrey would understand the calamity of those events in the psyche of his business colleague and the extent to which he would have gone to hide from his past. The two were similar in many ways, both hiding from a domineering father, but each a world apart in their business ethics. It would be a wakening for both.

The five years he had spent on the island had been tremendously rewarding. In addition, Aubrey, now 27 years old, was beginning to assert himself a little more, and was confident to allow the relationships he developed to grow into more meaningful experiences. In a tropical paradise with no more than their immediate physical needs to satisfy, he finally succumbed to the winsome allure of a young Zimbabwean girl.

She captured his attention, with her strawberry-blond hair blown wildly over her shapely neck, as the sun caressed her broad bronze-sculptured shoulders, shaped by the passage of time spent in the Zimbabwean swim team. Her zest for life, contagious; the fickleness of youth her prized possession. She was wholesome, and riveting to behold. The azure sky reflected in those sparkling orbs, alive, passionate and testimony to a soul, deeply etched by circumstance and unaffected by history.

They spent some time alone on the beach, whilst her parents were on a trip to the neighbouring islands. Bronwyn was her name, and she was remarkable in her understated beauty. The sun speckled freckles spread across her nose and cheeks like the mottled hew of a splash of Namaqualand daisies. Her high forehead and luscious locks, gave her a rather impish demeanour, which was difficult to resist. Aubrey found the time they had spent on the beach and frolicking in the sea, the most splendid distraction from the impending afternoon tropical shower. They had raced back to his chalet when the rain had started to fall, and with the dark clouds shielding the afternoon sun, they had made love on the low-slung mattress, hidden from sight by only the shade cloth hanging over the door, and the driving rain that screened the sounds of their passionate embrace. This was more of a moment for Aubrey, than it was for Bronwyn, but a bond was formed through their fervent love making, that would change both his outlook and the course of their relationship forever.

When Dave had come looking for him to help with a group of newly arrived tourists, he found Aubrey and Bronwyn in the midst of a post-coital slumber. He was visibly disturbed by the sight of these two love birds, but it did not register on either of them that he was enraged by jealousy. He had tried to seduce her the previous night, but her breeding, and the unfortunate comment by her father, overheard but misunderstood by Dave, had resorted in his first and only rejection for some time. The 'old man' had been just a little bigoted in his dismissiveness of Dave, being a typical father and choosing to be over protective with his daughter. What he had said, sounded like, "Don't you even think about fraternizing with that 'Mediterranean Sea captain', but to those brought up in the shielded halls of pre-independence Zimbabwe, it had a rather more racist implication when pronounced with a broad Rhodesian accent and direct reference to unbelief!

The embarrassment Aubrey suffered was not mirrored by Bronwyn. She had grown up with older brothers, who although protective were somewhat loose with their tongues and unashamed of their nakedness. Bronwyn had been dismissive of Dave's ill-timed incursion, choosing to stand entirely naked in front of them both as she retrieved her bikini and sarong.

Dave could not help but admire her leggy beauty, whilst Aubrey had been a tad bashful as he searched for his shorts. It was clear to Dave that he had been passed over for his younger protégé and it did not sit comfortably with his ego. Bronwyn departed for the evening, in search of her parents and siblings, albeit entirely un-phased.

"What the hell are you doing with her," he mustered after she had slipped past him in the doorway, and bolted with her colt-like legs across the beach, in search of her returned parents.

"What does it matter," Aubrey was now a little peeved about the intrusion and certainly the lack of respect offered for his privacy.

"It matters a hell of a lot," Dave had retorted. "Her father is a damn racist, and she probably is equally as bigoted!"

"Why?" Aubrey had not been privy to the previous evenings quip. Clearly, he was still smarting from the comment.

"Because I don't like people who make comments about others without even as much as the courtesy of hiding their bigotry, and especially when those comments are directed at me."

Aubrey, let it slip. He was dressed now and out the door, without so much as another thought. It was better if they just left it and did not discuss the matter further, even though Dave remained detached and pre-occupied for the remainder of the evening.

Several days went by, with Bronwyn finding any opportunity to be alone with Aubrey. They spent the mornings out on dives, with Bronwyn tagging along with Aubrey as her dive buddy. She held his hand as they descended into the pristine aqua-blue waters off Cape Maclear. The calm, clear waters of the island chains off the northern tip of the mainland attracted every conceivable tropical fish species; it was a veritable Eden. They frolicked under water once the other divers had surfaced, and Aubrey allowed his senses to be stimulated beyond all his previous imagination.

It was a balmy afternoon dive, when Aubrey had returned from his last trip for the day, and seeing the dive crew safely to shore, he slipped backwards off the prow of the boat and allowed himself the pleasure of a cool soaking, sinking below the surface and descending into the sandy shallow water. He often held his breath for over a minute and allowed his mind to vegetate with the solitude of the moment. The cool sea and the dancing light off the tranquil lapping waves calmed and numbed his senses. This was his way of meditating. A mindless submission to the external world; his rapture beyond the worldly reach of man's iniquities. He stayed down as long as his burning lungs would allow, laying on his back searching upwards, lost in time and space; he allowed the gentle surge of the tide to rock him gently from side to side, immersed in pleasure.

As he revelled in that moment of freedom, he felt something slid past his left leg. With his eyes glazed from the darting pirouettes of light, he raised his head and searched towards the interruption. There, in the magnified clarity of the filtered afternoon light, he saw that impish face looking down at him. Bronwyn had waited for him patiently on the beach and joined him once the others had disembarked.

Aubrey smiled and his greeting was returned with a dazzling show of the pearliest bleach-white teeth. Aubrey found her smile infectious and her inappropriateness charming. She held onto his leg and expelling the air in her lungs descended on top of him, her curly hair floating about her head like a shock of blanched Phylum Rhodophyta.

Aubrey pulled her to him and kissed her. The fresh water and her tongue mixed sensually with her soft tanned skin, to dissolve any remaining doubts he had; he knew he loved her. He would follow her to the ends of the world and beyond. Aubrey felt alive and invigorated unlike any thought he had ever imagined. Somehow, he would need to express those thoughts.

Bronwyn was due to leave the following day and it was to prove an exacting twenty-four hours. They were inseparable and Aubrey made promises to visit her in Zimbabwe. They were going to get together as soon as he had saved up enough cash to come out. Bronwyn was excited. They swapped addresses and would write as often as he could. The two love-birds were making their nest figuratively, now that they had consummated their relationship. Before he knew it, Bronwyn was gone and he felt alone for the first time in many years.

Because Aubrey had not been back to the home country since embarking on his long trip, it had seemed that he had been away a lifetime. The call had come from his father of all people, who had found out where he was by pure chance, when an article about Cape Maclear had appeared in a national dive magazine. There was a picture of Aubrey in his diving gear getting ready to escort a group of tourists out to one of the many reefs they chartered to. The picture was taken at a distance, but there was no mistaking Aubrey, who now tanned, muscled and bearded had become the quintessential beach bum.

His father had seen the article when visiting his barrister's office in The City. It had been the barrister in fact, an old friend of the family, who had pointed out the picture of Aubrey and suggested that Lord Pennington contact his son. The shame of admitting to having a son who, instead of heading up a successful brokerage firm, or leading audit firm, had resorted to sitting on a beach and wasting his life away, was too much for Lord Pennington. He had in fact not told his wife about the discovery, and had sworn the barrister to secrecy. That was how Aubrey's mom had spent the last year of her life – not knowing where her beloved son was. This had caused her to die of a broken heart and total sense of abandonment by both her husband and now her son.

When Lady Pennington died in the fall, Aubrey had been contacted by the family barrister and told of his mother's death. He immediately boarded a plane from Blantyre and after a stopover in Cairo, had found himself back home. The tension between father and son was unbearable and having attended the funeral and barely speaking to his father, Aubrey was just about ready to get back to the Cape Maclear. As he was making arrangements to board the first plane back to Malawi, he received a telegram from Dave with the news that he had sold their scuba company to a larger Tour Company based out of Johannesburg, and without as much as a formal thank you or goodbye, was informing Aubrey that the company was no more.

There was no forwarding address, and when he contacted the new Tour Company owners to enquire as to his share in the company, he received the news that the company had been sold in its entirety to them. Dave who had negotiated the entire deal behind Aubrey's back, had sold the company lock, stock and barrel to them, and they had not known of his supposed shareholding. According to the new Directors, the deal had been secretly concluded a month before, but only finalized when the money had been paid into Dave's bank account.

This was surprising and unwelcome news to Aubrey, who had always believed that he was a 50 percent shareholder in the company. Trusting Dave, he had never signed any share certificate, always believing in the strength of their relationship. Well how wrong he was. The company had been sold and there was nothing that Aubrey could do that would change it. Aubrey had been solidly diddled out of his share, and that was that. He could go back and try his luck at finding his ex-partner and forcing his share out of him, but as Aubrey suspected, he was long gone by now. He could speak to his father's barrister and attempt to recover his losses, but this would ultimately get back to Lord Pennington, and Aubrey was too proud to admit his naivety.

Aubrey considered going back and trying to start up a rival company, but without any real start-up capital, he knew this would be futile. All the money he was owed, had been held in the company account which had now been sold on, and Aubrey had no share or loan certificate to prove any of it. He had not withdrawn any money from the company in three years, since he lived frugally and wanted to keep the company flush and profitable. Believing he was investing in his own future, his share of the company, he estimated at roughly one hundred thousand US dollars, and it had all been tied up in the business. All the assets and all the cash were gone and it would cost him perhaps just as much in legal fees, to try to get it back.

Being a pragmatist as he was, and always with the spirit of adventure and youth on his side, decided to do the only thing he could. He had called Bronwyn once he was in London, and they had chatted before the funeral. She was a tour guide on a white-water rafting setup at the Zambezi River in what was becoming one of the world's most sought after destinations. Their torrid affair had left Aubrey somewhat overawed, and the invitation for him to join her back in Victoria Falls, was now to become a reality. So, with less than 200 dollars in his pocket, and a rucksack containing the contents of his current life, Aubrey left once again on another life changing adventure which would be the true dawning of his spiritual journey. This time it was Africa that was his calling. The Studebaker would have to stay where it was and Aubrey would have to send for it when he had the cash. He contacted his good friend Lovemore, and asked him to look after the car whilst he was gone.

Boarding a plane for Harare and a round trip to Victoria Falls, Aubrey set off on the next chapter of his life. Little did he know that this adventure would bring him closer to death's door and with a whole lot of political intrigue to boot? All he knew was that he was going to have a whole lot of fun, and he certainly was not to be disappointed.

Bronwyn met him at Victoria Falls airport. On the tarmac, she came running over to him, her enthusiasm uncontained. He had only known her two weeks at the lake, but his sudden arrival was a very welcome distraction for her in a town that lived, and breathed on extreme sports. Adrenalin flowed through the blood of its inhabitants, like the water that surged over the Victoria Falls. As majestic a place in the heart of the African landscape as any. Life stewed in the energy of the cascading river as it plummeted deafeningly over the edge of a precipice 380 feet, running along a mile-wide rock face. The Falls were carved into the bedrock of the Zambezi Valley, as though a giant and omnipotent God had scythed a zigzag series of gashes into the earth.

Devil's Cataract, the appropriately named western ledge had also been Dr Livingstone's first sighting of the falls, from the southern boundary. He had named it after first seeing it and commenting to his chief Induna, who had ported his belongings half way across the southern continent of Africa, that he had considered the eyes of the Devil at that moment; or so the legend went. The names invoked metaphorical god's and ancient tales of grand adventure. The place was alive with possibilities and everywhere, the locals were looking for opportunities to generate businesses from the growing tourism trade.

Victoria Falls was in the early days of Zimbabwe's re-introduction to the world's tourism market, one of the most magical places to be. In a pub called Explorers where the locals and tourists alike congregated after their adrenalin infused trip down the river, Aubrey and Bronwyn sat that evening and enjoyed a welcome sun-downer. They ate pie and chips and then spent the remainder of the night drinking the cool thirst quenching Zambezi beer.

The locals were the singularly most hospitable folk he had ever met. There in the confines of a somewhat ramshackle pub, with the stories of exploits and escapades drowning out the sound of the music, they met each of the rowdy crowd in turn. Aubrey was an instant success and his de-sensitised English accent allowed him to fit in with the locals. Bronwyn introduced him to all her mates and they listened intently as the latest tales of bravado were recounted.

The river guides were all local guys, some Ndebele some old Rhodesian whites, but the majority of them all very good natured, good humoured and great fun. The company that ran most of the river adventures had been set up by a couple of optimistic and motivated lads, who had seen the opportunity to get the adventure business well and truly established in Africa. Tourism was based almost solely on a strong US dollar. This gave them an excellent source of revenue, combined with an ideal opportunity to indulge in their own spirit of adventure. Their philosophy was simple and they kept the adventure spirit truly alive and hooked into every conceivable activity that could be made available.

Hence it was that Aubrey came to be a part of this burgeoning industry, in a country that had made his great grandfather famous and had in fact led to his family's title. There were no limits to how much money could be made and their enthusiasm was unbounded. These companies were on a roll and their initiatives were only limited by the extent to which the younger international visitors were willing to be entertained. They were printing money in an economy that was growing exponentially and the buzz was electric.

The Scandinavians, Germans and American back-packers were there in their droves. Their oversized, overladen, overland Unimogs and 60's style Bedford trucks, festooned with the stickers of every conceivable African country, a testimony to the enduring adventurous spirit of those heady days in the early euphoria of a new democracy that was Zimbabwe.

Any adrenaline junkie knew that a trip down the majestic river was the highlight of their African adventure. But a night on the town, quite literally was an experience worthy of all binge drinking exploits. There was every manner of young adventure seeker, and the pub's walls were littered with the oars and other memorabilia of their exploits. The drinking would go on until the early hours of the morning, and then, the tourists, back-packers and locals alike, would head off for some welcome sleep.

How miraculous a time it was in a free independent and promisingly beautiful country. Aubrey could understand the allure to which his great grandfather had been drawn. Those days were fraught with danger from wild animals and tribes, but now the only danger came from the alcohol infused hangovers that woke them in the midst of a hectic schedule of river trips, that would have sunk anyone with less stamina.

To wake after a long night of youthful indulgence and find himself on the river the next morning was a shock to the system. Having trekked the hundred meters into the gorge with a twenty-foot raft, weighing over two hundred kilograms was Aubrey's baptism of fire. He would still have the energy to make a death defying plunge through the greatest run of rapids in the Southern Hemisphere, and in Aubrey's mind it was worth every ounce of courage he could muster. How he survived was a miracle. Others had drowned before, and many were still to find themselves a victim of the treacherous river god Nyaminyami, who the locals said would seek out the unworthy, and drag them to their deaths, always without warning. Educated they were, but superstition had an entirely irrational life of its own. The Ndebele river guides would wear their symbols of this ancient water God around their necks and they became a popular memento. With the head of a fish, its body was said to be that of a snake. Rising rapidly from the depths, it would drag an unsuspecting rafter below, and their body may only appear days or weeks later, on the rocks below the last set of rapids. Intact, but nonetheless dead, this great river monster never ate their victims. Aubrey came to appreciate their culture and revel in their unceasing enthusiasm.

He soon put the disappointment of Malawi aside and with the spontaneity of a youthful charisma, forgave Dave, but stored those thoughts of retribution for another day.

"So what did you think of our river?" Bronwyn had asked when he had caught his breath, after a 400 foot climb out of the gorge.

"Unbelievable! That has to be the greatest rush I have ever had," he smiled, holding her passionately and kissing her unabashedly in front of the motley, but exhausted tourists.

"I thought you would enjoy it," Bronwyn beamed. Her man an instant convert.

"Do you want a job?"

Aubrey would begin to understand the forces that drove those ceaseless volumes of churning water through those narrow gorges, and around the most oblique of bends. The Zambezi Gorge was unchallenged in its geographical magnificence, and worthy of its reputation. The water plummeted down a series of dog-leg gorges and the river was currently at its lowest. They had made some portages along the way, but to each of the guides, there was always another challenge to be had. Aubrey was intoxicated by the grandeur of the gorges and natural phenomena that was now to become his home.

One day later, Aubrey was in the rafting shop in the Vic Falls central arcade. The manager, a somewhat gregarious character who Bronwyn had introduced as Marc, interviewed Aubrey for a position on one of the rafts;

"Have you had any experience on white-water?" Marc was a Scotsman, who had spent his childhood in Harare and ventured to Vic Falls after a failed university stint in Natal. The notorious seaside haven of Durban was where young Zimbabweans went for their gap years before finding work. Marc had found the social scene an allure, and his forte in hospitality a tremendous success.

"No, but I have spent my life on boats, sculling and eights!" Aubrey returned.

Marc looked up at Aubrey's bulk and through the loose-fitting T-shirt, could see that he was physically capable of becoming an oarsman. He would remember that moment intuitively, regarding Aubrey with a fearful respect.

"Sculling? You shouldn't have any problem with a kayak then!" Marc sussed him out.

"I would love to give it a go," Aubrey was keen to try his hand. The kayakers had the range of the rapids and were integral to the survival of any tourists who found themselves in the river.

"Okay, we need to train you up and we will get you started on the lower rapids." He proffered his hand. Job interview done.

"Thank you," Aubrey returned his smile. He was part of the family.
The next five days was spent on the upper sections of the river getting his balance in the tiny fibreglass kayaks, then onto the lower stretches of the river to attempt his first rapid. Aubrey took to it with aplomb and was up for his first gig before long.

The days merged into months and the months seemed hot and unbearably humid. Christmas came and went in the tiny tourism enclave and Aubrey was having a riot of a time. Bronwyn and he made a great partnership and they moved into their own digs, on a dusty road, in the neighbourhood. The house which they rented from the company was basic, but Bronwyn kept it tidy and hosted their friends for weekend braais. He soon settled into the routine.

The place had a spiritual side, which Aubrey soon came to appreciate. When faced with moments of sheer terror, or left to contemplate a moment of awe-inspiring beauty, Aubrey never lost his sense of wonderment. Africa was pitched and steeped in mythology. The place was to grow on him more so than he could have ever contemplated. Even the beautiful and gentle Thai people, baptised in their ancient philosophy of Buddhism, were no match for the spirituality of this grand and unchallenged place.

There was never a dull moment, and Bronwyn soon had him into the swing of things. Aubrey soon found himself not only intoxicated with the tangible air of excitement and adrenaline that was Victoria Falls, but also spending all his days on the river, kayaking and escorting tourist boats on the infamous river. Aubrey was in his element. His experience grew rapidly, and in tune with the dynamics of the surging water, Aubrey was able to quickly adapt to the brutality of the river and develop a reputation for his skills. Catching water born rafters, flipped out on the more aptly named rapids he was able to make a significant contribution to keeping the rafters safe. As they were thrown from the relative safety of the raft, Aubrey would spin on the bow of the kayak and within seconds he would be alongside the swimmer. With kayak as ballast for the shaken but visibly grateful tourist, and the calmer waters in the clefts of the rock face offering some relative safety, Aubrey would catch them and get them to the river's edge. If they were thrown overboard on the wilder rapids and became 'long swimmers' he was able to chase them and catch them before they could disappear below the water. Holding onto the prow of the fibreglass boat, and be taken downstream to join the rafting crew. Being a long swimmer meant the tourist had a somewhat alarming trip through the remainder of the rapid with only a life vest to keep them buoyant. It was Aubrey's job to make sure the experience was as least likely to result in no serious injury. Aubrey became extremely adept at getting between the heaving waters and rescuing the hapless tourists.

It was just such an occasion, Aubrey found himself in, on a three-day excursion down on the lower stretches of the gorge. Suddenly a large South African with a pot belly and an aggressive outlook, had fallen overboard, and Aubrey went immediately for the rescue. But weighing well over a hundred kilograms, Aubrey went under, as the man grasped at the kayak. Aubrey instinctively went to right himself, but as he did so he caught his paddle on a rock which effectively limited his leverage, and whilst the man mountain clung to the overturned kayak, Aubrey was left submerged. Intuitively, he gathered his bearings, knowing that the man was on the bow of the boat, Aubrey brought the paddle in sideways, and in a short sharp stabbing action, aimed at what he knew would be the man's solar plexus, he thrust the edge into his sternum.

Immediately the man released his grip on the kayak and with a nimble backwards and upwards movement Aubrey had righted himself. The man was floating close by in a quieter eddy.

"Stay calm and keep breathing," Aubrey shouted. He tried to keep his voice passive. But it made no difference. The tourist was thrashing at the water, trying to catch his breath. But as Aubrey manoeuvred to catch him, there was a sudden movement into the water to his left.

"Flatdog!" Aubrey shouted, his voice raising an octave or more.

Aubrey had only seen crocodiles from a distance until now, but he knew without a doubt there was a beast of a croc headed for them. Using the boat, he quickly paddled to get between the croc and the tourist.

Naturally the man's reaction was to panic and thrash all the more.

Aubrey took hold of the handle and smacked the water with a loud clap. The croc had surfaced ten feet from him, its natural buoyancy lifting it back to the surface after its dive from the rocks. Aubrey again lifted the paddle and as the two-meter prehistoric brute neared him, he smacked it on the back of the head. The beast rolled over and dived, and in an instant, was gone.

Aubrey spun the kayak and signalling to the oarsman on the boat, he deftly nudged the prow towards the South African and calmly said;

"Hold the end, but loosely!" his voice once more level and measured.

The guy was so scared Aubrey could see the fear in his eyes.

"Don't try to fight it, just breath slow and deep." There was still danger below, but Aubrey could do nothing if the attack came from there.

"Wrap your legs around the boat, and keep as still as you can," the man nodded his understanding. He kept his eyes on Aubrey as though his very survival depended on that calm, Englishman's every syllable.

Aubrey swiftly turned and with the buoyancy of the kayak now restored and the man clinging on for dear life, he stroked powerfully back into deeper water and the safety of the raft.

"Drinks are on you," smiled Aubrey, as he returned the gasping man to his hysterical wife.

This was the humour and camaraderie that he faced on a daily basis, and was the life blood of their existence. Just how close both Aubrey and the tourist had come to a life-threatening experience would be debatable, but it had re-inspired Aubrey, and formulated a bond which would last his lifetime.

Chapter 9

An Awakening

Back in Reading and in the present, Aubrey found himself so strongly attracted to Natasha that he had an immediate physical reaction that often happened around attractive women. He immediately felt a stirring in his groin. He learnt not to bring attention to himself by adjusting himself in his jockey shorts when this type of thing happened. The offending appendage would simply become the focus of attention, so he remained impassive keeping Natasha's focus so as not to draw more attention to his state of arousal. Aubrey had a proclivity to be aroused in an instant, but this was different, as he was hit by the pheromones, jolting him into a state of sexual awakening. It spilled through his entire body and ended in the obvious sense of wetness in his under-shorts that accompanied such carnal reactions.

Natasha smiled back in acknowledgement, and if she had noticed, she certainly made no attempt to arouse him further. She then resumed her study of the text before her on the screen.

Aubrey concentrated on the section pertaining to cancer. After all that was where it had begun. He remembered the oncologist in Kinshasa referring to 'cancroids' or some variation of the skin cancer that had developed on his arm. But then it had spread into the deep tissue and that was when he had found out some years later that it had metastasized. As Aubrey read through the text he rationalised that the reason he could think of sex at such an inappropriate time, was because he had lost all sense of fear of the cancer. This, after he had been told by the Oncologist in Kinshasa, "he should not worry about dying of cancer, and rather focus on 'living with cancer.'"

"The symptoms were classic and treatment was improving all the time." He was a French speaking, African Congolese man who had studied at The Royal College of Medicine, and having worked in London at Saint Thomas', the calling of his country's needs had drawn him back after twenty-one years.

Aubrey had felt some relief. Mom had died of Chronic Myeloid Leukaemia, after years of denial, but she was a victim of her own fear. Mom, who had been a fighter for charities and every other down-at heel, had not owned her disease and had let the cancer spread to her liver and kidneys. A typical prognosis for someone, who had suffered years of psychological abuse! She had died of neglect, and this was what was eating Aubrey. Aubrey would have to suffer his own illness, but did not want to give up as easy.

"I am not sure what the confounded name is", he apologised. "But it was on a Discovery channel program." He knew that in order to learn a little more about the condition he would have to research the scientific facts.

"That's cool," Natasha seemed intent on helping. "What did the treatment entail? Maybe then I could Google the form of treatment?"

"Yes. That is clever." She was obviously a budding medical student.

"The narrator mentioned an extreme form of detoxification." He added.

"Ah, yes!" Natasha was now keying in the words, and looking intently through the sub-scripts.

Aubrey had only told the Professor as he wanted to keep this news out of the mainstream and certainly did not want to share this with his staff at the Estate. Having just returned, Aubrey would need some time to settle and did not wish to upset the family of people who now relied on him for employment. He would break it to them, when he had found a credible treatment regime.

He could feel the physical wafting of those pheromones again. It reminded him once more of his antics amongst the scholarly works of Bacon, Shakespeare and Dunne. They would have approved the impropriety of his indiscretion. Aubrey nearly let out a guffaw, but managed to catch himself as he refocused his attention on the task at hand. There it was; Natasha had searched the sub-text for treatment. She brought the cursor to bear on the word, which now appeared directly in front of him. There was the title he recognized. This was the treatment he knew he had been searching for!

Aubrey's reverie returned. He quickly scanned through the index and having made the connection between what the Oncologist had mentioned to him back in the Congo, and what was now being quoted in that published medical journal, Aubrey was keen to get to grips with the contents. He would however not be doing any reading here in Reading. He would need to take a copy of the journal home to peruse at his leisure.

He had always believed in synchronicity and being a man of little patience and a now seemingly endless state of mutually erotic interest, he decided to take the bull by the horns.

"Would you mind if I asked another favour from you?" She smiled again; there was a mixture of interest and sympathy in her eyes.

"What would that entail," she smiled bashfully, before dropping his eye contact.

"Nothing untoward, I promise!" He grinned mischievously.

"Okay, but I can't promise you that I would be good at it!"

There was that flirtation again! Aubrey was beginning to realise Natasha was a veritable tiger. Her flecked green irises flashed a challenging signal.

"Well I would not be asking you, if I didn't think you would be good at it!" He tested her limit to this playful guise to what he imagined awaited them both.

She smiled once. Turned back to her computer screen; clicked the print function, then stood and said:

"Where are we going? Somewhere nice, I hope!" Aubrey jumped to his feet. He had not felt like this for a long time.

"How about London?" He offered breathlessly.

She smiled again and nodded. Closing the computer screen, she stooped, picked up her canvas bag and motioned to him to follow.

She led him to the study desk where she asked for her prints, then swiping her student card through the electronic card reader and effectively paying for the prints, waited for the Librarian to return them. She reached into her bag and taking her purse out, she dipped into the side pocket and taking a twenty pence coin, she popped it into a charity tin for abandoned animals. With the Librarian, having returned with the copies, she handed them to Natasha, eyeing her suspiciously before turning her stern look from her to Aubrey. He smiled playfully at her and then winked, puckering his lips by the merest degree, he suggestively turned to Natasha saying, "What a delightful woman," before turning and making their way out of the central annex and escaping to the stairwell.

"I think I need to thank you," he smiled wryly, as they reached the ground floor.

"Not at all," she responded, not too meekly. "I should thank you. I was getting so bored with studying," she reciprocated, with no further ado.

They were half way down the stairs to the car park. As they rounded the stone wall of the library precinct, Aubrey almost froze as a blue flashing light caught his attention, but putting his arm around her shoulder, he continued nonchalantly. Approaching the mayhem that was ensuing in the far corner, he squeezed her just a little harder than was necessary.

There were now three squad cars encircling his Rolls Royce, and a very unhappy bunch of uniformed officers, peering into the windows of the vehicle. One officer had taken the initiative and was busy trying the driver's side door, which opened on first attempt. As Aubrey, had not thought to lock the car, and had left the keys in the ignition, an unnecessary force of habit which was all the more significant now. After all, he had spent years in countries where, unlikely as it seemed, no one ever had to lock doors.

Aubrey assessed the situation in an instant, and realizing that the car would appear to have been abandoned, he quickly side stepped the mayhem, before taking a path down the side of the car park. They walked for a few paces before he said;

"It looks like we will have to find an alternative form of transport," he grinned."

Natasha looked suspiciously at him from the corner of her eye, retorting;

"Has Aubrey been a naughty boy?" Having realized that the car being detained was Aubrey's, she only allowed herself a moment to look over her shoulder at the chaos in the car park, as they got to the exit.

He grimaced. "Does that turn you on, or am I now not going to get lucky!"

"Not at all," she had summed him up back in the study room.

"I know we have only just been introduced, but is there any possibility you have a car in the vicinity?" A direct question and one which would have most people turning tale and running for cover. Not Natasha, this girl had spunk.

"Yes. In the car park! I came in from Oxford to get some studying done," she smiled wryly. Not at all fazed by what appeared to be a very peculiar situation. She had already assumed, correctly, that the Rolls belonged to him, and that he was a fugitive from the law. This was about as exciting a situation as she may ever have been a witness to, and it was strangely alluring. If he was a fugitive; he was certainly well-groomed and exceptionally well spoken one! 'And hey, whoever could afford a Rolls Royce must be someone important. She would help him out.'

"How about that trip to London?" he invited more than asked. "We can have dinner on the town and a night of wild passion to follow?" He would have to make this appealing if she was to be his alibi.

"We can stop at the bus shelter and I will pop back and fetch my car?"

Aubrey smiled gratefully and tagged in next to her as they exited the University grounds undetected and headed for the closest bus shelter on London Road.

They walked to the bus shelter and its cover gave Aubrey the opportunity to assess the situation. He had learnt from his days in the Zimbabwe, you never give the initiative to the cops, because they would always take the path of least resistance and assume you are guilty no matter whatever the violation may have been. These cops, however, would not be easily bribed and no twenty-dollar inducement was going to get them to back off.

Aubrey could only guess that the cops had tracked the vehicle from the highway on their extensive CCTV network. Because of his reckless driving, they would have followed his trail from the off-ramp and when it had run dry at the university entrance, they had used manpower to find the Rolls within the parking area. No amount of explaining would get him off a night in a police cell. His only option would be to claim his innocence and that the Rolls had been stolen by a bunch of varsity students out for a lark. Fortunately, the likelihood that they would be able to prove otherwise was strongly in his favour. He would need an alibi, and decided to head to London and book them into a hotel for the night, and only report the stolen car tomorrow.

'Yes, that would work,' he thought.

Although it would mean that he would have the staff and maybe the Professor going crazy looking for him the whole night. But then, he thought, they would track his credit card to the hotel, and he would have his midnight slumber interrupted by a bunch of cops barging through his door. He would have to report the incident to Highpot when he got to a hotel, but he would need to get there undetected. Natasha would have to help. He now had a moment of unadulterated doubt. Would she come back; and if she did, would it be with a posse in tow.

Aubrey had been sure that the bus as with every public amenity in the UK, had a CCTV camera, and although he could not be sure they had identified him in the car, he would assume they had not. He stood with his back to the shelter while he waited. He had seen a programme on Sky, where the cops had tracked some guys who tried to blow up the underground, literally all the way back to their front doors, or so it seemed.

Here in the UK, he was a captive to a system in which anonymity was no longer a given, and every move you made could be traced. He wondered if it were better to have been a victim of a system which was now the most repressive regime on the planet, or to be part of a system which could repress one's natural desire to be a maverick, by inducing the fear of the law. Here he was similarly a victim of a system that only rewarded absolute obedience. It was a strange paradox, but it was the lesser of two evils. This was indeed the question. Only time would tell how long he would be able to stand the claustrophobic climate of this civic society; or the enigmatic energy of an emergent Kleptocracy. He would take the car with Natasha, pay for her petrol in cash and give her the cash to make all the other necessary transactions for them. Or maybe he should simply take the bus.

Aubrey need not have worried, she was game. This was a lass with a bit of pluck! He always seemed to attract them somehow.

She was pulling up to the bus shelter before he could change his mind. When Natasha skidded to a halt in front of him, he leapt into the passenger seat, and before he could put his seat belt on, she had jolted off to re-join the slowly circling traffic on the roundabout ahead.

"Thank you." He was grinning. The dampness on his brow, the only sign of emotion.

"No problem at all," she smiled back. "Besides, it was starting to get a little stuffy in there," referring to the Library and the body chemistry that had become evident.

"Yes, I guess it was getting a little heated!" He was beaming from ear to ear. Natasha turned to him with one eye on the road, and gave him a wink with the other.

She looked over her shoulder as they hit the exit to the motorway. Joining the slow traffic, he unexpectedly had an opportunity to witness the chaos he had single-handedly created. The west bound Motorway was a scene of bedlam. There was a tail-back as far as the eye could see, but most importantly, there were the three cars being towed away. The drivers of each, including a rather bewildered patrolman, stood behind the hastily erected cordon of cones whilst his colleagues directed the mass of vehicular mayhem. Natasha looked at him quizzically. Aubrey sunk lower in his seat and reflexively covered his face, with the palm of his right hand. She watched his reaction intuitively and with no further ado, she smiled back and edged into the traffic, headed for London.

"I guess that I have some explaining to do?" He was apologetic.

"No not at all! I am a little rebellious myself," she admitted. "I'm guessing this has something to do with you and the cops back at the university?"

"Yes, I am afraid so," he admitted his transgression.

"What happened?" She was slightly amused.

"Nothing untoward! I was simply driving too fast." He recalled the speedo on the dash reflecting one hundred miles an hour. "Besides! Why does the Government not legislate for the restriction of a car's speed to the maximum speed limit, if they want people to obey the speed limits?"

She looked at him mockingly.

"I'm being serious!" He defended himself. "What is the point of buying a car that can do one hundred and sixty, when you are never going to be allowed to drive it at that speed?"

"I don't honestly know," she smiled, before gunning the little car's motor and slip-streaming the traffic. The tiny Toyota was clear of the slower moving gawkers and into the mainstream with a minimal effort.

He realised in that bold move, she had somehow, inadvertently answered his question.

Strangely, he was not at all nervous about her driving, and she seemed completely at home behind the wheel. When she swept through the traffic and out onto the open M4, Aubrey noticed the speed climbing as Natasha darted through the lanes, heading directly for the fast one. He settled down, confident that she was in control. This was a first for him, and other than his mother's sometimes erratic driving when they would take her old Austin Healy out for a summers day spin, he had never been a passenger in a car driven by a woman. He felt strangely liberated.

When they got to London, she found a parking in Bayswater Road and they walked the half a mile to the Holiday Inn on the northern side of the road. A quaint Victorian affair, as opposed to the ugly 30 story monstrosity they had built for the American tourists on the southern side of the road within a stone's throw. They checked into the room, using his credit card and once they had reached the room, Aubrey made a call to Highpot.

"Highpot," sounding slightly alarmed, "someone has nicked the Rolls!" There was no response from Highpot. Obviously, they had already been in contact with him.

"Where is 'Your Lordship'", he was being too formal. There was someone with him at the Estate.

"I am in London. But when I went back to the car she had been stolen." No chance for speculation.

"Yes Sir. Did you know that the keys were in the car?" Highpot sounded slightly quizzical and incredulous.

"Did I?" Consternation verging on self-recrimination! "I haven't even checked yet. What do you know?" Aubrey thought it best to play along, and sound a little concerned. The cops were going to grill him anyway!

"Yes, Your Lordship, the Roller has been found in Reading!" Sounding very confused!

"Oh, my heavens, I cannot believe my stupidity. They must have seen the keys and stolen it." He was firmly putting the blame on who ever had 'stolen' the vehicle.

"Don't worry your Lordship. I will take care of the matter and send a vehicle to fetch you." Situation resolved.

"Yes, thank you, Highpot. But make that tomorrow morning please. The Holiday Inn, Bayswater! The English one! About nine?" Aubrey was insistent.

He replaced the handset in its cradle.

End of crisis! Aubrey turned to Natasha, a bashful but knowing look on her face. He had managed to circumvent the long-arm of the law, and since he was in such high spirits he was happy to take Natasha in his arms, and make the most of his evening in London. They were starving, so ordering room service, they settled in for the evening, determined to get to know each other a little better.

Aubrey was still having breakfast with Natasha when Highpot arrived in the morning, minus the Rolls, which had been impounded for forensic investigation. He introduced the two and then almost immediately gave Natasha a good-bye kiss on the cheek, having made a prior arrangement for her to visit Finsbury on the weekend.

On the trip back to the Estate, with Highpot and Shaun, Aubrey was quite audible and animated. How had the cops known to contact the Estate so quickly and how was it possible that they had already been there before Aubrey had even reached London?

Highpot was less enthusiastic about the whole affair, but his seventy years of life experience had given him the benefit of a knowing but tolerant nature. He had reflected on the whole matter with the degree of concern it required. Having dealt with Lord Pennington for the better part of fifty years, he knew a good scam when he saw it. Aubrey was told succinctly and with no real drama, that the Roller had been fitted with a satellite tracking device. This had been activated by the cops when they had inspected the vehicle in Reading, and by contacting the service provider in London they had managed to get an instant ID on the owner and an address. Suspecting that they might have a stolen vehicle on their hands, they immediately dispatched a squad car to the estate with a local constable, to find out if the vehicle had been reported missing. They had just arrived when Aubrey phoned from London, therefore saving the staff a worrisome night. Thankfully, but miraculously no one had been injured, apart from a few dented egos, and several dented cars. The traffic cop had been admitted to Royal Berkshire hospital for observation, but otherwise no permanent injury.

By the time they hit the gate to the Estate's entrance, Aubrey had learnt enough, to realize that he had nothing to worry about. There had been the typical red tape, with the officer asking Highpot for some information, and the Rolls had been impounded for the lifting of fingerprints. But other than that, there were no real consequences to the event. The motorway accident had left, two vehicles in the scrap yard and three others at the panel beaters and a massive insurance claim no doubt. All were luckily insured, but there was the matter of a statement which he would have to make for the report, a tidy affair which Highpot would likely take care of. Job done. Aubrey was pleased, but had bigger concerns!

Armed with the knowledge he had from his visit to the library, Aubrey would now be able to get some research done. He was in no mood to have the little time he had left on this earth, getting involved in these time-consuming episodes.

"I say Highpot, would you mind terribly." As he climbed out the estate's errand car. They were agreed. He would write the statement, which Highpot would deliver to the local constabulary.

Highpot smiled. He was good at this. The whole ordeal had perked him up somewhat.

"Of course, Your Lordship." He held open the door, as Aubrey clambered out the back. Life was slowly returning to normality, and duty called.

Highpot was tasked with the job of meeting with the constable and filling in the necessary forms. This was because it was a NIP job which Aubrey had little time for. NIP was an acronym for 'non-intellectual progress' and unlike the more commonly used 'non-income producing', sales talk, this was a far more important pursuit. Aubrey also asked Highpot to find out the details of the other accident victims, and would make an anonymous payment to each of them to cover their insurance excesses and ease his own conscience.

Without transport Aubrey asked Shaun for a lift to the village.

"How was your stay in London?" Shaun ventured.

Aubrey looked over at the driver, and smiled. "Well thank you Shaun.

Shaun ventured nothing more. He stared ahead at the road, but there seemed to be a wrinkling of the skin around his eyes; then it was gone.

"In fact, I have an admission which you may not mention to Highpot." Aubrey felt liberated.

"No need, Your Lordship," Shaun interjected. He half turned. There was the crease around his eyes again. Aubrey smiled back. He would take this as the opportunity to begin building a relationship with Shaun.
"Thank you, Shaun." He was silent for a moment. Shaun fixed his head towards the road.

"You know Shaun, I am not particularly fond of authority." Shaun took his eyes off the road, and actually looked into Aubrey's eyes for the first time in a month.

"Yes sir," there was little more to say. Aubrey smiled into those hazel brown eyes, recognising in an instant, that they reflected the soul of Lord Pennington. The sins of the father were forgiven, and Aubrey could now get on with living. The connection with Shaun, did not seem to be dictated by anything other than a warm, sincere disposition.

Shaun was not as seemingly docile as Highpot and although Government educated, there seemed a bond between them that struck a chord with Aubrey. Somewhere in the depth of Shaun's soul, Aubrey could sense a reaching out of sorts; a search for something, which Aubrey felt was like his own. Aubrey said nothing more; the summer sun blazed through the windscreen, bathing them in a warm glow.

Aubrey would make it evident that he needed to chat, conversationally on their trip back from the village, so now Shaun would wait for him in the coffee shop whilst Aubrey met with the Professor.

As Aubrey walked in they were met by the Professor at the door. Aubrey introduced them.

"Yes, how do you do?" The Professor reached out a gnarled handshake. He had seen Shaun a hundred times in the village, but never been introduced. Turning to Aubrey, he winked knowingly at Shaun.

"What. No Roller today? Have you managed to wrap her around a tree already," he sniped. He was fishing; Clearly the accident had already made the gossip rounds in the village.

"Not quite", replied Aubrey, "but as close as hell."

"What?" Feigned consternation and raised eyebrows from the Professor, but Aubrey just shrugged it off and said. "Can we talk in private?"

The Professor, seeing Aubrey was in no mood to divulge more, quickly motioned to the back office. He loved the sense of drama this afforded him, and was aware that the patrons would be discussing the incident in detail.
It was all in a day's work. Gossip and speculation! He was born for this moment as a coffee shop owner. The village folk were naturally inquisitive, and so the rumour mill was subsisted. The Professor would not disappoint,

and the rumour that there had been an altercation with the law, had already circulated down from the local constabulary to the coffee shop. So, hushed whispers and sideways glances followed Aubrey and the Professor's retreat into the little back room office.

"What is going on?" enquired the Professor. "The whole place is abuzz with the talk of high speed chases through the country and Hollywood-style prangs on the M4."

"Not quite as dramatic as that old chap", dismissed Aubrey, passing the printout across to the Professor. He scrutinised the document with no further comment.

The Professor read through the pages, which was emblazoned with a stamp, 'The Faculty of Science and Medicine, University of Reading.'

The Professor raised his bushy, grey eyebrows looking up intuitively. He knew the stolen car thing was a rouse. Looking at Aubrey, who chuckled like a small schoolboy caught in the act of some mischievous behaviour.

Without commenting, he went straight to the text, where he read the top inscription. Turning to the light from the window at the rear of the office, the Professor read;

'Modifying Cytotoxic T-cells.'

If the medical condition Aubrey was in was not so serious, it would have appeared more hysterical, but Aubrey, just shrugged his shoulders.

The cancer diagnosis had taken the shine off his somewhat laissez faire attitude. But nothing seemed to worry him too much, and despite being angry at the timing of it all, it was that anger that motivated him now. He had been off the wagon for few months and had not let a drop of hooch pass his lips since the diagnosis of liver cancer was presented to him in Kinshasa. He was in a buoyant mood none-the-less, and what he had read from the article in the medical journal had presented him with options.

The Professor was deep in thought. When he had re-read the article he said;

"What now?"
Aubrey deep in his own thoughts just murmured a quiet "Not sure".

When he had been a youngster he had spent hours on the shooting range aiming at moving targets, so that as a teenager his father would allow him to go pheasant shooting. Despite all that practice he had never cracked the nod to go out every spring with the shooting parties. However, he was quite glad, in a way he had not, as it appeared to him in later life that the whole process was quite ridiculous. A bunch of elderly, paunchy old men in a tweed and leather venturing out onto the fields, while a bunch of healthy vigorous young men traipsed through the undergrowth with sticks beating the undergrowth in a hope that the quarry would venture forward to the hunter.

Aubrey stared out the window and recalled a day when he had been out in the fields, the great white hunters sitting in their armchairs on the great terrace surrounding the manor house, drinking their Sherry. He had snuck off on his own, watching as the fledgers had disappeared into the wood just some two thousand yards to the left of the duck ponds, on their next quest for the illusive pheasant.

Aubrey had gone down to the furthest duck pond and while he was searching the edge of the pond had heard a fluttering noise from one of the pump houses that serviced the fountains in the ponds. He had gone to investigate the noise and that was when he had seen the pheasant, which had become ensnared in the wiring in the base of the plant. What it had been doing there he could not tell, but perhaps it was trying to escape the bedlam out in the woods. Being young and wanting to impress Lord Pennington and his party, he had immediately set upon the poor creature with a broom handle. The shooting from the field began at the very moment he struck the creature a fatal blow to the head, thereby saving it from being further traumatized.

He had reached in and untangled his prize from the wiring and holding it by its feet, headed back to the party. When he had arrived, the shooting had already ceased and not a solitary pheasant had been downed. It was with great consternation, a smattering of humour and a few red faces to boot, that met him when he held his prized pheasant aloft in victory. The shooting party was mortified and they set upon him immediately with questions as to where he had found this creature. When he told them, they were stupefied and once the ridiculousness of their own circumstances set in they began to guffaw.

All that is, except his father. Lord Pennington had immediately ordered the farm hands back to the fields to drive the pheasants.

It was unsurprising that his father had never extended an invitation to him when he had reached the respectable age for pheasant shooting.

Well, he had probably saved a few pheasants from the pot no doubt, but now he made an oath with himself to make pheasant hunting on the grounds of Finsbury Hall a thing of the past. Aubrey would do something noble, like turning the area into a conservancy for bird watchers and ramblers alike.

Sitting in the back office with the Professor, he was now quietly pleased that he had never had to endure those savage affairs. He was not quite sure he could ever have grown to love them. And after all he would only have partaken in those grandiose events to please his father! What an irony that would prove to be.

He was so preoccupied with his own thoughts he had not heard the Professor's further comment.

"What are you thinking?" The Professor repeated.

"Ohh. Nothing important. I was thinking about the pheasant hunting seasons at the estate."

"What brought that on?" The Professor was intrigued.

"It just occurred to me that death is so brutal, that it gives pause for thought, to those who espouse euthanasia."

"Man is sufficiently evolved above wild animals, which tare each other apart for survival. But it is Man's capacity to distinguish between this barbarism and a gentile acceptance of our place in the universe that is a subject of his conditioning."

"Is that the conditioning of a sophisticated society that still eats meat, but has washed their hands of any responsibility towards the barbaric act of factory farming?" Aubrey saw no difference, but still loved his red meat.

"A civilized society can only be differentiated from any other by the way they are taught to behave regarding animals. Any culture that had no regard for the animals that shared their common space is doomed to fail."

"Do you mean that some societies are doomed to fail?" Aubrey questioned.

"Only a civilization that placed a high regard for other mammals, would become as nature intended, in balance with their environment. Any civilisation which holds scant regard for the survival of other creatures on this earth, are not to be trusted!" The Professor replied.

This of course was a far cry from his experience with people, but Aubrey could see the Professor's point. If a human had an aversion to animals, was it through a bad experience as a child that may have altered the natural state of their tolerance? Or as he now suspected, that they were simply unable to relate to animals on a spiritual level.

"Muslims who avoid dogs because of religious zeal, have simply not evolved sufficiently as human beings." The Professor did not look up from the article.

"Do you believe it is a transition of beliefs that will alter their opinion on co-existing with animals, and not conditioning which has led to their unnatural aversion?" Aubrey enthused.

"As the early Christians had done, there is a need to convert those who destroyed animal for sport, or greed, to become more in tune with those animals that share this small planet."

"Don't get me wrong! I am not advocating a vegan way of life," The Professor was quick to point out that he was no bunny hugger.

"After all, if a society like the Hindi of India can have a reverence for their bovine brethren in such a populace society, why then can the Chinese not share their common ground with dogs. Instead their canine brethren are simply treated as an alternative food source, and this was at odds with natural selection." The Professor continued.

"What do you mean by that?" Aubrey was intrigued.

"They are doomed to fail as a society, unless they can be more intuitive when dealing with these hugely intelligent creatures. Their survival instinct is out of synch with their moral soul, and this would doom them to fail as a society, because it is a depraved concept. Animals will survive beyond mankind, and only those humans who could adapt quickly beyond their environment, will succeed. This is a biological fact, that had been proven repeatedly in the millennia man has inhabited this planet."

"But what about the extinction of thousands of animal species? The Elephant for example!" Aubrey had attempted to find further ways of protecting the Elephant in Zimbabwe, but the Mugabe regime had successfully overturned the CITES agreement, instead of embarking on mass relocations. They were intent on annihilating the Elephant for their own financial gain.

"This may be at odds with the teachings of the Biblical Genesis, but any man, or woman, who does not heed the call to nature, but takes the literal meaning of the first chapter of Genesis to heart, is misguided. The book of Genesis was written to provide a moral code for man to follow, but conflicted with the true meaning of pastoral care. Nowadays this signifies a moral code by which humans may follow the guidance of a spiritual care giver, but its true meaning derives from the care of animals." The Professor paused and looked up.

"But it has now been adopted to include the Christian virtues of care giving to a congregation, or guidance to students. If that is so, then the Bible is at odds with nature, and the early relaters of the Biblical message could not have known God's true intentions. This is because anyone who could possibly know God would realize it had not been God's intention to give dominion over the Earth and all its creatures, to a species that held scant regard to sustainability and survival."

Aubrey was reminded of the Professor's arguments in favour of environmental issues, all those years before. The Professor continued reading.

"If our capacity to differentiate ourselves from wild animals, is indeed relative to our consciousness, it stands to reason that a society that slaughters animals in an inhumane manner, is indeed 'less conscious' than another, but does this make them 'less evolved'?" The Professor continued.

It did bring back memories he had of the ritual slaughtering of cattle at wedding feasts in Africa. Aubrey had been wholly repugnant of this practice, but being a guest had said nothing. This had made him an accessory to the crime, and to him this was reprehensible. He had resisted future invitations, but this had only come as part of his own spiritual awakening.

"If savaging an animal for a meal," Aubrey questioned, "made humans less evolved? Is it any wonder, then that civilized men can savage each other in the Boardroom, and this is considered 'a game'? If families can literally, go hungry as a result of these boardroom antics, would you say that this behaviour is any less repugnant than that of the tribal practice of slaughtering animals?"

"The Jews did so for religious reasons not so long ago. Now they do so symbolically in the Boardroom."

Aubrey was staring out the window once more.

"But that stands to reason why it is given headlines in the morning financial papers with literal translations, 'A blood bath', or 'blood on the walls'. Does this make those protagonists any less savage?" The Professor mused.

"Probably not; but it seems of no consequence to them, as their blood sports are considered the mark of civilized behaviour."

"This 'sport' you refer to has become a mark of respect amongst the financial elite. I don't believe it is sustainable however!" The Professor tweaked his overgrown eyebrows.

"If that is so, I really wanted no part in it. It will come back to haunt them however. If the very nature of greed has its origins in those great feasts that resulted in gluttony; then consequently that will result in death."

"If the mark of an excessive society was the over indulgence of its people, then America with its gross obesity dilemma is a sign of its greed. It would be interesting with the melt down of the world's economies, whether that might still be a symptom in five or ten years!" There was a wild look in the Professor's eyes.

"Africa and particularly South Africa is an example of how a society changes as economic opportunity changes. The level of heart disease in South Africa, is now directly proportional to the time that the ANC has been in power, and the excesses of that over indulgence has already taken its toll. This could be used as a barometer of how the balance of economic power in a society favoured one population over another." Aubrey was forthright.

The Professor who had concluded his reading, looked up, and gave Aubrey a congratulatory smile.

"So! What do you think?" Aubrey asked.

The Professor could hardly contain his enthusiasm. Some scientific terminology remained difficult to fully understand. However, it gave them an opportunity to learn more, and to understand the results of the research conducted. This was a significant step forward in his healing process. What they needed now was more information. Were there going to be any trials? What did the procedure require and who would perform them? All of this he would need establish.

"Thank heavens for the internet" he smiled at Aubrey, as he booted up his computer, and began a systematic search through Google. The power of the information highway. No single device, nor form of communication, had ever brought the world together quite as successfully, transcending both national boundaries and social borders.

"The internet will bring an end to wars, and the Biblical 'Thousand Years War' will not be necessary." The Professor firmly believed that all of man's ability to wage war and destroy would come to an end once he had learnt to make better use of communication. To him, it was as simple as that. He believed he would live to see the end of war and poverty.

"But!" The question would be asked. "Would Aubrey live to see this too?"

"Would I what?" Aubrey quizzed.

The Professor glanced across at Aubrey in the middle of his download, and realized that he had been mumbling as he worked.

"What was that?" he remarked in return.

"You said, 'would Aubrey'," Aubrey was sounding concerned.

"Yes. Would Aubrey have a look at this." Neatly escaping an explanation.

Aubrey leapt to his feet, and came to stand behind the Professor at the desk. He was already into a research document which was very detailed.

Before very long, the Professor had downloaded twenty or thirty pages and stored them as files on the screen. He was now working back through each with diligence. Aubrey had learnt to think laterally from the Professors' lectures, but had not learnt the patience required to process those thoughts. He had always been too impulsive and it was this impulsiveness that had always got him into trouble. Aubrey was now the passenger on this surfing expedition, and it was fascinating to watch how he scanned, copied and pasted all the relevant text, while the printer spat out all the necessary information. The web had always been a complete mystery to Aubrey, but he had been intrigued by the global hook it had demonstrated. The irony if there was one, was that the World Wide Web had been created by the United States military, to create seamless communication between all its global bases and outposts. The one tool, that had been created by the military to better wreck its havoc effectively around the world, had secured its' own ultimate demise.

The power of the web, had led to communications between people previously unable to navigate the labyrinth that constituted world telecom channels. The expense of an efficient infrastructure had also prohibited the spread of information into the third world, and this information and ultimate knowledge was what would drag these people out of the depth of poverty and into the New Millennia. Aubrey remembered hearing statistics from the Congo, where a population of over 70 million had only 4000 operational landlines. Then came the cell phone operators, and instantly people were communicating. The fact that many those cell phones in the DRC were stolen from South Africa was of secondary importance. They were however responsible for untold numbers of deaths in that country, during armed robberies and hijackings. But these hand sets were themselves creating the flow of this vital knowledge. Access to communication was what would bring the ultimate peace this world was so desperately seeking.

Aubrey sat with the Professor and they poured over the information from the net. It was fascinating, how a science that had just emerged as a credible treatment for Aubrey's unusual illness, was now published in twenty journals and all claimed to have the answer. Then it hit Aubrey like a bolt of lightning. There it was and he could immediately see the solution.

Written on the head sheet of one of the pages was a clinic in Rembrandt Street in the centre of Amsterdam, and it was offering a trial for the treatment of liver cancer. 'The Modifying of Cytotoxic T-cells, the adding of the T-cell receptor to the Cytotoxic cells. The MART. One protein common on the surface of melanoma cells was genetically engineered to enhance the auto immune system to fight the cancer cells that form in the liver."

The procedure had been developed at Caltech in the USA, but like every great invention, the US Federal Department of Action, had not yet approved the procedure., The less strict laws of the European Union, had allowed a small Dutch company to provide the trials and this in turn would offer Aubrey a solution. Aubrey needed to contact them as soon as possible and establish how he needed to proceed.

When Aubrey returned home that evening, he reflected on the day. Aubrey recognised that society looked for winners, and gave scant regard to those who finished second. The great old tradition of winning no matter the cost would always make the difference between notoriety and non-existence. He was however a believer in his own destiny. Conformity was what had led to his mother's death, and society had no time for those who fell by the wayside.

Aubrey knew that no one ever became the subject of books by finishing second; except in death. Human nature always credited the one who won. Forget the good guy who did what was right; he would be kept in our hearts with a fondness that bordered on pity. But the guy who was in first place, from Hitler and Mugabe, from Amundsen to Hillary, no one remembered the also-rans. Scott failed and perished in his quest, whilst Idi Amin was regaled because of his crimes, but no one took him to the International War Crimes Tribunal, even though he was still alive, and larger than life! They make movies about him, and Hitler. No doubt Mugabe, who was Africa's greatest tyrant, was still in power despite losing elections. He may be reviled in celluloid in years to come, but as memories fade and wounds heal, he will be remembered; not forgotten. Who cared about the little guy who lost his way, his livelihood and ultimately his life? Blair would be a long-forgotten politician with blood on his hands, but an extremely profitable career in book writing.

Aubrey agreed that there was a need for society to be ordered and organised, but always wondered, why it was that the very people who went into law enforcement and political careers, seemed to be the least suited to their jobs. Or was it simply that they got where they were through dedication and circumstance, but then forgot the reason for their journey, once at the top? Absolute power corrupted, but the system allowed them to. Tony Blair's legacy, once the Iraq war was over would be scrutinized, but no one ever speaks about the arms procurement exercise that lead to the awarding of the F35 multi-purpose jet, which won the tender for the U.S. air force and navy weeks before the invasion of Iraq.

A company owned by U.S. Pensioners won that tender, but as Aubrey could attest to, the war industry was an unstoppable juggernaut, with some Institutions and Funds, with assets valued at over 200 trillion dollars, hoodwinking the American public into believing they were investing in technology, transportation and utilities. Nowhere in their company profiles did they declare their interests in the arms industry.

Those he had been introduced to through his father's social gatherings, were strictly to be avoided. If the truth be known, he had an aversion to those sycophantic toads with their spiffy outfits and stiff-necked attitudes. They were dinosaurs in an age of automated intelligence, where the common man had no need for their sanctimonious behaviour. Megalomaniacs always resorted to extremes, where public personas and reality always seemed to be juxtaposed.

The alternative was a charismatic leader like Jacob Zuma, who took five wives in an archaic interpretation of his cultural heritage; and blended this all with a voracious appetite for all the trappings of a first world lifestyle. This came at a price and morally bankrupted the nation. He was always going to be vilified and hauled before the courts in South Africa to answer charges of corruption and bribery. He appealed to the masses, but appalled the Intellegencia. It was about his legacy within an Afrocentric Political landscape. But time was a great leveller, and Aubrey would want to see the outcome.

Having spent his entire life avoiding the authorities, he certainly did not want to be pursued by them. Aubrey was the type who could sweet talk himself in to or out of just about any situation. He had been in situations that others would simply have surrendered to. He could sweet talk the soft serve off a child's ice cream cone without hearing a whimper, but was not going to have some local constable raising his blood pressure. As selfish as it may have appeared, his objective now was to get to the Professor armed with his newly researched information.

Chapter 10

A Humid Homily

Victoria Falls had become the adventure tourist capital of Africa. The young Scandinavian backpackers arrived in numbers, and with them a blossoming of international relations. There was never any doubt in Aubrey's mind, that if he had not been quite so besotted with Bronwyn, he may have dabbled a little more energetically with the blonde beauties that fraternised the afterhours Shebeens. But for the few temptations that he never acted on when Bronwyn had travelled to Harare sourcing permits for what was to be their fledgling business, Aubrey had remained steadfastly faithful.

This was where Aubrey now found himself, in the heat of a humid, but distinct summer of 1990, surviving the oppressive heat, followed by balmy afternoon rain showers that arrived like clockwork. In fact, they were so consistent, that one could set one's watch by the timely arrival of those downpours. Despite the odd bout of malaria that hit him three times in those first years, Aubrey was feeling strong and enthusiastic, having already forgotten the past, and having found a comfortable niche for himself, knowing exactly what they wanted.

He befriended a chap who had been at school with Bronwyn, and still had the 'hots' for her. His name was Timothy, and he was somewhat of a rabble-rouser. Aubrey was sucked in by his endearing charisma, and the two of them formed a strong bond. When he flew in from Harare on business, the town of Victoria Falls became their veritable playground.

Like every new emerging frontier type society, the 'Falls' was low on limits and regulations and high on bribes that could turn prospective businesses into reality. The drinking binges which he and Timothy would have on the town became legendary, and so the summer of '90 came and went merging with the African winter of '91. There was little trace of a change in temperature or climate, other than the early morning mist that sometimes greeted them both as they emerged from a stint of all night gambling at the local casino. The climate was that of a sub-tropical rain forest, the closer one was to the Falls, but dried out considerably, the further one ventured from it. 'Mosi 'O Tunia', or the 'smoke that thunders', was the name affectionately given to the Victoria Falls and the humidity was stifling. Quenching one's thirst was the colloquial way to deal with the tormenting heat. Iced cold beer was the sanctuary to which they escaped on an inclement afternoon, seeking the shade or an air-conditioned pub.

Timothy was easy to like. He had a great sense of humour, a devilish sense of adventure, and a quick eye for an attractive girl. When the lads were together, they somehow managed to get themselves into trouble. They were not that different or outrageous than most the frontiersmen that frequented the pubs and hotel bars. But it helped that they were able to bribe the local policing authorities easily enough to ensure no time was spent in the 'choocky'; an affectionate name for the local jail house.

Once, after a night out on the town, Timothy had been banned from one of the local casinos. His gambling habits were becoming more than just a casual flitter, and breaking the bank a fairly common occurrence. He decided in his infinite wisdom to get into the casino, whether the pit boss liked it or not.

Now ordinarily, Aubrey whose reputation to that point was innocuously clean, would have taken Bronwyn's advice and left early after their evening revelries; but for the fact that Aubrey did not need to be up early the next morning. After some drinking at Explorers, with their spirits up and Timothy with his never-say-die attitude, they headed for the casino in Timothy's 4x4. It had a bulbar on the front and a lot of horsepower underneath the hood. When they got to the casino, they saw the casino manager standing at the top of the stairs looking out for them. Someone had tipped off the management that they were on their way. The only thing to do was to charge the place, and enter the premises forcibly. After a turn of the car park, Timothy revved the engine and before Aubrey knew what was happening, they were assaulting the stairs at a pace that had the manager fleeing for his life, and the security staff diving into the bushes next to the stairs. Up they went over the granite adorned stairs, with the engine howling in support, and the great rubber tyres bucking them ever upwards until they ended up in the lobby of the casino, pitching to a halt. Nonchalantly, they walked into the Club Privet, and not another word was said.

Timothy, whose company controlled all the tourist franchises and was earning US dollars faster than the Zimbabwe Reserve Bank could stash them away, virtually owned the Town. Even then, their hard-earned foreign currency was like gold. The casinos were only too happy to exchange these hundred dollar bills, which seemed to be the preferred choice of payment. Most indiscretions could be overlooked for the allure of the last bastion of civilisation; the Greenback.

With a rafting trip costing eighty dollars for a day on the wildest ride in the world, these bills were as plentiful as the ticks on a herd of cows in a Gongozoro kraal. Timothy controlled all that cash, and there was not more than rudimentary auditing to be seen there in Vic Falls. It was his paradise to exploit, and as long as the money kept rolling in, everyone in authority turned a blind eye. These were the heady days that consumed them, and their appetite for spirited adventure had no bounds. Parties would go on until the sun came up and to Timothy commitments were a distant bed fellow. This was how he carried on for some years, until the ultimate sacrifice would see Timothy hitched, and his antics curtailed.

Aubrey held one of the few distinctions from the rest of the crowd that he and Bronwyn befriended, and that was a passion for the Elephant. He knew that the Elephant was truly the ancient King of the Wild Animals. They had an innate sense of family bonds; a characteristic Aubrey admired and in fact made him quite envious of them. On his days off, Aubrey would go up to the Hwange Park, a conservancy about 100 miles from Vic Falls, and the biggest National Park in Zimbabwe. It was not entirely safe to go there, as the government of Robert Mugabe, who had already been in power for eleven years, had been responsible for the annihilation of over twenty thousand ZIPRA loyalists. Joshua Nkomo, who had been one of Mugabe's contemporaries and a fellow freedom fighter, were conjugated during the fight for the vote, and so-called democracy. But the moment the 1980 election had been fought and won by Zanla, they became bitter rivals; fighting for the very land that they purported to have liberated.

Despite these obvious distractions, Aubrey was able to meet with a number of local herdsmen on the borders of the Park, and he was taken along the ancient paths that had been the sole domain of the great African Elephant. The migratory paths of the great herds of Elephant, had for thousands of years taken the route through the Hwange National Park, into Botswana, and through the Okavango Deltas to the Chobe. These migrations had been the preserve of the herds, in times of plenty; and drought.

It was on these trips that Aubrey began to understand the strengths of those bonds, and how they could be a powerful ally in teaching humans the merit of family. This was not too unfamiliar territory for Aubrey, and would be the catalyst that would bring him full circle one day. It was however very prevalent in the bonds that held the local tribes people together; however Western culture was already taking its toll on these family values. Sitting with the local chieftain, Aubrey was to retrace the history of colonial servitude.

Wellington was a Bulawayo educated and privately schooled fifty something year old man, whose involvement in the freedom struggle had left two of his sons' dead; not from the fight with his colonial masters, but at the hands of

Mugabe's Fifth Brigade. These notorious North Korean trained 'gooks', were the scourge of Matabeleland and had committed the atrocities, which now became known as 'Gukurahundi'. This was the infamous purge of all opposition to Mugabe's rule, literally translated as 'the early rain which washes away the chaff before the spring rains'. Wellington now had no heir to the Chieftainship, other than three daughters who did not qualify in a Patriarchal society of Ndebele custom. As a consequence, he had done what any self-respecting Chieftain would do, and he married a younger woman capable of birthing him a new heir. This had not been so successful a pursuit, as two more daughters had followed, so he married a third wife who was also unable to provide him with his heir. Despite this the whole family lived in relative peace and prosperity on their ancient tribal lands.

Wellington stood a full head above Aubrey. His broad shoulders gave him the appearance of an NFL line-backer with full padding. His broad nose and equally square jaw were cloaked with a dark black skin which was parched from the harsh dusty climate of the Matabele summer. Standing effortlessly, the wooden stool used in customary meetings around the fire, discarded, he greeted Aubrey in a welcoming embrace.

"Greetings my brother," his hand a solid extension of those sinewy forearms.

"Kunjani, it is a great honour to finally meet you." Aubrey held that vice-like grip in equal measure.

"Thank you. You are most welcome here." A low stool was proffered for Aubrey to sit; his knees bent and he sunk slowly to the earth, maintaining his balance from the core muscles of his abdomen.

All about them village life came to a standstill, as Aubrey was made to feel comfortable, and now at a vantage point of waist height, he was able to meet the gawking faces of a myriad of children. Some dressed only in scruffy shorts, snot-nosed and dust stained.

"What brings you to our humble village?" Wellington raised his head, once he was on a similar level to Aubrey. The breadth of his shoulders seemingly all the more pronounced.

"Ndlovu," Aubrey used the local name. "I have come to ask you for advice, and to the learn the ways of the Elephant."

Wellington smiled, his thick lips peeled back, revealing a set of magnificently white teeth. There was an audible grunt, as he mimicked Aubrey.

"Ndlovu." It was repeated with a tone of reverence.

"Yes. You have come to the right place. You are most welcome."

Educated he was, but Wellington had no desire to pursue the Government and have the land that fell within the Hwange Park returned to him. He was a pragmatist, and seeing as the Park was a great source of tourist dollars, and his family could go about their business without any restraints, he had opted to farm the land that was still available. This had ensured he would not fall victim to any further purges and ultimately, he could pass on his vast knowledge and wisdom to his sons. But it was Aubrey who was to become the son he could never have. Aubrey now knew that this was how life had continued for centuries before the advent of the colonial shackles that had brought his family headlong into conflict with the Ndebele. No amount of political conniving could change those simple facts. There was, however, a sense that if only the experiences of this quietly, unassuming man could be learnt from his fellow Zimbabweans; then, and only then would peace prevail.

The term 'freedom fight' seemed to be purely semantic as far as Aubrey could see, and the 'fight for control' would probably have been more accurate. The only fight that was needed, but that would never be fought, was the right of the indigenous population to live in a country ruled by free and fair elections, and as voted for by them.

But this fight, as in so many political upheavals around the world, came down to fundamental economics. Aubrey could see that the liberation struggle had been funded by political interests in China and in Russia. Political systems that had wanted a piece of the economic pie. In a country, rich with natural resources and already capitalised by the British-owned conglomerates, there was to be a fight for those resources, which would inevitably tear the country apart.

They spent the evening around the camp fire discussing the political fallout of the war for independence. Sadly, with a palpable irony, the colonial power, namely Britain, had negotiated a favourable deal for themselves at the Lancaster House agreement that had sealed the fate of the country; ensuring economic wealth remained in the hands of the few, while completely destabilizing the democratic freedom of the country's people. It was truly ironic, that Aubrey was the great grandson of one of the worst of these colonists. Even more paradoxical was the fact that he too had been seemingly disinherited and was penniless in the country that had forged the golden melting pot, from which his great grandfather had drunk. Or so he believed.

But now the political tables were turned and Aubrey instantly recognized the re-emergence of the tribal divisions that had led to war among the African tribes in the first instance. Along with the sheer stupidity of a colonial master, who had forced the two tribes to work together in an attempt to share a land, whilst intrinsically, in opposition to one another. The Ndebele of the south were war-like, having descended from the Zulus of South Africa, and Dingaan the son of Shaka Zulu. The northern tribes were mainly Shona, and had their origins in those tribes that had migrated into what was now Zimbabwe from the North.

There was no disputing the divisions. Wellington was Ndebele and his knowledge of the bush and its animals was in his blood. He was descended from the tribe, who had fought the colonists in three failed Matabele wars, and he came from a long line of Shamans. They were at one with the land and he could sense the beat of the African bush. Aubrey marvelled in his knowledge of the land and its fauna and flora. Wellington knew where to find the hidden roots, which had the medicinal properties to heal all forms of ailments; yet this knowledge was being gradually lost, and with Wellington's ultimate death, that wealth of that information would be lost forever.

The colonialists had swept in and demarcated the area as a conservancy, after the pioneer column with their ox wagons and the superior fire power of the legendry Enfield and Winchester rifles, had begun decimating the local elephant populations. Cecil Rhodes and the British South Africa Company had originally signed an agreement with Lobengula, and for a few pounds and a trinket or two, he had signed away their cultural heritage. No one seemed to care now, but life would never be the same again. The settlers had taken what they wanted as they drove their large wagons north of the Limpopo, unrelentingly in their quest for the gold, Rhodes believed to be there.

It was ultimately the land and the prized ivory that was so abundant that they settled for, unable as they were to find gold in the quantities prevalent on the Witwatersrand. The swathes of elephant herds could be tracked through the bush in those early days, by following the almost mile-wide track of felled trees stripped of their bark. It was possible to follow a large herd, ambushing them from downwind and even after two to three days of shooting, never getting to see the front of the herd, as it stampeded on through the bushveld. The elephants only stopped, when the guns had fallen silent. Then the herd was a thousand less in numbers but still so abundant that the ground would shake from their defiant trumpeted roars, and the screaming of calves that had lost their mothers in the ambush.

The young calves were of no value to the settlers. They could, but ruthlessly would not spare the cartridge needed to put them out of their misery. Thus, they were easy prey to Hyenas and other scavengers descending on the inhuman spoils of those hunts. The calves, unwilling to abandon their mothers, and incapable of defending themselves, would stand by those rotting carcasses, in an obtuse show of devotion to their mothers. In the baking heat of summer, they submitted one by one to the hyenas and jackals.

The famed Colonial hunter, Courtney Selous, was challenged to a shooting dual and in the period between the January of 1877, and December 1880, personally notched up 548 kills. These culling trips were focused purely on the ivory, as the Elephant posed no other commercial value to the colonialists. This meant that the hunters went after the bulls, the older Matriarchs, and any younger males that had ivory worth reaping. This would leave the herds decimated by not only the loss of their leaders, but by social disorder which would render the herds completely dysfunctional. It would also leave the landscape strewn with the rotting corpses, and the Elephant populations in disarray. No other pursuit had brought more devastation to the African Continent.

It would take over a century for the herds to recover from that assault, but now they were to be further hunted to extinction. Human suffering aside, the continent was the poorer for their loss, but nature had its way of rebalancing, and Aubrey had an idea. If it was Aubrey's Great Grandfather who had raised that challenge, then it would now be up to Aubrey to remedy the damage done.

Aubrey now stood on the banks of the Ndowenda water hole in the midst of a staggeringly beautiful phosphorous sunset flaming across the western sky. He felt the remorse that a thousand settlers had paid no heed to, and he fell to his knees openly weeping for the losses and the sheer arrogance of it all.

Whenever Aubrey had returned from his trips to Hwange, he always seemed distant and brooding, and Bronwyn understanding his need for a private release for his hurt, always allowed him to go on these trips on his own. While he was off on these trips, Bronwyn would be busy researching the permits needed for their fledgling business. They were looking to introduce domesticated elephants, as an Elephant Safari business at the Falls. Aubrey hoped that the local elephants would be able to make the transition from wild free-roaming elephant to bring attention to the Elephants plight, by educating people. Popular thought said that the local elephant could not be trained by humans, but Aubrey had seen otherwise. He did not want the subdued, subservient Elephant that had been used in labour camps all over the Asian continent, but a proud, family of Elephant that would be trained without the harsh methods used by the Mahouts of India.

"I will need to take another trip to Impingweni," Aubrey told Bronwyn, after his latest trip to Hwange.

"Where is that?" She was in good humour and they were relaxing on the veranda which encircled their tiny cinder-block home. Standard, as all the other homes in that small township on the outskirts of the town, the home was cool and spartan.

"It is an Elephant Conservancy about 50 miles south of Bulawayo on the Plumtree road." This was to be the source for their Elephants.

"Why don't you come with me on your day off," he ventured further as an afterthought.

"Yes, I think I will," she had heard how he had seen first-hand, these beautiful creatures being trained and how, with the correct incentives, the great African Elephant was capable of learning from humans.

"Those Elephant are able, through the persuasion of a kind, gentle trainer, to understand the needs of humans. But ultimately, they co-exist. It is almost as if they are patiently waiting to be free again!"

"If there is a way that we can educate people, and somehow convey the message that nature and man can coexistence, then I want to try." Each was diverse in nature, but inextricably linked. If those Elephant could be nurtured, he might be able to leave a legacy that had sadly eluded his great grandfather.

Aubrey would sit and watch these elephants in contained habitats, feeding during the early morning routine; noting how easily they had allowed humans to enter their world. The largest beast that walked, and could have easily trampled any one of them, had been able to find their balance in a foreign world, because survival seemed paramount. They seemed to have the capacity to understand this. They would bide their time and await the call which would come. There was something biblical about the Elephant's submission to humans. It harked back to Genesis, and the biblical account of the Great Flood. He figured if Noah had tamed the elephant so effectively at that time, then he certainly could give it a try in this time, if it meant their survival could be guaranteed.

The difference between Indian and African Elephants was not as vast as scientists would have us believe. The Indian Elephant had been domesticated for thousands of years, yet they remained faithful to their Mahout. Why should these Elephant be any different? Hieroglyphics on ancient Egyptian artefacts showed the role that Elephants had played thousands of years ago. It seemed that Africa had simply forgotten how to utilise these beasts. The Elephants would take to the Induna, or trainer. They readily accepted food and commands from him, provided the persuasions were done gradually and incrementally.

There was a reason however, why the local tribes had never domesticated the African elephant until now. Firstly, they had no need for their service, as they lived in mud huts; a consequence of their shifting cultivation practices. These were easy to build and even easier to move when their land cultivation methods left the arable land, fallow. These practices were still being employed by the local farmers, centuries later. Many believed that were it not for the introduction of large-scale commercial farming, there would be very little arable land in use.

"How is our application to the Tourism Department going?" Aubrey had tasked Bronwyn with the paper work.

"The forms have all been submitted, but the department head has been unable to get to discuss them with Timothy yet."

Bronwyn and Aubrey had ended up taking the path of least resistance. Unable to ensure the business would get the necessary permits, Bronwyn had approached Timothy with Aubrey's idea. The funding required for his venture was made available and the bribing of officials to procure the licenses to get the business started, took less than a month. But now the official had become greedy and he wanted more.

"What did Tim say about it?" Aubrey, although not bothered with the bureaucracy, realised that high-level talks were required.

"If anyone can get us the licenses; Timothy would be the one to do it," she was confident he would pull through. The red-tape involved was not the issue. Africa was rife with corruption, because by making the process as complicated as humanly possible, these bureaucrats knew they could milk the system for all it was worth. Unfortunately, it would become their ultimate downfall.

By economic necessity, the country could not afford to have vast sums of funding, disappearing into the pockets of officials, only to be splurged on consumer products that all had to be imported anyway. There was no sustainability in African Economics.

"Where are we going to get the funds for the elephants themselves?" Aubrey ventured.

"Timothy has suggested that we offer the company ninety percent of the stock and they will fund the capital" Bronwyn was nervous of what reaction this deal would illicit from Aubrey.

"That is fine, but then we need a management fee and a stock buy-back option."

He really only had one choice, and to make his African dream come true, Aubrey made this ultimate sacrifice. But he was learning from his mistakes.

They would effectively become employees in the business of their own creation, but Aubrey knew that the alternative was that he would lose the licences and the option to run the business would be offered to somebody else, who did not share his passion.

That was something he really didn't want. They would build in a clause which would allow him to buy back shares, so that he and Bronwyn would have a greater interest in time.

It was thus, in the African summer of 1990, he procured eight Elephant from Impingweni, and Aubrey and Bronwyn finally got to start their fledgling business.

The idea of riding through the African Bushveld on an elephant soon captivated the minds of visiting tourists, and the local alike. The Elephants were an instant success and the business took off, boosted by the marketing expertise of the parent company and their network of tour operators. The steamy afternoon rains had settled in and Aubrey knew he could rely on the humidity to slow the African Bushveld to a leaden quietness and quell the thirst of the antelope as they grazed from the saturated grassland.

It was just such an afternoon that Aubrey had introduced his first batch of fledgling tourists to their first excursion. With the Elephants saddled and the motley bunch of American tourists mounted, they set off with Aubrey riding shotgun and Blessings, his head Induna on the lead Elephant. They headed for the water hole, drenched by the afternoon shower and providing ample sustenance to the large herds. They sat from a short distance and witnessed Africa in its true magnificence.

He loved getting close to the herds of Buffalo, Wildebeest and Gnu on Elephant back, without disturbance to the animals. It was a privilege to be on the back of the real 'King of the Beasts', riding through the African bush alongside herds of antelope on either side. Aubrey found it something quite extraordinary that they only looked up to acknowledge the passage of these immense but gentle creatures. Blessings' was also trained to approach the grazing animal herds down wind, so as not to unnecessarily spook the wild herds of Impala and Blesbok. Their first outing was a splendid success and the tourists were animated to the point of being overwhelmed.

Within weeks, the parties were being exposed to the raw intensity of Africa, without disturbing the ecology of the land. They were accepted by the herds and treated with respect by a local pride of Lion. Aubrey was out with an influential group of tour operators from London, when, as they skirted the vast herd they came across the pride, waiting in ambush. From a distance, they watched as the females ambushed the herd of buck, and witnessed at first hand the kill. This was a coup for them. The photographers clicked away with abandon as they witnessed the strength and beauty of those magnificent animals in their natural environment. It was an awesome spectacle.

When they returned to the Boma with their cameras filled with shots of that incredible wildlife, Aubrey smiled inwardly knowing that they had experienced the true nature of Africa. As they related their stories, Aubrey secretly wished that he could have given his mother the privilege of this visual feast. But he would not dwell on this success for long, and now had to spend a lot of time trying to find even better ways of interacting with the wildlife. He often changed his routes into the bush, so as not to make the tours a constant cycle of repetition. The animals were creatures of habit, and Aubrey did not want to turn this experience into a zoo-like spectacle.

He took the Elephant on different routes, with his Indunas' learning quickly to circle the herds with their young calves in the spring months, before the unrelenting heat of summer would descend. The tourists were provided with the spectacle of newly born Impala frolicking in the early morning dew, with their mother's twitching nervously; ever vigilant.

The maternal instinct of these creatures was so evident and it was remarkable to see how instinctual parenthood became. He liked to watch as they grazed on the sweet succulent shoots of grass emerging after the early spring rains. The mothers were always keeping one eye on the cavorting youngsters as they bucked and kicked with the wild abandon and exuberance of youth. Then with a bleat of caution the mother would reign in her youngster, giving a quick glance to check that the leading bucks had not seen or heard any danger and a shimmy of her tail, before once more resuming her grazing.

This was their life for the next three years. Aubrey was very passionate about his work with the Elephants, and had developed quite a reputation. He was able to build an incredible bond with the animals and his favourite was little Jimmy. At six months 'little Jimmy' weighed in at a hefty 250 kilograms and was the cutest little character that Aubrey and Bronwyn had ever seen. The mother was Lesidwa, the giant thirty five year old matriarch of the group, who had been bred in captivity and had somehow fallen pregnant.

Aubrey suspected, that it was not one of the younger bulls in the herd, as none had exhibited any of the tell-tale signs, such as 'wet-face' or musth. But a more dominant wild bull, who had been attracted to the camp due to Lesidwa being in oestrus. She may well have inadvertently attracted the bull whilst out on safari, and the bull would have countered by displaying his readiness to mate, by releasing the scent of testosterone into the wind. Either way, this all happened while the outer perimeter fencing was still a work in progress. It had taken some time to cordon and build the large Boma where the elephants slept at night.

One evening, Aubrey had been summoned out to the camp in the middle of the night. Blessings had radioed him when the matriarch had broken through the large wooden poles of the Boma and had taken off into the bush. Aubrey, had raced back to the camp. It was a dark, foreboding night, punctuated by the flash of lightening on the horizon. When Aubrey arrived at the camp, the Elephants were anxiously stomping their turf, fearing that they had lost their Matriarch. Aubrey soon discovered that a wild herd had been in the area for a few days, slowly picking their way through the thick lush vegetation on the outskirts of the reserve. The Indunas had chased her into the night but she soon disappeared.

The rest of the Elephant could sense the wild herd and being territorial were highly alarmed. Ndlodlo, the senior male, had stayed quiet remarkably, like some kid brother tasked with keeping an illicit affair quiet, when his sister elopes off on a hot date. Aubrey had known that Lesidwa's pheromones had attracted a lone bull which had been shadowing the wild herd. If he was the dominant bull in the area, it would be his bragging rights that would entitle him to the spoils. The need to breed was a powerful reminder to Aubrey of the cycle of life. The eight-inch diameter poles of the Boma had been no match for Lesidwa's strength and determination. Although she had not yet calved, she was a Matriarch at the prime of her breeding span and the man-made barriers were no match for her physical desire.

When the search party eventually tracked her down she had already finished her mating ritual and was calmly grazing a mere 200 meters from the camp, a very satisfied look in her eyes. She stood defiant, as if to redefine her place as the alpha female in the herd, and to remind these mere mortals of their inconsequential role in her domain. She had been roughed up a bit by the Bull, and had taken a few gouges to her flanks, a sign that the wild Elephant had not taken too kindly to her more domesticated role. The balance of power restored, Aubrey welcomed her back into the Boma and said nothing to the Indunas.

Somehow Aubrey's even-handed approach to the entire episode had sealed his position as the head of the company that was Elephants of Africa; a small but tightly knit group of individuals who had become unified by a common passion. They all breathed, ate and lived only for the Elephants that were in their care.

Aubrey had always known that Bronwyn was a pretty persuasive gal, but what he did not know was that she came from a family in Harare of four older boys and having been born last, she had been brought up as a bit of a tomboy. Bronwyn's mother was a lovely lady called Val, and her husband a typical brute of a man, who had ventured out to Africa with his new bride at the time of the Mau Mau uprising in Kenya. Having arrived by ship, as so many of the Colonialists from Europe had done in the fifties and sixties they soon found their colonial way to Rhodesia, the last resort of their African odyssey.

Bronwyn's mom, had visited them at the Falls, and they had welcomed her with open arms. But Bronwyn's dad Tony was a bristly old character. He was rather old fashioned and while Bronwyn was living in sin, Tony could not countenance her relationship with Aubrey. Aubrey suspected that the fact that they were not married may not have been the only reason, but that it may have had more to do with the reminder of his own guilt at having to elope to Africa with Val, since she had been pregnant at the time. The fascinating story about their trek through Africa was a story unto itself, with Val relating the story of how Tony, with his knowledge of animals, had become one of the major purveyors of wild animal through Harrods in London.

The stories of his antics could keep them entertained for hours as they sat around the large wood stoked fire, until the embers were burnt to coals and the sun was on its way up. It had been a pity that Aubrey had not yet met Tony. He sounded like an interesting fellow and he would have loved to get to know him better. The sad story of how they had eventually arrived in Rhodesia was a legend in itself, that would someday make an interesting anecdotal story to be passed on to their children and their children's children. When they had arrived in Zambia on the Copper belt in the sixties, having escaped the carnage of Kenya, the family had settled in a tiny mining community in Ndola.

Tony had soon set about his passion of getting the wild animals he required for his export business to Harrods. Since the import of wild animals was quite fashionable at that time, any import of wild animals had to be sanctioned by the British government but no quarantine periods were required. This was before the advent of the rabies outbreaks, which had been caused by the common practice of wealthy land owners trying to buy and domesticate African wild dogs. To this day there are rumours of unspeakable creatures that roam the moors of England giving rise to the legend of the ware wolf. Tony had been an institution, infectious in his grandiose ideas, but misguided in his delivery.

Tony had been responsible for single handily exporting hundreds of wild animals to the UK. Now, under normal conditions this would have been fine, but the desire to own exotic animals, by the filthy rich in England, was becoming a ridiculous pursuit of the sublime to the ridiculous. When the trade was finally eradicated at the end of the sixties, Tony had exported leopard, cheetah and even elephant to the basement division of Harrods. The most bizarre of all the creatures was of course the Aardvark. It was commonly referred to as the Anteater and was a strange creature of the African plains, with a long trunk-like nose and mouth with a long protruding tongue. Requiring a staple diet of ants to sustain these animals in captivity, whole ant hills, built like miniature condominiums on the African savannah, were cut from their resting place and exported in crates to the UK. Whenever a red ant infestation occurs in the south east of London today, the locals have the likes of Tony to thank. But these stories were urban legends and how embellished they had become along the way, would never be known. It was by meeting Val, that Aubrey became aware of the serendipitous nature of their relationship.

Val and Tony, when visiting Cape Maclear with the family some years before, were in fact returning residents. Unbeknown to Aubrey, the story of Tony's acquisition of the Golden Sands hotel, in the early sixties, and his subsequent development of the site, had never been discussed by Bronwyn. It was only when they sat in the Boma, watching the Elephant as they mingled outside their pens, feeding on the sweet roots of the elephant grass, that Val began to recount the story.

It was no surprising that Tony was embittered and disillusioned by his fate. Africa was a continent of vast inconsistencies and diabolical politics. It was unsurprising that the continent still laboured under volatile financial injustices, even fifty years after the installation of democratic mechanisms. Africa was not ready for democracy, and the multitudes who still awaited their liberation, would need to wait for an age longer.

Chapter 11

The European Odyssey

Natasha had met him at the Estate on the Friday. Aubrey had sat Natasha down and explained everything to her, with a minimal amount of fuss. Even despite the prognosis, she had been extremely positive. Realising his needs, she had already researched the development of Cytotoxic T-cells in this modification process. The treatment available at the clinic in Amsterdam was still extremely dangerous, but it was a risk she felt he should take.

"I must go to Amsterdam soon," he explained.

To which she had insisted that she would accompany him.

"I have a mid-term break, and would love to help!"

Aubrey was somewhat relieved. He had not wanted to do this on his own and there was no one else he could call on. He had not kept in touch with anyone after university and it felt good to know there was someone who could help.

They had spent a very relaxed but active weekend at Finsbury, where Aubrey had introduced Natasha to the staff and the wonders of its magnificent gardens. They had explored the gardens, sitting under the Elm trees in the outer field chatting with Goodness, and reminiscing about the grand old Madala; the African continent. Aubrey had allowed Goodness, with his infectious laugh, to tell Natasha all about the Falls and their ancient beliefs, while he had day dreamed about his explorations, and more importantly, his Elephants.

It was just the simple process of chatting and laughing that bolstered his spirits and gave Aubrey the opportunity to spend some quality time with Natasha. He was not given to emotion, having been weaned off that possibility by an uncaring father; but it was Natasha's empathic concern which she held in large reserve that now resuscitated his desire to survive. Natasha would make a good doctor one day, because she actually cared. For her this was an opportunity to really put everything she had learned thus far; to good use.

They had booked the fare from the Professor's office on Sunday morning and grudgingly, the Professor had bid them adieu, from the steps outside Finsbury Mansion.

With a moments grace, Aubrey had retrieved a beautiful silk scarf from his mother's wardrobe, untouched in years and soft as the day it was spun. He placed it around Natasha's shoulders and tied it neatly in a slip knot.

Realising its relevance, Natasha leaned forward as they climbed into the waiting roller, and kissed him. The waiting compliment of staff smiled affectionately.

Aubrey noted the furtive glances between the Professor and Sean. This had seemed somewhat puzzling, but Aubrey put this in his memory bank, determined to make the Professor explain this odd interaction when they returned.

With Natasha by his side, they were on a bus headed for the southern port of Dover on Sunday evening, along with a bus load of some one hundred multi-ethnic Europeans. It was to be an interesting journey because Aubrey had never travelled by bus in Europe. There was no such thing as polite queuing when one boarded these interstate buses, and Natasha and Aubrey were jostled aside. Moreover, there was a good chance that if they had stood on ceremony, the bus might have just left without them. Luckily, they were travelling light, Aubrey only with his rucksack from Africa, and Natasha, not having planned a trip to Europe, had brought just a carry on, so they fought their way back into the queue.

They were certainly not disappointed, if it was an expedition they were looking forward to. The bus driver, a Dutchman with a rather caustic attitude, booked them in with all civility dispensed of at the door. Aubrey had only just managed to secure the last two seats directly behind the bus driver. Being a European bus, it was a left-hand drive, which took some getting used to for Aubrey. The driver on the other hand, swept through the outskirts of Gatwick airport harrowingly close to pedestrians and other road users. He sped unperturbed onto the motorway with his country and western music blaring. The incongruity of it all would have made the trip entertaining, had it not been that this immediately put Aubrey on edge. Natasha picked up on this, and trying to calm his frayed nerves she held his hand quietly as they cavorted from lane to lane.

The driver whose name tag read only 'Maarten' was, typically Dutch, but clearly inspired by too many badly dubbed Dolly Parton and Burt Reynolds movies. He had a radar detector on the dash to avoid speed traps. Not a good sign. Lit by an array of red and green lights, every time the gadget bleeped he braked with the twenty tonne vehicle swaying from side to side along with all its passengers. This was one trip in which Aubrey was not happy to be a backseat driver. The position, right over the driver's shoulder gave them little room to avoid seeing the traffic in front, and before long, Aubrey had closed his eyes and placed his fate in the hands of God, and more deliberately, he realized God had left Natasha and his life in the hands of a natural born maniac.

Maarten obviously felt obliged to cast aside all in his path, in order to make the deadline, and the Chunnel crossing at Dover. Either way Aubrey was fast reaching a point of stress induced neurosis, which had him so far over the edge, that had their not been a seat between him and the driver, he might have easily thrown Maarten aside and taken over the driving duty.

But, if there was any consolation it was that he could not feel the full effect of the swaying of the bus, as he was seated directly over the front wheels, and this lessened the effect. Peering over his shoulder every now and then as they lurched from side to side was nonetheless a sobering experience. Thankfully at the pace they were going, the port of Dover arrived none too soon, and they were spared the humiliation of Aubrey throwing up all over the Maarten's back. The thought did occur to him, however, that it was nothing less than what he deserved.

At Dover, they entered the long queue of buses for the Chunnel train, into which and through which they would travel. It was remarkable that there was no passport control, other than at the check-in counter at the bus terminus. This was a far cry from the long queues of Congolese families, he had witnessed at border crossings in Africa. Mothers burdened with toddlers carried in the traditional piggy-back method and the rest all waiting patiently in line; their fathers, nowhere to be seen. Those queues of humanity, controlled and regimented.

Not so here; where one boarded a bus, and travelled freely to any European destination in a matter of hours. There was a disconnect and it was obvious why Europe and the UK were a catastrophic mess, because the immigration tide seemed to be in only one direction. But anyone could leave the country with just about anything they wanted. The bus laden with suitcases of every type and size were not even given a cursory glance, not even at Gatwick, where they had boarded. Aubrey was sure this had something to do with the fact that there was no contraband worth smuggling from the UK.

Then the bus moved forward and Maarten in a faultless English presentation, perfunctorily and with little interest shown, began to explain the safety procedures. Aubrey and Natasha sat and watched, mesmerized as the bus was driven onto a huge carriage, with doors the size of an aircraft hangar.

They were effortlessly opened and closed by massive motors, unseen and unheard. The whole procedure took less than two minutes and before they knew it they were a bus, encapsulated in a train, which was being driven through an under-ocean tunnel. The joys of modern technology, and an experience which would not be forgotten by Aubrey, Natasha or any of the other first-time Chunnel travellers.

The thought entered Aubrey's mind, that if a terrorist had really wanted to cause chaos, this would certainly give him maximum 'bang for his buck'. The journey was over in little more than half an hour and as quickly as that thought had occurred, they were officially on the European continent and it was gone. They moved off the train and onto the motorway with spectacular European efficiency, and were soon zipping through northern France in the direction of Belgium and ultimately, Amsterdam.

"Wow," said Natasha. "This is my first time abroad!"

"What?" said Aubrey, distracted by a very vocal conversation between the two occupants that were seated behind them.

"This is your first-time outside England?" Amazed he just looked at Natasha; he had never thought to ask her.

"Yes, did I not mention that on the weekend?" Natasha was sure she had mentioned her excitement at the prospect of travelling to the continent.

"No, I think I was distracted," was all that Aubrey could say, as he tried to catch the gist of the conversation behind him.

It was in a foreign language, but seemed heated nonetheless. When he zoned in on a conversation like now, he was unable to concentrate on anything else, and was therefore not really following what Natasha was saying.

"Incredible!" was all that Aubrey could muster.

Things were now quieting down a bit behind him, but Aubrey was still conscious of a more hushed discussion. Aubrey let the distraction go, and having no concept of what time it was, shook his wrist watch below his cuff to glance at the time. It was 1.30 in the morning and the whole trip had taken them from Gatwick to France in less than two and a half hours.

They were now charging through the French countryside, the Industrial outskirts of Calais behind them. The prospect of reaching Amsterdam in the early hours of the morning, which would give them the entire day ahead, suddenly made Aubrey feel exhausted. He needed to sleep for an hour to refresh and recharge his batteries, but between Maarten the cowboy and the travelling Wilboughries behind him, that didn't seem to be an option.

Even the head-to-head squabble with a bull elephant, which had stood in their bush-path one afternoon, on an African excursion from their tented camp, had not given Aubrey the sense of unease that he now had. Maybe, it was just his anxiousness about travelling to Amsterdam, and the prospect of what he might learn at the clinic, that made him so uneasy.

Natasha had been chatting away excitedly about her first European observations and he had been nodding in approval, but none of it had really sunk in. She was decidedly chirpy, but Aubrey was definitely somewhere else, his mind distracted.

It made him think of a trip to Harare, when Timothy had invited Bronwyn and himself to stay at his residence in Highlands, one of the more affluent residential areas. They had been invited to a party with Timothy and told it was to be a theme party. Hosted by a good friend in a neighbouring suburb, Aubrey had thought it peculiar that grown men would get dressed up to go to a party, having given up on that lark in his university days. However, in a small town like Harare, it was a symptom of the boredom of living in a cloistered community, where everyone went to the golf club on the weekend, and took turns to host a party.

No one had much respect for the local authorities as all dealings with them were based on bribes and favours. Unremarkably, it made sense, that in a town of less than forty thousand previously advantaged non-blacks, their sole aim was to enjoy their colonial heritage and live life to the full. The party was to be a 'camouflage party'. This required dressing up as a soldier, and any type of military regalia was appropriate. Having borrowed an old Rhodesian Light Infantry uniform from Timothy, Aubrey had squeezed into the tight khaki shorts of that time, and donned a camouflage vest and webbing, which etched itself into his 44-inch chest. He had seen photographs before of the young men with their fresh faces and fresh ideals about to enter a reality they did not understand, and some of whom would never emerge from that reality again.

The merit of those young men's sacrifices was to be the significant contribution of slowing and blunting the massive communist wave that had been rolling in from the north and east. Those young men, barely 18, had sacrificed their lives for an ideal which none of them could have understood.

The tide of terrorism, condoned by the Western powers at the time, had simply feathered the nests of foreign arm manufacturers, who often supplied both sides to that war. Funded through communist states which were desperately clinging to power, the war had been a source of significant unease for both the UK and US governments. They had looked the other way when isolated and geographically ensnared Rhodesia had stood alone to face the onslaught of communism. But it was the significant assets of the British owned businesses that had been at stake then, and still were to this day.

Timothy, who had pulled out his father's Selous Scouts Captain's uniform, looked rather dapper in full regalia and so they had all headed off to the party in Timothy's Isuzu double-cab. The journey was to take them out through Gun Hill, where the old settlers had set up camp, and down along the pot hole rutted Borrowdale Road, which was once the major thoroughfare to the north. They passed by the rather dilapidated Borrowdale Race Course, the sole form of legalized gambling in Harare and where countless poverty stricken, but nevertheless satisfied working class men and women had gone every Saturday afternoon to lose yet another weeks' worth of wages on the horses.

"You see those flag poles?" Timothy pointed as they swooped through the left-hand bend towards Borrowdale shops.

"Yes," Aubrey acknowledged.

"When we were teenagers we used to climb the race day flag poles on a Friday night and 'scale' the sponsor's flags." This, Aubrey realised, was an interesting euphemism for stealing which was not lost on the others in the back. Cheryl and Bronwyn had laughed uproariously.

It was symptomatic of a system born of a low moral conscience. Symptomatic of the reversal of power which had ensured the white population at least, held little regard for the authority of the day, because life held little future prospect. This was an indictment on the best and worst of colonialism and Aubrey now understood why these ex-Rhodesians were so passionate about their country. It was a testimonial to why so many of these born and bred Rhodesians had hung around despite valiant efforts by Mugabe and his cronies to dislodge them. It was a reversal of racism which was purely based on wrestling control of economic prosperity from the former colonials. Aubrey sensed their frustration with a Government intent on implosion, but it had not prevented him and Bronwyn from pursuing their dream.

Driving through the suburbs they had arrived on a plateau north of Harare in the Domboshawa hills. This place belonged to an old girlfriend of Timothy's, but he and the family had kept in touch despite his new marriage. The community was tight, and everyone knew each other except for Aubrey. So, after countless introductions, none of whom Aubrey could initially remember, he and Timothy headed for the bar with the lads to have a sundowner. The view was magnificent, west facing with the setting sun, and Aubrey who had been captivated by many an African sunset, could more than ever appreciate why these new Zimbabweans had made their home in this Eden. It had been paradise regained, but for how long? The government of Mugabe was on a roller coaster ride of abuse and extravagant self-indulgence that would leave the country on its' knees.

The boys stood at the bar and as the western sky had blazed in salute of that sunset, Aubrey and the rest of them toasted the old flag, and with an uproarious lilt to their voices they sang the unofficial national anthem, made famous by Woody Guthrie and adopted by the patriotic Rhodesians.

"This land is your land; this land is my land, from the western borders, to the Eastern highland. From the Great Zimbabwe, to the rolling waters, this land was made for you and me!"

It was a fine tune which had originally been written by Irving Berlin. It could still be considered appropriate in a country which was rapidly being decimated by greed and lust for power, but which lacked the passion of the early days. It was almost as though Mugabe was intent on eradicating all signs of the Old Rhodesia, to satisfy his megalomania.

"Don't you think Ian Smith, at ninety-something, must be shedding a tear for the immensity of the carnage being inflicted on this country." Timothy lamented. As rhetorical a question as they all would have mused over, it was lost to the spectacle enveloping the western sky.

"We have survived communism, but 'those' intent on retaining power at all costs, will bring this beautiful country to its knees." Timothy could not have known how prophetic his words would be. All Aubrey knew was that he had flown in the face of an accepted reality at the time, and challenged a cancerous scourge that was greed and corruption.

This ideal, had been laid out a century before by Rhodes, who was disparagingly called 'the vicars' son', by the author Rotberg. But his Nationalistic pride is considered no less distasteful in this modern time, despite the failure of a staggeringly robust financial system that had been handed to Mugabe on a plate.

Rhodes had been the founder of Rhodesia, and the reason why so many years later the population of Zimbabwe was still 'arbitrarily and indiscriminately' in the hands of yet another dictator. By signing off on that grand colonial scheme, the British government had laid the framework for a hundred years of tyranny, which had disenfranchised the common black man.

But the British it seemed were still intent on controlling events in this region through their control of the mineral rights in a country with vast reserves of resources. Despite the Lancaster House Agreement, which Mugabe had signed-off on, he wanted more, and Aubrey suspected it was more to do with retaining power, than anything else. Smith and the British were perpetually accused of racism, the age old and somewhat tiresome criticism of Mugabe and his henchmen; but it was an orchestrated attempt to impose their rule of law just as the colonialists had done. Their brand of racism was simply clothed in a cloak of despotism designed to look like Liberation Politics.

"No matter how bad things get, there will always be a silver lining in Zimbabwe!"

That silver lining included the magnificence of an African sunset, the camaraderie of a band of brothers and the cool, slow chug from a glass of golden lager glinting in the savannah sun.

They had stayed until the early hours of the morning, and with no concerns for the rule of drinking and driving, had set off back to the house in Highlands at about three in the morning.

But as Timothy cut back onto the Domboshawa Road and along the Helensvale road, he could clearly see an accident or road block up ahead near the Police station. With no more than a cursory, "shit there's a road block ahead," which seemed a common occurrence, they turned left onto a side road and came out into a valley that took them back past the old Salisbury Drive.

"The Third Marques of Salisbury was the British Prime Minister during the expansion into 'Rhodesia'," Timothy had mentioned as they hit the intersection with Highlands Road. He was a student of history.

"The British South Africa Company pioneered its way through the heart of Matabeleland, and had set up camp in what they called Fort Salisbury." It was a strategic, settlement designed to consolidate the power of Rhodes' BSAC.

The road had been named after him by the colonial government as it ringed the entire city, like an old outspun laager. As they came up to another intersection, they were confronted by what looked like yet another incident up towards the Lewisham riding stables.

"What the hell is going on?" Aubrey had voiced his concern, but Timothy nonchalantly swung the wheel and they were speeding up past Oriel Boys School and on their way through the suburb of Chisipite and back onto Highlands Road.

Before long, they were turning sharply into the suburb of Highlands and out of sight of any potential road block. They had driven in silence.

As they arrived at the rambling single storey settlers' mansion, Aubrey was agitated.

"What's going down?"

He was summarily dismissed by a cursory wave of the hand and a "goodnight all," from Timothy, who headed straight for bed propped up by his wife Cheryl.

As morning came to the sleepy city, all hell broke loose. The Sunday morning routine was interrupted by the wail of sirens and the soft padding to-and-fro by the domestic staff. The beautiful wooden floors, sanded and varnished only projected the alarming sound of scurrying feet. Timothy's voice could be heard issuing urgent instructions, but it was the sound of his own door creaking open, that had ultimately roused Aubrey. Louise, politely peered around the door, sheepishly apologizing for waking them.

"What is it?" murmured Bronwyn, lying with her head propped up on the crisp white feather pillows, she to having been woken by the activity outside.

"No real problem," replied Louise, "I would just like to get the laundry sorted and the kitchen staff ready to prepare breakfast. Any specific orders for you?" Cheryl adeptly changing the subject, whilst scrounging for the discarded clothing, strewn hastily across the bedroom floor.

"No. Thanks my angel," came the drowsy reply, and she was gone again.

They had slumbered for a little while longer; Bronwyn curled up in Aubrey's arms, before finally rising. They then padded down to the bathroom off the main passageway, which Aubrey noted had a cool red concrete floor and spacious white enamelled bathroom tiles. It was a blend of minimalism and functional opulence. The bath was deep, and the two of them had enjoyed a good long soak, rinsing off all the congealed smoke and sweat that had matted their hair from the previous night.

When they had ventured down to the open veranda to have their breakfast with Timothy and Cheryl, they were met with a forced calm and a resoluteness which bordered on paranoia. Then over breakfast Timothy began to relate the story to them of their lucky escape of the previous night.

During the evening, and unbeknown to the four of them, the barracks at Cranbourne had been raided, and the ammunition depot blown up by an ex-Koevoet commander of the South African Military. The espionage team led by the cavalier Major Bredenkamp, had destroyed the entire arms depot, setting the now defunct old RLI training camp aflame, and rendering the Zimbabwean army defenceless, but for a few rifles and ammunition that had already been issued from stores. The army, out for revenge, had set up road blocks on all the main arterial roads, into and out of Harare, fearing a coup d'état was imminent. Any one remotely suspicious had been arrested.

"What! Like a few inebriated fellas' in old Rhodesian army uniforms?" interjected Aubrey, as they went completely silent realizing the gravity of their situation. They had potentially escaped with their lives, a fate worse than death; but Aubrey was strangely elated. Once the palpable realisation of just how close they had come to being shot became evident, they all burst out laughing in unison, with the adrenalin infused terror of the moment.

Back in the bus, and ten thousand miles from there, the reverie of his previous close escape did nothing to quell Aubrey's current concerns. He found himself on edge again as the bus continued its ascent northward, dreams interrupted by the noisy conversation still active behind him. He was irritated.

'The raucous conversing behind him had reached feverishly high notes. This time there was an edge to the younger man's voice. Having spent many a night in the bush with his Indunas, in life-threatening circumstances with prowling Lions and Hyena nearby, his neighbours voices were of no comfort to Aubrey. Aubrey could now make out the odd sound of an electronic signal switch being activated by the two, but what concerned him more was the conversation itself. He could distinctly hear the older man repeating the words under his breath "Allahu Akbar, Allahu Akbar, Allahu Akbar."

Aubrey gently removed Natasha's resting head from his left shoulder, and cautiously placing the rolled-up scarf in the crook of her neck, he eased her head up against the window without her stirring.

In a flash, Aubrey, had picked up Natasha's carry on from the floor between them, he went for the pepper spray he knew she had in the sleeve of the bag, and armed with this he sat back prepared for the worst. As the chant became more vocal he tried to identify which of the two was seated directly behind him, peering out into the darkness, but secretly looking for a reflection in the large window beyond Natasha. Hoping to identify the whereabouts of his scheming assassins. The darkness outside afforded him the opportunity to see a distinct reflection of the two of them seated behind him, lit by the yellowish glow of the interior bus lights. The younger man was seated on the aisle seat and the older directly behind him. Aubrey could see they were conversing with a third man who was seated on the opposite side of the aisle.

Aubrey recognised a fanaticism evident by the contorted look in the older man's eyes. Through the distorted reflection, he could see the evidence of a box containing the instrument of death, held in the old man's lap. Aubrey was not about to become the victim of another 7/7 attack. He sat primed in a state of adrenaline infused anticipation, his finely tuned body prepared for the danger he sensed.

The bus lurched again and Aubrey, not having paid attention to where they had been driving, caught the glimpse of an exit sign from the motorway reading 'The Haag'.

"Of course," he rationalized under his breath. They were going to make a statement by hitting the capital of the European Union. This was where the despotic Milosevic had been dragged after his arrest in the old Yugoslavia. This was where Mugabe should be as well - he thought. The terrorists were going to create havoc in the very place where the human rights lawyers were sentencing old tyrants to death.

"But it did not make sense," he rationalised. This would not further their cause, but simply show the desperation of a dying religion, unable to evolve into a modern world.

"They were not welcome to do so on my bus!" His mind was racing as quickly as Maarten was steering the bus through the outskirts of the Dutch capital.

"What could he do to prevent three fanatical bombers from exploding their devices? How could he effectively tackle all three while preventing at least one of them from detonating his bomb?"

He peered over his shoulder as the bus reached a traffic circle, and as the bus swayed through the obstacle, he was able to see the two seated behind him. They were both wearing leather jackets. Standard black, untailored. Typical of the sort of thing you might see up on Oxford road in one of those gimmicky tourist stores, stocked with t-shirts with an inane message, 'I went to London and all I could afford was this lousy t-shirt'.

The probability was they would easily detonate as they reached the bus terminus in the centre of the city, killing and maiming all on board.

"But why?" His logical brain could not fathom why a bus load with a mixed racial background would seem an appropriate target!

On the pretext of getting something from the overhead locker he would make a cursory inspection of the terrorists behind him, trying not to raise any suspicion.

The bus was now belting its way to the heart of the City. He had no time to act. If he did nothing now then he, along with all the passengers, would be left powerless. He grabbed the back of the drivers' seat, and swivelled out into the aisle.

The only problem was that Maarten was not in on the plan, and his driving antics sent Aubrey reeling against the driver's seat.

Maarten, obviously irritated shouted, "Please sit, we are coming to the stop now."

"That could be too late," Aubrey thought.

Resolved not to wait until Natasha and he had become a statistic, he continued to extract himself from behind the driver's seat, and with one final surge, slipped into the aisle. Any thought of making this move discreetly, was now completely lost. The bus pitched again to the right this time and Aubrey was catapulted into the seat of the terrorist, who had not yet moved.

Aubrey was now provoking suspicion, but felt that he should not catch their bemused expressions with any eye contact that might give him away.

He reached into the overhead locker and rummaged around, for what, he did not know! Then trying to look casual he surveyed the area behind the seats.

He was aware of their stares now and could not help but catch the intense glare of the older man who had been seated behind Natasha up. He was the one who had been chanting 'Allahu Akbar'. Aubrey caught sight of the box on his lap. It was a book! A Koran!

The glare from the older man gave way to bemused concern. Aubrey was now staring directly into the man's steely eyes. He was calculating what Aubrey knew. Assessing whether he was a threat. Aubrey knew body language enough to know the advantage was lost.

The older man leaned towards the younger man next to him and in Arabic, made a comment while looking over at Aubrey. Aubrey felt exposed. As if they were now all looking through him and gazing at paradise. Any moment now the bomb would go off, and Aubrey would be spared the treatment he was about to endure in Amsterdam. This was the end game, either Aubrey must act now or all would be lost. With the pepper spray in his left hand, he froze.

Then he was spared the ignominy of having to confront them when the younger man, pointed over his shoulder while looking directly into Aubrey's eyes, and in a broken English, which had a European, possibly Dutch accent, said.

"The toilet is back there, "pointing towards the middle section of the bus where a set of stairs led down to the convenience.

Aubrey completely deflated, smiled back at him, as the blood rose into his face and with no further ado he sat back down into the welcome seat making sure not to rouse her.

The situation defused, he suddenly realized the European summer was upon them. The sun was creating a yellow stain on the eastern horizon, visible through her window. Aubrey realized with relief. The men had been praying.

Natasha, her head propped against the coolness of the window, with the silken scarf profiling her visible perfection, looked serene. Aubrey gazed upon her lustrous clutch of hair, pulled tightly into a pony-tail, and marvelled at how she slept, her long shapely neck exposed by the angle of her head. Aubrey gently pulled her back into his arms. He felt ridiculous, but somehow enlivened. Was this the emotional feeling that came from protecting and nurturing? He was certain that it was.

They arrived in Amsterdam after several other stops on the way. Natasha awoke slowly, her eyes fluttered, then her chin chiselled its way further into the crook of his neck. He smelt of aftershave and testosterone. She kissed him on the neck, the stubble of a one-day beard, scratchy and erotic.

Aubrey could not help but notice that the Dutch were prolific bicycle riders. Everywhere there were bicycles and bicycle paths and a host of early morning risers on their bicycles. After all, The Netherlands was very flat so it made for easy cycling.

"Have you ever seen so many bicycles in your life?" He remarked, as they sped towards the bus terminus. The Malawians had been prolific bicycle riders, but that had been more to do with poverty. What an example these people led with their vigorous cycling lifestyle.

"Even the kids are on their own bicycles." Natasha smiled. Whole families were popped onto bicycles. Mothers with a toddler up front on a chair, an older sibling on the back seat, and an infant in the buggy towed behind. Great swathes of cyclists could be seen as ocean waves washing past them as they commuted.

Aubrey was quite taken with this.

"I think that the bicycle should be seen as an extension of a societies evolution." As countries emerged from decades of impoverishment at the hands of a select few, so they progressed to mini-buses and cars.

"It is the necessity of large oil conglomerates to peddle their oil. Economic prosperity comes with the development of those natural resources, yes. But economic freedom comes from being able to discern what was more important."

It was one of Africa's greatest ironies. The biggest culprit in Africa was owned and run by the Dutch Royal family.

It was poignant that a country so obsessed with health and education, could allow their politicians to rape and pillage another country with their greed and avarice. They would always tacitly condone this by looking the other way. What a pity that this highly evolved society had not seen this obvious violation.

"Now there's a business with wheels," he chuckled under his breath.

"What is?" She was now fully awake.

"Exporting bicycles to Africa. Why not give them something they truly need!" Aubrey smiled. Natasha caught the gist of his argument.

"Why don't they use bicycles then?" Natasha had no concept of how Africa had been transformed during the period of Liberation and subsequent globalisation.

"It's all about consumerism." He explained.

"Governments tax the fuel with a levy which doubles the price of the stuff. They generate so much revenue from this, that they encourage the large fuel companies with incentives."

"There is even a law in some African countries that prevents a petrol company from providing a self-service forecourt." This would conceivably reduce the price of the fuel to the consumer. But no discounts on fuel are allowed and it benefits the governments two-fold. The petrol companies provide employment, the employees are taxed and the petrol is sold at a premium to maximise their tax revenues.

"The average indigenous African is fast becoming as overweight and unhealthy as some Americans." He added. Natasha nodded.

"It's a vicious circle," Natasha was beginning to realise that a paradigm shift was required.

She was more concerned about the health of people. The Dutch were a large people, in stature. Their physicality was the one advantage they had from a health perspective.

Arriving at the bus terminus, Natasha, an old hand at catching public transport, then led him off to the information desk where a rather severe looking Dutch woman, manned her kiosk. She stood in a blue lapelled jacket, giving directions. Within a minute, they had purchased tickets for the trams, and were beetling off to a hotel in central Amsterdam.

Chapter 12

The Morning After

The morning's voyage had brought them through the precipitous entrance to the Zambezi Gorge. The decent was tenuous, but made even more difficult as they manoeuvred a twenty-foot raft down a precarious path. This was the physicality of rafting. Aching muscles and the grogginess of a Mampoer hangover were quickly forgotten.

The White-Water Derby, as the sponsors had dubbed it, was a three day long high stakes adventure through twenty-four rapids, with no holds barred. The event had seen their motley crew of eight, plus navigator take on fitter, and more experienced teams from all over the world. They had descended on the Great Zambezi to take part in the biggest event ever staged at Vic Falls.

'The Devil May Care' team as they had named themselves, was made up of Bronwyn, Aubrey and six other Vic Falls residents who had volunteered for the race. Mike, a great hulk of a man was the team leader, seated at the back, riding shotgun. His job was to steer the raft through the rapids, as best he could. This first rapid, the Morning Glory, was enough to wake anyone up, even the devil!

"Pull, pull, pull," he barked as they neared the lip of the drop.

Aubrey and Bronwyn were up front, 'high-siding' the raft, and facing off against that cascading drop. Fearsome enough at any time of the year, the organisers had seen fit to run the event in September.

Bronwyn was screaming; a look of terror permeated her passively blue eyes.

"Okay steady, steady. Left, left and pull. Pull!" Mike's command was obeyed and the team of oarsmen on the right dug deeper into the surging morass.

The exhilaration was etched into their water-weary faces as they plunged down a five metre sheer drop onto the next level of the gorge. The river was running low and the rocks further exposed, gave added credence to the Zambezi's reputation as the premier white water rafting venue in the world.

Aubrey waited for the call and as it came, he threw every ounce of his ninety kilograms against the rubberised PVC prow of the raft. The team of eight joined him and they all rushed forward. With the oar still clutched in his right hand, he bounced back, the inflated tube offering little give. This was called high-siding and their combined weight, thrown against the prow of the raft, added further impetus to their descent.

Their added velocity crashed them through the first wave, the raft rearing once like a prehistoric Tyrannosaurus, and then plunged back into the surging foam. Aubrey steadied himself on the bucking prow and reaching over the side, as far as his balance would take him, he paddled with every sinew in his shoulders and arms screaming for release.

But the power of that torrent of water just seemed to take them away from where they were supposed to emerge from the cascading white water.

Bronwyn screamed again as the wind took her barely audible howl of terror, and whipped it away into the depths of the ancient cavernous walls of rock surrounding them. Aubrey transfixed by her stunning beauty, marvelled at her courage. She stood shoulder to shoulder, her wiry hair, knotted by sun and wind, streaming behind her.

But fearing they might hit the turbulent side of the wash that formed beside the rapid, they extended the paddles over the raft, and gave one more mighty pull into the water, as they slipped through the epicentre of a great wall of water.

Aubrey took another deep breath as the second wall of water hit them. Dousing him and shaking out the last remnants of the previous night's mampoer and filling his entire body with surging adrenaline. They emerged out of the white-water cavern, upright and amazingly with their full complement of crew still on board.

The raft buffeted violently to the left, catching Bronwyn off guard and she reeled from the force of the torrent of water hitting her from the side. The immensity of that weight of water sent her careering towards Aubrey, but he saw her coming and deftly caught her and pulled her to his chest, checking her fall. She managed to grasp his waist with both her arms so as not to pinion his arms. The raft dived again into the turbulent foam beyond the plume. As they hit the calmer water they steadied themselves once more, front and centre.

Bronwyn shrieked, hugging Aubrey, and as they barrelled down the river, she raised her arms in triumph. Her spirit was so infectious that everyone joined her in celebration. On the side of the river, a photographer had snapped a picture at the very moment Bronwyn had stood to roar her approval.

Bronwyn encapsulated the spirit of life in Africa, with the opportunities for young women and men. Everyone in their team had made Victoria Falls their home, and from the modest dwelling that Bronwyn and Aubrey had rented for themselves, to the communes that most of the younger crew lived in, the essence of what life in this bourgeoning democracy held for them, was electric.

Bronwyn had been the girl to whom Aubrey would entrust his life, and she in turn hers. They had a loving and warm relationship which most envied, but which was the start of something more powerful. If ever there was a couple who espoused the sheer glory of what it meant to be in community of spirit, they would be it. Their day was filled with the excitement and adrenalin of the rafting, and the quieter moments between rapids, where he held her in his arms and they gazed heavenward at the magnificence of that deftly crafted work of God and nature. Combined the Powers had etched this grand chasm out of the African soil, and it was splendid.

Aubrey was reminded of a quote from a long-forgotten poem he had learnt for English Literature, which he had rather ineloquently attempted to regurgitate at a school literary awards evening;

'He grasps the crag with crooked hands,
Close to sun in lonely lands,
Ring'd with the azure world he stands; The Eagle."

It was a poem by Alfred Lord Tennyson and personified the nature of that Eagle in almost revered tones. The Eagle is seen as a romantic outsider as he watches from his mountain walls and Aubrey would recite this to Bronwyn, as they stared mesmerized by the call of a fish eagle on the cliffs above them; the haunting lilt of its cry a plea to the world for common sense.

This was nature in all its splendour, doused in the evocative spirit of oneness. Aubrey envied its view from the insurmountable rock face above them, and wondered at the majesty of its domain. No human endeavour could ever hope to immortalize that dominion; there he stood with the vista of a billion years of natural made beauty spread out before him and not a shadow of doubt as to who owned and occupied it. He was the emperor of this Kingdom, and the master of his destiny. No wonder he stood so regal, unsullied by the human world that transgressed his territorial rights, patiently awaiting the departure of this intrusion, confident that the next visit to the water would yield his next meal.

That call was so African, that no visitor could resist the echo of its hallowed shriek; no memory could forget its chilling message.

That evening, they had met at the newly rebuilt Kingdom Casino, and with awards being handed out for the event, they had placed a credible third. Out of a field of thirty crews, all of whom had prepared for months for the race, this was no mean feat. A spirit of adventure, and a monumental effort, tinged with a smattering of luck, had seen them through quite proudly. However, if the truth be known, it was the invaluable experience of Mike, who had worked the river since the early days, and his intuitive knowledge of the rapids, that had made all the difference.

He was a great bear of a man, with forearms the size of Aubrey's calf muscles, and hands that looked like meat cleavers. Yet for his size, Mike was as gentle as a lamb. He had lifted them onto his shoulders one at a time in celebration, when they had reached the finish line earlier that afternoon; and when it had come to ascending the cliff face to exit the gorge, he had mustered enough energy to carry an exhausted Bronwyn, on his back, all the way up a sheer eighty degree, almost seven-hundred-foot climb.

Aubrey had always had a great deal of respect for Mike. He lived in a ramshackle home on the outskirts of Vic Falls, which he shared with his long-time friend Andy. Mike was a teller of tales which would confound and entertain them for hour after hour. He and Andy were inseparable and he had become known to the locals as Manqoba, 'the one who conquers'; and Andy was Mukani, 'the wise one'. They were always ready for a good time, always handy in a bar brawl, and courteous, especially to the girls, who would ask for their help and be provided it, to a fault.

Aubrey had often spent the weekends with Mike and Andy, when Bronwyn was in Harare visiting her cantankerous old man, with whom Aubrey had not exactly hit it off. He would find every excuse not to go with on those weekends away, preferring to hang out with Timothy if he was in town, or with the lads. They were the four musketeers when they got together and always had a great time. In their best form, they would drink from Friday evening to Sunday afternoon, when Bronwyn returned. They would end the weekend by breakfasting on the local beer and catching the occasional burger at the pub in town. Mike could lift the wooden beer crates fully laden with bottles, with his arms, raising them to shoulder height with a flick of his wrist. Aubrey was always in awe of the sheer physical presence of the man, but was even more amazed that he was passive unless provoked.

In one encounter while out on a boy's night, he had witnessed Mike take a beer bottle to the back of the head. Mike, who had shaken off the infringement, turned to his assailant, who stood his ground, but shell shocked by the fact that Mike had not dropped. Lifting the guy with one hand to the throat, he had tossed him like a rag doll across the bar counter. They had all drunk a toast to Mike while the culprit lay almost comatose on the bar floor. Never shy to have a party, they had quickly become the best of friends.

They were playing coinage one evening, a game in which the players sat around a bar table, bouncing a coin as accurately as possible into a beer mug in the centre of the table. Since the other team members had to down their drinks, on every successful effort, this game very quickly led them to a highly spirited and inebriated state. They would often while away the evenings playing the game, when there was little else exciting on the go. On this particular evening, the four of them had gone down to Explorers, intent on a good evening. Timothy was in particularly splendid form and had instigated the evening's proceedings. They would have a drink, bounce the coin and then brag about experiences with the bevy of beauties that were always in transit through Vic Falls. As the drinking took effect, their stories would become quite outrageous, particularly Timothy's.

It was now that they challenged themselves to a dare which always had to be bettered by the loser. The first to lose in the best of three rounds of coinage, was to have a 'down-down', but was also to take on a challenge devised by the rest of the team. Andy lost and was sent on a quest to grab any lady's brassiere he could get hold of. This was to be done 'calgut', a local colloquialism for running naked through the centre of Vic Falls in pursuit of his prize. Well, to the uproarious delight of the occupants of the pub, he immediately stripped, and with little hesitation headed out the door and straight across the road to the camp site, dotted by tents and camper vans of every size and variety. There was a group of exquisitely beautiful blonde girls from somewhere in Scandinavia. The girls had screamed in appreciation as he had descended on their camp site.

With no more than a casual remark, he had managed to secure his prize from the bevy of beauties, and deftly slipping her bra out through her arm sleeve, he spared her some modesty. He returned proudly to the lads with his trophy in hand. But not before inviting the girls to join them back at the bar. With no more than a furtive glance to each other, they had accepted Andy's invitation, and joined the lads.

"Where are you from?" asked Aubrey when the party had resumed.

"We are from Denmark," replied the blond closest to him, with a heavy accent, and even heavier set of legs.

"A beautiful country," remarked Aubrey, who had visited Copenhagen with his mother years before.

"You have been?" Incredulously the girl had assumed Aubrey must have been one of the locals, and they were, it had to be said, not well travelled!

"Yes, many years ago." He made small talk with her until late into the evening. She was a student at university in Copenhagen and this trip was a precursor to their final semester. Those European students, who feared nothing in their quest to embrace the cultures of Africa and enjoy the fruits of a liberation war; hard fought but sadly forgotten by its protagonists, soon realised that the imagery of a glamorous and extreme adventure into the heart of Africa, was not the same in reality as it sounded from the glossy brochures peddled to their fraternities.

Africa was not for the faint of heart.

The coinage had continued, with Mike setting the tone of the evening. The girls all took to the party game with aplomb, and soon were out-drinking the lads and out cursing them. Aubrey was losing interest in this cultural exchange as the clock turned through twelve and he began to fade. Being a small town with little else to do of an evening, the pub was spectacularly the only place to be, unless gambling. But the evening wore on until the time came for Mike and Andy to carry the girls' home to their tents. Adventurous in everything they did, the lads soon left their mark on the Danish contingent. Aubrey and Timothy, taking their cue, had headed on to the Casino, and a quieter exploration of their manhood.

Mike, who had been up since the sun rise, was outside making Bacon and Egg sandwiches, when Aubrey and Timothy arrived back. Everything about Mike was understated, except for his stature. He had fast become a very loyal friend to Aubrey. An unmistakably good friend. But it had to be said, as Aubrey did so often enough, that if he was not careful he would end up getting some of these girls into trouble, and in the process, end up with a litter of progeny to boot.

But in these halcyon days of indifference and ignorance, the disease that was to become AIDS, had not yet raised its ugly head within this community of transient lifestyles. The world was going crazy, life was to be lived, but no heed was paid to the issue of morality and mortality. It had no consequential impact as yet!

Biblical in its foundation, and catastrophic in its inevitability, AIDS was yet to devastate that community of Vic Falls. The tourists flocked in and the prize was there for the taking. Africa was a continent that lived on its edge, as a Frontier society with little regard for a future, which was uncertain to say the least. Where contraception was a concern for more erudite populations, the lads at Vic Falls were not concerned with the ravages of an unknown and mostly misunderstood disease. But Aubrey had seen the danger early and was aware of its devastating consequences. He was already seeing the effect on the villages around Hwange and the effect it had was Gomorrahish.

"Did you have a good evening?" Aubrey quizzed as they sat down to enjoy the fare.

"Pretty damn good as far as fraternity sex goes," he rebutted a mischievous twinkle in his eyes.

"I assume you were careful?" Aubrey was leaning towards moralising, but his sorority brother was to have none of this.

"What do you mean by that?" questioned Mike, over a strong cup of coffee.

"I am just telling it as it is Mike! You and Andy are heading for a disaster if you keep this up." Aubrey was trying not to sound too high-minded. He was certainly not without his own vices. Mike just raised his eyebrow, and smiled.

"Keep what up?" He was being sarcastic.

"It is a known fact that these girls don't have the same level of hygiene as, say the local girls!" Aubrey was trying to intonate that there was reason for why he was with Bronwyn.

"Are you trying to be my 'big brother'," quizzed Mike who was without his side kick Andy to provide moral support. The incongruity of that statement was not lost on either of them. He chuckled over the lip of his steaming coffee mug, giving Aubrey a conspiratorial sideways glance.

"No! That's not possible." He retorted. "But I am going to tell you that there is a thing going around which is called AIDS, and some of these girls are not too fussy about who they sleep with."

"Thanks buddy," retorted Mike, slapping Aubrey decisively, whilst almost dislocating his shoulder and dislodging his hot brew.

"No! You know what I mean?" He was unapologetic. "Listen to your friends sometime. I am just concerned that you have not stopped shagging your proverbial end off since I have been here, and that's an awful lot of shag!" He grinned.

"Yes, I know what you are trying to say," replied Mike. "It is a little difficult to resist though."

"Yes, I can imagine! But I am just saying that Tim here can tell you first-hand experience of the damage it can do; especially if you get one of these girls pregnant." Aubrey was aware that Mike had no propensity for carrying contraception. Regardless of that, the risk was more than an unwanted pregnancy.

"Okay, point taken." Mike was through with the lecture. "Let's talk about something more pleasant! You should have seen the look on those girls faces when we got them home to their tents. I thought they were going to have a multiple orgasm!"

They all barked out a raucous laugh, and Timothy sat, thankful for the change in conversation.

They had the day ahead of them and a tight band of brothers they had become. Aubrey however had those nagging doubts in his mind that always preceded some form of discussion. It would have to wait for a more appropriate time though. The day was upon them, and with little or no sleep, they began their day with a 'regmakker'!

Bronwyn had returned from Harare that night, tearful. She was late courtesy of an ill-mannered bunch of Mugabe's henchmen, who had thrown them all off the flight even though they had already boarded.

"They simply commandeered the flight, as Mugabe had to fly urgently to Johannesburg." She was visibly shaken.

Although she had been inconvenienced by this thuggish behaviour, Natasha was more upset about her old man.

"He does not get it!" She turned to Aubrey when they were alone in the car. Aubrey had fetched her at the airport late on Sunday night.

"Who, Mugabe?" Aubrey was furious for her flight having been delayed.

He had left the camp early, and because it was on the airport road, he figured he would pick up Bronwyn and they could go straight home. Mugabe had a penchant during those growing days of megalomania, to do exactly as he pleased. It was 1994, and the South African elections had given him 'Dutch-courage'.

"No!" she wailed. "Dad! He has no understanding of reality."

"When I ask him to come up to the Falls, he feigns work commitments, and when I ask him to call you to discuss the wedding arrangements, he mutters something under his breath." Natasha furrowed her brow. Her cute little button nose with its display of freckles turned upwards, and the look of discontent all too apparent.

"Oh!" Aubrey looked away; the twin funnels of light emanated from the bakkie, searching the road ahead. Aubrey kept his eyes focused on the road, and his grin firmly checked.

"He is impossible, Mom has told him a million times!" It was obvious to Aubrey; but clearly not to Natasha.

She was mad at her Dad. She was less concerned about a dictator, who clearly had no grasp on reality and it was fast becoming evident, there was trouble brewing.

Once the ANC had been un-banned, it was obvious that the threat of South African troops taking him 'out' was no longer an issue. Mugabe now turned his paranoia, which had lately become a growing obsession, to closer quarters. Like all his actions throughout his tenure, they multiplied with his further isolation from the ordinary Zimbabwean. He was internalizing this obsession with threats of a coup d'état, by having any detractor locked up, beaten up or killed. It was an interesting analogy, that Hitler had been on the receiving end of countless assassination attempts, yet Mugabe had not. His coups were only in his mind, and those of his ever increasingly power hungry lieutenants.

"He won't listen, and he dismisses my ideas because I am a woman. He has walked all over my Mom since the day they met, and I am not going to let him do it to me!" She was alluring when she was so angry. He smiled.

Woops, wrong thing to do!

"And what are you grinning about?" He would need to proceed with caution.

"Nothing!" He defended himself just before an angry slap aimed at his arm came whizzing his way.

"You men are all the same! You have no concept of the real world." Aubrey would later remember their little disputes, and marvel at how she could become so angry at the world of parents and family, when he was grappling with the world of megalomaniacs and greed.

They rounded the top of a small hillock and Aubrey had to brake violently.

On the road ahead of them were the wild elephant from Mfowenzi. This was a small group of ten whose breeding cows were in search of new feeding grounds. Tar roads and fences aside, these elephants knew no bounds.

They sat silently in awe of these huge beasts, and between them they became aware of the bonds that bound them together in their reverence for the mighty Elephant, and the love that they shared was for once put firmly into perspective.

"Look, the two younger juveniles are heavily pregnant," he observed. The Matriarch led them hurriedly across the road, disturbed by the lights from the car.

He slowed, pulled over and stopped, dimming the headlights and switched the parking lights on. In the pale moonlight, they watched as the breeding herd hurried across the tarmac strip. They were intent on the feeding of their unborn calves; the intrusions of this man-made kaleidoscope a mild distraction.

To the Elephant, mankind and his array of mechanical machinations were simply a materiality to be avoided, but never feared. The Elephant were the true rulers of their land; a preserve for their heritage and inconsequentially concerned with anything, but their own fraternity. Mankind was to them an inconvenience. Bronwyn put aside her verbal tirade, slipping across the seat and silently accepting Aubrey's embrace.

The elephants had been a tremendous success, and with little Jimmy now three, he would venture out with the herd when they set off on the safaris through the surrounding bush. Carefully following Lesidwa, he would make sure he was the centre of attention at the break during each safari. He was a treasure and the little guy never ceased to amaze Aubrey with his antics. Jimmy had become the favourite of all the Indunas and they would watch him play soccer with a basketball which had been especially bought for him by Bronwyn on a shopping trip to Harare. He would play against the Indunas in the paddock reserved for the Elephant's training, and seemed to understand the distinction between the field of play and the two draped flag poles which served as goal posts on either end of the paddock. This was very evident in the way he would dribble the ball towards the goals, and provided he did not stand on it by mistake, he would then kick it between the posts.

"I simply love the way he raises his trunk, as though he knows he has scored. It is almost triumphant." Bronwyn commented.

"These are learned sequences, and he is only responding to the delight of the Indunas. They always cheer his goals."

Aubrey, on the other hand, knew better, intuitively appreciating the behavioural characteristics of the Elephants.

"Look at the way he plays to the crowd. He is taking more and more of the activities and memorising them. But we must be careful not to turn him into a circus Elephant. I don't want to see him bowing and kneeling, or performing like one of those poor beasts."

"He is left footed," Aubrey realised. Jimmy would always favour his left foot. This gave him a more endearing character as far as they were concerned.

"If he is left footed, then it stands to reason he must be right-brained!" Bronwyn commented. "Is it possible that is why he learns quicker, because his right lobe is more dominant?"

"Possibly," Aubrey regarded more cautiously. "It may mean he is more creative!"

Lesidwa would tolerate Jimmy to a point. Aubrey and Bronwyn took turns to categorise the behavioural antics of the Elephant.

"The trunk can also be a determinant of left, or right brained activity." Aubrey noted.

"Watch how they turn the tip of the trunk when scenting, or feeding." Aubrey showed Bronwyn.

"Ahh! Yes, I see what you mean," Lesidwa as the dominant female had a definite propensity to using her trunk in an upward, left habitual feeding motion. "The brain function determines the use of the trunk."

Lesidwa's trunk snaked past Aubrey, slapping Jimmy on the flank. She was using her discretionary rights of discipline.

Of the younger females, there was an expectant mother, who was called Maweti. She was aptly named after her ability to make a racket by sounding the alarm at night if any predators had come close to the Boma. It was open ground between the forest canopy, and the camp, but it did not stop hyena and jackal from venturing into the camp at night. She would always let the Indunas know of their presence, with a raucous trumpeting, but it was her close relationship with Bronwyn that was noticeable. She had an uncanny habit of recognizing Bronwyn's voice the moment she stepped out of the bakkie.

The mere sound of her voice would bring Maweti to life, unmistakably aware of Bronwyn's presence; she would remain within the herd and their protective circle, but nonetheless cognoscente of Bronwyn and uncannily awaiting her approach. If it were at all possible to predict behaviour among these large and graceful animals, Bronwyn would claim so because of this very special relationship. There was a maternal affinity between them that was quite uncanny, and it would leave Bronwyn quite broody.

The two of them, that is Bronwyn and Aubrey had been together for nearly five years now. They had taken a home together and the business was doing well enough. They had even been able to afford to buy some more shares in the company, however grudgingly Timothy had been to part with them. The sweltering heat of summer had brought with it a level of peace in the sleepy town of Vic Falls and this in turn had given Bronwyn a sense of anticipation. The female 'Maweti' was about to calve after twenty-two months of pregnancy and she was larger than any Elephant they had ever seen. The other Elephant were to tiptoe around her, and even Jimmy would curb his boisterous behaviour when in her company. It was as revealing as a sitcom; but oh! So much more rewarding.

Aubrey had realized that there would be no need to separate her from the herd for the birth, and accordingly they kept the herd together in the Boma awaiting the birth with anticipation. The sense of behavioural modification that occurred during her lengthy gestation period was a marvel to all who witnessed it. Although not the Alpha female, she was elevated in the social hierarchy, and Lesidwa was happy to accommodate her within the herd as such.

Aubrey observed the complex social structure with growing appreciation. The matriarchs were the providers of stability within the herd. Provided they their routine was not interrupted, they held dominance over the rest. Bronwyn enjoyed a maternal instinct and an affinity to the mother when she was in calf, and she would sit with Maweti and softly talk to her. On the night, the new born was calved, Bronwyn had anticipated the very moment of her birth and 'Maweti' had dropped the next youngster into their collective world with not the slightest problem. The herd clamoured around, forming a protective circle as the afterbirth was to become a source of attraction to the scavengers. In their natural environment, the herd would subsequently move on, so as to allow the jackals the prize, but within the confined Boma, they would have to contend with an unnatural circumstance, not entirely ideal. Bronwyn had the remnants of the birth sack cleared away and the infant was suckled for the first time, as the pale hues of a pink dawn broke over a hushed and reverent camp.

It was a time of change for the entire fraternity of Vic Falls and the birth was received with the charm and grace afforded a royal delivery. These Elephants were the royalty of a wild and untamed place on earth, but the arrival was no less significant than the deployment of a cadre of war veterans, installed by Mugabe and a precursor to the savagery that was to ensue.

The birthing of democracy in Zimbabwe was no less arduous than that of a mother with Nuchal cord complications, whose umbilical cord strangulates the young foetus. Tribalism was still a very real aspect of the political landscape and Mugabe was being threatened by an emerging political foe, for which he had no immediate answers. He had savagely eradicated the threat of a federally diverse society with Gukurahundi and now he and his cronies were beginning to see the birth of the Movement for Democratic Change. It was a real and potential opposition. It was being formed on tribal lines despite a need for a credible opposition party and this gave him the excuse he needed. Aubrey's and Natasha's home and livelihoods were about to be threatened by two very sinister and unusual forces.

The very ideal, that Mugabe had fought for during a protracted liberation struggle, was coming under threat from a third force. Economic prosperity required that all the Zimbabweans who fought for their rights to freedom of expression and freedom to work towards a better future, were being hamstrung by a political elite who did not wish to share their new-found powers. The one great sacrifice Mugabe had endured whilst imprisoned in Rhodesia, was the death of his son and the only real heir to his kingdom. His son had died in Ghana from cerebral malaria during Mugabe's incarceration in jail during the sixties. This fact had festered in his mind for years after the liberation of Zimbabwe, and it now reared its head in the form of erratic and randomly outrageous ramblings by Mugabe. The vultures were already circling and Mugabe's detractors were beginning to recognise his weaknesses. This third force would prey on the one thing that Zimbabwe had in abundance; mineral wealth.

The second issue was one very near and dear to Aubrey and Bronwyn. During the rise of the new democracy in the eighties, Mugabe had done all the right things to portray a sense of normalcy to the Western World. They were the country's major contributors and Britain had vested interests in the mining and agricultural sector. However during this period, Ivory trading had become a major area of economic prosperity for the Asian continent. The Chinese were after the vast reserves of Ivory in Africa, but the Western World conscientised by a growing green movement, had embarked on the CITES agreement, to ensure Elephant and other endangered wildlife were protected. With the rising economic prosperity in Asia, demand was now being placed on supplying more Ivory to a growing market. It was this demand that swayed opinion in Zimbabwe and yet again, the greed of many would sway the decision to scrap CITES.

Growing Chinese industrialisation had no conscience where economic prosperity was concerned. Despite being host to a famously evocative symbol as the brand image for the World Wildlife Fund, the Chinese had little or no respect for nature outside their own borders. So intent were they to prosper, and so entrenched in cultural traditions that were now taboo in Western society, the Chinese could not set aside the practice of 'Li Shang Wang Lai'! To a sophisticated Westerner, it was a bribe; to them it was honourable! They were the inadvertent third force, working to undermine the apparatus put in place during Africa's drive towards liberation from Colonial powers; yet Zimbabwe and many countries like it were now selling their souls to the devil. It required the confidence of an African leader to stand up to the bully-boy tactics they adopted; but who was powerful enough to do so?

Bronwyn and Aubrey had spoken about children, and they had agreed that the time was fast approaching when they might consider the option. Bronwyn was now twenty-seven, and Aubrey having been away from home for twelve years was now, was thirty-four. Still, he was in no rush, but Bronwyn was going through the broody stage of life, with all her friends in Harare now either married or with children. She was constantly being invited to christenings and was the Godmother to a beautiful little girl born to a single parent mother. Samantha who was a friend of Bronwyn's from school.

Bronwyn's father had objected to her being involved with a single mother, but Bronwyn being as strong willed as her father ignored him and dragging Aubrey with her for the occasion, attended the Christening in Harare. The night after the ceremony, lying in bed with him, she had broached the idea of children.

"The old man, is a stickler for procedure and decorum." Aubrey had commented, after their return from Harare.

"Yes, I told you he is difficult," Bronwyn had answered.

"He is going to expect me to ask him for your hand?" Aubrey knew if they had wanted to marry, Aubrey would have had to ask for her hand in marriage. For all intents and purposes, this should surely have been a simple process, but the chances that Aubrey was going to grovel at the old mans' feet for his daughters' hand, was about as remote a concept as the Borje Dubai was to a Harare street beggar.

"I know you feel strongly about all this nonsense. But if it makes him happy, please just do it for my sake!" Bronwyn appealed.

"Your father is a manipulative old goat. He would bleat like a motherless kid and scavenge for your sympathy, yet he has been fiddling around with other women for years!" Aubrey could see the irony.

Aubrey had met Bronwyn's four brothers on this trip. They were as complex as their father and about as lethal as an unexploded mine field. As they had grown up, the threat of physical violence was no-longer an option for Tony to control them.

Of the four, Aubrey had been more comfortable with Jeremy. He was in Harare for a visit, having established himself as an artist in London. He and his partner David, were to be a source of great anxiety to Bronwyn's old man.

"Blood was thicker than water and all that," he had told Aubrey. Having manipulated Val for years, she was still deeply in love with him. However when his ruse was uncovered by Jeremy, his father's mind games, of which there were many, became the weapon of choice.

"He was shagging Violet, our domestic servant for years, when we lived in Duiker Street," Jeremy had no time for social graces.

"Jeremy!" Bronwyn had howled in anguish.

"Sorry Sis, but a turd is still a turd, no matter how you dress it up." Aubrey sensed the collective anger of thirty-two years, bottled up and ready to explode.

He had vented this anger at the world, and his art had exploded onto the canvas for a horrified Church to disseminate. The Roman Catholic's had been his focus of attention. It was their preservation of abstinence and no contraception that had bottled up his fury for all those years. The Church was complicit in the deaths of millions who would now suffered the ignominy of AIDS.

"He will expect a lavish Church ceremony so that he can walk you up the aisle and croon to all his peers." Jeremy had lamented.
Aubrey could feel the hunger that Jeremy suffered. A hunger to right those iniquities.

"Bronwyn," Jeremy raised a slightly comical left eyebrow; one that was heavier than the other. "You yourself told me that the only time he had gone to church was when Mom was overseas." It had been after the death of her own mother, and Bronwyn had still been a child. Fearing divine retribution or some similar calamity, which in itself was remarkable for a devout atheist, her father had dragged the children off to a church in Harare.

"Yes, but we were all so young we did not know what it was all about!" Bronwyn defended.

Never having set foot in a church before or afterwards, until now, Aubrey questioned the rationale. He had questioned her role as a Godmother to her friend Samantha's child, but all in all, Aubrey understood that she felt a deep sense of loyalty to her friend. Samantha was intrinsically pure, but for the advances of a smooth-talking guy, who had plied her with liquor and compliments, and seen her 'knocked up' after a rather passionless tryst in the back seat of his Datsun.

Bronwyn preferred to commune with nature instead, which she found much more authentic. Her Church was the open savannah plains, with wild herds of Wildebeest, and the ozone smell of the early spring rains on the dry red earth. Hers was the canopy of a southern sky, with its helter-skelter smattering of the bright milky-way, visible to the naked eye. Hers was the beauty and grace of the spring Zebra foals, clearly marked with the stripes that mesmerized the eye and calmed the soul. Bronwyn felt the urge for the sanctity of life, but for her she would have foregone all and the pitter-patter of little feet, if it were the precursor to a love that could transcend the lost affection of a distant father.

Aubrey understood the conundrum. Bronwyn herself did not want a church wedding, but felt the need to placate a societal demand towards conformity.

He felt guilty for being so cynical, but knew the rational. The big church affair was to ensure that Bronwyn's mother got to enjoy a church wedding, since she never had one of her own, having eloped to Africa all those years before. Val had been a veritable angel of a woman for putting up with Tony for so many years. Tony who had been a prominent business man in Harare, also needed the affirmation this ceremony would have afforded his position. Bronwyn, the youngest of the five siblings, had been the only girl, and the older brothers were all married off, and a distance from their controlling father.

Aubrey would ordinarily have foregone the futility of this charade, had he not seen how important it was to both Bronwyn and Val. However, the talk was on a very superficial level, as their engagement had not yet been confirmed. However, to all who knew them it was inevitable.

His features, beginning to look somewhat craggy, showed strength of determination. The pale light of a waning moon exposed the line of his jaw and the shadows thrown across his face, told Bronwyn he had doubts. They sat silently, gazing up at the evening sky, their silence a snare to a baited prey.

For Aubrey, the long expeditions he made into the Hwange National Park, were his commune and when he went he felt a dramatic change in his psyche. The 'bush' seemed to revive his spirit and he always returned home more upbeat and spontaneous. It was she, in point of fact, that had sent him away on these excursions, when his mothers' death had seemed to finally catch up with him, and the loss had seemed to overcome him. He would take the loss far more deeply than he cared to admit, so Bronwyn knew intuitively that his drinking was just a cry for help. So, when the depression had set in, it was she that had sent him to the Park.

These trips with only a rucksack on his back and Wellington as his guide were his opportunity to put his world in perspective. Aubrey made a bee-line for Hwange and his mood would change immediately. After the billowing summer Cumulonimbi, had drenched the afternoon dust and the cooling winds had spirited the remaining clouds from view, he would feel as if a portal had opened and whipped through his body, restoring his soul's energy. The haze that followed simmered on the dark red earth, as into the evening the cooling winds would bring a renewal. A cold snap set in, on those moonless nights, with only Wellington as a companion and a log fire to warm them, he would feel himself returning to the Earth.

"The Mugabe people were here again this week," Wellington was dismissive.

"What did they want this time?" Aubrey felt the pain, which could not escape his friend's furrowed brow.

"They said that they were looking for poachers, but the guns they were carrying were not for humans!" Aubrey remained silent.

"My feeling is they have moved north of the park, heading for the northern migration route." Wellington would need to tread as carefully as an Elephant.

"I am with you Shamwari," Aubrey need not have said more. Wellington smiled.

"You know how we catch a baboon who has been stealing our millet?" The question rhetorical, Wellington continued. "We find a disused red ant hill, then dig a hole wide and long enough for his arm, and make a small donga at the end. Into this we place a handful of groundnuts. Just as many as he can grab with his fist; and then leave and watch from a distance."

Aubrey grinned. He thought he knew where this conversation was going.

"Now the baboon is an inquisitive fellow, and when he sees the groundnuts being deposited, he will immediately investigate. Once he has smelt the groundnuts, his favourite snack, he will grab the handful but will be unable to remove his fist from the hole. He will panic, but not let go of the groundnuts, at the cost of his life."

Aubrey searched Wellington's eyes for a sign. It was the older man's tell. He had sad eyes. But what Aubrey witnessed was a steely reserve. The sadness was gone, and in its place, was a desire to right the wrongs of the past fifteen years.

"Do you have a plan?" Aubrey was game. He was tired of the wholesale butchering of Elephant, for personal greed.

"The migration paths lead to the border, and there is still a sector of un-cleared mines." Wellington was a survivor. The local villagers had an intimate knowledge of the safe zones, because their lives depended on it.

"If we take the route westwards, we can cross the border between Botswana and then double back to the Umfuloweni district. The mines have yet to be cleared, because of a logistical problem with the Botswana Parks people. But if we get to the area before the Tsoetsi's, we can skirt the area, and remove the U.N.'s warning signs." Aubrey could not believe what he was hearing.

"Yes, but what about the villagers? When the signs have been cleared, they will return to the area to grow their mealies!"
"No, the area is so remote, and they know the dangers. However, I intend to replace the signs. We will dig holes and bury them for now." Wellington must have been planning this for a while.

"How do you intend to lure Mugabe's men into the area? There is no Elephant spoor." Aubrey was now a co-conspirator.

"That is the easy part. I will skirt the mine field and make it to the eastern border before the Tsoetsis. On the way, we can collect some fresh Elephant dung in this large sack. When they get within a few kilometres distance, I will place the dung on the old path leading into the mine field, and then radio you. Then you fire into the air, several shots, as if you are culling Elephant. Two, three shots, followed by another two or three."

Aubrey was catching on quickly. "What if they know about the mine field?"

"They don't, it was I who sent them in this direction," Wellington had a look of pained inevitability in those dark eyes. "Once they are into it, there is no way out."

Aubrey, was hooked. They would sit silently for an hour contemplating the magnitude of their scheme, while the log fire crackled and hissed with the hard Mopani logs that had died and dried out naturally. Gathered from the scrubland around the camp, they peppered the silence with their collective pops and squeaks.

The fresh wind snuck through the outer perimeter of the camp, bringing with it the surrounding smells and noises, and the air was clean and animated with the possibilities of Elephant. Their dung, rich in tannin from the stripped bark of the acacia was not unpleasantly strong, but mingled with the more rancid hint of Hyena. Then the bittersweet essence of ripening Morula fruit, that once fallen wafted on the evening news, enticing the Elephant from miles around. In stark contrast, were the throaty noises that hinted of the distant prides of Lion, carried for miles on the prevailing evening breeze. Sounding a mere stone's throw away, then seemingly lost in the racket of the evening Christmas beetles, their hind legs rubbed over the top of their wings, rasped in concert to the countless millions of years of mating rituals; the cacophony of their chorus so abrupt, and penetrating.

This was communing with nature and Aubrey lay on his canvas bunk, feet towards the fire, his senses alive with the prospect of a bright future and a cloudless sky, he would fall asleep as the log fire burned down to embers. In the distance the rhythm of an owl hoot calling out sparked his subconscious mind, and he dreamed of Angels, carrying him on their winged flights.

A spiritual voyage through the vast Ethernet of mysticism. The gentle breeze wafting through the camp bringing all the wonderful energy of the bush, always felt like a spiritual wind bringing succour. There had been moments when he was convinced he could hear his mother's voice urging him on. Gently reminding him that he was protected. She seemed to remind him that the ills of this devious world could not ultimately render mother and child apart. These dreams enlightened as Aubrey fell into a catatonic state of spiritual slumber, un-conscious but cosseted and safe. He would awake fearing he had lost her, without explaining why he had left without an explanation. However, his mood would lift and he would walk away from the embers of the campfire, a new man.

Wellington and he carried out the plan with selfless precision. The Tsoetsi's lured by the sound of gunfire, were intent on plundering any ivory from what they had thought would be harmless villagers, poaching for their own needs. Instead, they walked into the minefield, and never re-emerged.

After returning home, he had found himself driving behind an ancient Renault Four. The car was a remnant from the seventies in Rhodesia, when the French had been the only European country willing to forego their global standing, in order to supply the taxi industry in Rhodesia. The slow-moving car had blocked his path on the road back to Vic Falls and as he had attempted to overtake the heavily loaded vehicle, the sunset was directly in his eyes. Blinded he could not see a thing. The westerly passage of the road brought them over the top of a blind rise, and as he had darted into the right lane on the crest, he had seen the heavy vehicle highlighted by the setting sun, which was bearing down on them.

The glaring sun, masked its approach, but it was in the wrong lane, having driven into the on-coming traffic lane, to avoid a huge pot hole. Aubrey instinctively swerved onto the opposite embankment, catching his slid as he slewed from the road and onto the shoulder. Skidding onto the dirt, the four-wheel drive saved him as he narrowly escaped the head-on collision.

He had felt the presence of a hand on his shoulder. It was the Angel that had made him impulsively veer off to the right. As he did, he avoided the oncoming truck, but was merely now a voyeur to the inevitable accident. The two vehicles collided head on, and with the truck being the heavier, it had stopped the car in its tracks.
The Renault had catapulted through the air. As the bakkie ground to a halt in the surrounding bush he had looked up into the rear-view mirror and witnessed the whole accident in breath-taking detail, spotlighted by the low setting sun. Every detail of the calamity was exaggerated as the passengers were flung through the air, catapulted in every direction.

The accident was devastating. The driver of the truck was killed instantly by flying debris from the car piercing through the windshield, and the occupants in the front of the R4 were crushed to death. The passengers in the back of the truck, of which there were two families with children, chickens and goats, were dispersed like rag dolls into the surrounding brush. All sustained horrific injuries in the process and were instantly killed.

All that is, except for a young boy, who seated right at the back of the truck, was somersaulted through the air and was caught like a pitcher's glove in the folds of an acacia tree twenty meters from the accident. Having sustained cuts and abrasions he had remained there, comatose and beyond sight.

By the time the emergency crew was called out from Vic Falls, the scene of the accident resembled a Beirut bombing. There was not a bit of the mangled

R4 which resembled its original shape, and the truck looked like it had sustained a direct hit from an incoming rocket propelled grenade.

The remaining passengers of the truck, strewn all over the area had thankfully not suffered.

The only piece of good news was in the early hours of Monday morning, while Aubrey and the emergency crew were cleaning up the last remains of the accident. They had heard the pathetic cries of help from the tree. The young boy, now having recovered consciousness, was in deep pain, and with the cold morning air was starting to experience hypothermia.

Aubrey climbed the tree, brushing off the thick acacia thorns and with no fear for his own hide, had gently recovered the boy and had him wrapped in a blanket within a very short time. The boy was given an intravenous drip, but was in a state of severe shock.

Back in Vic Falls, Aubrey was treated like a hero by the locals and tourists alike when the news had made the local paper. He in fact felt nothing like a hero, fearing his own impatience may have caused the accident in the first place. Aubrey was choked with guilt, but his guiding Angel had been with him and he was sure it was his mother's spirit.
Despite having been oblivious to this possibility, and a rationale that had initially escaped him, he was now coming to terms with the likelihood of having a guardian angel.

But the idea sat with him resonating on an entirely new level from that night onwards. He had been aware of the sense of a guide during those lonely nights at boarding school, when his father had him packed him off to Windsor. Aubrey could not have known at the time his father's ulterior motives, but it made sense to him now. He was a little six-year-old, and he was even small for his age. The bullying he endured whilst there was traumatic. Each and every boy was subjected to certain humiliations, which would ultimately scar the weaker and burden the stronger with guilt. The older boys in the house had suffered the same humiliations, so it was obvious they would in turn re-enact them on the younger and weaker boys when their turn came.

Their favourite ritual was to lock Aubrey in his metal locker, in which each boy was expected to keep their valuables. He had been terrorized by this ongoing ordeal, until it ceased after the night the boys had shut him inside, and sent him flying down the stairs of the dormitory fire escape. The dorm master had heard the chaos and had rescued Aubrey from the trunk, shaken and humiliated by the dark patch of dampness in his trouser pants. It was the claustrophobia that haunted him now, and the wide-open spaces were his antidote.

Introverted, the sense of abandonment was evident and his nights became tarnished with fearful bedwetting. This was a direct consequence of a fear, manifested it seemed by real malevolence. Understandably, he had established a dialogue with a fictitious friend, and often went on long walkabouts through the school grounds talking to himself. Only now did he realize that these circumstances were all inter related. The visit to his Uncle's funeral months before and the suspicions of his father, explaining why he had been packed off to boarding school, all stood as stark reminders of how sinister a world he lived in. It was this fictitious friend who now shielded him on one shoulder, and his adoring mother who sat firmly protecting his other. He was his own trilogy, but for now he had other issues to ponder.

At night, his guide would give him solace and somehow awaken him at the first sign of trouble so that he was never caught unawares. The bullying was bad during the days, but intensified at night, culminating in boys marauding through the dormitories in gangs looking for victims to humiliate in some pre-adolescent way. This usually took place after lights out, and took the form of indecent acts being requested from the twelve year olds, who represented the senior group in the lower school dormitory.

Then, when the victim refused, a perfectly natural choice for a child unaware of these sexual urges, they would then force those boys into some lewd act of depravity, en masse, resulting in tears and regular bed wetting thereafter. When the bullies entered the dorm with lights out, they would go for the first victim they encountered. Luckily for Aubrey his bed was in the far-right corner, and at the first sign of trouble Aubrey would be woken and often found himself leaping over the low wall which demarcated that area between the first graders and the second-grade boys.

Aubrey was fortunate not to be subjected to these humiliations, surviving the first year and the better part of the second year by always making a quick escape. He would be woken by a kind of whisper after having a dream in which he would be falling into a deep cavernous pit, dark and sinister. The repetitive dream was always accompanied by a sense of fear. Falling backwards, he would awaken with a start as the cavernous hole beneath his bed opened and swallowed him. With no bottom to the pit, Aubrey felt hopeless and weightless. Just when he had thought he would never reach the end of his fall, a giant hand would reach out and he would be whisked away into the light. This would always end with him waking, and he would hear the boys coming.

On the northern side to the second graders dorm, was a balcony that lead up to a brick buttress which reached out into the inner courtyard. Aubrey would sneak through the entrance to the balcony along a narrow corridor and slip out into the night air. If the weather was dry, he would often sleep out on the balcony having taken his blanket with him. This certainly beat having to deal with the bullies.

There was no specific moment when he could remember having a conversation with his guide, or when he stopped doing so. He just somehow fell into a different routine, and the conversations ceased. It was as if one door had closed, and now a different channel had opened, but he had never been able to understand why. Now he knew why. His guardian angel had always been there but up until now he had never needed it.

Suddenly, his conscious self, had been able to make the connection. He had communed with the spirit world all this time, but now he was seeing it in a conscious form for the first time. Aubrey was not sure why, but he now had two guides. He realised that the decisions he was making, the circumstances he found himself in, all had some influence from these spirit guides. This was comforting but also quite alarming. He could not share this with anyone, least of all Bronwyn, as she would surely think he had lost all conscious reason. But how wrong he was! It was at this point, he surmised, one had to lose the conscious self to gain access to the spiritual world.

Only now did he realize that these circumstances were all inter related. The visit to his Uncles funeral months before the bullying had started; the suspicions of his father, so thereby explaining why he had been packed off to boarding school in the first place and the pink and purple striped trunk which was inevitably going to draw attention to him, all stood as stark reminders of how sinister a world he lived in. It was his fictitious friend or Uncle who now shielded him on one shoulder, and his adoring mother who sat firmly protecting his other.

Now was the time for Aubrey to make the decision that would haunt him for the remainder of his life.

"We need to adopt Edward," Bronwyn had contended. He had been staying with Bronwyn and Aubrey for six months, as there were no immediate family in the region. The uncle who had been working at the old Victoria

Falls hotel as a chef had died from a lung infection at the age of thirty-five, leaving his own wife to fend for their five children.

"There is no additional space in that family, and the money they had, came from the brother-in-law's salary." Bronwyn was adamant. If they did not help; who would?

"That income had previously been subsidizing the extended family," and Aubrey now felt even more guilt.

Consequently, in two cataclysmic events, accident and nature, had removed the bread winners from the family and subjected the remaining families to a life of hardship. The cause of the brothers' death from tuberculosis was not diagnosed at the time as death from AIDS related causes, as the onset of the virus was only just beginning to take hold. Could the system that impoverished and decimated a once proud nation, have been a consequence of their adherence to the physical and not the spiritual, and could this symbol of HIV, stand as an metaphor for the loose moral behaviour it fed on?

Aubrey would be at pains to understand these ramifications.

This one single factor would be responsible for over three million deaths during Mugabe's tenure as President, and with his other dereliction of duties as leader of the country, had meant that the conspiracy to wipe out the populations of Southern Zimbabwe, had well and truly commenced.

The governments of the SADC region were complicit in the death and annihilation of the population of Matabeleland, through disease, famine and forced migration to South Africa. This once proud population was to become a tribe that would wonder through the Southern African region in search of work, food and a desire for self-respect. It was their liberation struggle leaders who now precipitated the next Diaspora. The ills of a past system of repression called apartheid, although unpalatable to historians, were nothing in comparison to this.

Yet this was somehow acceptable to those leaders and populations of the emerging democracies of Africa. The continent's leaders, and their unwillingness to recognize the virus for what it was, and treat it accordingly, was cause for some serious debate. But that would only come after it was too late. There was a plague spread by cultural myths which now decimated whole families. And it all came down to patriarchies that had a tendency of not questioning their leadership. This allowed the local governments to get away with murder on a grand scale, certainly not seen since the extermination of the Russian peasants in the Stalin era. No single cause could be of more concern for the survival of the African people, and no single focused endeavour was being carried out to prevent it.

The attempts to place a band-aid on the severed leg of Africa, by non-governmental agencies, was essentially valueless, and much of the funding would end up in the wrong hands. Whether or not the SADC region of governments would ever be held accountable for their actions, or, in these cases, in-actions, was debatable. The irony was almost palpable. There were no attempts to combat the disease through prevention and education, and when it did eventually come it was too late. The 'Bread Basket of Africa' was fast becoming the begging bowl of the region, and not one civilian could stand up individually or en masse, to do anything about it, for fear of being exterminated.

What it needed was the collective will of the people and instead of heading for the temporary and transient prosperity of South Africa, they needed to sort out their own home-grown dilemmas first. The plague would be exported through the porous borders of the south and the poor, as always, would be the catalysts. The uneducated, the desperate and those with no will to fight for what they had fought for before, would drive this plague further south and into the prosperous nations to the west and the south. Like a cancerous growth, the Diaspora would infect the entire continent, and ultimately cause a political upheaval to rival all revolutions that had gone before.

The young boy Edward, had been infected with HIV through birth, and his health was somewhat compromised by the unavailability of anti-retroviral drugs, and the care of doctors who would assist. Bronwyn and Aubrey automatically became the care givers like so many thousand other families in Southern Africa, as the demand for foster parents increased. These families often devastated by the bread winner dying, and then the mother becoming sick, left hundreds of thousands of teenagers in charge of younger siblings, and there was no system in Zimbabwe to care for them. Extended families already overburdened by this onslaught, became victims themselves, as the scourge filtered through the population, antagonized by insufficient medical care and inadequate nutrition. This Government was creating mass Genocide on a problematical tribe, with whom Mugabe had already had his differences. To the politicians of Southern Africa, this was inevitable, and by turning their heads, they were complicit in this Genocide. It was then left to those who cared to do what they could.

So with the possibility of losing everything that he now cared for, Bronwyn and Aubrey would have to make a decision. They would have to abandon their beloved Elephants. Aubrey's hand was forced in a way that he would come to resent.

It was ironic he thought, 'Human life was somehow more important than Elephants.' But it would not deter him. Aubrey and Bronwyn headed south to Mpumalanga Province in South Africa and a meeting with Thys van Schalkwyk.

Chapter 13

A quest for absolution

The hint of sea salt evident on the breeze wafting in from the Zebrugge channel, gave Aubrey a sense of his whereabouts. He had taken a mid-morning nap, fighting off the exhaustion of the tenuous bus ride. Awaking after a few hours, he was dis-oriented, but nonetheless rested.

It was Monday and the clinic was open. Aubrey lifted his head, looking for a sign that Natasha was nearby. She emerged from the bathroom, the steam still lingering off her skin, an aurora of allure. Peach; smoking hot.

"Good morning sleepy head," she cooed.

He smiled. The light from the open balcony door was now high enough to catch her ghostly silhouette as she appeared. Aubrey marvelled at her slim waist and ample bosom. She was surprisingly uninhibited for an English class. They had only known one another a few weeks, yet she stood naked before him, her body, soft and statuesque.

Natasha leaned in and kissed him. He immediately went to pull her back into bed, but with a filly's fleet-foot she pranced away before he could.

"No!" She squealed. "This is for later. We need the blood in all the right places now."

He grimaced. He would need to be up soon, so they could get themselves to the clinic for the series of blood tests and bio-pathogenetic tests. They needed a blood count and an idea of his white blood cell count.

"It is the CD8+ T cells which are recognised as the Tc cells which once they become activated have a pre-defined cytotoxic role within the immune system." Natasha had explained.

He was already feeling like a trapped laboratory rat and they had not even begun their analytical journey. It would be a long week, but Aubrey summoned the strength and began it by leaping out of the bed, and chasing Natasha back into the bathroom.

The clinic was a good walk distance from their canal-side hotel, and he would need all his energy, sadly. He slipped past her, into the shower with a partial pat to her exposed rump.

There was now an air of expectation as they sat at the bistro outside the Rembrandt Plein Clinic. This was a typical Amsterdam coffee bistro with aluminium framed, wicker basket chairs and small round tables squeezed tightly on the cobbled pavements.

Aubrey had ordered a cappuccino, but the taste of which was vile because of the toxicity of the medication, that he could barely stomach it. Natasha had ordered a more soothing green tea, which lingered on the palate but invigorated the senses. They had been in Amsterdam a week and the side effects of the treatment were beginning to take effect. Aubrey had felt bilious the night before and was now suffering a morose headache because of the infusion of the Cytotoxic-T cells the day before. When he had started the treatment, he was not entirely detoxed and the specialist oncologist had warned him that his liver would start rejecting the T-cells thus. The biliousness had brought on an episode of up-chucks, the likes of which he had not experienced, even after the consumption of an entire bottle of Tequila, one evening at a party for a friend on the shores of Lake Kariba.

Natasha had gotten him up at six and out of the hotel on Rajiksplaza, heading back to the clinic, before he could object. On the opposite side of the plaza, a small group of patients waited outside the front door of the clinic, with its picture-postcard blue weathered wooden door. He imagined that it had seen more than a few summer rain showers. They had been waiting about one hour now, and Aubrey, feeling weak from the side effects of the medication, had been unable to stand, whilst waiting so they had gone across the road to the bistro.

Earlier during the week, they had walked through the Bloemenmarket and the old bric'a brac traders on the canals that encircled the city like a spider's web. They got caught in that labyrinth of street markets and confusion, whiling away the hours in the pursuit of a bargain for Natasha to take back to her grandmother. Her Nan had always wanted a Dutch pendant with the windmill motif, so they had scoured the basement shops and canal side street traders for many happy hours. In the process, they had walked themselves fit. Aubrey could feel his calf muscles having developed into large sinewy balls, and even on his shins, two distinct muscles were evident, when he flexed his toes upwards towards his knee. But even so, he had felt his physical fitness flagging as the medication took effect with the onset of another bout of nausea.

As the doors opened at nine a.m., the small group of trialist's, slowly and deliberately plodded through the door in single file. In their bags clutched to their chests like the crown jewels on the Queens royal cushions, were the samples, with their specimen jars sealed. Feeling a sudden giddiness, he once more caught his breath in anticipation of having to endure yet another day of prodding. He was not given to this explicit bodily function analysis. Even when in the bush, he was quite modest and would venture far from the camp to carry out his ablutions with little fear of the wild scavengers; intent rather on his privacy.

He had been similarly pre-occupied with the unsightly aspect of body fluids when at boarding school. He would wait until late in the evening to use the latrines. That had been the best chance of avoiding adolescent pranksters, who would catch their hapless victims astride their porcelain thrones. Sneaking into the cubicles with a wad of tissue paper doused in water, they would plunge the poor fellow into a state of uproarious objection, by pelting him with the sodden mass.

So here they sat on wicker chairs, a rucksack with its regulation samples neatly tucked up against the leg of the table so as not to create any potential obstacle to a carelessly placed foot, which would send it flying across the bistro's pristine cobblestone floor.

Aubrey turned to Natasha. "I just can't face another day of this Tash," a look of sheer resignation on his face.

"Let's get out of here," and he was up on his feet and rounding the table to the street before Natasha could object.

"Wait," she cried, "We should still at least get the results!"

"No, I don't care, Tash. I'm really tired and it has no relevance to how I am feeling right now," he concluded.

"I would just end up feeling worse, having to stomach another lot of that medication."

"But Aubs," she objected, "you have come this far, don't you at least want to know if it is working?"

"Actually Tash," he dismissed her objection, "I think I would rather not find out anyway! Even if I have a positive result, those T-cells are now swimming around inside me doing their job," he argued.

"If it is negative, well…" he paused to contemplate the alternative, "I would rather not know!"

She followed him dutifully, as they headed back to the tram stop. They had spent the early part of the week walking the streets of Amsterdam, from the port side Red Light District, where they had tried their first joint, in a hashish smoke clouded café, the blue ether haze suspending reality and rendering the occupants in a semi-comatose state within minutes.

"The hashish will reduce the side effects of the medication," the Doctor had said, in an inimitable broad-minded commentary when Aubrey had objected. It had for six days, but now he was feeling the effect of the powerful drugs more than the medicinal properties of hashish.

They caught the forty-eight tram that took them deeper into the city and dropped them outside their beautifully decorated hotel. With its narrow sash windows and window box flowers, colourfully underlining the darkened wood, the view of that little street evoked powerful images of the history of their surroundings. When they got to their room, Aubrey laid down on the bed and burying his face into the pillow, fell into a fitful slumber, mentally and emotionally exhausted.

When he woke, he realized that it was already midday. The Dutch summer sun was pensively poking its' pale yellow face through the lace curtains. Aubrey roused himself, but when he turned to seek Natasha, she was not at his side. He felt a twinge of panic, but just as he had tried to calm his unusually strained nerves the electronic door mechanism clunked, and there was Natasha, standing in the doorway. She had a tray of food in her one hand, balancing the vitals in her attempt to open the door using the key card. She was seriously in need of help as the precarious angle of the tray was about to send all the contents tumbling to the carpeted floor. Aubrey leapt to assist her, but as he hit the floor running, the nausea took over and he collapsed in a heap.

Natasha somehow managed to dislodge herself from the doorway and with the tray now deposited on the entrance side table, she had him in her arms in no time and he was propped up against her bosom. Helping him to his feet, thankfully, Aubrey did not feel the urge to vomit, just a soaring sense of dislocation from his surrounds. Natasha gently led him back to the bed, and before long, he had a pillow propped behind his neck and was being hand fed the minestrone soup.

Warming his empty stomach, he felt its sustenance and succour fill his inner core and his stomach expanding to meet it. Surprisingly within minutes the vitals steadied his nerves and radiated towards every sinew.

Warmed and relaxed his thoughts drifted off to that comfortable place he had so often dwelled in the past. This was where he could get lost in the recall of his adventures in graphic detail, that would always bring him comfort. He let out a chuckle, more to himself, than in recognition of his recent escapade on the floor. He was in his zone and chuckled again when another thought occurred to him; He remembered the Afrikaans term 'binne oneprêt,' which literally translated as 'an inside fun'. The Afrikaans language, being of Dutch origin, had wonderful literal translations like this. Mirth, as the English would refer to it, was a state of internal joyousness.

He lay in bed and recalled the time he had been with Bronwyn, Timothy and Cheryl at the Falls for the grand opening of one of Timothy's new ventures. This new adventure concept involved tethering a helium filled passenger balloon with a winch to the side of the Victoria Falls, so that tourists could get a bird's eye view of the magnificent spectacle from the air. A basket suspended precariously from the balloon, accommodated six passengers. The idea had not yet been tested in an African environment, and none so dramatic as the backdrop of Livingstone's waterfall.

The concept was sound and safety measures had been fully installed, so when it was time to try out this brilliant new addition to the business, Timothy; not one for taking unusual risks with his personal safety, was more than willing to venture all in this high stakes game of business.

But here was a venture no one else was entirely convinced of other than Timothy and he was not about to let a good idea go to waste. If the balloon was an instant success, he would be a hero; but if it failed, there would be a few red faces around the boardroom table come Monday morning.

They decided to launch on the business on the Saturday, a week before Queen Elizabeth was due to arrive in the Falls for her first Commonwealth visit, since Mugabe had taken control of power in Zimbabwe. The world's media would be focused on Victoria Falls and the historical importance of the name had meant that the event would raise the profile of his company. Not that the Queen, on a visit to her old African dominion, was to take any part at all in this excursion herself mind!

But it was intended that she would have a guided tour of the Falls, and the balloon would be very visible from her vantage point, at the 'Boiling Pot'. The media would be in attendance, so this would be a marketing coup for the company. As Timothy had said, "you can't buy publicity like this; it's pure genius!"

Well, the balloon had been filled with the precious helium in the early hours of the morning to allow for the heat of the Africa sun to slowly heat the canvas polymer skin, and ensure the gas expanded correctly within the envelop. The balloon started filling on cue, and the massive gas bottles, especially delivered from the US at tremendous cost, began emptying their contents into the balloon. Up she rose into the magnificent early morning mist surrounding the Falls.

Timothy was not known for his technical knowledge, so had brought with him an expert from the States. This guy had coached the local handlers personally on all the procedures that needed to be followed. The stage was set for a grand lift off and so with what press was already in attendance, and a few loyal supporters from the surrounds, the balloon began its' ascent. As the local dignitaries looked on, the balloon had a moment of sheer brilliance as it caught the early morning light, reflecting the candescent red orb of the sun against its almost translucent skin.

But just as the balloon looked set to soar above its' awe inspiring surroundings, the wind buffeted it, and with a gust of hot air rising out of the Boiling Pot below, the balloon shot straight upwards. Fearing that the tether might snap, the expert from the States shouted a command to the valve release jockey, who sat with a rope in hand that allowed the gradual escape of the gas, if needed. He panicked at the severity of the barked command, and snapping back on the release rope, pulled too hard, and the valve was torn from its' housing.

With the buffeting balloon now precariously in the updraft, she literally fizzed like a party balloon as the escaping pressurized air sent it on a darting, dancing journey. But the balloon had nowhere to go, being tethered to the ground, so it just shot sideways, then back down and up again, sending the gathered spectators diving for cover. Eventually bouncing back into the ground, it slammed into the rocks, tearing clean in two. In a grand finale, as all the escaping helium shot out in one massive 'fwwuummp', it disappeared over the edge and into the abyss.

Gone forever!

To add insult to injury, an enthusiastic member of Timothy's team had been waiting for his cue to release a bevy of large, brightly coloured party balloons, likewise filled with helium, and they triumphantly rose above the dampened audience in a gesture of fortitude. Timothy too, had reached the end of his tether, and uncharacteristically disappeared while the photographers were getting their action shots of the disappearing balloons and the dejected canopy as it floated down towards the Boiling Pot, and a vortex pulled it under and it disappeared into the depths.

Deflated and disapproving, Timothy left on the next flight for Harare. He was very scarce from then on and the Falls became quieter for his loss.

A warm tummy and pleasant memories had left Aubrey uplifted and as he recalled that hilarious moment, the very act of laughing, lightened his spirits, and as the endorphins kicked, he felt slightly euphoric.

"Who had said laughter wasn't the best medicine?" He was perched at the head of the bed with his back against the headboard.

He grabbed the remote, turning the TV on and muted the sound. Natasha lay peacefully reading. He flicked through the channels. There were the usual Dutch speaking programs, a few in German, and then he reached the inevitable Sky News channel.

He sat and watched the weather report which the English, by rights, seemed fixated on. Aubrey always knew that the weather was not just, 'what went on outside' to the English, but was an event in itself. Whole channels were dedicated to predicting, following and analysing of the weather. A conversation in England could not occur, short of a detailed discussion about the weather, and it now seemed that they were exporting their weather to the rest of the world. That is, the owners of the news channels were. One could not imagine why, as the weather in the UK was inevitably bad anyway.

'Not that the English could change the weather; or could they?'

'No. But they could change the way they think about it!'

These random thoughts distracted him and he sunk deeper into the envelop of pillows, the visuals on the screen, a series of blurred dreams.

Not only was the news being regurgitated hour after hour, but was now, always immediately followed by reading the ticker-tape news scrolled along the bottom and repeated second by second as developments occurred. Aubrey flicked on, but as he did so he caught a glimpse of something written on a ticker-tape type broadcast on the bottom of the screen. He flicked back.

There was a breaking story about Amsterdam, and the ticker-tape was in English. He read the moving display as it streamed across the lower screen, purporting to be about a suspected bomb threat in Amsterdam.

Aubrey watched, wide-eyed, a sense of déjà vu. If only he had acted on his gut instinct. The square, where the camera was trained looked distinctly familiar. It was now vacated, and a police cordon surrounded the main area, while sniffer-dogs worked the vicinity.

For him there was an underlying sense of unease. It was not dissimilar to that fatal few seconds before a skidding vehicle, careens into the back of your car on a highway.

"Police in Amsterdam have isolated a threat contained in a canvas bag at a street café in Rembrandt Square," the ticker-tape reeled off.

It was the Square they had been seated in less than three hours before.

"All precautions have been taken to clear the immediate area there appears no further threat to the clinic." Aubrey lay on the bed mesmerized. Tables and chairs, lay strewn across the Square.

"Bomb disposal experts at the scene confirm sniffer dogs had identified a potential threat."

Then the broadcast cut to an earlier interview about the potential target of the threat being a clinic which was operating illegally, using cutting edge technology.

"We have contained the threat and are planning to explode the hazard, just for safety precautions," a Dutch spokesperson for the Police was saying.

The camera focused on a table, now deserted, under which there was a remotely controlled bomb disposal machine delivering a package of explosive to eradicate the threat. Aubrey's eyes were fixed to the screen. He was not sure if he was watching live coverage, or a repeat.

"Tash, Tash," she looked up from her book in time as a controlled explosion took place. Not realizing where this was, Natasha sat watching as there was a detonation and a puff of smoke rose from the area surrounding the tables. Natasha felt like she was in a movie, the scene was familiar and the event was quite cataclysmic, but it took a full minute for her to decipher what was going on.

"Oh my God!" Natasha sat, her jaw dropped. Her eyes bugged out, just in the instant that it seemed some divine cosmic force must have guided them both to leave the Square earlier.

"That is my duffel bag they have just blown up!" Aubrey exploded.

"What?" She looked at him. There was a sadness in those eyes, watching as his faithful duffle bag was incinerated in a blast of plastique explosives.

Then their eyes locked; a moment of sheer terror crossed their minds and then simultaneously they burst out laughing.

All the while Natasha was saying, "Shit, Shit, Shit!" under her breath.

Perhaps it was more nervous energy than the intended irony of the circumstances. Either way they couldn't stop. Natasha howled as they clung to one another, giddy as a pair of adolescents.

Aubrey chuckled uproariously. It was destiny, or was it infamy? Natasha hiding her mouth, her hand clasped over it so as to control her shrieking. Both came to the same realization in that same instant. They had just witnessed the explosion of Aubrey's samples.

"So now there is definitely no need to go back to the clinic!" Aubrey felt liberated.

"Babes, those were your …" She could not bring herself to say the word.

"I think we had better make ourselves scarce," Aubrey was a pragmatist.

The commentator was interviewing a police spokesperson, who surmised that a definite terrorist threat had been thwarted. It would not take them long to discover otherwise, and Aubrey's DNA was analysed. With Natasha in his arms, transfixed by the screen, Aubrey was planning their next move.

They had discovered an ability to laugh in the face of adversity, and the irony of being a witness to an event that they had inadvertently created made the anonymity of their position all the more wicked. They were both left suspended in a state of surrealistic hypertension. The incongruity of what had just transpired made irrational behaviour their only recourse.

"Why would they consider your duffel bag a bomb?" Natasha could not perceive the amount of time and effort afforded this event.

But to Aubrey it was abundantly clear.
"There is a disconnect in this society". People who had famed themselves on the fairness of their facilities and the favour they offered those who had

emigrated to their shores, was in stark contrast to the lack of reciprocity of the governments from whom these immigrants had fled.

"There is, as the Professor would say, a rendering of the collective conscience, towards the paranoia that now prevails in our Westernised societies." Aubrey knew that when the framework of the society for which so many had strived and sacrificed becomes the victim of external ideologies, that system, either must extrapolate the good from their circumstances, or live in mortal fear.

"It is the job of the media bosses to maintain that state of constant fear, so they can maximize the effect their coverage has on the viewing public; all in the hope of maintaining ratings."

However, it did have one major advantage that empowered and informed, and to Aubrey it appeared that the hope was in time, there would be a gradual enlightenment of those less informed. Contrary to popular belief, that empowering the public personae would avail the majority of the opportunity to make decisions for themselves; what was happening was the exact opposite. Mainstream media held the attention of the viewing public, in an obtuse form of servitude. The Westernised press were directly responsible for the demonising of a people, who had fallen neatly into the trap set. When the Cold War ended and the Berlin Wall was deconstructed after years of trying to keep people apart, the media needed something to turn their attentions to. This was opportunistically created by a source for which the media required little effort and the protagonists became vilified by a rabid press, intent on generating continued revenues. Aubrey knew that he himself had fed into that trap, by falling victim to the very form of bigotry that the media perpetuated. In a peculiar form of irony, he had fuelled that prejudicial thinking through his own ignorance. Trusting in the human spirit to find common ground was the only way forward.

As a consequence, and with the possibility of the authorities finding out that the bomb was no more than the last movements of a dying man, Aubrey and Natasha hurriedly booked out of the hotel, and with every look in their direction a condemnation of the guilt they felt, they took the tram to Central Station. On the harbour and boarded a train that would take them as far as possible in any direction.

They were headed for Berlin before they knew it, and the last bastion of the once despotic system of communism.

Aubrey was all too aware that he was not blameless. Whilst the idealistic world of the Dutch countryside flitted past their window, Aubrey sunk into deep thought. The canals, and the farms whisked by. The windmills and the whimsical lifestyle of an industrious nation, who had reclaimed their land from the sea, made a poetic analogous setting.

His life too, had seemed a series of intense challenges whilst developing a strong sense of the divine. Every facet of his complex being was a direct consequence of powerful forces that directed him. A finely tuned intuition had brought him through those many trails and this was simply another in which he would have to trust his instinct.

He was conscious that every decision; each twist and turn of his life and every consequence of his projected thoughts, had a direct channel from which they were derived. He was not just the facilitator of a mysterious power. Circumstance and opportunity had meshed perpetually to bring him to a point of consciousness, which few mortal men would, or could ever reach.

He caught his reflection in the window, as the Berlin express sped through a twisting tunnel under the Zebrugge channel. He saw his life story etched in the deep lines of his face. A face which was his passport to redemption. He studied those crows feet, attempting to pull his bagged eye sockets further away from his nose. A nose which, although straight and narrow, had begun to flare and protrude, as an eagle may survey its territory; a statement of aloofness. Or was it more his own sense of alienation?

He had yet again shown his unwillingness to become subject to the niceties of an investigation that might leave more questions than answers. In those eyes, a coolness hinting of disdain. The world he sought, was a million miles from here.

It was best he beat a retreat, and live to fight another battle, no matter where, and the results of which would be uncertain. But uncertainty was his succour. It fed his mind with opportunity. Westernised and sanitised living was too far from his reality. Aubrey recognised his desire to return to a world, where uncertainty was to him as staple a diet, as maize was to its inhabitants. In that tunnel, a study of introspection, he knew he was truly Whafrican.

It was not in the pallor of his skin, nor the sun-stroked whiplashes across his brow; it was in the blood, unseen and unchecked, that coursed his veins.

The drugs had taken a toll on him as they worked their way through his system. But Aubrey, despite his obvious loss of vigour was buoyed at the prospect of another adventure and the spontaneous love of a woman, intent on being his caregiver.

Luck, or maybe fate had always somehow bestowed the support of a strong woman in his life, when he truly needed one. She was his third real love, and despite his unwillingness to solicit providence, he would not claim superstition; more a fascination with fatalism. Aubrey could now put aside his failings and snipped the apron strings that bound him to his mother's love. Instead he could freely embrace the unadulterated affections of Natasha, who feared naught and curried no favour.

What he had seen in Kisangani several months before would see him travel half way across the vast Congo, and would haunt him forever. He had attempted to finger the perpetrators of a vicious cycle of corruption, but had achieved nothing. The nepotism and corruption of that society was like the cancer that was slowly eroding his body. He needed to fix himself first before he could fight the battle against ingrained Kleptocracy.

The Congo had been just such an example of this 'Kleptocracy', extending the personal wealth of the ruling class at the expense of the proletariat. Corruption cheated the Congolese of their rights to a better future, and channelled funds out of the treasury, and into the hands of individuals with no reinvestment in the country's future. This process was underpinned by the wealth of mineral resources and the desire of many countries to profit from those raw materials. The multinationals exerted undue influence, and mining contracts were awarded. The proceeds filtered through to vast conglomerates whose rabid appetite for profit further fuelled the corruption.

In yet another twist of fate he had cut short another treatment and headed into an unknown future, having left before agreeing to the treatment regime in Kinshasa, and the corruption of his body, became a corruption of his mind.

Travelling with Natasha really perked him up, and her constant upbeat banter was a blessing. With her unsuppressed optimism, he could only feel uplifted. She was like a child, excited at the prospect of travel and undeterred by cynicism. With Natasha's unbridled enthusiasm and her humour as constant companion, he could not help but feel a new zest for life.

With the spirit of adventure still well and truly alive in his blood, he and Natasha had soon put their escapades behind them and arrived in Berlin on the 9pm train from Amsterdam.

They booked themselves into a small hotel on the outskirts of the Bundaslagen, and with their spirits high and Aubrey feeling a lot better after a sleep on the train; they went in search of the Berlin nightlife. They were not to be disappointed. The place buzzed with an expectation that they had never experienced before. They passed the clubs on Wetenbuitenstraat, and discovered the delights of a late-night coffee shop with strudels brimming with stewed fruit. Aubrey was regaining his strength and was now famished. He could have eaten his way through an entire delicatessen, but for Natasha's desire to get back to the hotel.

Because of the injections of Cytotoxic-T cells or cytokines, which had inhibited the cancer cells in his liver, the infusion of these genetically modified cells, and a combination of the nitrogen mustard based oral therapy to retrograde any further cancer cells, Aubrey had momentarily lost his libido.

The past week in Amsterdam, had been the first time he could remember ever having been impotent, since discovering the pleasures of Onanism. The priests at his boarding house had referred to this subject of adolescence in veiled Biblical terms and Aubrey had been more than inquisitive about the pleasures it had brought him on those cold lonely nights away from home. In a dank soulless boarding hostel, filled with similarly inquisitive boys, he made a pact with the devil which had succeeded perfectly at the time.

Natasha rushed him back to the hotel room, and they had not waited for the lift to reach its bumping, grinding ascent to the third floor of the hotel. Choosing to lose their inhibitions whilst in the mirrored eight by six-foot vestibule.

They made love in the big soft cushioned bed, with its' pristine white down-filled duvet, and oversized pillows. They had then turned their predatory lust into a marathon session. All those lonely nights in the library and subsequent visits to book shops all over the southwest for Natasha, had not been in vain.

"There is a medical term for someone who could be aroused by the written word," she had offered up, halfway through an inspiring foray into cunnilingus.

She did not know if it was possible that others may have discovered the pleasure of the inscribed word as a source of such primitive sexual arousal, but it certainly worked for her.

"Of course, this must be a common occurrence", she had confided to Aubrey, as the endless shelves of semi-erotica posing as 'Romantic' novels, would attest to.

"The new shopping malls with all their bookshops have their origins thanks to the entrepreneurial skills of a South African businessman," Aubrey had told her.

She was absorbed by this little-known fact.

"He conquered the South African market with his vision of safe secure shopping, and promptly exported the concept to Britain. It is remarkable, given that the necessity for shopping malls had not existed in the UK prior to the nineties." The expansion into the country, driven by the need for housing outside the cities had fuelled this demand which was now taking over the rolling farmlands of Britain.

"My Nans' family, originally came from the city," Natasha ventured.

"Living in the country would be ideal if it weren't for the crime that accompanies it. The need for safe and secure shopping precincts led ultimately to massive shopping malls where people could remain indoors."

"Perhaps there is a method in their madness." The already weather beaten British, starved of the life-giving substance of the sun's rays, were now being enticed to stay under cover to an even greater extent. Any vitamin B enriched sunlight which was available to enhance their already gloomy lifestyles, was now snuffed out for ever.

"Well then he is now providing a sexual satisfaction to many who suffer from this condition called 'oeuvrephillia'!" Natasha offered.

'Yes', he thought.

"It sounds quite romantic", she added, indulging Aubrey in her conjecture.

"Well, thankfully there is a light at the end of that sad tunnel," Aubrey sparred.

"It is a bit ironical, that this guy is now a member of British High Society and a leader in charitable ventures. He has been cheating on his wife of fifty years, unashamedly and in the most solicitous manner."

"Well," Natasha was quick to point out, "the word 'philanthropic', occurs in the dictionary right next to 'philander'!"

When their lovemaking had been explored from all conceivable positions, Aubrey lay satiated and exhausted and had fallen into a deep sleep. He awoke around lunchtime the following day when Natasha had returned with some of the delights on offer in the local delicatessens and a cup of the roasted coffee from the corner bistro. The coffee smell roused him from the most peaceful sleep he could remember since his days at Cape Maclear. He had often slept in late on his day off from those scuba diving excursions. Nitrogen-induced sleep, which followed the extended dives they had conducted to please their burgeoning clientele, was followed by dipsomania, which starved his body of oxygen. Therein lay the crux of his problem, and through introspection he had inadvertently provided yet another answer to the quiz of life. Somewhere in his memory he recalled something the Professor had said. Aubrey would ask him.

They spent the rest of the weekend in Berlin, and with a glad heart and fond memories had booked themselves directly onto a cheap budget flight to Gatwick, and returned home to the Estate, rather than risking the long bus ride back through Amsterdam.

His thoughts for now returned to where his Elephants were. He wondered if his Elephants would remember him. It was the ill-fated business venture to South Africa that had been his undoing. What had transpired after the accident in Zimbabwe, and the subsequent need for Bronwyn to find medical assistance for Edward, had unravelled a perfectly good situation. They had met with Van Schalkwyk on his private game park in the hills of Mpumalanga, buoyed by the opportunities offered. For Aubrey, this was a chance to take his business to the next level, and for Bronwyn and himself to escape the controlling grasp of her father.

Neither of them had any idea of who they were dealing with, suffice to say, they had just received an enquiry from a game farm owner in South Africa. Neither of them knew the country, nor how cut throat the Game industry in South Africa had become. All the farms were vying for the lucrative American market, with Dollars to blow, and an exchange rate that made a business like this extremely attractive. So, with their hearts firmly on their sleeves, the two young entrepreneurs had made the fateful trip. They were intent on a better deal than they had been able to secure at the Falls, and this was an opportunity for a new beginning. They both had in mind that their destiny lay in the heart of a free democratic South Africa, with ample opportunities and best of all, good medical facilities.

Chapter 14

Back to the lion's den

Aubrey and Bronwyn had travelled down to South Africa in their Isuzu bakkie; the young boy Edward on Bronwyn's lap. A pioneering spirit etched in their conscience. They would secure a deal to bring the remainder of the Elephant from Impingweni, and thus ensure the continuity in a chain of events that had led them to their destiny in the south. Fate had dealt a significant blow to their lives, but it was a journey Aubrey was certain would lead somewhere good. The rationale behind this spirit of adventure was as genetic as it was a conscious decision. The desire to get away from Tony, gave Aubrey pause for thought. It would come down ultimately to the feeling in their hearts, that would drive them on again, and again.

It was the same pioneering spirit that had seen David Livingstone, traverse the sub-Saharan continent and it was ultimately where he succumbed to Malaria on the banks of a lonely lake in the interior of Africa. It was that same passion that had seen his loyal entourage carry his body a thousand miles through the most treacherous terrain, and mosquito infested lowlands, despite the anger of local tribesmen who had tried to stop them. They would deliver his body back to the authorities at the coast, and have it shipped to Britain for burial. That spirit of adventure was the driving force behind the opening up of the interior, where even Arab slave traders had feared to tread. So powerful was that yearning for exploration that he had lived and died to bring Christianity and medicine to the people of Africa.

Aubrey reflected on the history of that continent. It had been erased from the collective conscience of a post-liberation population, intent on eking out a living for themselves. It was the power struggles of a sycophantic leadership, which would attempt to eradicate all references to these truly heroic figures of African history. But Aubrey knew that somehow their testimonies would be recalled. Time was the greatest healer, and sooner than later, the memories of those pioneers who had opened the heart of Africa and changed the course of history through their Christian zeal and mammoth efforts, would be remembered.

The continent had sustained its populations naturally through the millennia, but modern medicine would change all that, finally eradicating small pox, black water fever, and typhoid forever. Malaria, the most prolific killer was replaced with a more vigorous viral infection that was spread by the most obvious form of transmission that not even God, infinite in wisdom, would have created.

This disease was rampant and severe, but seemed to only have devastating effects where populations were closer to the poverty line than not. It was natural selection manipulated, having its way with the world's populace; a sinister form of population control.

Aubrey for certain could not know, but it was the reason that he and Bronwyn would ultimately find their way to a clinic outside the rapidly growing town of Nelspruit, in an area of South Africa, close to the Kruger National Park. Until recently it had been the centre of pestilence and disease in the form of Tsetse fly. Previously an uninhabitable region, that saw only the local tribes numbered in their hundreds as opposed to the hundreds of thousands now making their mark on this South African landscape. They were there to get medical treatment for Edward, and meet with Thys.

Thys was eager to learn all he could about the Elephant operation at the Falls. He personally had never been there, but had heard first-hand accounts of how successful it was. It was this veritable cash cow and the opportunity to be the first in South Africa to set up a commercially viable Elephant safari operation that had seen Thys jump at the opportunity. Aubrey knew he would have to play this deal well in order to secure their fifty percent stake. They had a little money saved and a war chest of experience and knowledge, that would see them through. Aubrey needed to give as little information to Thys as was necessary, but he did not understand nor appreciate the nuances of 'Non-Disclosure Agreements'. Both he and Bronwyn were green when it came to negotiations. They had been stung once before, and Aubrey was very conscious of this.

Thys had served his time in the old National Party of apartheid South Africa, and had known who and how to spin the deal to get where he was. The land he owned on the outskirts of the Kruger Park was a private concession which the local Parks Board were keen to see incorporated into the overall tourist offering. He was forging a new grand design on the African continent with the thatch roofed double storey ochre painted homestead, and a paved drive of red clay brick which stretched the hundred metres from the double gated, electronic fenced gate house.

It was built to impress, and Bronwyn having spent the last five years in their ram shackle corrugated iron roofed abode in the indistinct sun blistered suburb of Vic Falls, was overawed. This was a far journey from there, and the house was perched on the southern slip of a large granite outcrop overlooking a water hole twenty minutes outside Hazeyview. The game lodge was spread out before them, with equally impressive views, and each lodge had access to the open-air thatch roof Boma. Resplendent in artefacts from the local tribes, the wooden deck soaring outwards beyond the cluster of similarly opulent lodges, giving the impression that one was suspended above the watering animals.

"Meneer Pennington," Thys offered as they stepped out of the bakkie, the windscreen covered in insects.

"Thys," Aubrey returned his warm greeting.

"You have travelled a long way. I am sure we can offer you some drinks?"

"Yes, thank you." Aubrey was thirsty. The ten-hour journey from Beit Bridge on the Zimbabwean border, had been non-stop.

"I think the ladies would like to have a walk to the room," announced Thys as his wife and daughter arrived on cue to show Bronwyn the chalet they would be spending the night in.

His dismissive indication to Bronwyn was not as charming a gesture as would have been expected. She was as active a partner in the business at the Falls as was Aubrey. Feathers would be ruffled if Thys had any other ideas.

The facilities were perfect and Aubrey could immediately see its commercial perspective, but the bush veldt was somewhat sparse. The Elephant would need vast areas to roam within the private reserve, and admittedly the winter months in the Lowveld area was dry and the vegetation looked inadequate. The contrast with the riverine vegetation of the Vic Falls setup, gave doubt in Aubrey's mind as to whether they could sustain ten Elephant on this land. The area was a natural habitat for Elephant, but that was if there were unlimited reserves of food. These Elephant would be constrained to an area fenced to protect the existing game from poachers, which were not a problem Aubrey had contended with at the Falls. This private Game reserve was too small, but Aubrey did not say anything.

They had settled for their sundowners and a relaxed chat. The prospects for a commercial venture were outstanding, but Aubrey had some questions.

"How much land is available for the Elephant to forage during the day?"

Aubrey was certain they could split the Elephant into two groups, with four to six Eles doing the morning excursion, and the others feeding during that time. He would then bring the others in and have them stabled while the Indunas watered them and removed the large ungainly saddles.

"During the day?" Thys had been unaware that they would need to feed during the day.

"Well. For a sustainable business, these Elephant will need between forty to fifty kilograms of leaves, bark and natural fruit for them to sustain a daily outing of two or three hours." The statement hung, suspended like the winter dust clouds that settled on the Lowveld horizons.

Aubrey would use the same format as he had embarked on at the Falls, and the Eles would be given horse cubes to supplement their diet at night. The building of the stables was still a subject they would need to discuss.

"Oh!" Thys fell silent for a moment. His mind was working despite his outward charming smile.

"Do you have costings for the feed?" Thys was foraging. His penetrating blue eyes searched Aubrey's.

"Yes. That would be a prerequisite to any formal business transaction." Aubrey had a spread sheet with a financial assessment of the business. His Eles were his primary concern, and this was not going well.

Thys was a manipulator, having got his way all his life. He had already surmised that a bunch of Zimbabwean refugees, in a beaten up old bakkie with tyres that should have been hanging from his tree for his Pitbull's to savage, would be easy pickings.

Aubrey smiled with a grace that smacked of supplication. He would accept the hospitality of his host, willing him to make the first mistake.

Thys could drink any man under the table, by all accounts. Aubrey had seen his fair share of the bottom of a glass, and being a scotch drinker, his liver had been conditioned to withstand that abuse, for now. Aubrey matched Thys, taking the mampoer offered with his beer, and chasing it with that kerosenetic liquid. The fumes shortened his breath, and would have been a suitable paint stripper.

Aubrey sat at the bar with the winter sun blazing a trail across the eastern hills. The remnants of the sunset, a purple hue hanging as a curtain to remind him of the prevailing South Easterly. Suspended in the troposphere the earths' radiation was caught like a buck in the headlights of a game-viewing Land Rover. Unable to move from the virtual barrier of light and dark, these particles were trapped in the troposphere, in its icy embrace. The dust mixed with the ions in the upper atmosphere, reflecting the sun's rays in a virtuoso display of iridescent orange, through the spectrum of light until the Tyrian purple of the climax, stretched out before them in a show of meteoric import.

The significance of this display was not lost on Aubrey, and he made his mind up, that the setting was magnificent, but the magnanimous display of hospitality, like the sunset, only clouded the reality of their venture. His Eles would be lambs to the slaughter, becoming mere beasts of burden and this circus, once the fanfare had died down and the spotlights snubbed out, could not hide the underlying motives, just as the phosphorescent display had finally ended.

Thys likewise had realized that despite his visible show of camaraderie, he had not had the meeting of minds he would have wished for. Trying to glean as much information as possible, he realized he would not need Aubrey.

Bronwyn arrived refreshed and ready for dinner, providing a welcome change in the evenings proceedings.

"Mefrou Pennington," Thys had cooed, the fumes of liquor, a lubricant to a charm offensive that ensued.

During dinner, Annelie Van Schalkwyk, wife and gracious provider, had sat silently, and smiled politely at her husband's jokes. She, it seemed, had been the back bone on which Thys had planted his seed, raised his seven offspring, and single-handedly lifted them from the poverty of a mine shift workers home in Vereeniging. Her brother was a Councillor for the Nationalists during the apartheid government. Contracts for the vast road infrastructure that was to be the eastern corridor to Mozambique and the port city of Maputo, were being handed out and Thys was on hand to benefit.

The Portuguese had acquiesced during the liberation struggle in Mozambique, which had seen a savage civil war tear the country apart. The Frelimo, backed by the Chinese and Russians, and the RENAMO backed by a South African Defence Force intent on stopping this brand of communism in the region, had fought a bitter war, and the transportation of provisions and armaments had required an effective road network. This was a job for a man with no predisposition towards ethics and the right Government contacts.

It resulted in Thys, project managing the building of a highway, and with it, the substantial financial rewards from a treasury, abundant with tax payers' funds, and financially secure due to International Monetary Fund loans.

South Africa, because of the Nationalist governments' grip on the resources, and their willingness to repay the IMF commitment with interest, had been seen as a good investment. Thys with his ear to the ground, had likewise been a certain bet, and the gifts bestowed on those councillors who had backed his tenders, had been very rewarding.

So, the cycle continued, and in an evolving society, where the handover of power through the councils after 1994, then the Provincial departments, emanating upwards to the highest levels of Government, simply became a transfer of opportunity for those taking over the old Nationalist government practices, to be installed as the recipients of business as usual.

Thys was one of the fortunate few, who had retired early enough to escape detection from the previously corrupt system, and who had the foresight to find a piece of land that was outside the scope of the Land Restitution Program and would not be subject to a claim from local tribesmen. Like the colonial masters who dealt with the Aborigine of Australia, the local ward councillor had ensured a Drankwinkel, or bottle store, had been allowed to flourish on the outskirts of Driefontein. It was close to his land, and in this manner, guaranteed that the local chieftain would remain a firm supporter of his acquisition.

This was the bottom rung in the evolutionary ladder of politics, but it was effective. The locals lived and worked the land, becoming game trackers, cooks and domestic servants, in a growing tourist trade that saw huge sums of cash generated for the local economy. Everyone benefited, and turning a blind eye to the effects that alcohol was having on their communities, the chieftains would become complicit in allowing the unemployed to become victims, and alcohol became a dependency.

The breweries that flourished in a fermentation of cultures and rural values, would ultimately become the largest companies in a country that had forty-three million expectant citizens, and only a handful of real recipients. But alcohol was heavily taxed and so became a staple source of income for the treasury. The wheel turned and yet again in a society where democracy and the vote was offered as a reward, the poor would be enticed to vote for the ruling party, because the game of politics was a fine balancing act between providing answers and hood winking the proletariat.

The next morning, with Thys having abandoned them, they were left to the quiet, polite hostess, who stammered her way through a breakfast of gargantuan proportions, and a good mug of coffee, and the inevitable rusk or two.

It was this balancing act that Aubrey would ultimately base his decision on. In the bakkie, on their way back to the guest house in Nelspruit, he told Bronwyn.

"Did you see those dogs chained up at the back of the house?" Aubrey was shocked to see how they had been scarred by obvious bouts of cage fighting.

"Bronwyn, I cannot see how I could work with Thys." It was straight forward, unequivocal and despite Bronwyn's misgivings about the dogs, he had made it clear that he would not have anything to do with Thys.

"But Aubrey, what are we going to do now?" She was ever the practical one; whereas he was the dreamer always assuming the best and hoping for even better.

"If we cannot work with Thys then who can we approach?" They did not know anyone in South Africa. Their enquiry had been through a brother of Thys, who had been at the Falls. It had been his idea to get Aubrey and Bronwyn to come to South Africa, and it had been him ultimately who had double crossed them.

But Aubrey was right, and now they had to think of an alternative. They had packed everything into their bakkie, and had set off on this journey with no fear of the outcome. Chasing a better life was all it was, and Edward would need their help. If Aubrey could not work with Thys, then there would be another opportunity. After all this was Africa, and they knew Elephants, and the tourism trade was crying out for their help.

Whilst they were in Nelspruit a newspaper article had attracted Aubrey's attention. They had been staying at the guest house, using their savings to live, and Aubrey had been out looking for work. He was selling his idea, when a disaster of seismic proportions hit the game industry landscape. It had every Game Lodge owner running for cover, and anyone with Elephants was a target of bad publicity.

The Tuli block in Botswana had seen a massive need for culling Elephants, but a small group of young Elephant had been saved from the cull, and relocated to a facility in Brits, just outside Pretoria. The Elephants then became a subject of media hysteria, and a massive public outcry because of their perceived mistreatment. Fair to say, from all accounts Aubrey would not have chained them in the manner that Asian Elephants are domesticated by their Mahouts. Suffice it to say this was a commercial venture with no real concern for those young Elephants. They would have been domesticated and sent to destinations all over the world, and had this initial foray succeeded, the venture would have become a multinational business.

Fortunately enough, a vigorous SPCA had descended on the farm, and with the help of concerned citizens the operation was shut down. However, despite the publicity, this event had two casualties. One was the Elephants themselves, which unbeknown to the altruistic public, then suffered further trauma by being shipped again to other parks; but the other casualty was Aubrey and Bronwyn. The bad publicity damaged Elephant backed safari tourism for several years. Considering these negative newspaper articles, Aubrey had a good excuse to stop the business idea in its tracks, and they would move onto greener pastures. Despite these setbacks, Thys had surreptitiously gone directly to the owner of the Impingweni Elephants, and regardless of the controversy he had bought the remaining ten Elephant.

Thys was not someone who would flinch at the first sign of a skirmish, and he certainly would not allow the liberal minded bunny huggers from the SPCA stop him. He forged ahead, arranging for the transportation of the herd and he would secure his Indunas by offering jobs to the Zimbabwean handlers whom he had met at Impingweni.

He was hard pressed to get clearance certificates for their export from Zimbabwe, with every official from Harare to Beit Bridge expecting a back hander. Thys, knowing a thing or two about bribery, was able to surreptitiously import the Elephant from Matabeleland, whilst Aubrey and Bronwyn had already packed up and left for Port Elizabeth.

The journey would be stressful for the Elephants, but they would make sure that it was equally stressful for Thys. Having got them successfully through the border post, undetected by the media vultures looking for a follow up scoop, the Elephants arrived in Hazeyview with their handlers, and none the worse for it. It was Thys who had taken some strain, and in the early hours, before the Elephants were to be off loaded into their new paddocks, he dropped dead from a heart attack.

Bronwyn had been pessimistic, but was not entirely deflated. She had been in touch with her Mom who had given her a lifeline, by announcing that they would be heading to South Africa, and retirement. Having bargained on the Zimbabwe economy collapsing entirely, Tony had taken his golden handshake from the firm, and they had settled in Port Elizabeth with a guaranteed British Pension.

Having given up on his dream of Elephant safaris in the South African bushveld, Aubrey was hard pressed to say no to Bronwyn when she had suggested they join the family. Like so many of the Zimbabweans before them, they had made the final trek down to the Cape. Reversing a journey that had begun a hundred years before.

When the pioneers had done this trek, a century before, they had done so with scant regard for the local inhabitants. Now they had to traipse the two thousand kilometres back to the south with a heavy heart, a sense of abandonment and a young orphan. This was the irony of Africa. It always has been, and likely always would be a transient society. The migrations of people had followed the changing environment since the melting of the ice caps twelve thousand years before. The nature of which is to seek opportunities in a hard and unforgiving landscape, of economic and political intrigue.

Chapter 15

Horribilis Annullus

Back at Finsbury, Aubrey had taken Natasha in his arms, knowing he would miss her effervescence and the support she had become to him. She had then driven the fifty miles back to her home to prepare herself for her next semester. Aubrey would see her the following weekend, but was not to know that her intervention would save his life. This would turn out to be the most cataclysmic event in their relationship, and from which they would draw the strength to continue fighting. He was soon to come to know the power of 'LifeZone', and the meteoric heights to which this small company, with grand ideals would reach.

With his dignity restored, and no further remorse for having terminated his treatment, he did one of his favourite things and took the Roller for a spin. The Rolls Royce had been safely returned to the estate by the local constabulary, none the wiser for Aubrey's escapade and he leapt into her after a hearty breakfast Monday morning, and headed straight to town and a debriefing with the Professor. No meeting with the Professor was a simple get together, and Aubrey had prepared himself for a thorough grilling. He knew that he was in for a marathon discussion and that he would have to explain the treatment in detail to the Professor. But Aubrey also took with him the knowledge that after the Professor had been completely briefed on the treatment process, he himself would be doing a little interrogation.

The Professor was in the coffee shop Monday morning chatting; a Beatlesque bevy of ladies surrounding him, cooing for his attention. It was their daily ritual, and the Professor had almost single-handedly been responsible for introducing caffeine to the population of Finsbury. Despite their previous tea drinking habits, the Professor now had a host of coffee addicts swilling the creamy cappuccinos and lattes until lunchtime. All on a perpetual high that had them tottering back to their village abodes, perky and uprightly nimble. One of the regulars was the eighty-something year old Margaret, who given the opportunity, would loiter behind the gaggle.

Without fail, Margaret would ask the Professor his advice on her financial affairs, and barring the calamitous failure of the stock market, or a meteoric event in the City, the answer would be the same every day. However, Margaret was a creature of habit, and staying later and a glass of wine as the clock struck the twelve. With the vigour of a twenty-year-old and her posture much the better for her imbibing the wine, she would head off up the road.

With shoulders trailing her hips by such a precarious degree, her body looked almost disjointed, Margaret would wend her way home.

She was a mischievous one, and was always ready for a modicum of gossip, as Aubrey knew very well. He had made his own decision to confront the Professor about his interaction with Sean. Perhaps Margaret may have some background information, as she was the unofficial Mayoress of Finsbury.

The Professor shook his head, and guffawed jovially.

"Undoubtedly, you have a leprechaun on your shoulder laddie?" The Professor mimicked his Irish Ancestry.

He was always amused by Aubrey's antics, never surprised by the sheer gall.

"After all the British had invented High Seas piracy, and taught the Muslim nations a thing or two about terrorism. We damn near had the trademark on Nepotism! All this in the name of colonialism, and the expansion of the British Empire, Eh!" He teased, reverting to his Cambridge eloquence.

"After all we introduced concentration camps in the Boer War and the forced removal of land owners when the Transvaal Government was installed. We bloody well deprived some of the Voortrekkers of their mineral rights to the Witwatersrand. Yes, the British had a lot to be proud of in their human rights record."

The Professor shook his head, wondered at the complete improbability of it all, and slapped Aubrey on the back. Notoriety was his middle name, and wondered if there was some gene that occurred in the Pennington blood, but stopped in mid thought, knowing only too well what the answer was.

"Do you make a habit of being chased halfway across Europe by the law?" He had heard there was a manhunt for unlikely looking terrorists, intent on bringing the Western world to its knees. Perhaps they might find a scapegoat?

"It was completely unintentional old man," replied Aubrey with a wicked grin. When he was in the presence of the Professor, he seemed to forego any niceties. The Professor was the Uncle he could always confide in.

"There has been coverage for the entire weekend! Do you realize the amount of manpower they have committed to finding these terrorists? I would love to see the egg on their faces when they discover the truth!" The Professor shook his head wryly.

"Except it would not be egg!" laughed Aubrey, and the two of them chuckled merrily through the rest of their meeting.

Aubrey then made some excuse about getting a bit of fresh air, and waited outside on the wooden bench in front of the coffee shop for Margaret. He sunned himself taking in the tranquillity of the village and its even quainter inhabitants. He could imagine JRR Tolkien sitting on just such a bench while he conjured up 'The Lord of the Rings'.

Margaret appeared like clockwork, right along with her faithful dog 'Changa', an old mixed breed collie, who had paws as splayed as duck's feet. The two stumbled out the front door of the shop, and with a brief pause and a courteous nod to Aubrey; she lit up a cigarette, and began to amble home. Aubrey, surreptitiously slipped off the bench, and joined her as they rounded the corner so as not to raise any suspicion from the Professor inside.

He caught up with her, and with a hearty, "good afternoon Margaret", he was soon engrossed in a conversation about everything from the weather to the new town's mayor, that no one was particularly enthralled with.

"May I escort you home?" He ventured.

"Oh, certainly. But I only live over there," she pointed down the street to a neat row of cottages.

As they walked, Margaret had an opinion on most topics, and with the trip to her humble abode taking no less than one hundred paces, Aubrey soon realized he was running out of time and space.

With only a mere twenty paces to go, Aubrey quickly changed the subject.

"What a wonderful village environment you live in, "Aubrey accentuated the positive.

"Yes, sweet pea," Margaret replied. Stopping to take another puff of her fag.

She remembered him well from his childhood and Aubrey's status as the local 'Lord of the Manor' had no standing, because at her age there were no sacred cows left in her life. With Aubrey already promoted to a term of endearment, he was in a perfect position to ask her opinion.

"Never trust a politician!" Margaret had suddenly exclaimed.

Aubrey was taken aback by this unexpected outburst. The conversation had remarkably changed from idle chitchat. He listened.

"You see the Belisha Beacon", she pointed to the traffic beacon ahead.

"Why do we need a confounded beacon? You know, those were introduced by the Minister of Transport in the thirties. My Aunt Agnus knew him as a young man, and he once remarked to her that he was thinking of going into politics, but could not decide on whether to go 'left or right'. I mean what a thing to say for a politician in charge of Transport of all things!" She grinned, raising her slightly hawkish nose heavenward in a gesture of resignation.

"He was a right leaning Liberal with a left tilt! A political chameleon! His claim to fame was a peerage offered to him by Churchill in 1954, which made him a Baron." Margaret certainly was a mine of information.

"I think Churchill felt sorry for him because the English never quite accepted his multi-faceted political persuasions." She paused so as to confirm his interest.

Aubrey listened intently. A wry smile invoking a cherry disposition.

"He became Secretary of State for war in 1937, after Cooper resigned because of Chamberlain's policy of appeasing Hitler. He called for conscription, but was shouted down by many who saw him as a warmonger. If he had succeeded, we may not have had to enter the war because Hitler may have been more cautious about entering a war with a fully functional British Army across the English Channel!"

She was staring out into the distance whimsically, having stopped to cross the road where the Belisha Beacon stood. This was her daily routine and it was clearly something she must have considered every day she did so. Changa followed faithfully by her side.

"He was however a political opportunist, and because he changed his name to the double-barrelled 'Hore-Belisha' at the age of nineteen when his mother remarried Sir Adair Hore; no-one ever took him seriously. His nickname was 'Horeb-Belisha' but he would have never made a difference, even if the English had just accepted his Jewish origins."

"But he did!" Aubrey stopped.

Margaret looked up at the beacon. She nodded.

Aubrey knew of a few African politicians who would never gain acknowledgement for their efforts. Maybe the Christian countries would never quite forgive the Jewish nation for the Crucifixion?

"He was defeated by Michael Foot in 1945 when he stood as an Independent candidate."

"So, he had four political faces, three posts, a double-barrel name, and one claim to fame. He really didn't have a leg to stand on!" Margaret chuckled ruefully.

Aubrey could not help but chuckle along with her. Maybe laughter was the best medicine?

"We have always had such a quiet life here in Finsbury," she remarked as abruptly as her previous observation had ended. Her mind clearly as sharp as the fine cut of her rakish jaw. This was no wilting wisteria. Margaret was a prickly English Rose with a refined, but showy exterior, full of fragrance and promise. She even had the pallor of a dark pink rose in full blossom.

"Except, that is for when the Nazi's bombed the local airfield," she added with an intonation in her voice.

"That was a noisy affair. My husband was based at Number 44 squadron in Lincolnshire, and I was in the WAAF. There were a lot of bombs, but it did not last too long thankfully."

Aubrey was now genuinely interested, "Oh that sounds remarkable," he recalled having heard a dinner conversation between Lord Fontenbury, and his father as a child, and being equally fascinated then.

"The Nazi's had made the Dunsfold Park airfield a target, you know?" Margaret added. "It was an emergency landing strip for the big bombers." A sense of pride evident. Time had not faded an acute memory of her wartime ordeals.

"My husband and I, we were based at Lincolnshire airfield when stationed with squadron 44 in 1941. My husband was a pilot on those big bombers, you know, the ones with four engines. Those were really loud." Margaret was quite animated now.

Aubrey could not help but be taken in with her enthusiasm. These were her memories and she had obviously been quite smitten with her husband.

At this point Aubrey would have liked to have asked about her husband. Was he deceased? Aubrey was tempted to ask, but was still caught up in the story. The golden rule of decorum, was to never be so impolite unless the information was offered. Remaining tight-lipped, an air of expectation hung in the silence that followed.

Margaret broke that silence, "My late husband and I were married in the local chapel in Lincoln, you know." He didn't but Aubrey kept quiet. This was Margaret's story.

"We were married on the 30th June 1941". Aubrey made a mental note that she would be at least eighty-seven now if she had joined the Woman's Auxiliary in 1941.

"We were only married two weeks, when he lost an engine over Germany. They diverted the aircraft to make an emergency landing here at the Guildford airfield base, but unfortunately, they had lost a fuel line in the flak over Potsdam. He tried to take the plane in but they were losing altitude quickly, so he had the crew bail out over Kent and single-handedly brought the plane in."

There was a pregnant pause. Aubrey could not bring himself to ask.

"Yes. He crashed into a wooded area north of here; on the Estate in fact!"

Aubrey remembered hearing about it. He had found some buried parts of that aircraft on his many excursions into the woods. He recalled Lord Pennington being slightly proud of him when he brought them in after one of his sojourns through the woods.

Aubrey smiled respectfully. She had lost her husband after only two weeks! He began to wonder if Margaret had ever re-married. But now they were at her front door in the narrow cobble stone lane that was set off from the main village road. The house was a Victorian cottage, which had subsequently been turned into a 'semi', with old wooden lintels over the doors and windows. They looked aged and weather beaten, the exterior edges finely worn so that each striation in the dark wooden beams was visible. The front of the property was very cottagey with two rows of thick rose bushes, nestled on each side of the front door. It did look cosy.

"Well, thank you for such an interesting talk," Aubrey began to make his apologies to leave, but he had not yet had a chance to talk about the Professor.

"Don't be daft," Margaret interjected.

"Come in and sit for a while. I will put the kettle on." She turned placing the cigarette butt into a trashcan on the concrete plinth beside the doorway. The lid clattered as she released it, and Aubrey was distracted for a second. He hesitated, but was intrigued enough to accept her offer. He wasn't quite sure and didn't want to impolitely barge into a complete strangers' home, but the urge to settle his provocative question was strong.

Margaret insisted, "Come on then", she remarked. "It's not like you have a lot to do this afternoon!" Aubrey laughed. Not having to put up with all the fussiness and protocol. She had no time for the pomp and ceremony, after all having lived four score and seven odd years, she likely figured that the best had past her already.

Margaret had a twinkle in her eye, "besides, you have not asked me your question yet!"

Aubrey paused. She was a wily old vixen. Had he made himself that obvious?

She was certainly very astute for her years. Entering the tiny cottage on Branbury Lane, Aubrey had to duck down as he passed through its' small doorway to prevent bumping his head on the old oak lintel. In the front living room, he sensed he was being drawn into the room. It was neat, and the furniture looked miniature.

There was a tremendous feeling that he was in the presence of someone he knew. It was as though this room had some supernatural force and Aubrey, began to float as though he were experiencing an out of body encounter.

It was as though he could see the room, just as that spirit might. His subconscious mind was open to the encounter, but his logical brain tried to fight it. This was an issue of control, and his sensual being needed this stimulation, despite the fear of allowing the spirit to have a hold over him.

Feeling the inner peace that the spirit conveyed, he succumbed to the power of the moment, and as he had done so often when alone on those treacherous journeys through the Congo, he surrendered to the spirit. Allowing whatever influence, it may have to lift him.

The sensation that it was welcoming, almost expecting Aubrey, like an old friend, gave him the fortitude to remain. Aubrey felt this sudden shift in his universe and he knew it meant, he would never be quite the same again. He hesitated again in the sitting area.

Looking around, he could see a framed grainy black and white picture of a young couple, dressed smartly in Royal Air Force uniform. The man peered out of the picture, his sixty-year-old gaze from the frame sharp, and penetrating. The picture enclosed by the aging glass was clouded by time and the adoring attention of a weekly duster. Etched with the imperceptible scratches, through which he stared, those eyes were still distinct, penetrating.

In life, they would have been the blue of the summer solstice sky having been drawn as northward as she might venture. The sun would illuminate this picture postcard caught in the frame of timeless eons, secure that life would remain abundant and true and Aubrey felt he was being watched, and that he knew this person; but how?

Those eyes were scrutinising but kind. The jaunty tilt of the chin, strong and commanding. The manner in which he held Margaret, her tiny frame childlike and supplicant, embraced in eternity. It was quite a peculiar feeling, and one that would remain with him.

Margaret saved the moment, returning through the narrow entrance of the dining area, with a chair that looked quite sturdy, and heavy. Aubrey instinctively rushed forward to assist her, but Margaret with her grip firmly on the old Victorian dining chair, dismissed his advance and shushing him away, placed the chair next to the now lifeless brick chimneystack. Ushering him to sit, she turned unceremoniously back to the kitchen beyond the dining area to prepare their tea.

Aubrey sat with an air of trepidation, and began to scout the room visually, trying diligently to avoid the picture on the far side. He found himself alone with his thoughts, gazing at all the memorabilia, which was in evidence on all the walls and mounted on the shelving behind the small couch. He felt as if he was a visitor to a child's Wendy house. Not unwelcome, but cramped; the furniture was old; but fastidiously preserved. This was a very peculiar home indeed!

Like a Victorian chamber of horrors, all the faces stared out at him, distant and haunting. But they were kind faces. This was a museum to her life. A life which would have been full and spontaneous. Richer for the warmth of all these friends and family, but somehow devoid of any depth.

The room was eerily quiet and despite the spirit presence, lacked some vital ingredient. Aubrey perused the pictures, particularly the older black and white ones. They were of an era that was steeped in a refinery, resplendent with well-cut suits, generous but elegant knee length skirts, and a smattering of sophistication that was so far removed from the cheap contemporary styles of a modern, functional fashion sense today. They were a cut above the sloppy Americanism of the 'saggers' of today; something that spoke to a civilized society. Theirs was a time of genteel manners, courteous decorum but savage wars. A room which seemed to say, 'Mankind will prevail despite the inhumanity of it all.' Life was richer for this conundrum, but poorer for its passing. This little village in the rolling English countryside, was a time capsule back to a gentler more appreciative epoch when men were intrinsically 'men' and women were caregivers and temperate and forgiving. Not the struggling neo-fascist feminism, which had driven a wedge between conventionality and the consumerism of today.

This room, suggested to Aubrey a life that was different then. The struggle for recognition was borne of the necessity of an era when women would don their overalls and crisply ironed woollen uniforms, to help defeat one fascist force, only to submit to another; more sinister and pervasive. This was a mausoleum to all those women who had foregone their traditional roles in society, and ventured out into the corporate and professional world to meet new challenges and make a mark on their society; only to submit to the greatest evil this world had known and would embrace. Consumerism was that evil, and in order to supplicate its desires, women would have to forfeit their long-established role as child minder. The world was poorer for it, and families bereft of good values, as television, video games and fast food became the substitute for parenting. To achieve the allusive goals of financial independence, something or someone had to be sacrificed. This was the cost this generation would have to pay, if only for a fleeting moment, Utopia was claimed, but paradise lost.

Margaret returned, having brought with her a tray, laden with cups saucers and a plate of biscuits. Again, Aubrey stood to assist her, but was waved away once more. This was a tenacious little old lady, who was still clearly quite capable. When the tea serving protocol had been dispensed with, Aubrey began the conversation in earnest.

"When I moved to the WAAF barracks of the Lincolnshire airfield, in September 1940, the Battle of Britain was over, but the war had only just begun." Margaret had revelled in various non-combat duties required by the Royal Air Force.

I met my husband Fergus on the base." He was conscripted to No. 44 Squadron, having been born in Rhodesia, the only son of Scottish émigrés. Margaret had fallen for him immediately and married him, despite her misgivings about marriage. She had always considered herself not the marrying type. However, she had been smitten by his charm, and his somewhat ribald Scottish sense of humour.

"Why did you marry then?" Aubrey.

"I admired his earthiness. Growing up in Rhodesia, he had no airs and graces." His good-natured sense of fun, which was evident in the picture that Margaret kept bringing to Aubrey's attention, lent a somewhat comical air to the conversation.

Each time Aubrey was directed to the portrait which he had earnestly been trying to ignore, it became apparent to Margaret that Aubrey would shift uncomfortably. Desperately avoiding eye contact with the man in the picture, Aubrey noticed when she pointed to his portrait, she would smile and consciously touch her Saint Christopher pendant.

Aubrey searched the remainder of the room. There were no divine symbols. The book shelves were spartan, but there was crossword puzzles, strewn across the coffee table. No sign of a bible, but this good luck charm was clearly important. Margaret seemed adamant and suddenly in desperation, she stood and taking the framed portrait from its central position on the wall, she offered it to him. This drew Aubrey's attention to the oval shaped mark that now appeared on the wall from which the frame had been extricated. An adoring husband was etched into her memory as vividly as that discolouration on the wall. Aubrey's question was answered. She had never remarried.

When this parody was concluded with, and Aubrey was forced to look at the intricately patterned gilt-edged frame, and its subject matter; he felt a chill descend his entire back, from the nape of his neck, where the fine blond hairs stood on end, all the way down his spine, ending with an involuntary shiver in his coccyx.

He now recognized his spirit friend. Like an adoring Uncle, he had stood guard over Aubrey on his forays into the woods. Aubrey had met him, face to face one early autumn evening, having ventured through the darkening wood. He had been making his way back home after one of his lonely vigils to the crash site, when out of the corner of his eye he had seen a movement in the undergrowth. He had stopped, having feared nothing previously, he knew he should have nothing to worry about. It may have been one of the grounds men on their way back to the servant's quarters. But he was now convinced that the six-foot-tall man who had regarded Aubrey then, was this man in the picture. He remembered that kind face, his head covered by a leather-flying cap, perched above his broad brow. Pleading with Aubrey, his eyes dazzled as the brightest stars in the clear night sky. He had seemed to beckon to Aubrey, rounding the tree, out of sight, and then was gone.

Aubrey, back in Margaret's living room, was certain that there was now a smirk on the man's face. One which had not been there when he had originally looked. The jaunty angle of his Pilot's cap and his slightly raised chin, appeared proud and all the more familiar. He was clearly still a massive influence in her life. He was now having a similar effect on Aubrey. After the conversation about the war began to trail off, Margaret told him what he wanted to know.

Human relationships were like a massive schematic of a rocket. The one characteristic combined with the next and they fuelled a reaction. With combinations of emotions, the whole thing ignited a response, which was fed by the chemistry. It either worked, or did not. Some were explosive; others less volatile, but all were designed to provide a harmonious conclusion with the corollary being a spontaneous union. If it was not spontaneous, it probably was not worth progressing with, and the thing should be shut down. It was as complicated a relationship as rocket science might be, but his innate sense was that Margaret had never been willing to try that experiment again.

This analogy was what he and Natasha had. Their relationship was animal in its simplicity; visceral in the basest of its effortlessness. It was what all should strive for, and should be spontaneous and work simply. If it did not, then it would ultimately fizzle out, or explode, destroying everything in its wake.

Ill health was one of the side effects of unhealthy relationships, and Aubrey knew that if he did not listen to his inner voice and go with the flow, his illness would remain, becoming more vigorous and damaging. He had to have come this far though, to understand the nuances of this life. He would learn from these experiences, and unlike many who pursue unworkable unions, which in the animal kingdom would not exist; Aubrey had listened to his spiritual self, in an effort to understand his primitive being.

Aubrey felt a need to restore the balance to his life. It required a paradigm shift, for which he searched. It was that inner voice which drove him from one exploit to the next.

Margaret and Sam had been ideally suited for one another, and despite the short duration of their existence together, it had been special. Theirs had been a brief, but exceptional union. She was a woman, who had selflessly given up on her ambitions, in pursuit of keeping his memory alive. But it was a common trait amongst English women, selflessly indulging their husbands for what little happiness they may encounter along the way. That in itself, was reason to give pause. In her own way, Margaret was indulging herself. It had probably started off as selfless sacrifice, but had ultimately ended as a shrine to her altruistic belief that their relationship had been the one special alliance that could never be reclaimed. Some would assume that a relationship could be replaced, but Margaret knew she could never hope to trade what they had shared, however brief. It was what had given her the strength to continue, despite the attentions of several suitors. Hers was a blissful existence, unsullied by outside intervention, and uncluttered by modern demands.

"I was released on compassionate grounds shortly after the accident, and because I had been born in Gravesend in Kent, I moved here, just after the war ended. It was closer to Tilbury on the Thames, where mummy and daddy lived, and I have been here ever since."

Aubrey, about to state his commiserations was halted in his tracks.

"Sam gave me this Saint Christopher the day he died, as it was his and said I would need it more than him!" There was a look of anguish for the first time, that spread across her forehead and then through her deeply set eyes; she appeared to display a hint of emotion. Then the moment was gone and Margaret stood, lifting the teapot.

"Anyone for a cup of tea? I certainly could do with another."

Aubrey wanted to tell her something, almost did, but then held back a remark. There was no need to tell Margaret that he had seen Sam in the woods. She knew he was there with them. Margaret was not alone in this Edwardian bungalow. She had her man close by, and no one else need know.

It was funny, he thought, how one could make an incorrect assumption about a person without truly knowing them.

What Aubrey did not, and could not have known, was that he was the first man to have entered that home in sixty-seven years! The char, who helped with house work, had only become an essential part of Margaret's life, when her knee had given up after a nearly fatal fall. But then she had spent two weeks in hospital, and had finally agreed to getting a domestic worker in on a part-time basis. It was this little indulgence she now accommodated in her later life, because she had been dusting his pictures, when the chair had collapsed underneath her and she had landed on her knee, causing her patella to snap like a twig.

Aubrey was now perched on the edge of his chair, with all her wartime memories and that picture keeping him captivated; so, when Margaret stood to replace it on the wall above the fireplace, he began to fidget. He knew it was time for him to ask the question he had really come to learn more about. The conversation had come around to some banter about the Estate, which Aubrey had answered in earnest, hoping his frankness would lead to a similar out pouring of candid information.

"I knew your mother, you know!" Was Margaret's comment.

"Did your mother ever mention that she had been to see me to honour my husband?" The question was pointed, but to a point Aubrey could not quite follow.

"No, I don't think she would have mentioned it to me. She kept her philanthropic activities quite private," was the only answer he could muster.

"No, I believe you were too young at the time to remember her Good Samaritan work?"

Again, Aubrey's answer was negative. "She was not one for talking about her charitable work."

"No, no, I hardly think it was charity." Margaret seemed offended.

Suddenly she leapt up, and mumbling under her breath, her chin set firmly in a dogged fashion, she became intent on finding something she had stored away on a shelf behind the armchair. With this air of indignation emanating from her pint-sized frame, she drew out a photo album, preserved in the plastic covering of an old faded blue photo album. Pulling the album up to her chest, she settled back into her chair. Opening the book, she flipped to a page and handing it to Aubrey. She was one feisty old bird, and Aubrey apologized.

"I'm sorry! I sometimes open my mouth before engaging my brain!"

She dismissed his attempted apology, drawing his attention to a small square picture with a watercolour effect; not sharp like the current digital pictures, but colour which gave the impression of a soft-focus filter on the camera lens. It was unmistakably his mother, standing next to a younger and seemingly taller looking Margaret. The low contrast and velvety effect gave each subject a softer, kinder persona. His mother looked to be in her late forties, maybe younger, her hair was drawn up in the style prevalent of the sixties. There was a framed object in the picture. As Aubrey looked closer he could see it was the same picture of Margaret and her husband Sam. In her other hand, a certificate which now had pride of place next to the photograph on the wall.

"It is signed by Her Royal Highness Princess Alice!" This was a statement of pride.

"She was awarded the Dame Grand Cross of the Order of Bath. The highest award a woman in National Service can receive!" Margaret was more intent on the honours of the Princess, than that of her own accomplishments. Aubrey was humbled by her selflessness.

"Oh, I see," Aubrey, eyed the picture. "I remember this event."

"Yes, I remember you from that day. We did not see much of you after then!" Margaret was perched on the edge of her chair now, once more animated.

"Do you recall what the event was about?" she reached out pointing with a crooked finger. Her hands were long, sinewy claws of flesh and bone. Blue and vascular, through the thin tissuey flesh. Pointing to the opposite page, where an equally grainy, yellowing newspaper article, written probably for a local paper, had been cut out and pasted. The journalists name was evident, and the article was headed.

'War Time Hero Honoured.'

"Lady Pennington, the founder of a group dedicated to honouring the memory of wartime hero's and those who had died in service to their country." Aubrey could recall all the detail when he read the article.
It was as clear as a summer's day on the South Downs. He remembered his mother taking him all dressed up in his smart St George's blazer and cap. But what he remembered more than anything else was the fly-by of a fully restored Lancaster bomber. It was not an original, as there were only a few of the MK 11 bombers preserved. It was a later version which had no longer used the famous Rolls Royce engines. These were the American versions, but it was still unmistakably, a British bomber. Resplendent in its camouflage fuselage paint and black undercarriage, to ensure it was as difficult as possible to locate from below. It was a night time bomber, and Aubrey had heard it coming before any of the others. It was a big four engine bomber, that made a din as it flew directly over the village at low altitude, and dipping its' wings left, and then right, it had circled effortlessly. It appeared above the unchanged English countryside, as it may have done all those years ago, and in a gesture of fortitude, returned back over the village to pay homage to the sacrifice of a generation of women, of which there has been no equal.

Thankfully, a nation had endured these sacrifices, in order to preserve a way of life, which had the Nazi's managed to gain a foothold on English soil, may have changed forever. Aubrey remembered being so excited that he had run into the street and despite his mother's stern look of disapproval, had jumped up and down with the other village children, shouting their enthusiastic approval, and tossed his cap into the air and lost it in the furore that ensued.

"Your mother was very kind," remarked Margaret as Aubrey finished reading the article.

"Yes, she had gone to a lot of trouble and I still have the award she gave me." Turning, she had pointed at the Certificate of Service and Recognition, with its' blue ribbon waxed onto the bottom right corner, signed by HRH Princess Alice.

Why had Aubrey not seen it when he had scouted the walls earlier? He had tried desperately to avoid the stare of the man in the picture and had missed the framed certificate that hung right next to it. Aubrey now looked closer. The man seemed to be smiling ever so slightly and the smirk was gone. He was smiling more in approval Aubrey thought, and Margaret's image seemed radiant and alive, as she did even now.

"Your mother scouted the military records you know? She found the picture amongst the wartime archives!" Margaret's approval clearly evident.

"Your mother was a really nice lady," repeated Margaret. Aubrey's mother being referred to as a Lady was pleasing to Aubrey. It had been her lifetime ambition, to be recognized for what she had always aspired to - and now she was receiving the tribute, although in death, from someone equally deserving of recognition. He had discovered a real gem in Margaret.

"The Professor! He was the journalist who covered all your mother's events." He had moonlighted as a journalist to make additional income.

"Of course", replied Aubrey. Now it was clear. The Professor had never disclosed this to the students at Kings'. This would have been undignified for a professor at Cambridge. He had used a pseudonym.

'Well', thought Aubrey to himself, 'so the Professor wasn't entirely telling the truth.' It was clear to him now that the Professor's history with Finsbury went back a little further than he was letting on.

'Yes', he thought, more than replying. 'This will require some diplomacy and a smattering of humour – to get to the bottom of it all,' he chuckled to himself.

"Are you sure I can't get you some more tea," Margaret pleaded more than asked. She was enjoying the company so much and this was such a momentous occasion for her, it seemed a shame to spoil the moment. So with a final cup of tea served in Margaret's finest china cups, they sat and reminisced about Aubrey's mother and the long lost aviator.

It was around three in the afternoon when Aubrey finally made his apologies and promising to come back. It was a promise in all likelihood he would no be able to keep. As he stepped out onto the main road with Margaret muttering something behind him, he took a moment to stoop down and smell one of the fragrant roses in the hedgerow. It had an aroma that only an English Rose could. Lightly scented, but unmistakable!

"Floribunda" Margaret offered without his obvious request, which would have followed.

"That particular variety is named after the Queen Mother, 'Auguste Seebauer', a particularly healthy and reliable hedge rose." She was standing beside him taking in the aroma of one of the blooms, which rose to meet her five-foot frame.

"Do you know that I planted this from a cutting your mother gave me?" She was clearly proud of her prowess as a horticulturist.

"Mind you though, in this soil you could plant a dead twig and still end up with a forty foot Oak." She was being flippant. Aubrey could see that a great deal of love and attention had been devoted to that hedgerow.

"That must have been over thirty five years ago," she surmised. "It was after the ceremony here in Finsbury."

"Incredible. My Mom had just such a hedgerow in her rose garden." Aubrey was brought back to the summers of his childhood, storming through the spatial garden, as his mother on hands and knees tended her plants adoringly.

"Yes. I believe it is quite spectacular. I would love to see it?" she asked.

"It must be some eighty and ninety years old," Aubrey recalled.

"The Queen Mother was one hundred and two when she died, and the Grand Dame Alice, who was our Commandant in the WAAF, was also over a hundred years old!" She stated it as a matter of fact, but the irony was not lost on Aubrey. It seemed that everything, and everyone who evoked happiness in this world, was doomed to live to infirmity. The onset of longevity amongst the English was a peculiar trait, which was borne of their humble lifestyle and gracious love of the world and all in it.

"It is a pity those confounded Liberals in the Government seem intent on destroying our wonderful lifestyle. I mean it is almost one thing after the next. Never mind," She was now almost begrudgingly happy.

"At least by closing the Post Office, we have been blessed with the likes of the Professor!"

"Yes". Aubrey smiled. The Professor had a lot of explaining to do.

He said his goodbyes, and with the afternoon almost lost, he made his way back to the coffee shop.

Consumerism at its best, intent on changing their world, was not all that bad. However his thoughts were with Margaret, who had survived her nearly ninety years as a stalwart of British Conservatism. She would probably still

outlive a great deal of those protagonists clamouring for change in their social order.
Still deep in thought, he paced the one hundred or so yards back to the coffee shop.

"The Professor has been looking for you," a young watron with a funky hairstyle breathlessly interjected, stepping between Aubrey and the office door. Aubrey was somewhat bemused.

"Thank you," he was about to make the final step toward the door, but the youngster stood his ground. "What was his name?" Aubrey could not remember, "Was it Michael or Mikey?"

Not being one to miss what seemed like a good bit of intrigue, Aubrey paused, raising an eyebrow, he waited for Michael to speak.

"The Professor has been fretting about you. He did not know where you had gone." It a hushed tone, and a discreet flicker of his eyes towards the office door.

The degree of informality was not troubling to Aubrey, but it was a departure from the stuffiness evident at the manor house. He was now a little perplexed about the Professor's relationship with the staff at his establishment. He seemed to have a familiarity with his staff, and particularly with this youngster, that begged the question. Sure the rumours had floated around the boarding hostel at Kings' that the Professor was a 'fag' and that one needed to be careful when left alone in his company. But that was a long time ago and it seemed to Aubrey, that he personally had never given a jot to the rumour. There had never been an incident where his tutorage was in question, and Aubrey had never been left feeling uncomfortable in the Professor's company.

Even on the evenings spent in his company alone in his study, discussing the merits of egoism versus egotism. Why then did Aubrey have a feeling of unease about this situation now? Was it that the Professors familiarity with these youngsters was just too cosy or maybe he was just a little jealous of the lack of boundaries that were so evident in this informal little Coffee Shop?

The Professor had always been a father figure to Aubrey, filling a void that had been left by his own father's indifference, and now he felt a little envious of the other younger men with whom the Professor had developed a relationship. The affable Professor was an enigma. Armed with a little more knowledge and some interesting titbits from Margaret, Aubrey thanked Michael for the forewarning and headed for the Professor's office door.

The Professor looked up cheerfully as Aubrey stepped in. He was seated behind his computer and a thick pile of books were neatly stacked against the far side of the cherry wood desk. Aubrey responded cheerfully too.

"Been having tea with Margaret," he explained before the Professor could ask.

He raised his eyebrows heavenward while giving the Professor a conspiratorial wink, indicating the intrigue that he had been a party too. The Professor responded nonchalantly.

"Ahh, so you have been to see the local celebrity." He remarked.

"But surely, you did not enter her humble abode?" The Professor likewise intrigued.

"Oh! Yes," replied Aubrey, giving more emphasis to the plot that was unfolding. "And guess what I saw?"

Aubrey now had the Professor's full attention. He was no longer perusing the computer screen, but watched Aubrey avidly, waiting for more information.

"What now?" He questioned, as Aubrey dragged out the suspense-filled moment, before continuing.

"A picture of my mother with Margaret, and guess who I found out was the journalist who took the photo?"

Obviously the Professor knew the answer to this riddle, but he was more curious to know what the inside of Margaret's little cottage looked like.

"Tell me everything," he breathlessly commanded more than questioned and Aubrey decided to let him off the hook.

"Very modest," he responded, "but what a history, the lady has."

"What did you discuss," the Professor needed to know more about the conversation. He knew what was coming, but needed Aubrey to say it.

"Well, it was mostly to do with my mother," remarked Aubrey.

"It seems she had done some charitable work for the community. I wasn't aware of the Village Guild Association and the work done for ex-servicemen and women."

Aubrey went on to explain that his mother had always kept her extra curricula activities very private because Lord Pennington often disapproved. Aubrey had not really been involved too much because of his incarceration at St Georges' and then Eton. Except, that is, for the time she knew he would love to see the flyover of the aircraft.

"Yes, your mother was a remarkable woman," replied the Professor. He had not had the question he needed answered and was not about to ask Aubrey directly. He skirted the issue to see if Aubrey took the bait.

"Did Margaret show you any more pictures of her late husband?"

"Yes, what a remarkably story," was Aubrey's response. "I can understand why she never remarried."

"Ah, yes, she was completely overwhelmed by their romance and then was left devastated by his death. She blamed herself."

Aubrey could understand that, but there was a nagging question in his mind. She had selflessly put aside all egoism to honour his memory. And in so doing had never entertained the thought of egotism, tirelessly holding Sam above all else, in a tribute to his contributions.

"Despite the fact that she has always said she was not the marrying type," added the Professor.

"Margaret had been besotted by him. I honestly think she used the whole disinterest in other men as a means to fend off any possibility she may once again find the bliss she had touched. Even if seemingly for a brief moment. But I expect she had a far more soulful relationship than one could imagine!"

Indeed, she had, thought Aubrey. That relationship still lived on and was not a figment of just her imagination.

"What does 'not the marrying type' mean, exactly?" Aubrey saw this as an opening to the conversation he now wished to pursue.

"It means she wore comfortable shoes and had a cat." The Professor would not be drawn. The Professor could see that he was not following the gist of the conversation.

"In other words dear fellow," he commented, "she would not have been happy living with another man!"

"So if she had met someone, it may not have necessarily been a man?" Aubrey belaboured the point, hoping to move the subject in the direction he needed.

"No, no she was a …" The Professor was about to demean their friendship by justifying an answer. It was obvious that Aubrey was not about to ask the question the Professor most feared, he turned the conversation to something more topical.

"Did you know that she is eighty nine years old?" The Professor was distinctly impressed. The grand old dame of Finsbury was everybody's favourite old aunty.

"Well, I did not know how old exactly, but that would seem about right," replied Aubrey.

"Margaret and I have been acquainted for more than forty odd years." The Professor explained.

"So how long had you known my mother?" Aubrey asked. It was a natural progression to the conversation.

The Professor shift uncomfortably in his seat.

"Your mother and I met at college," The Professor paused before answering.

"Really, that long ago!" was Aubrey's immediate reaction. "You never told me."

"Steady on," replied the Professor. "It was a while ago, but not what you think."

This answer raised more interesting possibilities than it answered.

"I met your mother at University, in Manchester. It was whilst I was a junior lecturer."

"Your mother and I became good friends. She expressed a desire for deeper learning, so I developed a mentoring program for your Mom and she became an Arts Major. She did not stop there and was referred to a fellow colleague of mine at King's where she went to complete a Masters in Social studies." Aubrey listened intently.

"While I remained in Manchester, your Mother had somehow concocted a plan and found me a position at Cambridge. Then my acceptance as a Fellow at King's and a lifetime Professorship." He continued. They had both got what they had always desired - The Professor got his professorship and Aubrey's mother became accepted into the society circles of her educated peers.

"Why Cambridge?" Aubrey had sunk lower into his chair.

"We were both Catholic." It made sense. They were both Northerners.

"So why did she marry a toff from the south?" Aubrey quizzed.

"Your Mom met Lord Pennington at the Henley regatta." Aubrey's mother had learnt the subtle art of association early.

"Your Mom was ambitious and discovered a means of using social engineering to her advantage. She realized that the only way to benefit from the class system was to play them at their own game." Aubrey wondered if perhaps there was a hint of the Professor's tutorage there.

There was a natural empathy between the two evident in their casual remarks, and open discussion. The Professor was frank in his responses to Aubrey's questions and likewise Aubrey had little to hide from the Professor. So they continued talking long into the night. It was around eleven in the evening when Aubrey and the Professor, well 'oiled', on a good cognac finally said goodnight to the staff.

Aubrey finally felt that he could broach the subject he wanted to, so with a casual glance towards the Professor, Aubrey asked.

"So Prof, is there anyone I should know about?" Aubrey could honestly not recall ever having seen the Professor with any romantic interest, since he had known him.

"Go steady, old fellow," was the Professor's instinctive reply, but Aubrey, determined to find out knew that he had the Professor by the proverbial 'jugular'.

"The only reason I ask, is that I happened to notice an exchange between yourself and Sean the other day which puzzled me!"

The Professor guffawed twice. Partly brought on by the fumes created when swallowing a considerable mouthful of the magenta liquid. Aubrey continued his interrogation.

"Now where on earth do you get these ideas from Aubrey?" The Professor rebutted.

The moment was slipping away from him, but Aubrey had the advantage. This was a fine line he had simply overstepped, but he remained quiet, raising his left eyebrow.

The Professor's usually calm, collected countenance was off-set by his ruddy complexion illuminated by a colour that spread quickly to his neck; so much so that Aubrey thought he already had his answer.

Catching his breath, the Professor responded.

"Aubrey, there are some things that must remain private; but seeing as you are being so brutally direct which I would normally ignore. I am going to give you this answer."

The office was hauntingly quiet; a far cry from the frenetic daily hub-hub.

"There are certain things I have kept to myself from the beginning. Certain issues have been kept private, because…well because that is the way they should be. My private life has never been questioned either professionally or otherwise, and that is the way I prefer to keep it. However," he continued, after a deliberate pause in which he rolled his head sideways to the left, his eyes followed the direction of his head.

Then, just as certainly, without turning his head back, his eyes fixed on Aubrey.

This was his 'tell', and Aubrey knew instinctively it was the truth.

"If you need to know. Yes I have had a very discreet and lengthy relationship, but not the one with whom you surmised it to be. The gentleman shall remain nameless for his own privacy and I shall not venture any more information, for his discretion. Suffice it to say, there are certain things your mother asked me to keep from you, but which, shocking as it may be to me now, I feel it is incumbent on me to tell you the truth."

The cognac had made his brain fuzzy and his thoughts quite erratic, but despite the alcohol, the Professor kept his response measured and even.

"Your mother and I had a very special relationship. She was a great friend to me right to the end and confided in me. The news I am going to give you now may be shocking for you and may change your life forever, so stop me if you must." This was not a threat but a warning of what was to come.

Aubrey felt the pang of remorse for having asked. He now realized that it was he that was now on the back foot.

The Professor continued, "Your mother had confided in me years ago, that there were certain family secrets which she would advise me of, but that I in turn was to swear secrecy to her. Which I did! But now she has passed on and as shocking as it will be to you; I feel it is necessary for me to advise you about. In light of your illness, and that there is no obvious heir to your fortune."

Aubrey sat forward in his chair, no longer lounging back casually. His attention was riveted to the professor's face, eyes and every word. He felt that he was indeed about to hear something of great import. Perhaps the very thing that Aubrey had always known about innately.

"Sean Hightop, (aka) Sean Bridges, his mother's maiden name, was adopted by Mr. Hightop when he was born." He paused; took a deep breath.

"As the son of an illegitimate union with one of the kitchen staff, Bessie, he was obviously an embarrassment to the family and Mr. Hightop chose to become his guardian and his father. Despite the obvious age difference, he in fact became a very positive father figure. So, Sean grew up on the Estate with all the benefits of having a real family around him."

The Professor was now whispering but Aubrey dared not interrupt. He knew, what was coming. But nonetheless Aubrey steeled himself for this information.

"So you understand now why there is a pact between Sean, Mr. Hightop and myself!"

The Professor was asking a rhetorical question, and Aubrey was about to glean the relevance of it. There was no conjecture required.

The Professor continued.

"Sean is not Mr. Hightop's son! But then you knew that didn't you Aubrey?"

It was obvious that they did not look remotely similar, and Aubrey had noted this fact on their very first meeting at the airport.

The Professor went on.

"He was brought up on the Estate as though he were one of the family."

Aubrey wasn't quite sure what the Professor meant by "the family", but still had not recognized the curve ball as it was delivered.

The Professor paused to let Aubrey take it all in. He was watching Aubrey for a glimmer of recognition to make the conclusion less painful.

Aubrey's pupils dilated. It was intuitive and the Professor knew at once, that Aubrey had visualized the subject of this conversation.

Aubrey's eyes darted back to the Professor. The affirmation was just a hint of a smile on the Professor's lips that told Aubrey he had seen the natural conclusion to his thoughts.

"You see, Sean's real father is none other than Lord Pennington himself."

'Yes. It was obvious now,' thought Aubrey. 'The image he had seen was a black and white picture of his father as a young cadet at Sandhurst, some forty years before. A picture Aubrey had seen in a family album once, but which bore a remarkable resemblance to Sean.

Aubrey sank back in to his chair.

Chapter 16

A sinking feeling

There was a errie clinginess to the mist that sapped the air, like the worms of the Mopani trees on the outskirts of the camp. The road had been severely rutted by the rains, and Aubrey slowed to a crawl, as he approached the large Baobab, which had always tweaked his imagination. It had stood sentry over their camp for the six years Aubrey had been in Zimbabwe, and even when the Zimbabwe Dollar had sunken like a proverbial stone in the murky waters of the Chinoi caves, it had not mattered. Foreign revenues were being emptied into that bottomless sink hole and the currency's fall was unfathomable. But to most whose livelihoods it affected, the damage it wrought was real. Aubrey had known that truth. The people in power had no intention of sharing their new economic prosperity with the rest of its citizens; and the world turned a blind eye, because the economics of this tiny landlocked African country was of no importance.

But as he rounded that physically impressive tree, whose size had ensured that the entrance, and exit road, were to resemble a traffic circle, broad enough to hide a car; he could not sense the joy, rounding that tree, had always brought him. This morning, he felt no joy at all. The tree stood, almost dormant, as it had done for countless centuries before. Only growing in spurts, as the rains brought sustenance. The roots beneath the ground held that immense girth upright, but this morning, for some reason, Aubrey, like the tree, felt drained and inert.

The Elephants were in the paddock, impatiently awaiting the next tour group. But, this morning, there was to be none. The business was floundering, the Elephants could sense this. There was a tangible dullness to the air, and it choked, rather than provoked the imagination.

Aubrey found himself missing Bronwyn, as indeed did the Elephants. She had stayed in Port Elizabeth with Edward and her parents, but left Aubrey to collect their worldly possessions and his thoughts. He was needed to continue looking after the Elephants, but what he truly desired, would have brought him into direct conflict with the company, who was now the only shareholder; and the potential risk of spending a long time in a notoriously unhealthy Zimbabwean jail cell.

Life at the Falls was becoming difficult. The grocery shop was a sad reflection of an economy on the brink. At six that morning, before the start of his day, he had taken his bundle of Zim dollars collected from the bank the day before, and arrived at the supermarket doors to ensure the bread, milk and other basics were available and fresh. This had been Bronwyn's job, and he now had a true appreciation of how bad it had become in the last year. Standing in a queue, Aubrey found himself fighting with the local inhabitants, for loaves of bread, which were far from plentiful. This function of his daily routine was becoming a bind, yet it was essential. He felt the effect like a Biblical chapter, and was all too conscious of the plight of the average Zimbabwean.

Yet it was humour which would prevail, and he recalled Timothy at a service at the Catholic Church in Borrowdale, where they had attended the previous Christmas midnight mass. As the priest, had called the Holy Eucharist, and the handful of congregants had stood, Timothy remarked somewhat irreverently, 'Oh God. Not another bread queue!' The thought had brought a momentary smile to his face; but it was short lived.

Despite finding the opportunity to laugh in the face of adversity, Aubrey was more than disillusioned and was now finding the going difficult. All the work that had gone before was to no avail. He could sense the decline in the living standards, and had not ever known this level of hardship. Yet the average Zimbabwean had been through this before, and regardless of the anarchical policies of Mugabe, they endured.

But there was a far more sinister force at work, he believed, and it was this effort to destabilize the economy that had truly seen the rapid decline that was now so self-evident. It was beyond rationale to expect a landlocked country with limited resources, and a socialist agenda, to be able to remain a powerful economic force in the region. Yet the irony was the sudden emergence of the Zambian tourism trade based around Livingstone. Large conglomerates were building hotels and casinos across the river, literally a stone's throw from the bridge which separated Zimbabwe and Zambia.

The hotels on the Zimbabwean side had low occupancy rates and the trade was simply moving to Zambia, a mere gorge separating the two. It may as well have been an abyss, because the tourism trade to Victoria Falls was drying up, like the proverbial main stretch of the falls during the winter months. The scale of the rift was astounding. The historical tables had turned, and where the Zambian tourist trade had always been the poor brother to Zimbabwe, there was now a sense that Zimbabwe was the forgotten comrade to its Capitalist brother across the divide.

That gorge, stood as a stark reminder of exactly who controlled the purse strings of a world economy. Mugabe was riling the West with his bombastic tirades, yet despite all his learned philosophy, he had not learnt from the lessons of history. Mugabe had simply backed the wrong horse and the North Koreans, stood as a testament to that futility.

As Aubrey circumnavigated the tree, he turned the steering wheel towards the boma and brought the Pajero to a gentle halt. Despite this, the tyres slid across the dusty car park. He climbed down from the driver's side. The wheels were turned full lock, to the left, but the tread was non-existent.

The Elephants swayed rhythmically, to and fro. The youngsters in the middle of the group, Lesidwa and the older females on the periphery of the huddle. It was as though they could read his thoughts.

Aubrey moved lethargically towards the group. There was no urgency; no expectant fanfare of trumpeted calls, or swishing trunks, stabbing the air and sensing his odour, as they had always greeted him. Eyesight was unnecessary, when the sense of smell was twenty thousand times stronger than human olfactory glands. But this morning there was no necessity for even that. The Elephant were aware of his approach, but they were not roused.

Aubrey leaned in against the large wooden poles of the paddock. They stood as an affront to the very freedoms that had been so passionately fought for, in the Zimbabwe of the liberation years. But, even those freedoms were selective and the desire for economic prosperity had tainted his own morality. Aubrey realised then, he had been misguided. How he had arrived at this juncture in his life? He would want to do some soul searching.

Standing with Timothy in the near-empty bar of the old Victoria Falls hotel that evening, Aubrey lamented.

"If there was ever an example of how two fundamental principles could be at odds with one another, this is a prime example."

"The difference between Livingston and Victoria Falls is becoming a real issue. The Tourist dollars are flowing to the Zambian side, so we have opened a concession across the bridge in Zambia." Timothy shrugged his shoulders.

"Money will always find the low ground. It flows like that river; but now it's all in the direction of Livingstone and Zambia."

Aubrey understood the economic powers that dictated the flow of this capital would always ensure it flowed in the direction of profit and maximum return.

"Zimbabwe has become the economic back water of the region," Timothy was pragmatic.

It was like the magnificent Chobe River that sustained the Elephant herds of Northern Botswana. It fed back into an environment that was parched of sustenance, devoid of life and withering in the harsh African environment. It could only sustain so many Elephant, and like the Zimbabwe they now encountered, Aubrey had realised their dream of a predictable future had ended.

"Do you know how much a paper toilet roll with one hundred squares costs?" Timothy was flippant.

"I know! It is more expensive than a wad of Zimbabwean 'one dollar notes', bundled together." Aubrey had noticed.

"Ya, but despite the obvious abrasive qualities, it would be cheaper to use, and let's face it." Timothy continued.

"I'm going to wait until the notes with Mugabe's face on them are worthless." Timothy dug his elbow into Aubrey's side.

"Listen, Tim." The last double scotch was warming the pit of his stomach, and taking the edge off of what had been a sad farewell to his Elephants.

"I have decided to travel to join Bronwyn in Port Elizabeth." This was the coastal city in South Africa, where Bronwyn's parents had decided to emigrate after Tony had retired from his partnership at an auditing firm in Harare.

"Okay, I understand." Timothy stared at Aubrey's reflection in the large ornate mirror across the bar counter. He was looking older than he remembered.

"I must warn you Tony was an influential member of the Southern African branch of Chartered Accountants. He has probably looked after himself pretty nicely."

"Yes, I believe he had made a few significant investments over the years." Having bargained on the Zimbabwe economy collapsing entirely, Tony had taken his golden handshake from the firm, and settled in Port Elizabeth with his wife Val, and his guaranteed Pension, astutely invested offshore. Able to buy himself the apartheid he could no longer enjoy in Zimbabwe.

There was nothing racist in his assertion, but that he would choose to live within the community he long aspired to. One which for the last twenty years had eluded him whilst working in the ivory tower that was his office in the now aptly named Samora Machel Avenue. Built in 1960, as an icon of capitalism, the offices stood for many years as the pinnacle of Africa Architecture, built by a leading assurance company, whose pension plans were now worthless. Communism was dead as an economic philosophy, and not even the grossly obtuse effigy of that man that stood atop the building that had housed its empire, could become a beacon of hope.

"He has an English pension and a house bought with the proceeds of all his business endeavours." Aubrey realised he was not envious. Val, Bronwyn and the young Edward, were now happily ensconced in South Africa, and Val deserved some happiness.

The Zimbabwean government blindly pursued their failing socialist policies and the country became poorer by the day. Not even the power of the all-conquering US dollar, which drove the economies of these third world Kleptocracies, would save them. It was obtuse to consider in this world of plenty, that there were so few who had managed to elevate themselves beyond poverty.

"Old Tony, certainly has an eye for real estate!" Aubrey leaned over his third tall glass. "He has invested into some property on the south coast, outside Port Elizabeth.

"Yes. I have had some dealings with him before." Timothy was vague.

"Well he certainly seems to have managed his finances well!" Aubrey rued the day he had not listened to the old man.

"He is shrewd, for sure! But I would not trust him too much." Timothy's quick glance was all the affirmation Aubrey required.

"He told Bronwyn to tell me to sign that N.D.A. with you," Aubrey shifted on his barstool.

"Wouldn't have mattered," Timothy shot back. "Look where we all are now."

"Eem, I suppose you're right. I have never had a keen business sense anyway." Aubrey took a slug. The ice clattered against his teeth. He winced. "Damn filling needs replacing."

"The company has transferred me from Marketing Director." Timothy never looked up from his drink. "Sideways promotion. The Board feels I am a little too exuberant with the company's money."

"What are we going to do with the Elephants?" Aubrey clenched his jaw, feeling the offending molar with his tongue. It did not feel like anything. It was numb.

"We may have to sell them to another concession, but I don't really have a say anymore." Timothy lifted a hand in the direction of Moses behind the bar. They stood silently as the drinks were delivered.

It was to this substantial home on the beach south of Port Elizabeth, that Tony and Val had retired. The economic wealth of Zimbabwe was draining south and knowing how to move funds from a country with very strict exchange controls was a definite asset. It was this stripping of the wealth of Zimbabwe which had led to the escalation in an already unpredictable financial situation, with everyone looking out for themselves, and a significant meltdown about to occur. Tony had spent the last five years of his working career channelling these funds for high profile clients, after seeing that emerging Kleptocracy in Zimbabwe wreak havoc on its economy. It was a rush to remit whatever funds could be transferred into accounts in South Africa, and Tony was well rewarded for his initiative. A life well lead, would be rewarded by a peaceful existence in post-apartheid Port Elizabeth.

Port Elizabeth nestled on the southern coast of the Eastern Cape of South Africa, was a natural harbour with a mainland curving north-eastward and acting as a barrier to the South-Westerly, as it blew in from the Antarctic. The city, founded by the 1820 settlers, and an industrial city with a predominantly working class population, had been the centre of the labour unrest in Apartheid South Africa. Now it lay as a testimony to the ravages of post-apartheid planning. The houses on the outskirts of the city reminded Aubrey of pictures of gulags in Russia. No names or signposts offered him direction. As with Harare during the period post-liberation, street signs, and old colonial names, were a luxury the incumbent political power had no need of.

This was the absurd vista that greeted Aubrey as he drove into the suburbs of Port Elizabeth twenty-four hours later. Every house was guarded by a private security company, and fences, palisade grills, and dogs, were plainly evident. It was almost as though, having relented to the political tsunami that flooded the country after 1994, property owners were now hunkered down, awaiting the next onslaught.

It was the systemic rationalization of a society which had become used to crime and violence. No other society was prone to these security measures in quite the same way as middle class South Africans. Where other societies relied on their taxpayer's money, to provide the security and safety of its citizens through an effective functioning Police Service; South Africans paid their taxes, but relied on a security company to patrol their homes.

Aubrey realised that no longer would the rule of law prevail. It was either to live like this, or be subject to the vagaries of a Mugabe regime, which had already set the bar in terms of how others would behave. By his corrupt and inept tenureship, he had managed to destroy an entire economy, and subvert an entire civilization. Aids, cholera and hunger were the norm.

The call of the African bushveld, had given way to the realities of a financial burden which now harkened. Aubrey had suffered the agony of considering the loss of his Elephants. It was inevitable; he had to choose between the love of the woman he adored, and the love he had for his Elephant. He knew, however, that his Elephant's would remember him.

He was just grateful that he was in Bronwyn's arms and their reunion was a passionate one.

P.E. as it was affectionately known, as a port city, with very little for a guy with no qualifications and a history in the tourism business, was not exactly welcoming. Despite this Aubrey pounded the pavements looking for work. With little or no tourism to be had in this lifeless city, the only other possibility was the Addo Elephant Park and their work with the local Elephant.

Consequently, Aubrey did what was expected of him and he ploughed the tourist shops and spoke to the tourism office staff on the beach front. He was looking for ideas, and a month had already elapsed. It was going to be a push to find anything suitable; that is until one day at a small steak restaurant at the local strip mall, he happened upon his ex-scuba diving partner David Cohen, sitting at the bar.

"Well hello David," Aubrey had offered, having come directly into his personal space as he sat, holding court on a wrought iron barstool.

Aubrey stood over him, giving him no opportunity to avoid the intrusion.

David flinched, like a boxer about to take evasive action from a blow.

"Hell.....hello Aubrey!" There was an awkward moment as he assessed the situation, as a startled antelope might regard an on-coming truck.

"What the hell are you doing in P.E.?" They had not seen each other for over six years and Aubrey was now bigger and far more self-assured than David had remembered.

A somewhat vivacious brunette, sat clutching her handbag on a barstool next to David. She smiled awkwardly at Aubrey.

"I am here with Bronwyn", replied Aubrey, motioning over his shoulder to the table where he had just abandoned Bronwyn somewhat hastily, to make his way to the bar.

Bronwyn was looking in their direction, but had not seen, nor recognized David. Aubrey smiled and waved, which had the desired effect of drawing Bronwyn's attention to the man sitting on the barstool next to him. Bronwyn could see the outline of a handsome face which had now given way to a more defined, sharper nose, which made a startling pronouncement.

"Bronwyn?" He followed Aubrey's gaze. There was no hint of recognition.

David had aged, and his features had become more haggard, the jaw line appeared weaker as the nose had begun to take over what had become a wizened, older face.

"We are living here now," Aubrey returned.

"Is that Bronwyn from Cape Maclear?" David was incredulous.

After his initial shock, the confidence tinged with a definite bravado returned. He had still not introduced Aubrey to the brunette, who soon began to lose interest in their conversation, and turned to chat to her female companion.

David could see Bronwyn still had the firm body of a woman in her prime, unaltered by the life changing hormones of childbirth, but she had a glow, which was more evident in the colder climes of the P.E. winter. Her freckles, once a blend of her sun-streaked complexion, were clearer, on a skin which now had the iridescence of a soap bubble, and the consistency of a ripe plum.

He stood to shake Aubrey's hand. David was now edging to get away from the bar.

"Let's go say hello." David suggested, as the barman passed the drinks Aubrey had ordered. With drinks in hand, Aubrey lead the way, with David leaving the bar without even so much as a cursory goodbye to his female companions.

Aubrey admired Bronwyn's elegant beauty, and her gracious hospitality, as she sat at the table, and welcomed David. He gave no hint of his previous discomfort.

"You remember David from Cape Maclear?" Aubrey introduced.

"Yes." She smiled easily.

"Well it turns out, he is now living in P.E." Aubrey's tone was matter of fact; Bronwyn saw the daggers behind those passive blue eyes.

"That is serendipitous. Of all the places in South Africa to live? What made you decide on P.E.?"

"This is the fastest growing economic zone in the country." David imparted knowledge with eloquent gamesmanship.

"Yes. So we have heard." Bronwyn nodded.

"So, what are you doing for work?" David would be gallant if required.

"Well, if there is scope to begin an Elephant concession on a private game reserve, we may explore that avenue."

"You know about Elephant?" David was interested.

"Yes, Aubrey and I have run an Elephant operation at Vic Falls for the past six years."

"At Vic falls?" There was maybe just what could have been a hint of something, which Aubrey read in his eyes. It was fleeting; but it was there.

"Yes, Elephants of Africa, we started it."

"Oh, so you are running a safari business?" The interest waned.

"Yes, that is, we were in the tourism business." Bronwyn acknowledged.

"You were?" David was not so effusive.

"Well we sold up, and are looking to reinvest here." Bronwyn smiled easily.

"Investing here?" David was gazing more intently, having shut Aubrey off from the conversion somewhat, repositioning his chair. He was a gambler. One eye on his cards, the other on the exit.

"We are thinking of an Elephant conservancy."

"I would not know too much about that." It seemed his interest was no longer piqued.

"So you are not in the tourism business?" Bronwyn ventured.

"No, well yes, if you call it that." He made no effort to elaborate.

"Hey Mom." The interruption came relievingly from Edward. He had returned from having played in the kid's zone with some local boys.

"Please may I have a coke?" He directed his question to Bronwyn.

David watched, the relief of having to impart any more information, was now superseded by the interruption.

"Of course you may." Bronwyn relented. She would ordinarily not allow him to indulge in the highly sugarised fizzy drinks.

"Here we go," Aubrey stood, offering Edward a ten rand note from his wallet.

The interruption was telling in more ways than one. Bronwyn watched David, as a hint of an imbedded prejudice seemed to cloud his dark eyes.

He was gushing and overzealous in his complementary offerings, but like the weasel he was, his guard was soon down. The drinks flowed, the excuses flowed, and the charm oozed. They reminisced about Malawi for the remainder of the evening, with David skilfully navigating his way around the subject that they all knew would come. Aubrey was content to allow them to talk, taking in the subtle intimations and carefully barbed comments, as Bronwyn milked David for all he was worth.

"So you sold your Zimbabwean business?"

"No. We got screwed out of our controlling shares and sold the remainder back to our partner," she jibed. David flinched ever so subtly, but it was there. Aubrey could see he was now completely on defence.
"Shit man, was that a lot of cash?" he countered with a swaying defensive side-step.

"Yes. Quite a bit, but we landed back on our feet," she was all attack.

"Ohh, I would imagine a good-looking gal and … guy like you will always get by!" He was show-boating for his audience whilst trying to smother the blows.

"Not if we don't find some work here," she jabbed tentatively.

"What exactly are you involved in?" Aubrey had unleashed Bronwyn.

"Oh, I am managing a dive shop on the beach front." Aubrey watched as he stroked his nose, suggestively. I was his 'tell'.

"A dive shop?" Aubrey was intrigued.

"Yes, but nothing much really. We still offer dives and courses, but the market has not been very lucrative." Aubrey said nothing.

"So, if the shop is not making any money, how do you survive?" Bronwyn was all empathy.

"Well, it is really a small part of a bigger business. We also supply curios from Central Africa."

"Curios?" Bronwyn smiled.

"Yes, but we have to get permits, and it is strictly controlled now." David looked past them both. A man stood at the bar. He was short, plump, and had a shaven head. Despite the air conditioning, Aubrey noticed him patting down his brow, as he spoke to the two female companions David had not introduced.

"Well, you guys should come down to the dive shop and maybe we can get you set-up." He was smiling as he lay back across the ropes.

"Yes. Thank you. But I am not sure if Aubrey wants to get involved in the dive business again." He flinched once again, having missed the low blow as it connected with his manly parts.

If her taunts had hit home, he was now showing no sign of his guilt. He sat poker faced whilst Bronwyn offered her opinion on how difficult it must have been to start all over again. She made no mention of the Rolex Seamaster on his wrist when she had asked for the time.

"I am sure we can help," he schmoozed. Then graciously offered to pay for their meal. Aubrey resisted and paid the bill as it arrived.

No sooner was the offer on the table, then David had stood. Thanking them, he returned to the bar, and a heated discussion with the bald, fat man.

Bronwyn chatting animatedly all the way home. They lay in bed, and listened quietly as Edward shifted and moaned in his sleep next door. Despite this Bronwyn seemed content. Aubrey listened as she spoke about their run in with David. She was an eternal optimist; Aubrey was not. As they were drifting off to sleep, Bronwyn said, unexpectedly.

`I don't think I will dive tomorrow."

"Uuhmmm." Aubrey was gone.

Aubrey and Bronwyn were to pop around to the shop the next day to meet David and have a look at the dive shop. Aubrey dreamed of floating, weightlessly through the pristine waters off Cape Maclear. He dreamt of the myriad of colourful cichlid fish that made up the abundant life around the rocky outcrops that were Otter Point, Thumbi West and the beautiful surge zones, deeply rooted below the surface off Nakantenga Island. The rifts and caves, with waiting faces, popped out at him as he moved seamlessly with the current. The tiny fish species of Lake Malawi, abundant and innocuous.

They arrived the next morning at the dive shop in the central business district, and immediately had been offered a trip out to one of the newly surveyed dive sites. Aubrey had not dived for six years, if he did not count the snorkelling episode at Kariba; but that was a whole story on its own. The prospect of diving again was like magic to Aubrey and so they launched off the beach destined for the dive site called White Sands.

He may not have dived, but his instinct was still primed. Bronwyn was not feeling well, as they reached the dive zone. She remained on board, whilst the young Edward was happily playing with some friends on the local beach. She was now aware, she should not have entertained this invitation. Her stomach queasy and the launch into the surf, a masterful display of boatmanship, had nonetheless left her feeling nauseous.

The South African coastal waters lay atop the enormous ledge that ran the length of the southern continent. The up swell from the vast Indian Ocean rolling in from the east, merged with the cooler Atlantic waters bringing a multitude of oceanic life that lay outside the perimeter of the continental shelf. This was a destination to which the abundant life forms from the depths converged, and was the birthplace of the dramatic stories of pre-historic creatures, which have captured the imaginations of marine biologists and formed the basis for the emergence of Algoa Bay as a prime scuba diving destination.

Mere seconds in evolutionary terms separated this world of majestic life forms, from a subspecies of ancient looking fish that had evoked such passionate debate over the last century. Caught in a fishing net off the coastline further north, was a fish once considered extinct. The Coelacanth had since been discovered in various other sites, at depths once deemed to be below human endurance. Subsequently those detractors had been proved wrong, but at the cost of human life. It was over a site which induced this type of passion for the unknown that they now waited, as David and Aubrey, and the dive-master Hendrik, secured their gear.

The South African coastline was a mysterious place, as the tectonic plates had lifted this enormous continent off the bottom of the Indian Ocean like a meat cleaver through a pork chop. The staggering oceanography of the continental shelf emerged from the abyss sixty miles from the coast. Here at Riy Banks, was the reef which lay at an average of 24 metres, and it was spectacular.

Thirty minutes from launch, where the warm Benguela current met the outflow from the Gamtoos and a number of other rivers, bringing with it the sediment from inland, and a rich source of food for oceanic predators. The sharks glided with impunity through this thick porridge of terrestrial fodder. Within this abundant food source, these sharks reigned supreme. On the perimeter of this outflow was the largest congregation of Ragged Tooth and Leopard Sharks.

The sun was almost at its apex when they had slipped into the water, and the sun shone through the murky water with a dazzling effect that seemed to accentuate every creature below the surface. It was an optical illusion, but as the three divers hit the bottom, Aubrey found himself in a veritable wonderland where nothing seemed real on that vast plateau beneath the quarrelsome ocean waves.

The abundance of life was staggering as the visibility at that depth was excellent. The dive site was just as impressive, with wide stretches of sand separated by gullies and huge sand castles into and through which the alien Manta rays flew, like Enochian angels skimming the tall Carnation Tree coral which mesmerised his eyes with in its bright red conglomerates. The rays fed from the vast store of plankton that welled up from the lower edges of the continental plateau and seemed to hover slowly, as if watching over them.

The dive was planned for forty minutes, but after three or four minutes of bottom time, Aubrey started feeling light headed, and as David and Hendrik seemed to disappear behind a sand bank, he was left on his own to enjoy this moment and be in touch with his extraordinary senses. He floated with the current, conserving his air by not resisting the ebb and flow of the warm onshore tide. By allowing the natural force of the current to move him he felt euphoric, like an ethereal being elevated above this world. He was caught in the rapture of the moment, taking in the immense splendour of the site.

Then when Aubrey thought he might pass out from his reverie, something innately spiritual occurred. He had begun to feel as though this out of body experience was exactly that, and a sense of foreboding washed over him. Pausing between a long hollow in-breath, he raised his head to look towards the surface, remembering to check on the whereabouts of the buoy-line which Hendrik carried. He could not see it, but he could fortuitously see the bottom of the dive boat to his left, whilst the sun blotted out his vision to the right.

As he stared transfixed by the sun's rays reaching down through the water he suddenly became paranoid. As a dagga addict, might suddenly lapse into a feeling of intense fear, after the initial ecstasy of his first 'hit', Aubrey became aware of a desperate need to breath. As he gazed towards the light, his claustrophobia became like tunnel vision, channelling that view towards the light. Around the disc-like sun that appeared to sashay across the surface, he saw angels beckoning to him. He began to smile to himself. This was what heaven would be he surmised.

He was in utopia, and from there no force of evil would reach to him. Aubrey was content. Above him the light called, and below the world was at peace. Aubrey would allow himself to float off into this oblivion. But for a sudden, dramatic thought. Where was Bronwyn? He wanted her to experience this with him! He focused once more on the boat where he knew Bronwyn sat calmly watching the distant horizon, and fighting her own nausea. In so doing, he realized that the angels floating above were in fact sharks. Paranoia set in once more. He could for a moment focus, and in that moment, he saw them, circling like demons, highlighted by the sun spiralling inexorably, they waited.

Aubrey immediately and instinctively hit his inflation valve, and as his buoyancy compensator inflated, he began to rise, immeasurably at first, and then as the air in his BC expanded with the lessening of pressure, he rocketed to the surface; straight through the centre of the spinning mêlée of sharks, but untouched and valiant, he remembered to raise his fist as he breached the surface, like some comic book hero.

Bronwyn saw him erupt from the oceans depths, and without a moment's hesitation was into the water and having dislodged his demand valve from his mouth, had him in a lifesaver's embrace, and was trailing him back to the boat, Aubrey gasping for air. He was hauled over the side unceremoniously by the skipper, grabbing him by the BC, he first plunged him back under the surface, swallowing a mouthful of putrid saltwater, and as the buoyancy from his jacket took hold, he popped back out of the water, his lungs racked by a coughing fit.

Back in the boat, his equipment quickly stripped from him, Aubrey was able to take in the fresh sea breeze. That, and the boats' severe rocking motion made him instantly nauseous, and he was up and with his head over the side of the boat, feeding the fish. The imperceptible effect of the oxygen narcosis left him with a headache, but thankful nonetheless.

Aubrey recognised the symptoms, but said nothing.

He lay in the boat, propped up against Bronwyn as she wrapped him in a large beach towel. Aubrey became aware of the wind. It was tearing at the boat's flag, whipping through the skipper's dirty blonde, shoulder length hair. Aubrey watched him, as he reached for the cooler box, and was aware of the control he had of his station, but there was no hint he was a threat. The skipper was a youngish, lean looking Afrikaner who was chiselled and sun-baked by the years on board boat. Aubrey could not however, see what was going on behind the dark, wrap-around sunglasses.

It was miraculous, how some fate of genetics had gifted those who had the stronger melanin in their skin, with the ability of not burning in the harsh sun. Aubrey was aware as the skipper reached for a fruit juice in the cooler box strapped to the central lockers, that there was panic in the shaking of his seafarer's hands.

This was no coincidence! Aubrey recognized the taste that permeated his throat. It was sweet sickly bile that even his nausea could not mask. Aubrey knew instinctively that his air had been spiked.

The thought remained with him while Bronwyn administered the fruit juice to his swollen lips.

"How are you feeling?" She asked.

"Much better," the sugar and fructose was having the desired effect.

"What happened?" She was not feeling well herself, but had been convinced to join them despite her protest. She was glad now for that opportunity. Her place was next to Aubrey.

Bronwyn knew that this was part of their cathartic voyage of discovery. This would be their nadir, and the turning point that would bring them back up into a world that seemed for now, devoid of meaning; but ultimately to a place that promised redemption, within a vast ocean of guilt. Aubrey was wracked by the guilt of the accident. Reminded of it every time he looked at Edward. She would have to help him overcome it.

Aubrey began his recovery, with several deep intakes of fresh sea air. Controlling his breathing in the manner as a yoga teacher might, Aubrey soon had his heart rate down. After several minutes, he was able to sit up without feeling any further nausea, and a full thirty minutes later, David emerged from his dive.

The skipper, nimble and athletic went to his assistance.

David shucked off his tank, handing it to the skipper, and then hiked himself back onto the boat, unassisted. Turning to see Aubrey seated on the floor of the boat opposite him, a look of terror invaded those usually sanguine eyes.

It was the second time in twenty-four hours. Without having given Bronwyn or the skipper any further reason for concern, he had purposely awaited David's return, allowing him to finish his dive.

Aubrey could see into his soul, and what he saw was worrying. David's reaction was all the confirmation that Aubrey had needed. This was the actions of a desperate man. Aubrey said nothing.

He should not have dived without a refresher course, but his enthusiasm to get back in the water had been impulsive. Aubrey now saw why David had taken no heed of this generally accepted practice. Aubrey was certain of his motives. The tank had been filled before Aubrey and Bronwyn had arrived so he had not witnessed this for a fact, but he was adamant that the tank had been filled with spiked air. Aubrey had seen it once before, when during a typical power cut at Cape Maclear, they had run the generator for refilling the air tanks off a car engine. Carbon monoxide poisoning was a classic cause of nausea and could be fatal if gone un-noticed.

His watery grave would have left no evidence of any foul play, had he not reacted to his gut instinct. The angels he had seen were in fact just that. Perhaps an active imagination, or maybe a Divine hand. The winter season and the cold waters off P.E. would have ensured his body would have never been found. Aubrey would now have to watch out for both Bronwyn and himself.

They headed straight to the beach. Aubrey was feeling sufficiently recovered by the time they off-loaded their gear at the dive shop, but David made too much of the need for Aubrey to rest on a couch, so despite making a valiant effort to appear undeterred, he feigned further nausea, scouting the back of the dive shop looking for a toilet.

A rear-facing window gave him a view of the service area behind the shop. The bakkie was busy off-loading the dive tanks with the service crew hefting the bulky tanks onto a wooden crate. Then, with an air of expectation Aubrey watched as the dive tanks were purged of their contents, with a perceptibly 'fffwwwuuuu'.

As the technician turned to the last remaining tank on the bakkie, he pulled the smaller unused nine litre tank from its' resting spot on the vulcanized rubber load bay, and with no hesitation released its air.

Aubrey could now imagine to what level David would sink, in order to cover his tracks. But now, it was about survival, and Aubrey was in no doubts as to what fate would have befallen Bronwyn, had he himself not been able to save himself and get back to the boat.

Driving through the back streets of P.E. to their apartment, Aubrey's mind was racing. The evidence gone, and only some unsettled gut-feeling, gave Aubrey the adrenalin to figure his next move. They were not safe in P.E. Certainly not, as it seemed, with David intent on ensuring their silence, and a obvious Israeli Mafia, who were a prominent force in the city.

It would not help to alarm Bronwyn further, so Aubrey did what was expected. He swallowed his pride, and called Tony, to arrange for Bronwyn to move back to the house on the coast. Tony was surprisingly magnanimous, and instead of lecturing Aubrey, he made a phone call and then called Aubrey back. It was arranged. Aubrey would drive to Saint Francis Bay, dropping Bronwyn on the way. There he would meet someone called Victor.

The winter sun was streamed in through the lace curtains, but he had slept through the sunrise that caught the east facing tower block bedroom.

"How are you feeling this morning babes," Bronwyn was at his side, a look of concern that gave her angelic eyes even more depth.

"I'm okay," he lied. But the throbbing in the back of his head was still there. He was lucky. Lucky to have Bronwyn, and even more fortunate to be alive.

"Thank you toots," masking his discomfort, as she handed him a cup of tea.

"Okay to drive, or would you like me to?" He had also slept through her rush to the bathroom earlier, but she gave no hint of her own discomfort.

She had been rising early the last few days, and had spent some time in the bathroom the previous morning. He would need to ask her what was up. But this morning he had an important meeting.

"What time is the meeting?" Asked Aubrey, his thought process a little fuzzy, but his objective nonetheless assured.

"Nine and we have to get through the morning traffic." Bronwyn was still by his side, as she watched him sip his tea. It was hot and the steam drifted off the lip of the cup as his breath caught it. She seemed hesitant, as though watching him for a clue. He watched her; the two smiling quizzically at each other. Then the moment was lost, and she moved back to the kitchen. She needed to think.

The meeting with a local attorney had been organized by Bronwyn's father, so Aubrey showered and got himself ready. Aubrey did not believe in fighting his battles through the courts. His opinion about attorneys was not a favourable one. There wasn't any difference as far as he could see, between the thieves who stole the money, and the thieves who stole it back. But as the fraud had taken place in Malawi under an antiquated and entirely different legal system, he did not see how they could make a difference. However, Tony had insisted on it, and his ex-client had been the leading advocate in Rhodesia during the hedonistic days of Smith and the UDI regime. Victor Rebock had retired to Port Elizabeth after the demise of the white government, fearing the obvious retribution from Mugabe and his Fifth brigade henchmen. Aubrey was intrigued.

It was into this intrigue, Aubrey was to find himself thrown. Having dropped Bronwyn at her parents' home on the coast early, Aubrey had driven the coastal road to Saint Francis Bay. The opulence of that setting summed up his position. Those white-washed walls stood as a beacon to all those, intent on maintaining their sense of separation from the rest of the world. The houses were all appointed with their backs to the trading town of Humansdorp. The pristine thatched roofs and expansive gardens, gave way to a sense of a bygone era. With estuaries, docks and a peaceful tide that lapped gently at each individual mooring, devoid of any boats, the gated community was in hibernation.

But as Aubrey arrived at the gated entrance to the largest mansion on the waterfront, he became aware of a sense of isolation. The place was eerily quiet. Not a soul seemed to be in evidence, and the cold winter wind whipped through the open window, as Aubrey drove up to the house. He discretely parked away from the main entrance.

The gate opened, and Aubrey drove through unannounced.

He was ushered into an ante-room on the first floor which overlooked the marina. From this vantage point, Aubrey could see the abandoned canals. Not a boat or a person could be seen. House after house stretched to the horizon, freed from humanity and detached from society.

"Good morning," Victor stepped into the room, a large man, braces festooning a neatly laundered work shirt buttoned to contain an immense beer gut; a large collar with neatly matching tie, threatening to choke a crocodilian neck.

Aubrey stepped away from the window.
"Good morning. Aubrey." He extended his hand. A gnarled, claw-like grip, maintaining a good arm's length between them reached out.

"Come inside," he turned, leading Aubrey into a vast office with walls awash with gold framed memorabilia.

"Have a seat," Victor offered him a green leather covered Eastman, with upholstered armrests, comfortable but business-like; having retreated to the far side of a substantial desk.

"May I offer you coffee?" Victor stood behind the glass covered walnut expanse, mirrored and imposing.

"Yes, thanks." Aubrey was still a little out of sorts.

"What is your preference? Cappuccino, latte or straight-up?" Cordial, but authoritative.

"Straight please." Aubrey was still queasy from the side-effects of carbon monoxide poisoning.

Victor lifted his hand from the desk, releasing an intercom button, on a cleverly appointed electronic gadget.

"Having usurped power from the minority white Government, it became clear after Independence that it was business as usual," Victor stated, seeing Aubrey was surveying the pictures behind his desk.

There were portrait photos with Victor and several vaguely familiar faces. Central to the collection, was a smiling and enthusiastic looking Ian Smith. The framed photographs a declaration of just how important a man he had been! He was pictured with every important politician from Smith, to Pik Botha. There appeared to be no one he had not met. The most remarkable picture was a black and white newspaper article from 1972, of a debonair looking Victor, seated in what looked like a courtroom, and standing in the background, a shackled and manacled younger looking Mugabe, his trademark Ronnie Corbet glasses evidence of his already failing eyesight. Aubrey found himself in discussion with Victor, whose passion for the old

Utopian dream of Rhodesia had not faded by any margin since his exile to South Africa.

"When Mugabe took over, his Government elected the Reverend Canaan 'Sodindo' Banana as a Presidential figurehead. That was when there was still the possibility of a democratic chance for success. The writing was on the wall however." He joked.

"If ever there was an example of a banana republic in Africa! But the Reverend's claim to fame was more to do with the crime which he nefariously committed whilst in office. It caused huge political embarrassment to Mugabe."

"Yes," Aubrey nodded. He had heard the stories of a sordid tryst between the President and one of his body guards.

Mugabe had to change the constitution in order to nominate himself as President." Victor peppered him with conjecture.

"Mugabe, who is himself is a promiscuous homophobe with the most obvious effeminate behavioural characteristics, had the Reverend jailed!" Victor was unrepentant.

"Perhaps it is a throwback to the Catholic Missionary School he attended, and their tutorage." He grinned. It was nonetheless an unfortunate association. Aubrey had to agree, but was non-committal.

"Mugabe has been a master of manipulation and has used public opinion in Zimbabwe to serve his purpose." A patriarchial society with no word for homosexuality in their vocabulary, Mugabe had fought the last election on the auspices of a 'white-orchestrated' attack on the fledging country's democracy. He had unfortunately used Banana's crime as an example of how the British were ostensibly undermining African values.

"Well. I suppose he should know?" It was a rhetorical jibe.

When Mugabe had swept to power in the election results of 1980, Victor had understood he would be targeted. The tactics of intimidation and point of barrel electioneering were never broached in the early days because of the popular support amongst liberation politics advocates. The British Government had wanted it to work, so had forced the Lancaster House agreement on the parties, much to the annoyance of many, including Victor. The main protagonists to Lancaster House were the British who had significant financial investments in Rhodesia at that time. They wanted to resolve the land issue amicably, because this had been the sticking point for negotiations dating back to 1930 and the Land Apportionment Act.

Despite the British having created that law, Whitehall had effectively usurped the Governance of Southern Rhodesia after 1918, disbanding the British South Africa Company founded by Cecil Rhodes, and laid claim to the sovereignty of Rhodesia. But the Ian Smith Government had resisted the now liberal policies of Britain in 1965, and unwilling to hand over power to the black communists, these dissidents under Smith had formulated a Unilateral Declaration of Independence, based on the American Constitution. Victor had been one of those who drafted this legislation, and theirs was a dream of self-governance, but clearly a century too late.

Because of Britain's continued interference, and notwithstanding an attempted blockade of oil shipments which should have strangled the tiny land locked enclave, the Rhodesians had thumbed their figurative noses at them and continued regardless. It was this sense of pride, and an irrevocable desire to forge a land of plenty from the virgin African bush, that had seen them resist those who were in no position to be dictating terms. The British signatories to the Lancaster House agreement included Sir Ian Gilmour, himself a somewhat Liberal member of the Heath Government. His family had presided over Craigmillar outside Edinburgh as the feudal lords for centuries, but perhaps he had suffered a change of heart!

For the bulk of the economic wealth to remain in Britain's hands, there were provisions made to protect the likes of Tiny Rowlands and other business-minded members of the old Rhodesian elite. Victor had represented many of these businessmen when they had swept all before them in their quest to build the 'Rhodesian Dream' of self-dependency in the 70's. He was instrumental in obtaining vast tracks of land for the then virgin sugar cane industry to propel the ethanol production used to supplement imports of the scarce supplies of petrol and diesel required to keep the war effort on track. These men fought a gallant but futile war to keep communism at bay and provide the time needed to get the South African question resolved.

It was the Hendrik Verwoerd Government of South Africa which had supported Rhodesia, during that period in 1965 when the Oil Embargo had been declared against Rhodesia. So, Britain was forced to keep the pretence of a blockade going until 1975, despite the assassination of Verwoerd.

When the Mozambiquean communist backed Frelimo forces of Samora Machel took power from Portugal, the embargo effectively ceased. Britain withdraw their Naval and reconnaissance aircraft from the Mozambique Channel, having played the game in the U.N. Security Council, and conceivably still had their diplomatic integrity intact.

But nothing was further from the truth, and those who had maintained this ruse for the ten years it continued, were in effect as guilty as the Rhodesian's who had hung on to power. No one escaped with their reputations intact. Not the Life peers in the House of Lords who secretly condoned UDI, and certainly not the Portuguese oil dealers, who made vast fortunes from the brokering of those shipments. It was to this end that Victor believed the war against Communism was worth fighting.

Zimbabwe had subsequently adopted socialist policies akin to those failed economic principles of North Korea, and despite this failure, the scourge had spilled across the border into the economic heart of South Africa. Communism had to be fought with the tenacity that an injured and cornered Buffalo would fight, when confronted by a gun wielding poacher. This was the evil that Victor feared, and the reason he maintained a powerful grip on the Third Force politics of Southern Africa.

"ZANU PF, which dominates the government, has gone on a spending spree and hundreds of millions of Pounds earmarked by the British Government at Lancaster House, has simply found its way into the hands of the political elite." Victor pressed on. These were the circumstances that had dragged Zimbabwe into this quagmire, and it was now a waiting game, as Victor and the 'Old Rhodesianna' block bided their time for a return to the homeland.

"Like Castro, Mugabe has defied the odds. If it were not for the tobacco industry and the British education system, Zimbabwe would be a lot worse off." Victor was interrupted by a polite knock on the door.

"Enter," his voice carried to the outer ante-room.

The door opened, and a butler, with a bowtie and neatly pressed shirt and suit pants entered. Victor waited silently whilst the coffee was served. As the door closed discretely behind the butler, he continued.

"Mugabe seems to always recover from his various illnesses and afflictions? I have it on good authority, he has been seeking medical attention in Singapore! Something to do with hormone replacement therapy, or some new-fangled treatment. No other dictator in the history of the African continent was so damnably persistent."

"Funded, it has to said, by all the money he has ferreted into accounts in the Philippines!" Victor smiled, a rueful twist of his moustached lip.

"The failings of the various Land Reform and Land Acquisition Acts over the past years of Mugabe's tenure, has proven once again, that the entire dispute over who owns the land is a smoke screen. Mugabe himself has shown through his inability to provide honest governance, that the way to divert attention from his own failings is to foist the dispute onto the shoulders of others," Victor continued his lecture.

"What was it that Professor Michael Freeden had said about politics?" Victor was now seated behind his ornate desk.

"Politics is often colloquially associated with an unscrupulous drive for power, but it is an inevitable feature of human organization, of the containment – or pursuit – of conflict." He stopped himself, gauging whether Aubrey was listening. He was.

"So, that is why Mugabe has been so entrenched for the last twenty years," remarked Victor. He has found conflict at every turn along the way, and even exported his brand of war politics to the Congo. Without that conflict, he has nothing." Aubrey understood the necessity to Mugabe of that Central African war. A conflict which had already claimed the lives of five million Africans.

"One family, who were unfortunate not to make it to South Africa intact," Victor was following Aubrey's gaze.

"The deceased President Wrathal. He was the second President under Smith's Government after Clifford DuPont. He was an accountant, who headed the large Tobacco Auctions Company." Wrathal had been in commerce, before learning the tricks of the trade during his stint as Minister of Finance.

"Back then, when Rhodesia was the bread basket of Africa, tobacco was exported all over the world. The economy enjoyed a brief but phenomenal growth during that time, and whilst other post-independence African countries were floundering in their own cesspool of liberation politics, Rhodesia was a beacon of hope." Ironically, it was this death-provoking cash crop, tobacco, which generated most of those profits and employed one of the largest agricultural populations on the continent.

"Do you know, that at the height of its success, the largest companies in Rhodesia supplied half of the tobacco sold to the West. Not surprisingly, the growth of the economy had been ballistic, and the South African government, whose economy benefited from those exports through Durban, was happy to supply the fuel needed to power a growing economy." Victor paused. "Provided palms were being greased." He gestured with his thumb and forefinger.

"But those deals were incestuous, and every senior person worth mentioning was in on the act." Aubrey contributed.

"Yes," Victor agreed. "Wrathal, was rewarded with the position of President, once he had served his time in Government. But he died mysteriously in the middle of the night! He was lucky to secure his family's inheritance on the Durban Berea, thus ensuring the deal making he had orchestrated was not in vain."

Aubrey had heard these rumours. Timothy, whose father had been the unfortunate victims of a scurrilous feeding frenzy in the years leading to Zimbabwean independence had related stories of greed and power mongering.
Aubrey was no longer listening, as he reflected on what Timothy had told him.

It was one of the less obvious abuses of the then Rhodesian Government. One of the victims that had been caught up in the pandemonium was Timothy's father. A local businessman, he had spent two nights in the Salisbury Central Police holding cells, and was fined five thousand Rhodesian dollars, having endured the wrath of Wrathal. All that for having not declared the six hundred Rand sale of a German Shepherd dog, sold to a South African breeder.

"What about the innocent Rhodesians, caught up in that corruption?" Aubrey ventured.

"Yes. It is always the innocents on whom the guillotine falls. Unfortunately, history is always written by the victors."

The value, which was a paltry amount in the grander scheme of things, was a warning to other lesser mortals who might not declare their foreign exchange transactions. They were so intent on securing their own financial futures that the fate of the common man never ventured into their equation. It was this glaring hypocrisy that now fuelled Timothy's drive for profit, and in so doing bred its own duplicity.

"Well they were almost right," Aubrey assessed. "They certainly cannot claim the higher moral ground. But it was those who held power who were merely intent on making an example of others." Aubrey offered.
"That incongruity will never be raised, because in plain and simple terms, it was every man for himself. Regardless of how hypocritical the vanguards of the Rhodesian Elite were, they had worked diligently to secure some eventual settlement." Victor smiled, almost apologetically.

Aubrey recalled a quotation. "Laws are like cobwebs, which may catch small flies, but let wasps and hornets break through." He spoke it unwittingly.

This quote silenced Victor. The Professor had taught him to caste a critical eye on what he saw, and to lend a cynical ear to what he heard. Principles aside, there was a sense of paranoia amongst whites, which had been foisted upon them by an effective disinformation campaign run by the Smith Government. The irony was tangible. Those war wounds would never heal, but for the Rhodesians who had witnessed these crimes, it was a taste of a future Zimbabwe.

"Johnathan Swift. 1707 CE!" Victor eyed him suspiciously.

"Mugabe is a vicious terrorist, whose bloody retributions among the Tribal leaders has left men and women disfigured as an example of what was to come if they did not support him. The worst of these crimes was the visceral act of slicing off a woman's upper lips if they were accused of informing on ZANU Patriotic Front." He continued. If Aubrey was some liberal leaning apologist for black patriotism, he would convince him otherwise.

Aubrey was now interested. The land was the sticking point. "Why could they not find some equitable resolution?" He had spoken his thoughts aloud.

"Because Mugabe does not want the land, it was never his intention to return the land to Blacks! He simply used it in political expediency, as a bargaining chip. This is why the British under Blair have withdrawn their support."

"Really?" Aubrey was a little doubtful. He had read up on the debacle that was Lancaster House, and his understanding was that the talks had nearly failed because of the land issue.

"Of course, he didn't care, it was a ploy to get his hands on the half billion Pound Sterling that the British Government had earmarked for land redistribution." Victor raised a dismissive hand.

"Mugabe has used up all the funds Britain gave the Government of Zimbabwe after 1980, and when the 'Willing Buyer, Willing Seller' clause of 1985 did not work, Mugabe simply forgot about it until he faced further opposition to his Governments policies."

"Yes, a friend of mine in Matabeleland who was forced off his land." Aubrey had seen the suffering it had caused.

"No!" Victor interrupted. "That was the result of the 1981 Communal Land Act, which was derived from a need to force the tribal leaders on the old Tribal Trust Lands to follow Mugabe's policies. By replacing the tribal elders with local authorities who were funded by Government, they were forced to do his bidding. This was his way of limiting the power of the tribal elders, and effectively sanctioning them for having supported the old Smith Government. What he did not realize was that he would systematically destroy a way of life that had been around for centuries. People were forced off the land by default, and they descended on the cities. This caused mass unemployment, and thus, created a popular opposition to Mugabe's own government." Victor was referring to the new opposition.

"Mugabe is to blame for the fiasco that has ensued. Not only did he create mass urban migration, but he then gave half the land acquired by the 'Willing Buyer, Willing seller' policy, to his political allies and never compensated the poor who had been removed from the land in the first instance. Mugabe bought his political future, by using the funds offered by the British. When New Labour found out, they simply withdrew support to his Government. They wanted some cockamamie policy of land distribution to the poverty-stricken, which was a waste of time, because the poor rural folk did not want the land. That would have never worked, because the rural peasants were already heading for the cities, and a brighter future. It was only Mugabe stirring up the so-called 'War Veterans' that had generated the land invasions we are now seeing."

"He certainly has played this card game well!" Aubrey had been non-political in the time he had been in Zimbabwe, but he could not help but admire the sheer gall of Mugabe. He had played them at their own game. The only problem was that he was running out of cards. His political future now relied on his ability to bluff, and he certainly seemed to have the rest of the African countries on his side. For now, at least!

"Yes, but at what expense? He has destroyed the country's economy, and its ecology. Farms which were commercially successful, have now fallen into dis-ruin, and soil erosion from shifting cultivation has damaged the rest."

"I spent six years tracking Elephant through the Matabeland bush and you can see the effects of poor farming techniques!"
Victor smiled. It was an affirmation of his deepest thoughts.

"So you would know all about Ghukurundi?" The stakes had just been raised.
"Yes. Let's say, I have had first-hand experience of what has been done in the name of democracy. Mugabe's henchmen have done a lot of damage. My only concern is for the Elephant though!"

"I see." Victor paused. Leaning back into his chair, giving Aubrey a penetrating look. Reaching forward, he twisted a brass key and slid the central draw of that ornate desk open.

"Here," he opened a lever arch file, crammed with file photos. "Is this your experience of democracy?"

Aubrey looked down. The file open, was a testimony to man's inhumanity to man. But it was the photos of Elephant, hacked to death, and tusks removed from bloodied heads, which caught his attention.

"Where did you get these?" Aubrey was no longer a passive witness to a political intrigue. He was now engaged.

"Let's just say we are actively seeking evidence against Mugabe and his henchmen." Victor's stern look, gave Aubrey the chills. He was now an accessory.

"Who is involved in this poaching?" Aubrey looked up, his gut wrenched.

"We suspect that the syndicates are shipping the ivory through South African ports. The new regime here, have empowered people in the port authorities, who turn a blind eye; for a consideration."

"But who are the customers?" Aubrey was incensed. This was evidence enough that his actions as an accomplice with Wellington had been justified. Any guilt he had suffered was evaporating.

"We suspect the Israeli Mafia, are in cahoots with the Triads!" It was the confirmation Aubrey expected. Was David involved?

Aubrey simply nodded.

"So, it's quite simple," he continued. Victor with the resourceful brevity of his legal education took Aubrey's silence as acquiescence.
"There was a society of men among us, bred up from their youth in the art of proving by words multiplied for the purpose, that white is black and black is white, according as they are paid." He quoted eloquently.
"Seeing as we have a similar appreciation of Gulliver's Travels!" Victor appropriately chose an analogy that was central to his utopian ideal.

"If only it were so simple? In Africa, there is no black and white! Only grey"

This provoked a reaction from Victor that Aubrey would do well to remember.

"Mugabe has a limited life expectancy, and once the economy collapses altogether he will be finished." Victor was confident.

"The only thing keeping him from a natural political death is the backing of Communist China. Whereas the Russians had empowered the liberation resistance with Kalashnikovs, the Chinese were delivering arms and ammunition to support Mugabe's repressive regime for exactly the opposite reasons. The old guard in China is busy building their economy, so they spout socialism and communist ideals to hoodwink the likes of Mugabe, while the rest of the world watches as they plunder the resources of the country. They are the greatest capitalists yet, and they make good bedfellows with 'Old Bob'." Aubrey now regretted having said anything.

"The joke is that, 'Old Bob' is in point of fact, a 'closet monarchist'. He loves the idea of the monarchy, and his greatest reward for his endeavours was to be knighted by the Queen. His argument is based on the premise that he should, like the Queen of England, be installed in perpetuity, to rule over his dominion. He would be quite a sad character, were it not for the unfathomable damage he has done. When they stripped him of his knighthood, they may as well have castrated him.... Maybe not? That job was done effectively a long time before!"

"That's why they say he hasn't got the balls to confront the British! He secretly wants to be one of them." Victor smiled at his own parody.

"Well, Mugabe certainly will not be able to trust the Chinese. Once they are well and truly entrenched in Zimbabwe, Mugabe will become expedient." Aubrey knew only too well not to trust the Chinese.

"The Chinese are too clever to buy into his ego. They simply want to do business, and Mugabe's spat with Britain is now creating too much publicity. They will orchestrate his demise, and the next Government that comes along will have the blessing of the Chinese, but it will be at a cost!" Victor had certainly not given up on his dream of returning.

"When do you think that will be possible?" Aubrey was sure that it was possible.

"Certainly not whilst the Chinese are there." Victor was adamant. "No amount of financial input will ever completely repair the damage done. However, when the time comes, and Mugabe and his repressive policies have been stripped away, the land will be available again for farming."

"So why bother. What's in it for you?" If Victor had no financial interest in Zimbabwe, other than the land, then the country held no immediate economic potential for him. Or did it?

"Because," responded Victor, "to allow him to get away with what he has done is pure sacrilege. Mugabe will pay for his crimes, and he will go down in history as a dictator."

No amount of debating was ever going to sway an ardent fanatic from his crusade, and Victor was no exception.

"He will be tried at the International War Crimes Tribunal, countered Victor; that or he will die by the hands of the desperate, before we can even get him there."

"Oh, so there is a process under way to bring Mugabe to justice. What will that prove?" Aubrey knew he was steering dangerously close to the edge of Victor's reason.

"Because, he deserves no less!" Victor became irritated.

Aubrey remained quiet, just raising his eyebrows in a mock salute to Victor's outburst.

"And because it is the right thing to do for all the farmers who have lost their land, their livelihoods and their futures in Zimbabwe," he almost spat the name out.

"So, if Mugabe is prosecuted, that will give the old farmers their land back?" Aubrey tenaciously persisted.

"Yes, of course it will," Victor was condescending in his contempt.
"All legal matters can be brought before the International Courts, and this land is the subject of an international ruling set for promulgation in The Haage. There are two thousand applicants on the role, and those will be heard in the not too distant future."

Aubrey had not counted on Victor's tenacity, but what he heard gave him pause to reflect. He could see that to Victor, this was no game.

"Now, what is it that you need me to do?" Victor swiftly changed the subject.

Aubrey, could confide the entire story of David's fraudulent behaviour in Malawi, but that would make him out to be an idiot. It was something he somehow knew, would place him at a disadvantage with Victor. But he probably knew the whole story, seeing as how tight Tony and Victor were!

"How much do you know?" was Aubrey's response? This would settle the question and answer the debate more tactfully.

"Enough to advise you, that you would not have a leg to stand on." Victor was economical with his assessment.

"I see," Realizing that Victor was not in this just for the fee. Aubrey was beginning to take a liking to Victor's abrupt, and scathing character. There was no bullshit with this guy.

"What would you recommend?" Aubrey asked next, now playing it tactfully.

"You have two options," Victor countered. "Either you can fight this at an entirely different level, or you can walk away! That is pre-supposing you have no written contracts or documentation we could fall back on?"

The question was rhetorical. Aubrey's silence sealed the conclusion.

"What is the first option?" He may as well get Victor's expert opinion since he was there. Besides, the idea of walking away, if there was an alternative option, really wasn't that appealing. David was due his comeuppance and Aubrey knew that this opportunity had not been offered in vein.

"There is a reason the two of you had bumped into each other again." Victor looked sternly across the desk.

Aubrey did not blink. Was Victor alluding to the fact, that the universe had brought them together? Aubrey was only beginning to appreciate there was more to the man seated opposite him.
There was no escape for David this time. But David had known that when he had tried to knock them off. Aubrey knew that to venture down this road would be dangerous. It was obvious from the precursor to this conversation, that Victor was a man who could make arrangements.

"Well you need to understand that anything I disclose here is not to be discussed with anyone. Especially not Bronwyn!" His remark was unanswered.

Aubrey would not want Bronwyn involved in anything sinister. He nodded.

"I have known Bronwyn since she was a child. What I would not want her to know is that we plan to take back what is rightfully yours, and that we may do so outside the parameters of the legal system. Are we on the same page?"

The pictures on the wall said everything there was to know about Victor. This was not someone you would double cross, and expect to walk away from. The severity of Victor's furrowed brow and piercing stare was all the confidence Aubrey needed. He just nodded, slowly and with an awakening appreciation of where their discussion was headed.

Yet, he could not withdraw himself from the discussion, despite his intuition, and the sinking feeling in his stomach. This conversation was headed somewhere he could never have anticipated, even had he known the full extent of Victor's reputation. The possibility existed that if he succeeded, he and Bronwyn would have sufficient capital to get back on their feet.

"Okay," began Victor, "this is where we need to discuss the extent of your loss."

Aubrey was not sure if he meant the monetary or the inherent value in the business.

"You mean how much the business was worth," he asked for clarification.

"No, no!" Victor sounded a little exasperated. "I mean, how much has the loss of your business set you back? No one can put a value to something you have worked your life at, and put your heart and soul into. You wouldn't want to forego the intrinsic value of goodwill, human suffering and sheer guts and determination in this endeavour, would you?"

"Well, it was not really my business initially, although I brought a lot of the ideas and innovation to the business," Aubrey now found himself making excuses for David.

"Don't get caught up in the niceties of the deal." Victor frowned.

"Was there an understanding between you and your business partner as to who owned what?" Victor was pursuing his direction of interrogation.

"In other words, was there ever a specific value placed on the percentage of your share in the business?"

'Yes, of course, there was,' thought Aubrey.

The two partners had often discussed their plans for the business whilst sitting around the beach fire at night. Generally, they would sit and talk about the days diving, or fishing, or just enjoying the evening in communal kinship. Often David would discuss what he planned to do if the business was sold.

Funny that, thought Aubrey. It had always been David who was talking about selling. Often Aubrey would simply dismiss the idea. He was content with the lifestyle, and was not planning to go anywhere else.

"Yes," replied Aubrey, "it was always fifty-fifty. We always reinvested our profits."

"So your investment was fifty percent of the value of the assets and goodwill?" Victor was unequivocally forthright.

"Yes. We never spent any of the money. There was nothing to spend it on!"

"That's what I needed," Victor smiled.

Aubrey nodded agreement.

"Then that is what we must recover." Victor did not elaborate.

There was a timely buzz on the intercom on Victor's desk. He answered it by picking up a phone and pressing a button. A brief conversation ensued from the recipient on the other side, and without a word, Victor replaced the handset.

Aubrey remained quiet for a moment. How could he put a value on the business without knowing what equipment they had? He felt a little sinister. As though he had somehow committed a crime. But, why should he? He was not the one who had disappeared with the full proceeds from the sale of a business which did not belong entirely to him. At least Aubrey had his self-respect, and no matter what happened, he would sleep well at night.

Victor got up suddenly from behind his desk.

"That will be all we need for now," he remarked as he shepherded Aubrey by the elbow out through the office door.

Victor led him downstairs and through the side entrance to the garage area. There were two very expensive German luxury sedans parked in tandem. He opened the garage door, ushering Aubrey out to his old Pajero, parked on the pristine paving stone of the driveway. He walked straight into the South Easter wind blowing its inevitable way across the well-manicured lawns of the estate. Skirting the side of the house, Victor said his farewells. As Aubrey drove to the wrought iron gate, he noticed another expensive looking sedan parked at the grand entrance to the house. It had not been there when he arrived. Victor had another visitor.

Aubrey drove back along the coastal highway headed for the flat in Port Elizabeth, not stopping at the house in Jeffrey's Bay. His mind was racing. Had he just unleashed the hounds of hell? If he had, what were the repercussions? His mind wandering, he missed the P.E. turn off, and before he knew where he was, a signboard announced 'Uitenhage'. The road had narrowed and he reached a bridge, under which flowed the dirtiest river he had ever seen. The effluents had turned the water a putrid green. The litter clogged the banks, and the stench was unmistakable.

A thought crossed his mind. Whatever it was that Victor had in mind, it was clearly not going to be above board. He has dug himself into a cesspit and there was no way out. Then it hit him like a sledge hammer. He wanted to go back but could not bring himself to return, cap in hand! A great aching knot tightened in his gut. He realised with one sickening realisation that his finger prints were all over the window and the door to the bathroom of the dive shop.

He drove on, almost in auto-drive, his mind wondering as he weaved past the slower traffic. He could see how the affluence of the South African Renaissance had not made its way to the working communities of Uitenhage. How the prestige of a nation with its own iconic figure of Nelson Mandela, had not yet been able to reach those who had waged war against capitalism.

It was apartheid all over again as the wealthy got wealthier within their walled communities and disregarded the poverty stricken, of whom there were now more than at the time of independence in 1994. When Nelson Mandela made the long trip back from his incarceration, the great miracle of the rainbow nation was born. The potential was immense, but unlike some democracies, there was no regulatory system to control the wastage of taxpayer's money. The newly enriched government had forgotten all too quickly, where they had come from, and in a systematic reversal of fortunes, the black elite now embarked on a similar form of disregard for the poor. To add insult to injury, the millions of Mozambiquean, Zimbabwean and Nigerian refugees and opportunists, in the cities of South Africa were looking for work and a roof over their heads; and they would ultimately usurp the jobs and wealth of South Africa's poor, because coming from those failed states, they had no sense of entitlement. Their expectations were for hard work.

He caught himself short, once again questioning the plight of this beloved continent. Africa was a complex and difficult place. No single expert had ever been able to put a finger on the multifaceted dynamics that was Africa. But like a rough diamond, the potential was there. It needed those with the skill to recognize what was within its very foundations, to hone and construct the veritable gemstone that lay within. Africa was a sleeping giant, awaiting that grand awakening, but it would take a man with courage and passion to raise it from its slumber. Was that man waiting in the wings for his opportunity to shine? Or was the next African leader likely to follow the hoards that came before, and plunder everything in their path, leaving nothing of value in their wake?

Aubrey arrived back at the flat, and parking, found himself looking up at the concrete monstrosity, built to house working class labourers in the seventies. How had he somehow found his way to this parochial place? Port Elizabeth was so named after the wife of Sir Rufane Donkin nearly two hundred years before. He had been the Acting Governor of the Cape Colony, and it was and always would be, the last place he would have chosen to live. He knew that to exist here on the fringes of society, would be as debilitating as to have stayed in Zimbabwe. He had chosen to get away from the negativity of that place, only to replace it with the hastily built accommodation of a block of flats, lifeless and devoid of any spirituality.

These living quarters, to a generation of young South Africans who would become known as the lost white generation, were akin to those sprawling townships of the city of Johannesburg. Never had there been any attempt to provide the framework of a sustainable community, at one with its environment, and at peace with its neighbours. The process was merely to exploit the work force, and a generation later, the children of these workers were devoid of the humanity that provides the life-giving sustenance of any self-sufficient society. These kids would become the drug addicts that spread their illegal activities into suburbs where the affluent lived. Equally drawn to the excitement of contraband activities, and the temptation of narcotics, whilst the dealers and peddlers made sufficient profits to live next door! They enjoyed the same benefits of a society, hidden behind high walls, beyond the scrutiny of others, whilst the crime that accompanied this addiction, robbed the very framework of the society it fed.

If, as he suspected correctly what Victor was up to, then he knew Bronwyn would be taken care of. Victor may have been an unscrupulous negotiator, but he was a man with integrity where it counted. Bronwyn would be able to afford somewhere better, and the boy would be brought up in a better environment. Aubrey had suspected that his condition would worsen, but Bronwyn insisted they would take care of him. If Bronwyn could not live with her parents because of the boy, well at least they would be able to afford a decent place to live once Victor had done what was necessary.

But, it was more complicated and he knew Tony would also not accept Aubrey, on principle. For Bronwyn, the hope of securing a bright future in P.E. was destined to fail, if Aubrey stayed. Sitting in the driving seat, looking through the cracked windscreen at that very moment, Aubrey realized that he had to leave. To stay would have been the beginning of the end. Guilt wracked, he realised he had no other choice. He felt like a lone Cheetah with the spoils of a short, but exhausting chase; and the circling, malevolent hyena pack. He knew that he should have said good-bye to Bronwyn, but she would have only made it more difficult for him to get away. He knew that she didn't want to leave, and he didn't want to stay. He knew he would regret this, but he would never know unless he tried. At that moment, in that parking lot, and with no thought of how or where to go, Aubrey found himself alone again and a traveller.

His journey needed to continue, and to stay would have curtailed the very essence of his soul. He was on the road to self-discovery, and Bronwyn had been an integral partner on this quest. Somehow, he knew they would meet again, but for now, he had to continue.

Turning back out into the lunchtime traffic, he drove out onto the north coast highway, and hugging the low sand dunes he drove the lengthy trip all the way through the Eastern Cape, then on through the treacherous Wild Coast ending up as midnight struck, at a casino on the border crossing in the old apartheid Bantustan of Transkei.

Aubrey slept in the Pajero overnight, catching a bite to eat at one of the fast food franchises that adorned the perimeter of the slot machine den. It was in the morning, a half jack of whiskey empty by his side, he began to feel remorse for his actions. He phoned the flat.

Bronwyn, who by now must have feared the worst, answered the phone instantly.

The beep-beep of the pay phone receiver drowned out her breathless, but husky tone; she had been crying.

"Hello! Aubrey? Where are you? Are you all right? God, I thought the worst Aubrey. I really did. I thought that you had had an accident. Where are you?"

Silence accompanied the monotonous magnetic tone.

"Aubs, Aubs can you hear me? Where are you? What's going on?" Bronwyn was now even more alarmed. He had no change in his pocket; no way of replying.

"It's difficult for me to say this, Bronwyn. I have been driving and thinking about it yesterday." He spoke out loud, knowing she could not hear him. He was now beginning to fear the worst for himself. That he would have that fit of conscience he so dreaded, and head straight back to the flat and into her waiting arms.

"Aubrey, can you hear me. Are you alright? What happened at the meeting with Victor? What did he say?" A million questions and he had no answers for her.

Aubrey sighed. The pain returned in the pit of his stomach. He had to leave.

"I can't stay in P.E. I'm going to take some time out, and really think this through." He vocalised his own thoughts.

She began to sob. It was his Achilles Heel. He had heard his mother weeping in her bedroom parlour as a child and had not had the courage to ask her why. Now he felt a similar pang of regret, but knew he had to buy himself some time. As Bronwyn was about to broach the subject that had been weighing on her mind the previous morning, Aubrey regrettably returned the public pay phone to its cradle; the world around him spun and he could no longer hear her frantic scream.

He returned to the rank smelling Pajero and headed further north to Durban. He was in no hurry to make the two-hour drive on a highway that was thick with the early morning commuters, and trucks destined for their urbane markets on the hundred miles of immaculately designed golfing estates, and Colonialesque towns with names that harkened back to the colloquial heartland of the English countryside. He had nowhere particular to go, so he drove quietly in the slow lane and took some time to gauge the spirit of this last remaining British enclave. When he eventually drove into the outskirts of Durban, he first met with the Bluff, a great imposing beacon to the weary sailors headed for Durban harbour. He had come up with a plan.

Reaching the Esplanade of Durban harbour, a rich semi-circular basin of mixed opulent Victorian buildings, ornate and picturesque which once housed the headquarters of the sugar cartels; juxtaposed by seventies style concrete monoliths. These apartment blocks facing onto a harbour with large bulk carriers laden with their containers of consumables, now housed the working class of a city that had re-invented itself with the birth of the eThekwini council. The harbour was the city's lifeblood and traders now plied their trade from offices that once housed the Colonial heritage of Natal English families. Except now, the trade was all from the East, and Durban Harbour was a conduit to the informal traders and hawkers of a country busy re-birthing. It was a strange mix.

He needed to stop for petrol again, so he pulled up underneath a hotel where a garage, like some halfway house for the weary traveller, was perfectly nestled. He filled the tank halfway, as a precaution to what otherwise may have become a wasted purchase.

Climbing out of the bakkie, he asked the petrol attendant where he could get some breakfast. The man dressed in his smart cotton 'pit crew' style shirt, pointed up to where the hotel beckoned. Having paid the attendant in cash, Aubrey drove up into a parking garage above the petrol station, parking the

Pajero; he locked it and slipped down the concrete slip road to the parking garage, and out into the early morning pedestrian traffic.

Looking right he gazed up at what was a cantilevered glass deck above the garage and a sign that read 'The Riviera'. It sounded grand but the cold lifeless concrete gave its sadness away. Above him, the façade had not yet had time to soak up the early morning sun. The glass windows reflected out onto the harbour, a myriad of reflections from the early winter sun, still low on the eastern horizon, but blazoning along the Esplanade. The windows of the hotel had been angled, each one catching as much sunlight as the oblique vantage would offer. This was a testimony to a post war architect's, interpretation of a twenty first century energy saving 'Green' design. The building had character, and no doubt its' proximity to the docks would yield the right patrons. It was a bit of a dive he thought, but he was hungry and the only alternative looked like a 'bunny chow' at the corner café. Alternatively, there was the Durban Yacht club across the way, with its flagstaff bearing the club ensign proudly over a smartly painted quarterdeck with emblazoned corporate umbrellas. No, he thought, that would not suffice. He was looking for real sailors.

The Riviera looked like it could pass for an establishment of this sort. He climbed the stairs to a balcony perched above the yacht basin, with a vantage over the harbour. He could see the harbour master's conning tower on the Bluff across the way, and a steady trail of tug wake, as the big ungainly boats shepherded their quarries out to the harbour mouth, then spun and high tailed it back for the next shipment. Agitated and busy, this was where he would find what he was after. As Aubrey stood looking out into the silver tinted gleam of the harbour water, it seemed to be winking at him as it reflected the sun off its disturbed muddy surface. It was low tide and the yacht club lay in wait. No sooner had he surveyed the harbour, than a voice called out to him from the balcony.

"Spectacular, isn't it?" It was a North Country accent, akin to his mother's family that spoke out. Aubrey glanced up, but could not recognize the speaker, hidden by a dark shadow. His pleasant baritone voice sounded from a table in the corner. Shielded from the sun by an umbrella, this brute of a man had all the makings of a seafarer. The wall caste a further shadow along the balcony, but Aubrey could not tell whether he had company.

"Morning," replied Aubrey, realizing that he was in the company of one of his kinsmen.

"Join me," a remark more than a request, "I'm about to order breakfast here." Sounding like he had a common knowledge of the culinary exploits of this establishment.

"Thank you, I will," Aubrey said, quite thankful for the companionship. He had not spoken to anyone since leaving P.E. twenty hours before.
"Where are you from?" The question was posed as if he were trying to place Aubrey's accent.

"Originally the UK, but more recently Zimbabwe!"

"Ha," he almost slapped himself on the back having guessed correctly, that Zimbabwean accent so distinctive.

"You guys," a colloquial euphemism for any person who wore khaki shorts, without underwear, and a pair of veld-skoens, "you all sound the same."

"And you," remonstrated Aubrey, now feeling he had to justify his existence. "You 'Jordi's' are all the same too", he laughed. "Never can go anywhere wi'out bomping into y'all." Aubrey smiled.

"Don't I know it," the bear wrestler replied. "Got a name," directed at Aubrey, but more an invitation for Aubrey to join him.

"Yes, sorry! It's Aubrey."

"Don't be sorry. You aven't done naught yet! 'Sorry' is a South Africanism, designed to ingratiate oneself to an acquaintance, without ever having done anything wrong in the first place."

"Why do all southern Africans use that term?" The question lingered for a moment, both men contemplating the answer, and a formal introduction.

"I think it is something to do with the good old 'Afrikaner' expression, 'ekskies', which broadly translated means 'I'm sorry'. But even the blacks have a use for it, but in a more charitable way" Replied Aubrey, reaching over to shake the seated man's hand.

"How's that." Questioned the man, having not yet returned the introduction.

"Africans will say 'sorry' if you hurt yourself, almost as if they feel the pain themselves, and somehow internalize their sympathy. It is an empathic way of sharing your hurt." Aubrey sat expectantly.

The man had forearms like the cartoon character Popeye, and a chin with a similar jaunty jut. Aubrey made a mental note born of experience.

"Devlin," not any more or less of a remark, that left Aubrey thinking he was referring to something on the menu. But there was not a menu in sight. This was his name and he had nonchalantly offered it, with no further comment. The name was even more incongruous then the voice, but Devlin it was, and Aubrey thought better than to argue it.

The pleasantries aside, Devlin summoned a rather shabby looking waiter with what could only have been a late-night hangover expression, referring to him by his first name.

"George, we will have two breakfasts and the tea George. Don't forget the tea!"

"Yes baas," was the only response, and off shot George to organize breakfast.

Assuming correctly, that there was only one breakfast on offer, Aubrey allowed the conversation to flow to matters that were more important.

Having assumed again, correctly, that Devlin was staying at the hotel, Aubrey asked.

"Are you staying for long," the seafarer symptoms were plain for the entire world to see.

Devlin had a rugged, weather beaten exterior that was only evident among the seafarer class. Aubrey had known a few since his early exploits on the voyage from Southampton, and this man was no different. Devlin, despite his craggy exterior, was as incongruous a member of that band, as had ever set foot on land. However rugged he was, he had a somewhat comical hairstyle that made him look as though he had just slept. He looked like a Manga comic character, with jutting jaw and the spiky hair presenting an amusing demeanour that Aubrey would be wise not to comment on.

Aubrey listened as Devlin explained that he was awaiting the return of his ship, the 'Santa Maria', a Columbian registered vessel which carried iron ore from Richards Bay to Rotterdam and then returned empty, to start the whole process again.

Whilst Devlin was telling Aubrey how he had been left in Durban to convalesce after a bout of bronchitis, Aubrey looked more closely. He was distracted by the tea arriving, so Aubrey peered at Devlin's hairline, and discovered that Devlin was wearing a rug, and it was a bad one at that. The piece was a clear sign of a degree of vanity, even those twenty years on board, had not vanquished. But like a woman, who takes out her Sunday best for appearances sake, Aubrey surmised that the toupee that resembled a splattered meercat, was only brought out whilst Devlin was on shore-leave. Just as Aubrey was giving himself a salutary smile at his newfound info, he was caught in the act.

Devlin looked up from the tea pouring, but luckily, he must have thought Aubrey was smiling at something else, and he just smiled back at Aubrey. The moment passed and Aubrey turned his attention away from the obvious incriminating 'syrup of figs' as it was affectionately referred to among the West End theatre fags. He allowed the conversation to flow again. The breakfast course followed.

"I work as a diesel engineer on most of the ships on the Rotterdam route." Devlin gave a brief recount of all the ships that plied that shipping route. He had been rather free spirited, working them all, preferring to freelance his services rather than work in the employ of a single shipping company.

The conditions are all notoriously bad," Devlin offered. His keen sense of seafaring had identified Aubrey as a kindred soul. "If it were not for my skills being in serious demand, I might have ended up in the hell holes of one of them vessels," Devlin gestured to a Singaporean registered vessel.

"Those captains make huge profits for their owners, and living conditions are bare minimum." Devlin related.

"What's the Colombian registered 'Santa Marta' like." Aubrey ventured.

"It's a bulk carrier with twenty-five crew, and only fifteen cabin beds. This is so that there is always someone on deck. She is a very sturdy ship, but has been ploughing this trade route for twenty odd years now."

"Twenty years?" Aubrey was surprised. "The shipment is headed to Rotterdam?"

"Yes, she has been doing this route ever since the sanctions busting days of the old Apartheid government." Aubrey was intrigued. He had known of those sanctions whilst he was studying at King's.

"Yes. The old Government was busy shipping iron ore and coal through Richards Bay since the eighties, directly to Europe. But I guess they had a different agenda then!" He smiled, a hint of a curl to his right upper lip

"What do you mean by a different agenda?" Aubrey questioned.
"Well it's to do with the fact that the Captain, when I first began life on board, used to confide some of the more explicit details to me. You see, I did not start off as a diesel mech, but was a young cabin boy for the first few years." He let the idea hang a little, to test if Aubrey was on the same page as him.

"Anyways, when I was on cabin duty, the Captain would offer me gifts!" He could not have been vaguer, but was using a conspiratorial tone.

"These were gifts given to him by the guys from the shipping company in Richards Bay. All sorts of useful and interesting gizmos and the occasional bottle of good scotch as well. These were in effect bribes, which I did not know at the time was illegal. We were basically running shipments through to the deep-water port of Rotterdam, which were paid for by German industrial companies, but shipped in a Columbian registered bulk carrier, through a company in Johannesburg, which was owned by a Jordanian businessman with connections to the Royal family."

"That's incredible." Aubrey was on the edge of his seat.

"Yes, but when the new Government took over, it just became another opportunity for someone else to make the profits. I guess that's how the world works?" He was quite blasé about it.

"I suppose you are right! The machinations of high finance have always disinterested me."

"The Santa Marta, strangely enough, was named after the Port of Santa Marta in Colombia. It was founded by a Spanish nobleman, who sailed with Christopher Columbus. He landed on the coast of Colombia on the day the Spanish celebrate Saint Marta's feast, so he named it after Martha from the Bible! You know; who served Christ." Aubrey did not, but he listened intently.
"His name was Rodrigo de Bastidas, but despite his name, he was not a bastard." Devlin smiled at his own joke.

"In fact, he was called the 'Noblest Conquistador', because of his human rights record with the native Columbians. He was however murdered by his own crew, because he would not share the gold he had traded because it was destined for Spain. That was the end of him, but ironically, Santa Marta is a bulk carrier that has spent the last twenty years shipping iron ore and coal from Richards Bay to Europe, all in an effort to defeat sanctions, and perpetuate the human suffering of Apartheid victims." He lifted his cup of tea.

"She has never set sail from Santa Marta, although that is her port of origin. But she was bought by the Jordanian shipping company, and now ploughs the high seas under a neutral flag. Bastidas would have been ashamed of his legacy, but at least he died a principled man." Aubrey loved an intrigue sipping his tea, whilst soaking up the story.

"Amazingly, he was murdered for the sake of his crewmen's greed, even though he was serving the Spanish Royal family!" Devlin was a good protégé of the master it seemed. Surprisingly, the Captain at the time had a moral conscience, and despite his proclivity towards the younger man, had been a sincere mentor it seemed.

"So, why do you say there is still a problem with human rights? Apartheid is over, and the South African government is now exporting freely to Europe!"

"Because we all serve someone, and the current administration is no different. The coal we ship is being mined in open caste mines on the Highveld of Mpumalanga, and the process of stripping the land to get to the coal is destroying not only the top soil, but is polluting the entire river systems that feed into the Vaal River catchment area." He paused for Aubrey to swallow a piece of bacon, he was furiously chewing.

"The amount of coal the Santa Marta carries, pales into insignificance with the bulk carriers that are destined for China, and the demand is growing daily. If you see the size of the rail shipments of coal from Witbank and the coal mining areas, you would understand my point. It is a chaotic situation, and the amount of damage it is doing to the environment is criminal. The new government is issuing mining grants to anyone who can get funding from the Banks, and the infrastructure has been overloaded. On my last trip to Witbank from Richards Bay, the roads were so bad we destroyed two tyres simply getting there and back. The coal trucks have ruined the roads, but that is nothing in comparison to the damage being inflicted on the land. Something has to give, and in ten years the population of Johannesburg will be drinking pure sulphuric acid from their rivers." Devlin had certainly not spent all his time in an engine room it seemed.

"So why do you do what you do?" Aubrey was confused. Surely if he felt that way, he should morally object to the process.

"Because, while I am here in Durban, I am researching a book that is to be published in South Africa, to divulge the environmental impact this coal mining is having in Mpumalanga."

"Okay, I see! What do you think the South African government will have to say?"

"That's the point, they are too busy empowering themselves. Having been previously disadvantaged, they have blinkers on. They cannot see the damage they are doing, or are simply ignoring the real threat." Aubrey was relishing the story.

"If the Government does not regulate the industry, despite their dependency on coal for power generation, the destruction this process will cause will leave the inheritors of the struggle for liberation, with nothing anyway." Devlin had a glint in his eye.

"That's why I am not releasing any information until I have all my research finalised. I am communicating with a Professor in Geology at one of South Africa's universities, and we will have the book published in a few months." A more incongruous author Aubrey could never have imagined meeting.

"There's a guy." He leaned towards Aubrey.

He is related to Zuma, and he has a hand in all these deals." Devlin made a gesture with his arms. "A big man, in the true Zulu tradition."

Devlin turned out to be such a dab hand at storytelling, Aubrey forgot all about his worries, and sat whilst he relayed one story after the other. By mid-morning, they decided it was time for him to head down to the docks to find a ship heading out somewhere interesting. He had looked a little dishevelled, so Devlin allowed him to wash up in his hotel room. With a clean-shaven face, and a perfunctory smoothing down of the somewhat creased pair of chinos he wore, they headed down to the western basin.

Devlin was well known and the deckhands were happy to let them aboard. On his third interview, Aubrey was given a passage on a Taiwanese freighter with a cargo of mining equipment destined for the Congo. The ship headed for Nigeria, had been requisitioned by a big mining company to; so, with an opportunity to head off into obscurity, Aubrey was told to report the following morning at five.

The two chums, now well bonded headed back to the hotel and a well-deserved sun-downer. The deck was empty, so they headed for a bar on the second floor. It was a Wednesday afternoon, and the bar only had a few stragglers hanging around at a table near a dance floor. There was a stage to the left, and as Aubrey sat down at the bar on a stool covered in plush burgundy velvet, Aubrey looked up at the ceiling, and was amazed to see that the whole ceiling was covered with cardboard egg boxes. He looked up at Devlin to say something, but Devlin was intent on ordering two large whiskeys from the barman, who looked about eighteen years old. In an instant, Aubrey realized why the ceiling had the egg boxes attached.

This was some rudimentary form of sound management, intended to mask the sound of late night revellers from the hotel guests upstairs!

The realization now dawned on Aubrey and all the innuendos of earlier seemed to make sense. It had not made Aubrey uncomfortable, but he was quick to surmise that Devlin obviously stayed at the Riviera because of its proximity to this bar. This place had all the trappings of a typical gay bar, and it did not differ from Bangkok, where she-males hung out in those seedy dives. It smelled of stale cigarette smoke permeating the velvet cushions of the bar stools, the rippled carpets and dralon drapes. They hung over a large window shielding any sunlight from the room; and the room from the rest of the world.

Aubrey accepted the drink from Devlin, and ended up toasting to their success, and his help in finding passage on board one of the ships. Whiling away the early evening, the two sat and polished off a half bottle of whiskey.

"Good God, it's six in the evening," Devlin remarked he had to change clothes and get some grub.

Did Aubrey have a change of clothes? There was no suitcase and Aubrey had not booked a room.

No, Aubrey thought better of the offer, and having realized Devlin's interest was not, as it seemed, unencumbered, he kindly turned down the offer.
Seemingly, Devlin brushed off any possible slight, as he had intuitively recognized all of the symptoms. Aubrey might be unwilling to change, as he

had not any clothes to change into. He good naturedly winked at Aubrey, telling him he would see him later.

With Devlin gone, the barman started chatting Aubrey up. The boy called Matthew was barely eighteen and he lived on the Durban Bluff.
"My mother is divorced," he confided. His sister, a lesbian cross-dresser who had many friends in the gay world, had effectively taken him under her wing. The mother had embarked on a crusade of self-destruction, and as with any underclass, he would not have appeared any different to Aubrey, were it not for the fact that his lifestyle promoted the use of drugs. Matthew, clearly turned tricks for the older patrons, who was feeding his habit from those proceeds.

Aubrey sat listening and realised just how his childhood may not have been any different, had he not been born to a wealthy sector of society. It was evident that the proletariat in a profit driven world would always be on the receiving end. Dysfunctional single parent families, were driven by a need to prove to the world that they could succeed. Aubrey realized that without the opportunities afforded by the presence of a father figure, Matthew was destined to spend his life in and out of rehab, and would amount to nothing, unless he had the help of someone like Devlin, to settle down with. That was only possible if Devlin was there and not permanently on the high seas.

"Your predicament is not too different to mine,' Aubrey confessed after his third double. He was a traveller on a quest to self-fulfilment, a short trip from Alcoholics Anonymous, but not the poison these kids substituted for the real world.

Devlin returned from his shower and offered to buy Aubrey dinner. Aubrey accepted.

It was as if a light had been switched on. They sat down in the bar, with a welcome plate of steak egg and chips. Matthew plied them with whiskey, and Aubrey lost himself in the haze of cigarette smoke, and sleazy 'come-ons' from the mid-week patrons slowly filling the bar. Devlin was in a party mood, and the evening was thoroughly entertaining.

Although Aubrey had refused to be drawn into a game of arm wrestling, knowing he stood no chance against the burly seafarer, Aubrey watched as one of the hustlers who plied his trade on Addington beach was game enough to take Devlin on. The crowd bayed in muted shrieks much to their amusement, and a crowd gathered at the bar.

He lost, despite a valiant effort born of a finely toned athletic body that had been hewn from endless days of surfboard paddling and countless nights of vaulting over high perimeter security gates to avoid the local police, who were sent regularly to purge the beachfront of these delinquents. The result was spectacular as Devlin with one arm still holding his whiskey, and the other under-pinning the two-handed effort of this young upstart, reduced him to cannon fodder.

Aubrey slipped away to catch a few hours' kip in the Pajero, as the party continued into the early hours of Thursday morning. Aubrey refreshed, rose at five and made his way down to the docks, leaving the keys of the Pajero.

Chapter 17

A breath of fresh air

Aubrey awoke in a confused state of anxiety. The dream he had awoken to, was a myriad of faces, voices and sinister shadows. In the dream, he was being chased, but the road was perilously steep, and all along its path were the skulls of the Elephant. He had tried desperately to reconcile the fact that he had a half-brother, spending two days after his return from Europe, mulling this thought over and over in his head. The impromptu tea at Margaret's cottage had uncovered more questions than it had answered. If Sean was indeed the progeny of his late father, then that would realistically entitle him to half of the Estate. This would elevate Sean from Chauffeur, to co-Landlord. Aubrey was however, troubled by the thought of Sean being the only real son of Lord Pennington. Troubled, but not entirely uneasy with this concept.

Sean could be the only realistic claimant to the title of Lord Pennington!

This was going to be tricky, or was it? There was no doubt that this would cause a huge scandal if it ever became common knowledge. To find out your real genetic father was the man who had spent twenty years treating you like a common servant was one thing; but to know he had sired you, and not given you any of the entitlement of your birth right. That would cause some tricky legalities, which Aubrey would not want to have to deal with.

Considering it all, Aubrey grappled with the news. He spent the rest of the week wandering the lanes of the village and chatting amiably to the passers-by, who would greet him "Morning Sir' or 'Morning Your Lordship." It was comforting for them to know that the Manor House was once again occupied with their own gentry. In time, they would come to appreciate the finer details though, Aubrey smiled to himself. No irony was greater than the prospect of these very people finding out that he was not who they thought he was and that the man who had been ferrying him around in his Rolls Royce was in fact, 'His Lordship'.

On the Friday afternoon, he was browsing the old antique shops of Finsbury when a sports car came whooshing past, throwing up leaves and dust onto his trouser legs before suddenly screeching to a halt some twenty meters from where he was. A loud voice roared back at him.

"Hello old man. What the devil are you doing back here?" The voice was affected and strangely familiar, but Aubrey could not place it.

Aubrey turned to see a familiar looking man, paunchy with thinning short, cropped blond hair. He was guffawing from the driver seat of a little black Japanese sports car. The timber of his voice was distinctly well enunciated, but the face was momentarily indistinguishable from all those overweight middle-aged gentrified men, who had a claim to some recognition in this society. He was clearly intent on catching Aubrey's attention.

"Good God man, it's me Jerry!" But Aubrey seemed slow on the uptake. To jog his memory, he yelled again. "It's me old man, or shall I call you Your Lordship?" He suggested, a mocking tone now evident.

Aubrey turned his body completely to face the stranger and with a jolt of recognition realized this was Jerry Laubner, one of the chaps he had known at King's. He had been at Eton, but because he was older than Aubrey, they had not met until attending university. He was only recognizable by the upturned cartoon caricature of a nose which seemed improbably pompous. His flushed complexion, made the flared nostrils appear even more grotesque. Aubrey could not recall the nose ever having such wide nostrils. It appeared as a bulbous addition to what had once been a chiselled profile, not dissimilar to many others in the Aristocracy he had known at Eton. His voice, sounded far more affected than Aubrey could remember, but was the only partially recognisable characteristic. Gerry had not been a sportsman, so they had little in common; except for the shared tutorage of the Professor.

Aubrey, with an awakening realization, saw that his passenger was game- fully ignoring the conversation. Instead, he was intent on listening to the stereo music, blaring across the conversation. He finally turned his head dismissively in Aubrey's direction. There was disdain in those eyes, made all the more comical by a silly little goatee balancing awkwardly on his lower lip and chin. Aubrey had recalled his father saying dismissively;

"Only queers wear moustaches! It's for tickling their fancies." Aubrey never understood that at the time, but to have a thin line of facial hair extending the line of the nose to the chin, did seem somewhat odd.

"How are you?" Aubrey replied rather formally, not sure what to make of the rather odd couple. Jerry, he had remembered had been dating a lovely girl at university. But from what Aubrey could now easily make out, the effeminate looking man next to him was an obvious queen. Aubrey, reluctant to have his quiet morning disturbed, was all decorum. He politely acknowledged the driver, as he reversed the little open sports car.

Aubrey ambled over to the side of the car.

"Hello, I must apologise," a warm handshake beckoning. "I honestly did not recognize you!"

"No!" Jerry sounded quite shocked. "I recognised you instantly."

It was one of those syllabified sentences, which drew the words out to emphasise a point. It was quite comical, but laboured.

"Ah, that's more like it," Aubrey conceded as he came into view alongside the driver. Mind you, Aubrey had not seen him in some twenty years and those years had not been kind. Jerry still in the car and having made no effort to switch off the engine, awkwardly offered his hand over the high sill of the door. The open top of the car allowed Aubrey, to reach in and shake his hand, however, when he waited for an introduction to the companion, there was none forthcoming. Aubrey was aware of the other man staring straight ahead and intent on ignoring the conversation as far as possible, which he did by busying himself with the drowning beat of the car's compact disc player.

"Where are you off to?" Queried Aubrey, shouting somewhat to be heard above the music.

"Oh, just on a country jaunt to see a friend, old man," offered Jerry. He most definitely was more affected than Aubrey remembered. The voice was pitched higher, or maybe it was because he was shouting to be heard over the monotonous beat of the music.

"Oh, that sounds like a lot of fun," Aubrey remarked, somewhat unconvincingly. What was the name of that lass he had been dating? Aubrey racked his mind, the music a considerable distraction! "Michelle!" Yes, he thought to himself, she had been a honey.

In a vain attempt to make conversation, Aubrey was about to ask, but thought better of it. The companion seemed irritated and turning up the music further, to make a point. The moment was not entirely lost on Jerry, and with a simple wave of the hand, he shouted to Aubrey.

"Sorry old man, have to run. Due at a party, you know," and with that the car's engine was revved, and as the engine berated the throttle, a hollow sounding exhaust vibrated over Jerry's voice.

"You're at the Estate? I'll give you a call. Got to go" and with that they were off in another plume of dust and a limp-wristed salutary wave.

Aubrey stood watching them go. He was chiding himself for having turned around to acknowledge them, when a thought crossed his mind.

"They were clearly in a rush to get to their party, and they both looked a little spaced out. He surmised that the two were probably off on some drug-induced debauchery, that Jerry had been famous for back in those days at King's. Aubrey had attended one of those evenings himself, but that was twenty years ago! However, in all likelihood, it was not marijuana they were after this evening. Thankfully, no one else had seen them talking, and Aubrey felt certain that Jerry's threat to call was just that; a threat. He stepped back onto the pavement and continued his late afternoon stroll.

At the Estate, Aubrey stopped in the kitchen to ask Highpot if he was busy. With his request being made this way, Highpot dropped what he was doing and rushed out the kitchen. Aubrey slipped into the study and Highpot followed, closing the door behind them.

"Your Lordship," he acknowledged as Aubrey entered, he sat down in one of the wingback armchairs, motioning to Highpot to come and sit next to him rather than at the old Edwardian oak desk. "Is there something wrong?"

Aubrey countered him, "Don't be so formal with me, Highpot, you and I go back too far for that. Besides, I have something important I need to ask you, and it can't wait!" Highpot was as agitated as Aubrey.

"Yes Your Lordship." he laboured.

"And cut 'the Lordship' crap. Please!" pleaded Aubrey. "We both know that it has no validity."

Highpot searched Aubrey's eyes for a hint of recognition. He had not ever seen Aubrey so tense.

"What is troubling your...," he stopped himself out of habit. "You?" he remarked.

He sat, carefully, without taking his eyes off Aubrey. Highpot was beginning to expect the worst. His mind was racing. 'Perhaps he was about to receive a rebuke, or worse still a dismissal!'

"Highpot. How long have I been back at Finsbury?" It was rhetorical. Aubrey knew the answer. It was no more than three months now.

Highpot was confused. "About three months Sir, I mean. I mean...He was now totally flummoxed.

Aubrey recognized his dilemma. "Just call me Aubrey while we are alone. Sir will do, with the others around."

That sounded so much more palatable. Highpot breathed out, settling back into the chair.

"What is on your mind...Aubrey?" It sounded strange but was something he could get used to.

"Highpot. We need to talk about Sean, and what we are going to do for him."

Highpot smiled, inwardly he was thankful. Aubrey would cut to the chase, as he had become accustomed to of late. But his mind was racing in all sorts of directions. 'If Aubrey did know the truth about Sean, what would his reaction be?'

"You know that I have never had designs on Finsbury, or the title it confers."

Highpot fidgeted.

"Highpot, or should I now call you Colin?" he asked, taking it as confirmed without giving Highpot a chance to respond.

"Colin. I have decided that I would like to relinquish my title, and I want to do it in a manner which will not bring scandal to the Estate." His mother would have concurred.

Aubrey explained himself.

"In effect Colin, I have had a great amount of trouble adapting to a lifestyle, which to be honest, I am uncomfortable with." Aubrey was troubled.

"Aubrey, if you are asking me what is required; I genuinely could not offer any advice. This is most peculiar! Actually, I don't believe one ever relinquishes one's title unilaterally, it is offered, and one accepts it, or not." Highpot was sitting at the edge of the chair facing Aubrey and his brow was deeply furrowed.

"Well, that's the point isn't it?" Aubrey was animated.

"I never accepted the title. It is naturally assumed that when I returned, the title was automatically passed on to me!" He grinned. It was somewhat disarming.

"Yes, but the issue is not whether you accepted it, but whether the title remains in perpetuity!" Highpot was more measured in his response.

"Well we don't live in a feudal society anymore, so I cannot see how we can be expected to keep up these pretences!" Aubrey was unequivocal.

"The title Lord Pennington was irrevocably linked to this land. Land title-ship is the conveyor of that privilege, as it has been for the last three generations. It constitutes an aristocratic claim in the first instance. That, or a title conferred by the Queen!" Highpot explained.

"So, Sean could be conferred that title, if I abdicated my land rights?" Aubrey surmised!

"No. But I don't understand. This was your mother's desire, to see you as Lord Pennington! Anyway, I would imagine he would not want any title." Highpot was sure.

"Can anyone claim a peerage without the Queen's blessing?" Aubrey speculated.

"It was often handed down through hereditary ownership of the land, that is until 1999." Highpot was anticipating Aubrey's question.

"After the law was changed, the House of Lords now has an election process for the remaining seats in the House."

"You mean that someone can buy this land and be called Lord Pennington?"

"No, I mean that it was often the case that the land conveyed the title to an outsider through ownership. But that has changed." Highpot answered.

"So anyone with money, could have bought the title they wanted?" The peerage had strange bedfellows.

"More or less!" Highpot could see the rationale behind Aubrey's questioning.

"That is it exactly!" Aubrey shouted triumphantly.

"What is?" Highpot quizzed.

"The land is the source of titleship. If the land was not relinquished by law, or by conveyances, it has not passed hands correctly and is therefore still owned by the rightful title deed holders." Aubrey smiled in celebratory mood.

"I'm not sure I follow you," Highpot was now confused.

"I am talking about the land in Zimbabwe," Aubrey explained.

"What land?" Highpot was unclear. He had thought they were talking about the estate.

"All of it!" Aubrey remarked. "All of it!"

Highpot reflected for a moment. He was now confused. Had they already resolved the problem of the title to the estate?

"Yes." answered Aubrey, having read his thoughts. They were etched across his forehead in deep furrows, like the bounteous farmlands of Mashonaland that had once fed a continent.

"The estate is in good hands, Highpot," We don't need to do a thing here!" He remarked rhetorically. Highpot knew instinctively not to question him further.

After their discussion, Aubrey felt somewhat relieved. He vegetated for the remainder of the evening, only allowing Highpot in to fetch the plates and cutlery once he had finished his dinner. When he went upstairs to bed, there was a card placed on the bedside table, with a little smiley face on it and a large italic 'N'. Natasha must have been passed earlier, or perhaps she'd had the card delivered? He opened the card. It was one of those black and white photos of a pair of period dressed children kissing on a swing. Aubrey could feel the blood coursing through his veins at the memory of the last sweet encounter he and Natasha had enjoyed. He opened the card.

'Hi Aubs, I thought a little message might lift your spirits. Please call, I need to tell you something. Your minx, N.'

With that, and a pang of guilt for not having called her earlier, Aubrey decided to call her despite the lateness of the hour. Highpot had not mentioned the card, as he probably felt Aubrey had too much on his mind already, or had Natasha requested the card be placed by his beside?

"Hi Aubrey," she answered on the second ring. "How are you?"

"Fantastic. Had a great day out walking!" he exclaimed.

Aubrey's spirits were decidedly lifted upon hearing her voice. He could never remain impassive when she spoke; there was something equally elegant and spontaneous in her lilting voice. She always put him at ease immediately.

"Oh, I am so pleased you had a good day?" she recognised his eagerness to talk.

"Yes, in fact I have had a lot on my mind this week, and I took a long and invigorating walk to brush out some of the cobwebs." He had felt alive after the long walk back.

She was elated again.

"Yes, yes. That's what I want to talk to you about!" Her voice was pure music to his ears. A subtle mix of angel, with a touch of vixen! Aubrey could feel aroused just listening to her. A wicked thought crossed his mind, but Natasha sounded as if she had some good news.

"What is it my sweets," his tone warmed to her instantly.

"You know I mentioned a holistic healer that I had met at a medical conference last year?" He vaguely recalled her having mentioned it.

"Yes. What was it you told me again?" Aubrey wanted to listen to her voice."

"Well," continuing with suitable enthusiasm, "I was chatting to him this morning, and he mentioned he has just opened a clinic in the Bayswater area."

That sounded expensive, but Aubrey was happy to oblige her, and cost was not the question. "What type of clinic Tash?" He was nervous of any experimental treatment.

"It is a very professionally run Ozone clinic. The way it has been explained to me, it is worth a visit." She could be very persuasive but Aubrey was really, just happy listening to her soothing tone.

"Can we go up to London tomorrow? Please. It would be extremely beneficial!" She was a tonic to his ears.

"Yes of course sweetie, any time." He just wanted to spend some time with her, and as he understood it the effect she had on him was healing his mind, if not his body. What was that tantric move she'd pulled when they were in bed in Amsterdam…? Aubrey was energized by her enigmatic energy.

"Great. Great! I'll meet you at the estate, nine o'clock." She sounded very positive. "I really hope this can help Aubrey! If not, it cannot do any harm." She need not have sold the idea any further; he was up for anything she had on offer.

They stayed on the phone, chatting for an hour. Aubrey was tempted to ask Natasha to stay up a while longer, but she would have to get up very early to get to Finsbury Estate by Nine. After reluctantly saying goodbye, Aubrey went into the bathroom with its large marble bassinettes and the gild-framed oblong mirrors which looked somewhat dated by modern standards. They had been installed by his mother after she had married Lord Pennington. He looked at himself in the full-length mirror beside the bidet and what he saw gave him some sense of ease. His reflection, boldly framed in the centre was proud, well contoured for a man in his mid-forties; and not a pound of flesh which was not where it should be. The walking was paying dividends.

Next morning, after a good night's sleep, he awoke, and did his thousand sit-ups. Natasha was there before nine, and the two commandeered the Roller from Sean, with no protests, and knew that a quiet weekend was on the cards. Aubrey and Natasha sped off like a pair of eloping teens, heading for London and the Bayswater Road healer. By the time they arrived on the outskirts of London, Natasha had briefed Aubrey completely on what the Ozone treatment was.

From what Natasha had said it sounded mildly promising to Aubrey. He would have an opportunity once at the clinic, to decide what he wanted to do. The treatment consisted of an intravenous needle connected to a continuously flowing tube of ozone. With a butterfly valve on the end, this was linked to a chamber filled with the highly-oxygenated air, allowing the three atoms of combined oxygen which formed under ultraviolet light, to form a molecule which was very unstable. Under highly sterilised conditions, the tube, once inserted through the main artery in the arm, became part of the blood flow into the body. When used in clinical circumstances, it was a sterilizing agent used commercially in hospitals for cleaning the air and instruments, but was now being considered as a way of supercharging the blood, by essentially oxygenating it.

"Didn't the oxygen when it reacted with the blood form air molecules in your blood?" was Aubrey's first comment.

"No, the oxygen is pure O3 which doesn't contain hydrogen, nitrogen or any other impurities, so when it encounters the blood, it's a blue coloured pungent smelling gas, which reacts instantly with the blood molecules, purifying them. In essence; it bleaches the blood."

"Bleaching!" Aubrey was shocked. "How and why would you want to bleach your blood?"

"The chemical reaction of the blood to oxygen helped clean out impurities and changed the colour of the blood from deep red, in less healthy person, to a bluish purple." Natasha continued.

Aubrey could not quite get his mind around this treatment process, but if Natasha said it was safe; he was game.

"At least I will finally be blue blooded, even if it is by transfusion!" he quipped. He chuckled to himself, keeping his eyes on the road, but a mirthful grin appeared on his face.

Natasha laughed with him, not entirely certain of the irony.

Sensing his good mood, she sat with her left knee turned in underneath her on the plush leather passenger seat. She was twisted towards him and had felt herself falling in love with Aubrey for quite some time. Adoringly she watched his face for the first time in days as it contorted into pure laughter. She was elated that he was enjoying himself, but little did she know why!
Natasha had not been privy to the convoluted politics of the Pennington household. This news was to come as quite a shock to Natasha, but one she would be extremely comfortable with. To her his position had never been the attraction. She had the opposite of an Oedipus complex, whatever that was called? She knew her fascination with Aubrey was more than just sexual. She was drawn to him in a manner which confused, but vitalised her. He was the father she had never known, the brother she had longed for and the confident she could converse with on the same level. She was attracted to

him, because of the forbearance of any ego and not for lack of self-worth. She only wondered why he had become sick?

When they hit Bayswater Road, Aubrey slowed down to look for a parking as close to the address as possible. Other vehicles gave them a wide berth as they tried to negotiate a parallel parking close to a major intersection. No one wanted to have an accident with a Rolls Royce. Usually it came at a price, and was likely to inflict more damage to the pockets of the other vehicle owners than they would have liked.

It reminded Aubrey of that wonderful urban legend he had heard at university. It was a classic story which should be taught in schools, as a lesson to all on the salacious manner of life. - A chap in a Rolls Royce is waiting for a parking bay to become available in a busy street, whilst he waits patiently for a lady who is being challenged by having to negotiate the exit to the parking. Finally, she exits and he is about to reverse into the now vacant bay, when a youngster comes along in a Mini, sneaking in ahead of him and usurping his parking bay. When challenged by the fellow in the Roller, the youngster flippantly quips, "You see what you can do when you have a Mini!" Incensed by the gall of this upstart, the fellow promptly continues reversing his Roller directly into the Mini, pushing it right out of the bay and onto the pavement. Howling in anguish over the damage inflicted to her car, the youngster yells, "What do you think you are doing?" To which, the fellow replies, "You see what you can do when you have money!"

Aubrey, now in an excellent mood, slipped the large vehicle, directly into the narrow bay, swivelling the large tires with a flick of the power steering. The two of them walked the final twenty meters to the clinic.

When they walked in, Aubrey's initial reaction was mooted by the tacky entrance hall with two brownish coloured dralon couches. It was not an auspicious start. In Aubrey's mind's eye, he had pictured a state-of-the-art clinical laboratory; so far, he was not enthused. There was an equally drab looking receptionist seated behind an old sixties style metal desk, like the ones he had seen at school in his early days. The desk served as a perfunctory receptionist station and she was humourless despite Aubrey's efforts to the contrary, remaining unmoved by his initially buoyant mood. Natasha filled out the proffered form, and sat there waiting, whilst the reception lady stared at each of them disinterestedly. No one came out to them, but during the five minutes that they waited, several other patients came in and with a cursory nod to the receptionist, they disappeared into the back.

Aubrey was becoming a little impatient, despite his attempts at entertaining them both. Finally, a geeky looking doctor, fresh-faced with little round glasses, but a considerable improvement on the austere receptionist, popped his head around the corner from the hallway. He was introduced as Dr Michael and had a firm handshake despite his rather frail form. Dr. Michael had a definite twinkle in his eyes which Aubrey hoped was a result of the use of the ozone, and not a consequence of the obviously lucrative business he was operating.

"We met during a medical symposium at the Homeopathy Conference in Brighton last summer," Natasha said, introducing Dr Michael, dressed respectfully in his white doctor's coat.

"We are just waiting for an opening in the general ward," he explained and with a smile and a nod to Natasha excused himself and disappeared again.

He returned, apologising for the further delay. Aubrey remained conscious of the sitcom developing before him. He disliked needles in the first instance and this procedure involved their use, but somehow, he was being entertained by the unfolding antics, of a peculiar situation.

Dr. Michael ushered them into his office, offering them a chair each, and apologising for his frenetic behaviour.

"We have to brief an American company with twenty million dollars to invest into our clinics," he seemed jumpy and his unease was not aiding Aubrey's mounting nerves.

"We have an urgent meeting to attend," he announced as a colleague arrived with a file. I will leave you in the capable hands of my assistant Donovan." He smiled once more, and disappeared out the front door, still dressed in his white coat.

Aubrey could not help but think that this introduction was a few slippers short of the mental asylum, but kept his mouth shut, to give Natasha, the benefit of the doubt. They rose from their respective seats and walking with Donovan, they were ushered through to an office, which doubled as both consulting room, and administration office, leaving Aubrey to ponder;

"Was his work that successful that he would be selling the idea to the Americans, or was this one of those pipe dreams, that, like a placebo, gave the patient the benefit of thinking they were being healed?" He was the proverbial doubting Thomas.

Aubrey, as sceptical as he was kept it bottled. 'If this unassuming man could convince some American company to invest that amount of money, there had to be something in it! Or was it just a ruse, to get each new patient thinking they had just encountered the 'Jesus factor' and like the Biblical encounters of healing, they had their miracle cure on tap. Was this a typical form of psychobiology?'

Donovan led them through to the back of the premises, where they were shown through to a ward. Eight beds stood alongside one length of the room. He ushered Aubrey through to a vacant hospital bed. He then turned to the elderly patient in the bed adjacent to Aubrey's and hovered over her as she calmly lay, fully clothed with an intravenous needle in her arm. Six other beds were occupied, and there was a buoyant, air of calm expectation amongst the patients. They all lay, in various aspects of dress, heads propped up on pillows, and a serene look in their eyes. Each one had their left arms extended alongside their torsos, the elbow propped on a cushion, elevating the intravenous needle that had been inserted into their flesh. A long thin plastic tube extended from the needle, and disappeared behind their heads, and unfathomably went nowhere. Aubrey could see that this room had been freshly painted and crisply clean, which was so dissimilar to the entrance hall. Aubrey was astounded; he began to suspect there was a motive, or was the entrance a work in progress?

Surveying the rest of the ward before sitting on a bed, Aubrey looked for at the other patients, one at a time. On the bed to his right was a shaven headed man, with a brace on his left ankle, a deep ruddy complexion and a pair of sapphire blue eyes. Natasha was all smiles and the chap smiled happily in return. What was he doing here? They exchanged a smile as well, and Aubrey now on the verge of no return became less concerned about those needles that hung like an array of tentacles on a giant squid, each reaching out in a cephalopodan display. It was an example of a singular colossal living organism, drawing its life blood through those searching, sinuous snorkels that disappeared inextricably behind each bed.

Just as Aubrey was about to take his place on the bed, he made as if to take off his shoes, and bending down to release the laces on his moccasins, he deftly lifted his head searching out the source from which these thin tubes emanated. They fed into a conduit in the skirting board, neatly disappearing it seemed in the direction of a large fitted cupboard near the entrance to the ward. The head of the beast was hidden from sight.

"You need not take off your shoes," offered Donovan, speaking in a hushed tone from the other side of the bed.

Aubrey started, having not seen him turn from attending the elderly lady, and looking below the level of the ward bed, saw the white sneakers that heralded Donovan's return. A little flummoxed, Aubrey raised his head back above the bed, where Donovan standing beside the bed, patted the plastic sheet that covered the end of the bed, and smiled at Aubrey. So much of his conditioned response was fear based.

"Unless you will feel more comfortable taking them off?" The voice was English, but with a hint of the Caribbean.

Aubrey raised himself up, and a little red faced more from having been craning his head below the bed, than from the less obvious embarrassment of being caught in the act of what? Only he could fathom the nuances of his sceptical mind. Aubrey left the shoes on, and climbed onto the bed. The supervisor was all smiles.

"Your first time?" he offered sensing Aubrey's discomfort. Natasha stood back out of professional courtesy. Donovan was at his side, and Aubrey, his golf shirt with short sleeves not having to necessitate the rolling up of sleeves, was immediately asked to lay back and relax.

"We won't have a problem finding a vein," Donovan held Aubrey's sinewy forearm with one hand cupped below the elbow, placing it on a pillow. He smiled amiably.

Withdrawing a fresh hypodermic needle from its plastic sheath, he worked expertly, gauging Aubrey's reaction for any hesitation. Wiping the skin with a sterilised cotton pad, Donovan had the needle inserted before Aubrey could object.

Aubrey sensed, rather than saw the red blood appear in the neck of the hypodermic needle. Donovan attached a slender plastic tube, having removed its cap. The tube extending away and behind him into that magic cupboard. Aubrey watched now with fascination, having survived the initial needle insertion. His blood flowed towards the butterfly valve in the tube, then, settled back as Donovan gently eased his arm onto an elevated cushion.

"We are only going to keep you on the ozone for ten minutes," Donovan smiled. "Just to get you used to the process."

Aubrey relaxed visibly, but was conscious that his initial reaction was a result of the conditioning of society to believe that only medical doctors knew best. He was humbled yet again. Donovan turned and walked away to attend another patient.

With Natasha now sitting on the bedside, she asked.

"How are you feeling?"

Aubrey was relaxed. He could not feel anything but the slight weight of the needle on his arm, and a sense of nothing else. He shook his head.

"Nothing yet!" If he was waiting for a magic bullet, it did not appear. He had no sensation of anything, but a sense of calmness.

"Dr Michael explained it to me a moment ago. It is like having a car," Natasha was paraphrasing. "You need to have a clean air filter for the lungs, clean oil filter for your kidneys, good clean fuel to power your body, and enough water to keep it cool. Without that the engine dies."

Aubrey was proud of her. This was an analogy he could relate to.

The chap next to him was watching, unmoved but clearly intent on their concerns. He made no attempt to intervene, but there was an unspoken regard, which he could offer, if they were to ask. Aubrey asked.

"How long have you been doing this?" He looked like a seasoned veteran.

"Oh, not long this time." He confirmed. "Just having some treatment to accelerate the healing of the bones." He indicated his ankle, bound by a fancy looking space boot.

Oh, you only broke your ankle?" Aubrey was somewhat disappointed. He expected the man to be there for sustaining treatment of life shattering consequences. The shaven headed man just shook his brightly glowing pate.

"Yes. This time at least." He let it hang.

"You have been here before?" Aubrey was challenged by a need to know how his previous treatment had panned out. "What was that for…. if you don't mind me asking?"

The nose bulbous, hung above a cheery smile. "Not at all!" There was nothing to hide. He raised himself slightly, creating a pregnant pause whilst he repositioned himself awkwardly on the bed, his space boot interfering with the movement, all the while keeping his arm elevated so as not to interrupt the flow of the life-giving gas.

"I used to come every day, whilst I was undergoing chemotherapy for cancer treatment." He did not elaborate. Aubrey wondered if that was when he had lost his hair.

"That was ten years ago." He continued in a matter of fact way.

"What? This clinic has been here ten years?" He was quite shocked. Natasha offered no comment.

"Well not here at least, but Dr. Michael had the practice at his home in Crystal Palace, for quite some time before moving here."

"Oh," replied Aubrey. Not sure what to offer next.

"Yes. The ozone not only helps with the healing process, but it is great for eradicating toxins from the body. The Chemo left me quite weak, so the oncologist recommended a vigorous treatment on Ozone."

"The process involves the oxygenating of the blood, to assist with the release of those toxins, but it also helps the tissue to heal, and when the highly-oxygenated blood enters the affected area, like with my broken ankle, it assists with rejuvenation at a cellular level." No diagnosis, no convoluted Latin phrases, just a sense of natural healing on a basic biological level.

"So, you are in complete remission?" Natasha asked, redirecting the shaven headed man's attention to the foot of Aubrey's bed.

"Yes. I had testicular cancer. It was caused by my own stupidity." He bit his lower lip.

The silence that followed was politely interrupted by Natasha.
"Introspection is a cathartic part of the healing process."

"Yes. I suppose it was my Achilles heel, so to speak." He shook his booted foot, allowing a moment for both Natasha and Aubrey to catch the joke.

"But seriously. I think if I had not been injecting myself with steroids, I may well have never had the cancer."

Aubrey contemplated the gravity of what had been offered; there was an awkward silence.

"My apologies! This is Natasha, and I am Aubrey." He waved with his right hand, unable to make any effort to bridge the gap between beds and shake hands.

"Good to meet you. My name is Lance." was again all smiles.

"Yes, the cancer has been stopped. Not that it ever is stopped!" He corrected himself. "But the ozone helped me recover very quickly. It is fantastic."

He certainly looked healthy, and his skin was ablaze with vigour. 'Perhaps this was an elixir woman wishing to remain looking younger should consider.' Aubrey was thinking.

"How long do you have the treatment for?" Natasha was doing her own research.

"Forty minutes. That is three times a week now. But I am also using the chamber at Cambridge, which helps knit the bones quicker."

"Oh, like a compression chamber?" Aubrey was aware of decompression sickness for scuba diving accidents, when nitrogen in the blood expands too quickly if a diver surfaces too quickly.

"Yes exactly. Do you dive?" Lance was happy to meet a fellow scuba buddy. They were a close-knit family.

"I used to," replied Aubrey, his last experience in Port Elizabeth still a distant memory that would haunt him for years to come.

"Fantastic. I have not been able to since I broke my ankle." He looked rather disappointed.

"How long do they say it will be before you can scuba dive again?" Natasha needed to know.

"Oh, less than a month! Perhaps six weeks at worst. I would just need to be careful of the ankle getting damaged again. Otherwise it is natural healing all the way." He smiled, his warm infectiousness growing on them.

"So, you have not had any other medical treatment?" Natasha was again all research.

"No! And I stay away from doctors at all cost." Aubrey thought that an odd expression. He wondered if he meant at the cost of losing his foot? No, it was obviously a reference to the chemo treatment. Aubrey now wished he too had such an obvious lease on life.

"I know how you feel!" Aubrey smiled. "I have been prodded and poked enough already." There was an unspoken camaraderie. Like soldiers on the battlefield, they suffered their various ailments in silence, lest the occupier's sense their wounds as mortally inflicted, and put them out of their misery.

"The early Muslims introduced the idea of alchemy to the world, over a thousand years ago." He elaborated. "They developed an idea that man could create anything from nothing, so ending poverty, pestilence and poor health. Their culture and traditions were not so dissimilar to the Greeks, and ultimately the great period of the 'Dark Ages' were not so. They were 'dark' if you happened to be a European living under the yolk of Roman Catholic oppression." But Aubrey knew this from his studies at King's.

"But if you were an early Muslim in the Middle East and its surrounds, the explosion of Sciences, Medicine and technology was immense. So much of what the Christian Church had done was of significant detriment to European cultures during a time, before the reformation." Lance was obviously a student of history. The diversification of these sciences, had brought significant development to the study of medicine and had it not been for the early Popes, who had fought valiantly to limit the power of the early Islamic nations, those strides that had been made, would have saved the continent of Europe from the 'Black Death'.

"The diseases of the eighteenth century, and ultimately the flu epidemics of the twentieth, would not have happened, because the Muslim world was structured and extremely aware of health and cleanliness issues." Lance was enjoying having an attentive audience! Or were they a trapped audience?
"Had the Christians not sunk so deep into the sanctity of their own righteousness, and rather embraced the cultures of the Middle East, the world would not only be a better place, but a healthier one!"

"Have you studied Philosophy?" Aubrey recognised the symptoms.

"Theology. It was a course in the history of the early church, that changed my mind." He did not elaborate.

"You study philosophy?" Lance ventured.

"Who me?" Aubrey shook his head. "Maybe a long time ago, but I prefer to think of the world with strictly less certainty. Perhaps with a slightly jaded opinion, born of experience."

"Oh yes. Perhaps there is something to be said for cynicism?" The thought of having a soul mate, to while away the boredom of a forty-minute session, was a tonic to Lance's mind.

"That form of repression was orchestrated by fundamental beliefs that spurred the religious wars that have ensued. The Christian fundamentalist, is as dangerous as any Muslim fundamentalist! Sometimes, I think the Church has shares in the pharmaceutical industry." Lance may have studied theology, but it may have been an awakening of a different sort.

Aubrey knew that his treatment and ultimate good health would have its foundations in faith and good fortune. Not in yielding to the cattle prodding of modern science. Faith in his spirituality and his angel guide.

This meeting was fortuitous and meeting Natasha had been fortuitous. He needed to follow his innate sense of self-preservation. Too many today, succumb to the so-called wisdom of medical practitioners, who are as largely ignorant as the public. He knew that mankind had abdicated their inherent senses for the greater convenience. That inherent knowledge was once upon a time as common to mankind, as instinct is to an animal in the wild. Today however, he felt that too much emphasis was given to the modern medical field.

"They have not learnt to take their own medicine, 'so to speak'," Lance laughed.

"The Roman Catholic Church has not yet learnt from those mistakes or is divinely pursuing its own agenda," Natasha offered. They both looked on interestedly.

"It has perpetuated a single act of lunacy that indirectly preserves its market share. By advocating the non-use of condoms, a vital preventative measure in the fight against the spread of HIV in Third World countries." Natasha's eyes narrowed; Aubrey could see the fire behind her contracted pupils.

"A lack of understanding and cultural stigmas prevents the poor from containing population explosion," Lance was in agreement.

"The marginalized poor always propagate large, seemingly unsustainable families which result in unnecessary hardship and suffering. The Church keeps their customers happy in the knowledge of divine salvation, often meaning they must forego contraception. AIDS is a factor that the Church has still not managed to come to grips with. Despite this knowledge, the Church has committed the most heinous of crimes, by advising the poor and poorly educated to abstain, rather than use condoms."

'A good diet, healthy lifestyle including better sanitation, and ultimately better education is the answer," Natasha offered.

"But alas, the Church is not putting its money where its' mouth is, creating a swathe of suffering. Humanity is being side-lined for spiritual purity, at the expense of humanism. What is required to combat the scourge of AIDS was a doctrine of human interests and values of a more secular nature." Lance was enjoying the debate.

"What planet are these people living on," Aubrey commented. "They clearly have no grasp on the reality of modern day living!" But then in truth they lived a rather cloistered life! Aubrey made a mental note to himself to re-explore that idea, the Professor had raised concerning a little-known work called, 'Of the Laws of Ecclesiastical Polity.' The key to his thinking was the juxtaposition of State versus Church and a more humane rationale that dealt with this scourge. Yes, a Renaissance! That was the key. They all remained quietly in contemplation. Nothing more need be said.

He was beginning to feel slightly depressed. Aubrey could do this to himself, and admonished himself each time. Here he was on the verge of finding a potential cure to his malady, and he had thought himself into a spiral of negative thought. He could not help it. There was a common trait amongst men whose childhoods were skewed by a dysfunctional family environment. They had difficulty understanding the merit of a positive outlook on life. These men were destined to be great thinkers, but they would always have difficulty putting those ideas into practical terms. This was why Aubrey had walked away from two exceptional ideas, several fantastic businesses and a wonderful woman. Aubrey would need to remedy that! But for now, he could not help himself.

The only thing Aubrey had immediately noticed was a sense of healing calmness about the people in the ward, unlike the energy you get when visiting a hospital. He always felt depressed when walking into one of those hideous Victorian style hospitals, like St Thomas' in London, which had been built in a period when medicine was verging on the explosions that would see Fleming and Pasteur create massive steps forward in research. That had been a hundred years before and they had not only survived the bombings of London during the Blitz, but also stood as memorials to the successive Labour Governments, that had expanded National Health services, whilst ignoring the possibility of alternative forms of medicine.

What was it that the Professor had said, 'If the state of a nation's health regime was evident from the smiles of its patients; then the NHS had failed dismally, because the average Britain had teeth to die for; literally. Their teeth stood as tombs to the diseases of their mouths, symptomatic of inferior dental practices and poor health education.' Was this then an attempt to thumb his proverbial nose at the Establishment and keep the alternative medical fraternity alive and kicking? Aubrey would wait and see; he was quietly confident Natasha knew what she was talking about.

Returning, a disappointingly quick ten minutes later, Donovan smiled at Aubrey with quiet self-assurance that reminded him he was in control.

After the treatment, Natasha again asked, "How do you feel?"

"No different," replied Aubrey, as they said their good byes and walked out.

"Don't we have to make another appointment, or is that it?" Aubrey, could not have been more wishful.

Natasha shook her head. "No, we will just pop in when you feel like it, and there is always a bed available at any time during the day."
"What about the payment?" Aubrey looked perplexed, as no money had exchanged hands.

"No, Michael gives the first treatment free, so that we can establish if you want to come back. If you feel up to it, we can come back tomorrow or later in the week if you prefer?" He considered for a moment, that she was taking ownership, alongside him, of this disease. It gave him an assurance that the treatment would go well.

It all sounded very casual, but that was how Aubrey preferred it. He could get used to this kind of less-invasive form of treatment.

"Do you want to have lunch somewhere nice," was Aubrey's immediate response.

"Yes," was Natasha's answer, and with that Aubrey opened the Roller's door for her, and she fell into the large black leather covered seat.

As they zoomed off to Harrods, Aubrey felt inclined to ask; "What did you make of Dr. Michael's discussion about the American deal?"

Natasha was taking in the scenes around her. She looked puzzled. "Why?"

"The mention of money at a first meeting may explain a lot about a person's motives!" He was deep in thought. If Michaels' true passion had been the holistic healing benefits of the practice, he would have had no need to talk about his success in large dollar terms at their very first meeting. Unless it was simply his conditioned justification to the years his ideas had been put down by the established medical fraternity. They, no doubt saw him as a charlatan because of an unwillingness to understand the methods he used. Or, alternatively they may not have wanted to know about his medical breakthroughs, as they themselves had been so successfully conditioned by all the large pharmaceutical companies. They might be taught by the medical fraternity to diagnose and dispense only the drugs they sold.

Perhaps not, he began to suspect there was method in their madness. If first impressions were so vital in any business, surely that would have been a real negative, but Aubrey considered the possibility that the entrance had been designed just such. It would stand to reason, that if they had just walked into a clinic, with its' treatment on the cutting edge of medical science, it would stand to reason the purveyors of that treatment might be reluctant to advertise, especially in the heart of London's more fashionable areas.

The roller whistled through the morning traffic, zipping into the congested Kensington Road, after Aubrey decided to cut through Hyde Park. Aubrey sped through London with the agility of a formula one driver allowing Natasha to sway from side to side, squealing every time they snaked past another traffic obstruction.

They were enjoying themselves, and the conversation had no place, now; in this old city, where old ideology and established rules were so deep seated.

Before long, they had arrived at the front of Harrods, with the long hand showing exactly twelve, as they walked through the entrance. That would allow them to get a seat at the deli, and gave Natasha the chance to shop a little. Big mistake! With his left arm hooked around Natasha's waist the two of them entered, and cut back into the food court hitting the main gush of morning tourists. As they slipped past a plethora of Japanese tourists, the food court appeared to their left and it was already busy with diners. It was the touristy equivalent of lunch at Buckingham Palace probably, having just been past the Palace and Big Ben. At the food court, they arrived settled on two bar stools at the deli counter, and were immediately assisted by an assistant in her crisply ironed Harrods uniform. The lady, a very tall blond Polish immigrant, immediately asked in her best English.

"Vat may I help you vith?"

Aubrey smiled and said. "May we see the menu?"

"Yez, off coursh," she admonished herself. Aubrey smiled to Natasha. With the menus whisked off the counter almost out of the groping hands of a small Japanese lady, they were handed to Natasha and Aubrey. She stood expectantly, but dutifully waiting for their order.

"Thank you …Greta," Aubrey had read her nametag. "We'll let you know as soon as we have decided."

"Yez, yez," she chided herself, flushing a little that she had not thought to give them a chance to read the menu.

Aubrey gave Natasha's hand a contented squeeze. He was very comfortable with her in many ways.

"Wow, there is so much, and it all looks so wonderful," she was beguiling to watch, so elegant in her effortless approach, and yet always so enthused with life.
Aubrey was elated by the pleasure he felt when with this charming free-spirited and beautiful woman. Yet, he had reservations, as he pondered the situation. Was he being fair to her, if the chance of a relapse was to become an issue? He was thinking of getting Natasha a gift. It was their one-month anniversary, yet so much had happened in that time and she had been instrumental in all of it. He wanted to thank her for all her support, but she was such an elegantly uncomplicated creature, he could not think what to get her. They had been chatting whilst looking at the menu, when a voice rang out from the right side of the deli counter.

"Good Lord, it's you again. Are you following me old man?"

Aubrey looked up. It was none other than Jerry leering at them across the deli counter from the seclusion of a hooded shaggy sheepskin anorak. He looked bloated, like 'toad in a hole', a particularly English delicacy. The sausage plumped by the fatty oil that it was saturated in and nestling in creamed potato mash. Aubrey wondered how long he had been watching them, before he chose to announce his presence.

Aubrey smiled, an easy reflective smile, and gave Natasha's hand another squeeze. He could not help but cringe as the man with the adolescent hoody, circled the counter and was upon them. It was just an irritation he could do without!

"Natasha, this is Jerry." as he hovered behind them and offering his supine wrist.

"Enchanted, Mon Cheri." The greeting was enunciated so that each syllable seemed insincere.

Aubrey spoke up. "Jerry was an old varsity chum, and was on an outing to the country yesterday. We bumped into each other when I went for my walk." No more was needed.

"Yes, and your old man here was out and about, without you!" Was it Jerry's way of making Aubrey feel he had to explain himself. If he had to it was shortly lived as Natasha quipped.

"What a pleasure to meet you," as she extended her hand, it was grasped none too gently. With his podgy hand in hers, he proceeded to drool all over Natasha like a slobbering puppy.

Aubrey gave Natasha a quick look, not sure what to say. Whatever it was she was thinking, he was sure he would be entertained with it later.

"What the devil are you doing in town?" Jerry was all questions again.

"Just a little treat for Natasha, to have lunch and take in a show." Was all Aubrey would venture? Jerry was the last person he wanted knowing about his condition. It would be broadcast all over the City before they had finished their lunch.

"Oh good, in that case I'd like to invite you both to dinner this evening, at my Pied-a-Terre in Notting Hill. You must come; it simply won't do to have you wondering around this monstrous city without a drink in your hand."

"Yes, well we are planning to take in a show," so as not to make too much a point of it, Aubrey wanted to short-circuit that idea.

"Nonsense, I won't hear of it," he countered. "Besides there are no good shows on, it's all that bloody touristy stuff they put on for our lesser brethren from across the seas." Jerry's family had immigrated to England, to escape the Nazi persecutions.

"Actually, we did want to spend some time together, as I have not seen Aubrey since last weekend." was all Natasha could say, sensing that Aubrey was beginning to feel irritated with the imposition. She wanted to keep him relaxed, and Jerry wasn't helping.

"By Gad! I haven't seen the 'old man' in twenty years, and now we meet twice in two days! Surely this is serendipity!"

"Thank you, but I think we need to take a rain check on that offer." Aubrey doing his best to be courteous, but firm. He liked to be spontaneous, but there was a limit to how much he would endure, and Jerry was about that limit. They had not intended to be in London for the night, and yet there was a lesson somewhere within this chance meeting, which required pursuit. But not now.

Aubrey, who had been seated facing Natasha, raised his eyebrows. It was a plaintive plea. Physiognomy aside, she read his thinking. This was one of the things she loved about him. He did not suffer fools, and Natasha could gauge his desire not to accept.

"Thank you, but I have already purchased tickets," Natasha lied.

"Oh, what a pity," Jerry lamented. "Perhaps next time?" He turned on his heels, and was off. Bags flailing in the process.

Aubrey had not said a word, but Natasha could pick up his mood, and with no further ado, they rose and escaped the madness through the side foyer, not stopping to witness any further charade.

It was a parody of everything the English held dear, but was the one saving grace the British could claim. The immigration of every other race to Britain's shores, had guaranteed that the justification of xenophobia, which now tainted virtually every Third World country in its post-colonial rush to democracy, had indeed not taken hold in Britain. London, in particular, was a cosmopolitan convergence of cultures, each with talents, values and variations of a lifestyle which seemed to blend effortlessly in a migratory buffet, evident from the surge of humanity that greeted them as they hit the lunch-hour crowds on Brompton Road. But the disease of xenophobia, seemed the preserve of the underclass, and it bubbled away underneath those streets.

In Baker Street, where they found a lovely bistro, they whiled away the afternoon, totally absorbed in each other and forgetting, absolutely everything else.

A great bottle of Chablis and many nibbles between the even more rewarding lip-smacking fares that were served up provided an adequate distraction. The discussion seemed to flow as eloquently as the wine, and before long, Aubrey who had not touched alcohol for several months, was quite intoxicated. High on both life and Natasha, he became more outspoken and quite witty. As he became inebriated, letting his guard down, he let Natasha closer than ever to the real vulnerable Aubrey.

They spoke about their respective childhoods and Aubrey's travels and Natasha's studies, leading them all back to that fateful meeting at Reading. Aubrey was more expressive in his current state than ever before and Natasha loved what she saw. Aubrey made Natasha laugh as he spoke unreservedly about David, and Timothy and the way their paths had crossed repeatedly, and how he finally came to be in England again. Natasha was overwhelmed by the nature of all his adventures. Aubrey had been halfway around the world, and he had so much to share.

"It is difficult to divorce the idea that the Estate should not be seen in exclusion to my mother's estate." The two, although separated from each other by an anti-nuptial contract, had shown the degree to which Lady Pennington had ensured they remain separate. He had never spoiled her up until then, because it had taken Aubrey until now to realize, that his inheritance from his mother was that, 'his inheritance'.

"My mother, I think, enjoyed the benefit of her title, which she had used to further her own family and business interests," yet Aubrey, who had been born into the marriage after an imperceptibly long honeymoon period, was now comfortable with the possibility that his lineage excluded any Pennington bloodline.

"My mother was a wile old vixen, taking liberties with my father. All the while it appeared, she had duped him, but not as I may have suspected for the money; she had not needed it!" His eyes glazed over imperceptibly.

Aubrey was becoming quite melancholy. The lengths she would have gone, to ensure that Aubrey be given an opportunity to succeed in a world of privilege. Yet on a whim, he had summarily dispensed with it in an edict which would be signed with his lawyers very shortly.

Aubrey was more assured of his position, and it was not the title he wanted. No recognition of class or privilege could replace the feeling he had for that ancient country of ancestors, and to it, he would return, empowered with the proceeds of an Industrial revolution, which had brought wealth and opportunity to his mother's family, and the trappings of a privileged life bestowed on the Pennington's by a grateful Queen Victoria, would not be required back in Zimbabwe. He had made up his mind, on a whim, whilst they had sat reminiscing over lunch. It had been something Natasha had said, and Aubrey knew intuitively that he was to return. The time was right, and Mugabe would be gone soon, and with that, the rebuilding of that beloved homeland could begin in earnest. No more would he be torn between the love of his country of birth, and an ancient but romantic notion that he was more at home in his spiritual home, with his Elephants.

When the coffee finally arrived, it was four thirty, and the kitchens were closing for the lunch trade and the waitrons were packing the tables and chairs. Just as they were about to leave, Aubrey dropped a most unexpected piece of news in Natasha's lap. He was quite determined and was going to take Natasha right then and there to Selfridges, as he intended buying her a gift. This was unexpected and out of character, but he now felt imbibed with the spirit of life. To date he had not bought her a bunch of flowers much less a gift from Selfridges. This was quite unexpected. Aubrey paid the bill and with the two in a convivial mood and arm in arm, they walked down the road to the department store.
Aubrey opened the door for Natasha. She giggled, and dressed only in her summer frock, and a pair of open sandals, she skipped delightedly inside.

At the ladies' department, she was given over to the assistants who happily obliged Aubrey, whose instruction was, "whatever she wants." Clearly, Aubrey was feeling extravagant, and Natasha just loved this new side of Aubrey. It was not so much the expression of generosity, or the opportunity to be spoilt; it was that both Natasha and Aubrey knew that this wealth was a tombstone around his neck, ready to drag him down. As he watched from a comfortable chair he thought about Africa. His wealth could be used so much more effectively, but now the thought reminded him of those barbaric 'necklacing's' of the revolutionary detractors. That was how the comrades had settled their scores in the pre-democratic South Africa, and it would be used again in the coming social revolution. This revolution would be for a truly free democracy; not the current system foisted on them by an 'Orwellian' African National Congress, which was entirely inadequate. The question would be, "Would the young, new comradeship, led by a 'Napoleonesque' Malema, see the real culprits; or continue with the zeal of their parents."

"All men are enemies. All animals are comrades." But just who would they see as the animals? Or were their snouts so deeply buried in the trough; that their eyes were blinkered!

It was a signal to those that might disagree with a liberation struggle mentality, that they would be the next, to be adorned by that inhumane symbol of power. Displays of wealth were a harbinger of the violence that pursued individuals or communities that paraded this success. In an uncivilized society, it was the claxon call to the 'have-nots', who would wrestle that wealth from, those intent, on not sharing its proceeds. Aubrey would know the damage done to societies that did not share in their combined wealth. It was the precursor to decay in moral values, and as he had seen in Zimbabwe, and was evident in Congo; the atrophy of a societies' core values, was directly proportional to how much obvious showing of wealth was on view to the proletariat.

No system could hope to succeed, unsullied by displays of grandiose wealth, whilst their brethren lived in squalor and inadequacy. Aubrey would spoil her, this once, but thereafter he would spare the considerable wealth accumulated by his mother's family, and use it proactively to promote the rebuilding of a nation, whose considerable assets, for now, lay in bank accounts in Indonesia and the Far East. Ironically, Mugabe would be forced to return to the East, from where he had received his entire liberation struggle funding, and unbeknown to the world at large, to a grave outside his native Zimbabwe. When the benefactors of his tyrannical rule of nearly thirty years, finally found the timing right, to denounce him as the dictator he is and was, the damage would have already been done. Mugabe would leave a legacy of un-chivalrous Kleptocracy, and like the marauding Vikings of the past, he had shipped all the spoils of his pillage to bank accounts, seemingly, he thought, beyond the reach of International authorities. He would however be wrong!

Whilst Natasha was shown all the options for an evening dress, Aubrey wondered off to the jewellery counter, and picked out a pendant, and a pair of matching earrings, with a unique blue stone which he thought matched Natasha's eyes.

"Tanzanite Sir!" Came, a quick comment from the behind the glass cases counter.

He looked at the colour, the cut and the exceptional quality and without hesitation he bought the matching stones. Remarkably, they were as valuable as diamonds, and because of their rarity, would become even more so. So, for Aubrey the irony was tangible. He would buy this jewellery for Natasha, and the stones would complement her beauty. How they became part of the great consumer cycle, no one would probably ever quite know or understand properly. Or maybe they would in time?

After returning to the Ladies apparel department, Aubrey discovered a perfume which he was immediately drawn to. It aroused him with pheromone intensity, so he bought it instantly.

He returned to 'the ladies in waiting', who had now bedecked Natasha in a bold print of yellows and blues. It was cut to the knee, with a wide black sequined belt, hung decoratively over the hips, which accentuated both Natasha's long tanned legs, and her high child bearing hips. She looked like Carly Simon in that music video he had seen in the seventies. She lit up the room like a Bunsen burner in a chemistry laboratory. Her azure eyes, were assured and fiercely off set by the bold colour of the dress. She had on a pair of open toed high heels with a braided strap, and this was delightful, but as he noticed, she was not wearing nail varnish. Everything about her was natural and she looked stunning. He sat and relaxed on the leather-clad ottoman, and as an artist might reflect on a painting in progress, he waited patiently as they regaled her in the jewellery.

The pendant set in a white gold claw and the earrings which she had to clip on, as she had never had her ears pierced, matched perfectly. Natasha cooed her approval; a gentle Turtle dove, wooed by her mate. As fetching in her new outfit, there was no denying it; but her true beauty was evident in that sad smile.

She was a gem, previously uncut, and with not the faintest hint of exaggeration, she had now been transformed into a genuine starlet. He appraised her genuine beauty, confident in the knowledge she was a catch, but not a trophy. Aubrey was speechless.

"All dressed up, and nowhere to go." She grinned, her impish smile an aphrodisiac.

Aubrey and Natasha swished out of the store, Natasha soigné in her new attire and Aubrey two inches taller, resplendent in his pride.

They hailed a taxi, then back to the car in Bayswater Road, and leaving the 'Roller' in the street where it was, they dropped off Natasha's packages and then taking the taxi, its' big diesel motor chugging away dutifully, they headed back to Leicester Square and a show.

Chapter 18

Welcome to Nottingham Forest

The red luminous sun crept over the Indian Ocean horizon, early morning humidity, smudged across an eastern canvas that was clouded in mystery. Aubrey had left the harbour aboard a cargo ship destined for the Congo. The thick haze, already hung like the blanket on a Durban July winner; steaming with post-race condensation. There was a smell in the air of rotting fish, which came from the harbour wall as the freighter rounded the entrance and made its way out to sea. The fishermen of Indian-descent and scourge of the harbour officials, lined the great concrete harbour wall with their three-meter-long fishing poles, trawling the ocean for anything they could take home to the many mouths that were waiting to be fed.

They were there before sunrise, sometimes a two-hour trip from their shanty abodes in the slums that were scattered from the edge of Durban's elegant Berea, as far north as the squalid townships of the North Coast. They came in their bakkies and VW hatch-backs, pockmarked by time, and evidence of the financial divide which still separated the colour bar of post-Apartheid South African society. How road-worthy those cars were, was of no relevance; they were the happy-go-lucky cousins in a society of erstwhile social misfits, eager to eke out whatever living was to be had, and undaunted by political upheavals. They knew their place in a forbidding system that favoured only one side of the political divide, and then the other. Foreigners in a foreign land, faultless of the futility of an establishment of Falstaffian proportions.

They slipped seemingly between the two; the underclass of both, intent on survival, but happy nonetheless. The fish they plucked from the diesel fuel laden silt of the harbour entrance, often ended up in the fish restaurants of the tourist destinations up the North Coast. This was where wealthy Jo'burg holidaymakers would spend their summer vacations. The lead saturated fish caused many pre-natal pregnancy terminations, that were so prevalent along the Natal coastline. There were also birth defects and pre-cancerous tumours that became an epidemic amongst the communities in which these fish became a staple diet. This caused all manner of health issues in new-born children and everyone, both poor and wealthy alike were affected by the scourge.

The poorer communities mostly suffered the effects of this poverty, as the migrant workers', who had worked well in harsh humid climactic conditions, had been brought in to work the clammy sugar cane fields of the Natal coast.

The Indians and Sri Lankan workers came from similar climes in Bangalore and the Pearl Island and were well suited to the plantation work. They stayed on to raise large families, many becoming victims of their own ignorance, and culture. The harsh conditions of the sugar cane fields, where cane rats, if they did not bite, spread their disease like wildfire amongst the working population. The Apartheid Government of the time turned a blind eye to the death toll, but somehow, these families survived living on the increasingly polluted fish reserves.

Of course, many were left destitute and without work, when the wealthy sugar cane plantation owners began turning their estates into large Balinese style residential communities, further enhancing their own wealth, but leading to distress for many. They turned the once pristine Natal coastline into massive housing estates that dotted the North and South alike, impervious to local authorities, who allowed one application after the next to transform the lungs of Natal into a dead-zone of environmental incompetence. The once densely laden vegetation that soaked up the saturation of a modestly sub-tropical climate was now replaced by tar roads and brick driveways, therein paving the way to an immense run-off catastrophe, which took with it the top soil from the rolling Kwa Zulu-Natal hills. This sediment in turn choked the river estuaries, and played havoc with the natural ecology. The irony was that as fast as the developers could build these units, the sea was reclaiming the land with its rising tidal system. Residential homes on the North Coast would be forced further and further inland, and more and more of the natural vegetation would be lost. Perhaps God, in His infinite wisdom, had a sense of humour after all.

Aubrey stayed on deck until the Durban Bluff began to fade below the horizon. The ocean was a millpond, calm and serene; a welcome sight to any a seafarer, and a potentially good omen. The voyage was starting well, and there was an air of expectation as Aubrey watched one chapter of his life drift away and as another chapter was about to begin. He went down into the cafeteria only once there was absolutely no sign of the Wild Coast to be seen. Then he had his breakfast, safe in the knowledge that there was no one to pursue him. He had not stopped looking over his shoulder since his meeting with Victor two days before, but now he could finally relax. The day-long trip took him past the Eastern Cape, but Aubrey had little time to view anything after a day of chores in the ships kitchens and swabbing the floors of the living quarters. Aubrey emerged on deck, just in time to see the sun set over the western horizon, where Bronwyn would likewise be sitting looking out over that same ocean and fretting over Aubrey's disappearance.

Aubrey suspected, that Bronwyn now had something else on her mind. The police would have been to see her, having had a report that a break in had occurred at the scuba diving store in Main Road. Bronwyn would not know, there were fingerprints all over the window in the bathroom that the thieves had used to gain access to the store. They would have been given a report by an agitated owner that Aubrey was involved. They would need to talk to Aubrey to establish if these were indeed, his fingerprints. Where was he, and could they get a copy of his I.D? Bronwyn, devastated, would immediately suspect foul play. Most of the contents of the store having been removed, and ironically, some expensive equipment like the computers and other easily movable electronics had been left. There would now be a warrant out for his arrest.

Aubrey allowed his furtive imagination to ponder the outcome.

"No! The equipment would have to be exported from South Africa, and it is possible it may have been shipped already. It was probably already on board a ship destined for the Far East, and the black markets of the Chinese Triads!" It may even be aboard a ship like the one registered to a South Korean shipping company that had left Durban harbour early that morning, headed for Thailand. The detective would investigate, but he had limited resources. "He would get back to her!"

She would have to hand in their passports at the local police station, and inform him if Aubrey contacted her. Aubrey had not confided in her, so that she would not have supported these actions. He knew she would have been partial to the conspiracy, so the less she knew for a fact; the better.

This way, he believed, she could never be implicated, and likewise he could never be found! Of course, Aubrey had been three hundred miles away up the Wild Coast, sleeping in the Pajero, when the break-in would have occurred. She would never be able to prove his innocence, and he had unwittingly created a smoke screen for the real culprits, by leaving the Pajero, which would ultimately be found in the parking garage of a less than salubrious hotel on Durban's Embankment. Bronwyn would be left in the long term to suspect Aubrey, despite her better judgement. She in turn would find solace in the knowledge that the proceeds from the sale of that equipment, would buy her, and the young child some degree of security. She would accept the proceeds from an unknown benefactor.

In the interim, Aubrey safely wound his way around the Cape of Good Hope, enroute to Kinshasa, the Capital of the Democratic Republic of the Congo. They skirted the coastline of Namibia, avoiding the treacherous Skeleton

Coast which was and still is the resting place of many an explorer. This was the romantic coastline on which tales of grand adventure had evoked the passions of historians and their subsequent novels. Africa in all its grandeur was a perfidious place, never failing to annihilate those weary but intrepid travellers, intent on the spoils of the vast fortunes that lay beneath and above its soil. Along this coastline at the wide mouths of the great rivers that snuck inextricably through the dry Karoo and Namib deserts, was the source of a greed which was to grip a continent and tear its innards apart like the spoils of a Zebra carcass, at a ferociously barbaric Lion feeding frenzy.

'Diamonds', which lay within the depths of the Kimberlitic pipes that emanated from the ancient strata of the Southern African continent, billions of years in the making, yet somehow torn from the earth in a quest to feed the desires of an avaricious human society. The earth had created a phenomenal process that had given up these buried riches, through a procedure of millennia-old erosion and depository aggregation. The entire process, which nature had construed as the appropriate means of divulging her secret bounty, lay in the relative confines of the alluvial shale on the seabed. But 'clever old man', had devised a manner in which he could rip those riches, not only from the easily accessible alluvial deposits, but would render the majestic earth asunder to grasp those that still lay in wait for future generations. North, and further north, past the great oil rigs off the Angolan coast, and on up into the lion's lair.

Although the inaptly named Democratic Republic of the Congo stood as Africa's salvation for economic prosperity, its wars waged in the name of democracy, were a testament to the savagery of its leaders and lieutenants alike. They had and continued to render untold barbarism on the general population and it was into this feeding frenzy that Aubrey would travel.

He had spent ten days on board the ship, and finally decided to disembark at the inland port city of Matadi. He had stood on the deck as the freighter had entered the narrow spit at Banana from the south, their prized cargo, enroute to the city of Kinshasa that stood some several hundred miles or so to the east, on the banks of the vast Congo River. The lower stretches of this immense river network, interspersed with islands and mangrove plantations, was the sedimentary deposits from the heart of Africa. She regurgitated the contents of a billion years of alluvial soil onto this low lying plain. The Lady of the Congo, as she was known, laid bare her assets for all to see. Like some salaciously, seditious harlot, she lay in wait, three thousand and some miles from her source, in the eastern rift valley. Inviting the explorer to enter her as Sir Henry Morton Stanley had done so some one hundred and twenty years before. The relative calm of her twisting confluence at the coastal entry, belied the treachery that awaited the intrepid voyager. The elevation of the river from her eastern source evoked great rapids and un-navigable stretches. So, with only a rail network from Matadi to Kinshasa, the equipment would trundle the remaining three hundred and sixty-five kilometres; one kilometre for every day and one kilometre for every soul lost to malaria and typhoid, in the building of that railhead. Aubrey looked up to the monument that stood as testimony to their endeavours, as a sacrificial lamb on the hilltop overlooking Matadi and wondered fleetingly, what lay in store for his soul beyond that hill.

"Howzit?" Daniel had offered as an introduction to Aubrey.

"Well, thank you. How are you?" Aubrey recognised the South Africanism.

"Where is this equipment destined for?" He was making conversation. The only English speaker at the port, Aubrey had been tasked by the captain to assist with the unloading.

"Inland." Aubrey welcomed the respite from the pigeon English spoken aboard ship.

"That's a big place," Aubrey gestured with a sweep of an arm, then turned to Daniel, reaching out with a friendly hand. "Aubrey."

"Daniel." Looking at the chaos unfolding on the keyside.

"I am headed to the Amatito mine on the Congo River." He was there to oversee the safe delivery of the equipment to the mine.

Daniel smiled. A lob-sided grin. Aubrey could see he had a lazy eye. Returning his handshake, Aubrey could feel the dampness of his armpits. Morning had broken over the equator, and the heat was already oppressive.

"You?" Daniel was asking. Perhaps he recognised the traveller symptoms; or just making conversation.

"Kinshasa." Aubrey stood shoulder to shoulder with Daniel. The great package swung pendulously on its crate.

"Why not fly this stuff in?" Aubrey watched the crane operator in his lofty rig high above them. He was shouting insults in French as labourers scurried.

"Too expensive," Daniel seemed un-phased.

"Also, there is no airstrip big enough for a C one-sixty." Aubrey stepped back as a low-level pass nearly took their heads off. Ropes flailed.

"How are you getting it there?" Aubrey could see no container, or trucks.

"Road, all the way." Daniel grabbed hold of one end of the wooden packing box as it came to an abrupt halt, roped secured. Twenty smiling Congolese, with white teeth hung perilously on in a Gulliverian embrace.

"What are the roads like?" Aubrey, intrigued, could sense disaster.

"If you're heading to Kinshasa, why not catch a lift with me and find out?" Daniel slipped a loose rope over the wooden crate.

"That would be great." Aubrey could hear the diesel motor as a fork lift rushed scurrilously along the keyside.

"In fact, I could do with some help getting this to the mine." Daniel's eyes pleaded.

"Sounds good," Aubrey smiled. "Where we headed?"

"Lualaba." Daniel arched an eyebrow.

"Where the hell is that?" Despite the oppressive air, Aubrey felt the nape of his neck prickle, sensing the thrill of an adventure.

When Aubrey and his new comrade reached the capital Kinshasa, they booked into the clean, whitewashed Napoleon Hotel on the outskirts of the city, which had been co-opted by the foreign work force as their regular watering hole. He contacted the mining company office there, on Daniel's recommendation. They were short of manpower and immediately offered him a junior management position. Knowing how hard it was to get good staff in a country which, was still in the midst of a major internal power struggle.

The interview and job secured, Daniel and Aubrey, found themselves catching a taxi from the headquarters in Libération Boulevard.
This was a city of contrasts, where the occupants of luxury BMW's and Mercedes Benz motorcades trolled the streets looking for something to plunder, whilst the poor eked out an existence from whatever economical trade was leftover. These gangs, somehow beyond reproach, kept a high

profile and drove around in off-road SUV's, with large bull bars designed to keep the occupants out of harm's way.

They all drive expensive SUV's." Daniel explained. It was a signal to the community that the occupants had arrived, and in style. The more bling the better, regardless of cost.

"It's like the notorious Chicago gangs of the twenties and thirties," Aubrey applauded. They always had black vehicles, and they were always visible, invoking fear and the respect of a gullible social working class.

"What is the education system here; French?" Aubrey could recognise the effects of a deprived education system, suffering the effect of three wars in three decades.

"French I'm sure," they passed Ecole Catholique. Religion offered what it could; but reality had a bruising effect on morality. There was something, somehow glamorous in the high speed, gun totting car chases that were the popular viewing alternatives on the TCM satellite channel. It was a badge of honour which was worn with confidence and commanded the support and respect of the proletariat.

"God!" I don't think I would last a week here." Aubrey watched as the streets heaved with humanity. It was a dog-eat-dog existence.

They like the "Children of the Arabat" needed to survive the purges of a dysfunctional and paranoid regime, which had garnered the support of allies to defend its revolution. It was an irony of Africa, that the very nature of its socialist revolution, had adopted the trappings of a Westernised World. It was available on satellite, from a multi-national conglomerate providing entertainment, glamourized on billboards high above the teaming city.

Somehow, those viewers neglected to understand the moral lessons of movies, that resulted in the less than appealing sight of fictitiously dead bodies, strewn across the running boards of old Cadillac's and the like. The truth was beyond fact, because the fiction was all too alluring. The gangster always had the pretty girls, the big bucks and the swagger. There was always cheap liquor and plenty of excitement.

This was the reality of a society borne of necessity, to repeat the mistakes of the past. They had to bump their heads despite the obvious, in order to appreciate those failings; but it was a society, nonetheless gripped by the power of the consumer world. This was the Congo, democratic and free. The frontline of a frontier society that had honed its knowledge on a similar society, that had been fifty years in the taming, but was now for appearance sake, below the radar. Hollywood had a habit of recognising the desirability of a good yarn. The political intrigue and battle for economic superiority being waged by old foes from either side of the Iron Curtain, had orchestrated the start of the Three African Wars, staged in the heart of Africa, on the Equator. This agonic imaginary line attracted forces from Rwanda, Burundi, Uganda and as far afield as Zimbabwe, where 'Old Mad Bob' had commandeered his own elite forces to protect economic interests for himself.

As their taxi jostled through the late afternoon traffic on Boulevard Lumumba, the he gangs seemed to create a great source of entertainment for the local street children. They jived and shoved for the attention of the drivers, who would employ these kids as lookouts for their burgeoning contraband business interests.

"They spend their days on these streets, instead of schools." Daniel could sense Aubrey's pity. "These are the poorer kids, whose parents cannot afford to send them to schools," Daniel offered as consolation.

"But even if they did, they would have to share school desks, three or four to a seat, and both paper and schoolbooks were a luxury." Daniel was no apologist, but perhaps this education may offer at least an income for poor families. These schools, which should have been funded by the wealth created by the large international mining consortiums in the DRC, found that instead, they existed on the charity of funding from other international donors, whilst the privileged few, who had the money, sent their kids to schools in France and England. Education was a badge of honour for the elite, whilst the cost of flying them back and forth to attend privileged colleges was a token of a trophy, of a life of opulence. Aubrey could hear the Professor at Kings' saying, "the fundamental problem with capitalism, is that it favours a society of opportunists!"

Socialism had at its very foundation, the development of a fair and just society, but even the most socialist society in the world, the U.S.S.R. had failed because of a disastrous education system. Aubrey remembered the hype created when the Berlin Wall began to show signs of crumbling and Perestroika had ensured the release of that great work of Fiction, 'Children of the Arabat'. He had just started at King's and it became a prized literary work for The Professor.

"This reminds me of a quote from a book I read at varsity." Aubrey was deep in thought. What was that comment, he recalled? He could almost recite it verbatim;

"The country needed industry: it was not going to be an Asiatic Russia with a few factories, the way it could be done in the Congo; it was going to be a European, industrial, socialist Russia. You couldn't achieve it with peasants getting their training haphazardly on the job; you needed a well-educated work force supplied with the amenities of modern civilisation." Aubrey smiled inwardly. There was nothing wrong with his memory. There was, however, something about modern industry, that could not be built "on the blood and bones of people."

"Ya, but what about Russia? Why did communism fail?" Daniel pitched his two cents worth.

"Because the power was concentrated within the politburo. Like the pigs in 'Animal Farm', Napoleon rather aptly named, it seems, suggested, 'All animals are equal; just some are more equal than others'."

"But isn't that the point of capitalism?" Daniel looked up as the passed the Palais Du Peuple, its dome soaring elegantly above the capital.

"Yes. However, the two are not mutually exclusive. But for capitalism to flourish in a properly pre-scripted society, it must be tempered with a smidgeon of compliance." Aubrey was enjoying his revival. This was where he belonged, in a society where contrasts were no longer black and white.

"Socialism is the fabric on which all society must prevail, because without it, the flipside is greed and malice. We may need each other to survive, but we tend to want to step over each other to get to the top of the pile, instead of picking our brothers and sisters up along the way and taking them with us."

"For Maslow's 'Hierarchy of Needs' to work in totality," he realised.

"Everyone needs to get to the middle of the pyramid first; then society can determine who remains up there because of hard work or talent!" Because, he realised, in a natural progression, the pyramid cannot remain balanced if it is top-heavy, it would stand to reason there will be an attrition rate.
"Without that balance, the social system will remain flawed, and humanity currently engaging in a 'Might versus Right' philosophy, will always become skewed in favour of a select few," Aubrey could sense his rising consciousness. They almost never had the plight of the less fortunate at

heart. Self-actualization was all very well, and the myriad of family trusts that stood as a testimony to mankind's penchant for benevolence was unquestionable. But it granted benefits to some, and may well enhance lives in respect of the charity offered, but Aubrey was far more concerned about the Foundations that would arise from a more intimate understanding of human nature. The Developing World would always be just that, a charity case; unless for every profit rent from the proceeds of international conglomerates, an equal amount was put back to balance the loss. Every investor to whom a dividend yield from an international company was due, singularly and without exception should morally put half back into the economies of those developing states. Aubrey maintained that belief because of how his mother's family had risen from humble working class origins, to become leading industrialists. But, Mother had sought self-actualisation by pursing the wrong course; it was up to him to remedy that.

Aubrey was now firmly ensconced back in his room and with only a rucksack on his back, he was able to shower and change into his khaki pants and cheap knock-off Jeep safari shirt purchased from a local trading stall. He showered, before heading back down to the bar, and a few welcome sundowners. With a celebration pending, he headed for the bar. This previously run down establishment was enjoying somewhat of a resurgence in business as it was within the perimeter of a housing estate, with high walls and security guards, which helped ward off the local clansmen.

Daniel, was seated at the bar with some ex-pats. Aubrey was introduced and they settled in for the evening.

Being a computer systems specialist, it was Daniel's task to install the new equipment and maintain it over the next few years. The profits these machines could illicit was significant, and was a massive boost to the South African based mining company. They were there to plunder the rich reserves of diamond fields, using these machines to extricate every stone from the alluvial shale. There was no room for any losses through in-efficient mining practices, as Daniel told them.

"The mine must operate at a much higher recovery rate." Daniel was now in his element.

"Why would that be such a problem," asked Aubrey naively?
"Because those licenses could be revoked at any time, depending on who is in power?"

"Ah! Good point I suppose," offered Aubrey, power struggles were on-going in Central Africa.

"When I was a young auditor of an international audit firm, I had the privilege of seeing a diamond mine in action on the Botswana diamond fields." Daniel related the story to Aubrey as it had sounded quite ridiculous at the time.

"When we undertook, a stock taking exercise, to value the worth of the uncut gemstones at the mine, I was lead into a sorting room, where there was a pile of uncut gemstones, weighing an estimated twenty-five hundred carats. It was quite spectacular to see," Daniel's smile was triumphant.

"They had to count each individual stone, and separate the stones by colour and size. So, I was given some story, for security purposes. I could watch them sort the stones, but would not be able to touch anything whist the stock take was being undertaken."

"It's just that I had seen them do something similar at a mine near Mafeking, where the quality and the value of the stones were very poor," he offered.

"When the mine was threatened with closure, and the mine boss was about to lose his job, the company had arranged an audit, to consider its viability. When the stock take was done, the so-called diamonds which had been put out for the auditors to evaluate was a pile of worthless silica at the bottom, covered by what gemstones they had! He managed to keep his job for another year before being fired!"

"Oh! So, you never actually got to touch the diamonds?" Aubrey was digging somewhere that Daniel was certain he now understood! What was the point?

"This new machine operates an x-ray spectrometer which detects the diamonds." Daniel was clearly intent on explaining that the same fraud could not occur here. This machine allows the stones which fluoresce under soft x-rays to be identified and are detected by the computer program in the machine. The belt carrying the ore runs at a very high speed, and when it reaches the end of the meter-long conveyor belt, it is catapulted through the air, over a splitter plate and into the reject chute below. The ore is separated from the diamonds at the staggering speed of one carat extraction per two tons of shale."

"That is an immense amount of stone that must be processed," replied Aubrey, who could not even imagine what an uncut carat of diamond, looked like!

"It's smaller than you think," was Daniel's reply. "The system is fool proof and leaves no room for even the smallest of diamonds to be missed."

"What happens to separate the diamonds from the stone then?' was Aubrey's obvious retort.

"The rock passes through the beam, and it takes about a minute for two tons of shale to flow along the chute!"

"As the rocks move below this 'eye' there is a photomultiplier tube next to each pneumatic ejector." Daniel was scribbling on the back of his cigarette box.

Aubrey was just about to ask.

"It's a big jet of air basically." Daniel caught his breath. "This tube sends an electronic signal to the jet each time it recognizes a diamond below, via GPS. These jets are positioned above the conveyor belt, and as the shale roles off the end, the position of the diamond is recorded and blasted out of the mass of shale, and into a trap at the bottom." The sparkle in his eyes was mesmerising.

A thought came to his mind. "So, what happens if the computer that runs this machine simply misreads the fluorescence of the stone?" Aubrey asked.

"Ah, yes," responded Daniel. "If the programs were adjusted to allow for a margin of less than one percent error, the slightly less dense shale carrying the gem stones would not get picked up by the laser, and could pass through the system undetected. But I'm not sure I know what you're getting at?"

"Well isn't that a problem right there? Aubrey asked directly.

"Well, yes. Provided of course you had no mechanism for further selecting the stones down the line, to counter such a problem… otherwise yes, the system could become very inaccurate and inefficient."

"But," He paused whilst he reflected.

"Essentially, there is one final counter-measure to any system flaws and that is the computer program itself! It runs twenty-four seven and all year. If there is a catastrophic failure on its readings at any time, it will simply switch off the entire production line automatically. My job is to maintain the equipment to ensure that the process has as few flaws and as little down time as possible."

"Besides," he continued, "the system has very few moving parts. Apart from the conveyor belt, the shoot allows for gravity to run the shale through the system, which keeps complications down to a minimum!"

"The machine is completely self-contained. Provided the seals of the computer are not tampered with, there should not be any disruption." Daniel was as confident as any systems analyst could be. This was his baby, and it worked splendidly.

Aubrey was fascinated. This new technology took mining to a completely new level, and he would be working on the mine which Daniel had brought in this equipment for. Aubrey was certain they would become good friends.

Aubrey sat talking to Daniel until evening, and they shared some of their own ambitious business ideas. Daniel was a thinker, like Aubrey, and knew how to get his mind around the technical detail; whilst Aubrey had a more global perspective on ideas.

"Laurent Kabila wrestled power from the local Generals, after Mbuso Sese Seko died of a debilitating cancer," Daniel told him. "Once he was gone, the little dictators had emerged one by one. Each fighting for their little piece of Africa, and a share of the plunder it represented. Global governments had not intervened, but the African ones had!"

He paused for good effect.

"Mugabe sent a regiment of his guerrilla fighters from Zimbabwe, to prop up the ailing government forces, in return for a stake in the diamond fields. His battle hardened Fifth Brigade had seen fierce battles in the mountains around Chimanimani, in the eastern highlands of Zimbabwe, and they were perfectly prepared for the Congo's jungle conditions." Daniel loved a good scandal.

"They were aided and abetted by the likes of that notorious Rottenbush character!"

"He is a really perverse business entrepreneur, who has backed Mugabe throughout his reign of terror. His modus operandi is to make money from any deal north of the Limpopo. Because the South African government of Thabo Mbeki did not have the stomach for that fight, they had not taken him on directly. They slapped him with a fine and held his assets in South Africa. But I guess they were too busy lining their own pockets, to be troubled by the chaos north of their own borders." Daniel took a sip from his beer.

"Isn't he the guy who owns a transport empire?" Aubrey was suddenly very interested.

"Yes. But because he was never brought to book by the South African's - probably too many skeletons in their own closets! – he simply moved to Zimbabwe and carried on business as usual." Daniel whispered in a conspiratorial tone, looking over his shoulder. The bar was occupied by a host of well-dressed and ethnically diverse men.

Aubrey looked around. This mass-scale non-intervention caused the suffering of millions, whilst power mongers such as Kabila, Mugabe and unconscionable opportunists like Rottenbush plundered.

"The diamonds were traded for oil and other luxuries whilst monstrous palaces were built in their grotesque opulence in the very counties which could least afford such extravagances." Daniel continued.

But, like the grand palaces and castles of Medieval Europe, the African Lords wanted to sit and watch their fiefdom from the ramparts - too scared to venture out and too powerful to be deposed.

"They pay-off the Generals, who in turn hold power through tyranny; and the vicious cycle continues. Without intervention, the Governments of the west have condoned the slaughter of millions, and are equally to blame for the carnage." This was Africa in the raw. Devoid of humanity, destitute of moral fibre and left to the dishonest dealings of power brokers. Aubrey would no doubt learn more about the likes of Rottenbush, and his insidious business practices.

By the time dinnertime came, the two had firmly established a camaraderie. He had finally met someone who shared his ideals.

The political situation in Africa had marginalized the efforts of men like Daniel. His contribution to the continents growth, and the hard-won skills development of men like him, would be required if it was to forge the melting pot of ideals and skills together to create that Rybakovian dream. Daniel was a distinctly fatalistic thinker, and could see clearly his role in this society, which favoured the powerful. The skills transference of technology was happening. But it was changing so rapidly with each new development, and provided men like Daniel had the knowledge to extend and hone their skills, there would always be a place for them in the African landscape.

But, what of Aubrey? His skills were limited, and he would need to find a place for himself in a rapidly changing social system. This continent had always been the destination of opportunity seekers, but had faltered as each new reach towards unlocking the continents mineral wealth, had brought the likes of Leopold II and his uncompromising greed; all the way down the line to the Portuguese Corner Café owners. Who, with their grasping mentalities, were irrelevant in a society which strived for basic necessities.

"Let's say we were able to change the way people viewed the white man on this continent!" Aubrey began a conversation over a dinner of chicken chow mien at the famous Chinese restaurant that had emerged in that boiling pot of cultures, in one of Kinshasa's trendier neighbourhoods.

"How are you going to do that?" Daniel may have been a thinker, but he was a pragmatist.

"Well, centuries of greed have separated the white man from our native brothers. Whereas the new elite take their share of the natural assets from a plethora of vast untapped wealth; and the common man flounders because of his ignorance and lack of motivation." Aubrey thought about what he had said. The DRC was just such a fusion of these cultural inadequacies. The power mongers, to whom the richness of this country's assets now filtered, were in an enviable position of place and circumstance. But like some timber log on the upper Congo river, which will finally reach the open sea, four and a half thousand kilometres downstream, the flotsam of incalculable natural resources, would somehow need to find its way into the hands of the less privileged.

"Eehhmmm, okay, tell me more." Daniel had a mouthful of noodles.

"If there is any hope for a future, it will require initiative to make it happen. But it's not going to come from the top though. They are too comfortable in the relative newness of their entitlement." Getting used to the lavishing of a multitude of sensual experiences, would take their focus off the lesser mortals that encompassed the proletariat. There was a need to catapult the common man somehow from his unexceptional life, and offer the proceeds of that untapped wealth to their door. How was Aubrey to achieve this?

"So, what do good people to do?" This was even more reason they needed to take control of his own destiny, and get involved directly in serving and assisting his fellow man.

"Well standing on the side-lines and whining is not going to be the answer." Daniel washed down his mouthful with an imported red.

"No!" Aubrey thought, as he and Daniel continued to chat. "We must make a difference!"

He vowed to himself to get a handle on this new technology, and use it for the betterment of the people who walked the scorched earth directly above the abundant riches that lay beneath their feet. How would that make a difference without the proper means of education, but it was just as he tried to figure the way forward, that the solution presented itself. 'Education!' That was the way to create answers to the vast injustices of this immense continent. Aubrey would need to figure out a way of getting the masses to benefit from it. Aubrey had a quiet thought that emerged as a guffaw. 'He would plan to become a modern-day Robin Hood!'

"We are Whafricans!" Aubrey looked across the table. Daniel smiled.

"Yes. And the black consciousness leaders of America, changed their destinies by resisting the status quo." Daniel understood the analogy, completely.

"This continent is being ravaged by greedy fat cats, who sit in their London or New York offices, slicing up the spoils of their exploits, and continuously dishing up more and more for themselves. All the while, they are whittling down the proceeds that are so desperately needed to feed the street children and the jobless mothers." Aubrey felt impassioned.

"Mothers who have been deprived of any sense of human dignity, by the very men who raped them literally and figuratively. Whilst the land is plundered. Do you know the rape statistics amongst Congolese women is downright evil? Over 1000 women and girls are being raped every day, and of the twenty children born to these mothers in Central Africa every minute, ten will not reach adulthood, or even early teens."
Aubrey shook his head.

"The remainder of the family will be severely poverty stricken for their entire lives, depending largely on handouts from food agencies." But that was the problem right there! The family structures were being torn apart and because of migratory labour practices, the men were abandoning their clans, and heading for the cities and the mining communities of a rapidly expanding resource industry.

"How would you reverse that trend?" The solution was too complex.

"We are creating a burgeoning market of consumers on one continent who are fed by a wholly deprived people on another continent." The imbalances seemed staggeringly untenable to Aubrey. He could not fathom how this imbalance and status quo had been allowed to continue for so many decades. He needed to do something, even if it was not the ultimate and total solution.

After having given him the entire brief on the machine, Aubrey understood how the system worked in general. What he figured would be needed was some way of getting to the technology that lay within the interior of the great machine.

'It's brain.' He needed to find out how to get that working to his advantage. Aubrey would need to milk Daniel for every bit of information, as he did not want to implicate him in this venture; but needed his assistance nonetheless. Aubrey and Daniel finished off the evening, before both retiring to their respective rooms, Daniel to sleep off his hangover, and Aubrey to lie silently scheming. This felt like a calling to Aubrey. He had never been as certain about anything in his life.

Morning dawned. The evening air had cooled, just perceptibly enough to allow a gentle breeze through the open window. The noises of the Congo, had filtered through the stained cotton curtains. Aubrey had lain awake, listening. A world of humanity never quieted, always on edge. The city was a cacophony of uninterrupted bedlam. But despite this, Aubrey sensed a melody to it all. It worked on a strange dissonant melody. Incongruous to some, it now appeared strangely comforting.

They set off on what would be a ten-hour trip across corrugated roads, and gun bearing check points, with each stop exacting a small donation. Henry was their driver. He had craftily shown Daniel and Aubrey how he would deal with the roadblocks along the way. He had loaded a stash of cash, in smaller denominations of U.S. dollars, into the roof lining of the Land Rover, above the sun visor. This ensured their 'rite of passage' and guaranteed that if an overzealous guard was to frisk them; he would not find any cash worthy of taking. Each set of roadblocks would get just enough of his bribe stash. Each stop cost two or three dollars and each time they successfully negotiated the next road block, with its oil barrels rolled across the gravel road, and branches of trees hastily propped up to create a barrier, Henry would then remove some more currency from its cover, and leave it just visible enough in the open ashtray, for the guards to see.

Henry always addressed them as 'Officer'. Or the clever ones were, "Bon Jour, Monsieur General," clearly playing to the fragile egos that stood guard at their posts. It was like any other venture if the truth be told. The simple requirement was to make a living, and with opportunities as remote as a New Zealand 'Dodo' on the slopes of Mount Everest, these enterprising young men had discovered a way of generating a livelihood.

Good manners and a sense of circumstance always satisfied them and Aubrey and Daniel could continue their journey unmolested. Apart from the badly rutted roads, the protracted negotiation at the roadblocks, caused most of the delay. The vehicle was never searched, as the commanders of these posts were keenly aware that the key to their survival was a symbiotic relationship that respected the balance of the nature of their business. Like a tick on a buffalo, they could only hold onto their posts, if the value of their service was to be respected. This was the way the system worked, and without being, too altruistic, Aubrey soon realized that as a buffalo might feed that tick inadvertently, they needed one another intrinsically. If the tick sucked up too much blood, it fell off, and the relationship ended, but the ticks never seemed to diminish in number; breeding continually. However, the system required the tick birds, which were attentive enough. This symbiotic relationship was supported by an army who would from time to time purge the parasitic ticks from their posts. There was more than enough sustenance for the relationship to continue in a vicious cycle. There was an inevitability about all of this that Aubrey knew was being sustained by greed. But who was the real host, never being in doubt.

The Congo. A vast forested anvil-shaped dichotomy. The lungs of Africa, which fed the bellows of a furnace of savagery. Three wars and five million deaths. Vast unspoilt vistas, devoid of human influence, blanketed by a lush green canopy, smothering untold treasures. Untainted by the Ice Age, harbouring God's own Eden. This was where Africa had been birthed, ten thousand years ago, after the last ice age. Where the great flood of humanity had embarked on its southward colonisation.

Aubrey watched quietly; respecting the knowledge that Henry had gleaned over countless trips. The balance of power was restored, even though it was on a micro-economic level. The system worked on a perfunctory level, and though Daniel was nearly relieved of his laptop computer, it all worked. The boy-soldier had to be reminded in no uncertain terms, that, if he was to deprive Daniel of his equipment, he would not be able to do his job; and if that happened, he would have wasted his time coming to this country altogether. Furthermore, should he be unable to get through with his laptop, they would be in for a serious beating from the mine manager.

Armed with a Kalashnikov rifle too big for his shoulders, he continually had to shift the weight of the rifles to prevent their shoulders from becoming permanently bruised. This 'General' was older than his comrades and held their attention unequivocally. Aubrey had an uneasy feeling, as the loaded guns were often inevitably pointed right in his direction, and always looked like they could erupt at any second in a hail of bullets. The thought of having this chap, who the driver affectionately referred to as 'Oom Piet', bearing down on them like a runaway bulldozer, inevitably resulted in the boy backing down. Aubrey looked forward to meeting 'Oom Piet'!

As soon as they were through, Aubrey watched over his shoulder, as these young men, thankfully released the weapons from over their shoulders, whilst sharing the spoils amongst themselves. A few U.S. dollars would feed their families for a week, with mealie pap and fish. The opportunities for these fatherless children to benefit from any form of self-indulgence, was always overshadowed by their commitment to their starving families.

Aubrey witnessed the devastation that was being wrought on the north of the country. Villages, which once dotted the landscape with settled establishments, were now devoid of inhabitants. In their quest to man the ragtag armies in the east, the army generals had co-opted every soldier they could lay their hands on in the countryside. Where they had resisted, the women were raped and a limb, usually an arm, was hacked off with a machete. Their faces cruelly mutilated once the deed had been done, so that they would be living testimony to those that resisted. In this war, which was fought within and without the country's borders, only the strongest would survive. Very few other wars on the African continent had been quite so pervasive or seen its inhabitants annihilated quite so thoroughly.

"Who is this Oom Piet?" Aubrey had asked half way into the journey.

"Ooh! Well he is your boss from now onward," Daniel smiled.

"He was born in the Free State of South Africa and grew up on the plaas. The farm was his Uncle's, because he was orphaned at birth." Daniel explained. "The Afrikaans have a closely-knit culture and 'Oom Hennie', his father's brother, had inherited the farm and taken care of young Piet. The youngest of them all, Piet was a rebellious young oke. He skipped the farm after completing only his Ninth-Grade exams, and at seventeen, he was already a strapping six-footer. With a penchant for rugby and the 'meisies', he headed for the big city of Johannesburg, looking for work on the mines."

"The story goes, that he started working at an independent mine which was not too phased about employing under age, or under-educated workers. He had been employed as a runner in the office, taking the shift logs down to the pit bosses." The 'Baas' as they were known, were the ruthless managers of the sometimes-ill-disciplined workers below ground.

"But Piet's real job was to play rugby for the mines' team, which had been top of their league for a good few years. Piet was treated like a veritable star, and he soon proved his prowess. Having grown up on the farm, he also had a good knowledge of the local black men, spending his holidays grafting with the farm labourers." Daniel continued.

"This he would freely admit to, but to think of him, as a 'kaffir-boetie' would enrage him and a fistfight would ensue. It was Piet's initiation to the working-class slums of Brixton and Feittas where the mining company's set up digs for their mineworkers."

"Well, actually it was called Vrededorp, or Freetown. The place developed as a working-class community for the old South African railways, and was a throwback to the days of Apartheid. You could work with blacks, but you were not allowed to live with them."

According to the myth that had followed Piet all his life, he was none too slow in adopting the camaraderie that saw him quickly elevated to a crew boss. His understanding of the languages spoken in the depths of the mine proved incalculable as the respect given was not a set right. It was to be earned through selfless work, and unfaltering diligence. His pit-crew was his family now, and given the strength of his devotion to that crew, he soon showed his worth. Piet was not to be underestimated, and the big Zulu's who stood chin to chin with Piet at the rock face, would attest to his unrivalled strength. This was his education, and no book learning would replace the knowledge of human self-sacrifice, as he would come to understand it.

"Well his legendary strength resulted from a story which had given rise to this folk story. It was after a tunnel collapsed on the forty-third level of the mine. The timber they had been supplied with from an independent timber contractor in the Zululand forests had proven too weak to support the tunnel roof. These struts were paramount, as they literally supported the thousands of tons of rock above each tunnel. Without their strength, the mine, simply would collapse." Daniel understood mining.

"The independent contractor had been trying to get contracts for the mine for some time, and in his eagerness to win the tender, he had discounted his price, by buying sub-standard 'green' timber which had not been allowed to be tempered long enough to reach optimum strength. The contractor was a buddy of the purchasing manager, and as they had both grown up together at the same Natal boarding school, they were 'tight'." Daniel emphasised.

"Unfortunately, the timber wasn't, and as the story goes, 'Piet' was on duty that morning. It was the middle of winter." The supports were brought down the shaft to open a passage to the new vein of gold in the reef which was to be mined. Piet had arrived at six that morning with the shift change, and as the timber was lowered to the forty-third level, he noticed that the timber yard had been over-supplied. Some of the timber was standing out in the open. Unseasonable winter rain had settled onto the timber, soaking the unprepared wood, which had been saturated all evening. When the early morning winter frost of the Transvaal Highveld froze the timber supports, as they lay on the open ground, unbeknown to Piet, they became as brittle as a fizz-pop sucker, and just as effervescent.

"As the supports were brought down to their level, the heat within that poorly ventilated tunnel grew to a staggering forty-five degree centigrade!"

"This had the effect of releasing the trapped water, and weakening the supports further." Daniel loved the detail.

The pit-crew had started to lodge these supports into the ceiling and they were twenty meters down the tunnel when Piet arrived. The crew worked, shirtless and unsupervised as they had done for twenty years before. The system was fraught with danger, but they had never experienced a tunnel collapse in all those years, despite the untenable statistics generally across the gold mining industry. These great sweating Zulus, fearing none but their ancestors, had already been at work for twenty minutes, when Piet noticed that the timbers on the left column of supports were not aligned. He had an eye for detail, and as he ventured into the treacherous tunnel, suddenly there was a massive explosion, as one of the supports buckled. Piet could see the two Zulu labourers deeper within the tunnel, but before they could react, the second support in the column began to bend.

He ran instinctively into the tunnel and throwing his immense one-hundred-and-twenty-kilogram frame at the support, managed to hold it for a moment as the two labourers, now in full flight darted past him into the open tunnel beyond. The series of supports in place began to heave under the additional strain, and without the necessary strength of the snapped pillar, they cracked and popped like match sticks.

There was a sudden rumble as the roof caved in twenty metres away, and like a concertina, the supports gave way one by one, and the mass of rock was hurled forward like an avalanche. Piet had waited just long enough to see his pit-crew safely beyond the perimeter, and like a juggernaut, he threw himself headlong towards the surrealistic phosphene light. This light created by the adrenalin coursing through his veins, and creating pressure on the retinas of his eyes, provided what was an out-of-worldly experience. He could sense the fear in his gut, but had acted instinctively as a mother might, when a child is teetering on the brink of a precipice. When the dust which was streaming through the tunnel in the stifling confines of the five-meter wide aperture had finally settled, the men had dragged Piet, coughing and shouting from the remnants of the rock fall, his legs broken and twisted in a grotesque angle from his knees.

"He never played rugby again, but that did not matter, as he was a hero. Piet had met a young girl on the mine who was the mine manager's daughter, and they had fallen for each other whilst he was in hospital recovering. Piet stayed in hospital just long enough to mend his broken bones, but not too long, that his memory of the event would fade. He tracked down Dave, the supplier, to his designer mansion in Sandton, and waiting for him at the gates, gave him a good 'doornering'."

Piet was forced to remain in the office during his recuperation, where he had his trusty 'sjaambok' mounted on the wall behind his new desk. From there he conducted his recovery for just long enough, that he would learn who was who, in the hierarchy of mining legends. This had taught Piet a good lesson, and one which he held dear for the rest of his working career. He soon became a reliable buyer, working his way up to his present position. He had earned the honour and respect of his work colleagues, and the mine bosses were in awe of his reputation. Like a veritable Samson of Biblical legend, he became somewhat revered with mining bosses vying for his services. This was in part because of the respect his deeds had earned him, but mainly because the mining magnates had heard of his reputation as a man who could be trusted.

The press had never been alerted to the inferior mine supports, and the dubious dealings of the mine bosses, looking to cut costs wherever they could. The sixties were a grand era in the mining industry, and every major mining house was expanding. The world was alive with possibility, with the space race creating demand for all manner of raw materials, and gold was high on that list. South Africa was a magic place if you were white and a man with unlimited potential! This was the man to whom Aubrey was about to be introduced.

Daniel and Aubrey finally pulled into the main offices of the mine at six that evening. The night shift had just begun, and the mine manager was happily ensconced in the clubhouse with his first brandy and coke. Oom Piet was a mountain of a man, and by all accounts Aubrey could now see why his strength was legendary. He was now in his sixties, and still built like the brick wall of an Apartheid era jail cell wall. Appearing to be as broad as he was tall. He was seated at the end of the bar, with his beer mug full of the 'Free State cheer'.

Daniel introduced Aubrey. "Oom Piet, this is your new shift manager, Aubrey Pennington."

Oom Piet, who had seen them coming, slugged down another big mouthful of his Klippies and coke. Daniel had successfully negotiated the space between the bar stool and the far wall, slipping into the bar stool at the very end, leaving Aubrey to the mercy of this man-mountain. He rose dutifully, surveyed Aubrey with a circumspect eye, and then completely surprised Aubrey by extending his hand and breaking into the broadest smile, minus a tooth, but otherwise very convincing. He had a handshake that dwarfed Aubrey's, but he did not try to overpower him in a forceful way. Aubrey appreciated this concession, but he was almost charming, which unnerved him.

"Gooie naand," he said politely, waiting for a response.

Aubrey responded, "goie naand meneer, hoe gaan dit?"

This was the extent to his Afrikaans, and Aubrey almost spat out the guttural 'gaan dit'. It did not role off his tongue as it did with all 'the Boere', who spoke the language. Oom Piet smiled even broader at Aubrey's attempt at Afrikaans, acknowledging his effort.
The problem with the 'souties' as the English were affectionately known amongst the Afrikaners, was that they would not speak the Afrikaans language out of principle; a throw-back to their colonial history. Aubrey would have a good laugh when told that the English were known as 'souties' because, unlike the Afrikaners who were committed to the 'motherland'; the English were just visitors, with one foothold in Africa, the other firmly in

Britain. But their dicks were dangling in the sea, covered in salt; and that was why they were 'souties'.

Oom Piet motioned to the bar stool next to him, and with an outstretched hand that resembled a meat cleaver at its broadness, ordering them drinks from the barman. He was now in his sixties, and still built like the brick wall of an Apartheid era out-house, appearing to be as broad as he was tall. This man with whom Aubrey was to work, and whom he immediately took a liking to, had a strong presence and a formidable girth. His eyes were direct and honest, and Aubrey knew instantly that he was not one to be toyed with. Little did Aubrey know that they were to build a powerful alliance of sorts, whilst Aubrey set about building his Sherwood Forest community. This was where they spent the rest of the evening, only stepping out into the humid evening air, to find their accommodation, once the bar had closed.

"The function of shift manager is one that requires no real training," according to Oom Piet; "Other than to have eyes in the back of your head". Aubrey was naturally observant and his enquiring mind was attuned to this function.

"These people will steal the shirt off your back, if you let them!" Oom Piet suspected Aubrey's English accent was a sign of naivety.

"Okay." Aubrey was not going to argue, but he questioned the psychology.

"You treat them well, but firmly and they do their job," was Oom Piet's advice.

"Show any sign of weakness and they stab you in the back!" Aubrey listened intently. His experiences had been wholly different, but then he had been working with educated Zimbabweans.

"You will need a translator, and someone who you can work with," Oom Piet explained.

What Aubrey could not understand was, 'if the work force were paid well, treated well and given reasonable working conditions; why would they need to steal?'

"They feel they have a sense of entitlement," Oom Piet answered his unspoken question. "Africa is full of these people, who have no education, no initiative and feel they should be entitled to more because it is their homeland."

Aubrey listened even more intently. There was only one major issue. To be completely successful in his venture, he would have to have alliances and those would ensure the longevity of his plans. He would need a specific ally. Someone within the work force to champion his cause, but he would certainly have to be extremely observant to ensure his scheme was to be successful. He was in no doubt that Oom Piet would not be a push over, given his experience in this business. He also would have his own trusty observers, and to be successful in Africa, those allegiances were vital. Aubrey would have an easy affinity for the job, but he would need to look carefully for the right person.

Bunked in for the night, the sleeping quarters resembled a ship's mess. The kitchens were self-contained within each dorm room, and Aubrey was immediately at home.

They started preparing the installation of the machine the following day, and it would be Aubrey's task to oversee this process with Daniel. Aubrey was to facilitate the day shift, in the management office. Daniel would only be there for the initial phase to get this million-dollar machine online. Once he had it up and running, Aubrey would be in charge, and would have to handle general maintenance until Daniel's next visit. There was a lot to learn in the meantime.

They were shown through to the sorting sheds with Oom Piet, where the heavy machinery had been deposited the night before. Daniel immediately set to work checking that no computer apparatus had been damaged on the inward leg. The equipment was stored separate to the main machine and this was all intact. Whilst 'Oom Piet' supervised the assembly of the machinery, and conveyor, Aubrey and Daniel spent the better part of the week ensuring the systems were configured properly, and Aubrey was given two-days of instruction on how to read the printouts and what to look for in the data. This was quite technical, and he spent some time pouring over Daniel's notes before he was sure he would get the hang of it.
"The mining operation requires very precise daily reports to estimate carats per tonnage and these reports are given directly to the mine manager." Daniel was a great tutor.

"There is an extremely narrow range of operation for error. Any deviation from the norm, will immediately bring up a red flag, and prompt an investigation." Daniel showed him through the process. It was very scientific, but the beauty about science was, it is always being improved.

Aubrey knew enough about using a laptop computer to work his way around the fundamentals, but a system rigged with enough storage space to detail every ton of rock from a day's production line, would be a different kettle of fish. He would have to 'up' his game to another level if he wanted to get to grips with this system. If ever there had been motivation for him to apply himself to his learning, now was that time.

Aubrey read through the operational manual and identified the pertinent aspects of the programmes and studied the system before Daniel returned to Johannesburg. He poured over the mine security and layout; dissected each minute detail and looked for opportunities. Once the facility started full operations, it would be too late to determine whether he would be able to institute a plan. A plan to get the stones through the system undetected and out onto the screed dump.

From there it would be shifted in large dumper trucks to a crushing mill, where it was crushed further to make gravel for the roads being built in the DRC interior. Once these stones were through the system they were of no economic value to the mine owners, so it made absolute sense to have them sifted by labourers, who were outside the phase three security zone.

Phase one and two, were the immediate area around the sorting rooms, and the perimeter where the stones arrived when they were brought through the first washing and crushing cycle. As soon as those stones were beyond the perimeter of Phase Two Security, they were outside of the security perimeter of body searches. The mine managers could go freely to and fro without any real security checks. Aubrey needed a system to get the stones beyond the perimeter and into the waiting hands of the labourers who would crush the gravel further.

"What happened to the previous shift manager?" Aubrey now asked.

There was no comment from Piet, but by his reaction it was clear that they had ended their relationship in disagreement.
Daniel looked across as an affirmation to Aubrey's question. He raised his eyebrows and continued working. Oom Piet was a very practical man, and had won the respect of his staff by leading by example. He was also, it appeared, very ethical and was extremely fair to all his workers, and they loved and respected him for that. He, however, did not suffer fools gladly, and Aubrey made a mental note to try and avoid disputes with the old man. Oom Piet was, however, not very familiar with technology and for the elaborate computer systems that ran the back end of the mine, they would have to rely on Aubrey.

Aubrey needed a good grasp of the local mine lingo, which was a variation of the Swahili spoken for centuries in the Central African. The language originated in the early days of Arabic trading down the coast of East Africa, and became popular in the dark days of expansion into the interior. The English had proved that their inability to learn the local dialects of sub-Saharan Africa was a limiting factor in the success of their Colonial conquests. To deal with their inadequacies, the British had created an understanding of this language and a unique dialect had expanded to incorporate certain English phrases.

Swahili was formed from several languages of German, Portuguese, Arabic and ultimately French, which combined into a bastardisation of them all. The language was a corruption of the Arabic word 'Kisawhili' which meant 'boundary or coast', relating to their five hundred years of trading. The Arabs had not ventured, as the British and Europeans had, into the interior, preferring to trade mostly along the east coast. However, during the slave trade, they had ventured as far as the Great Rift Valley, and so spread the language into the heart of Africa.

When the British, led by the missionaries, came to the Congo, they applied their own moral values. Attempting to end the slave trade, they needed to communicate with the local tribes, so they were forced to learn Swahili. The language expanded with the footprint of the colonialists, and in the halcyon days of pre-independence Central Africa, this was the language which originated in the homes of the colonial masters; it became known rather indiscreetly as 'Kitchen Kaffir'. This was the legacy of two hundred years of subservience, and would prove to be the ultimate un-doing of the English as Africa's masters. The resentment had grown pre-Independence and this language had been lost to a generation of Africans as they made a determined choice to speak their mother tongues. But for the old colonists, who still controlled the mining interests of most Central African countries, the political dictatorships that had followed had given pause for thought. Amongst those who had seen the English as the demons from across the sea, they could now recognize that it was not a black versus white syndrome. It was a 'might versus right' symptom of human society.

But it was a chance conversation with one of the mine's charter pilots, that got Aubrey thinking. Richard, was a thirty something year old charter pilot, who had learnt his flying skills in the South African Air Force before 'ninety-four'. After which all conscripted military service was suspended, and because of the new government, conscription made way for a peace time career military force.

With his military training behind him, Richard, as he was to become known, became a charter pilot. He converted from the one engine Pegasus Trainer, to the commercial twin engine Cessna and ultimately the King Air, which was used for the flights into and out of the Congo. Military air force pilots were in big demand, and this was where Dick had the skills needed. He had also seen a short stint as a commercial crop sprayer in the Limpopo district, but had ended his career, when as a spray jockey; he had managed to catch his aircraft on an electrical pylon. Luckily for him he had managed to land it successfully at the local aerodrome despite the obvious damage inflicted. Having virtually shorn the portside wing from the fuselage, Richard became known as a bit of a cowboy, and with his interest in flying none to diminished by the experience, he took to flying charters into the Caprivi Strip, between Namibia, Angola and Botswana. This took guests to the lodges dotted around the Zambezi and Chobe, where he had honed his flying skills for his current undertaking.

"So, you have been flying for the mine for a while?" asked Aubrey, who had been introduced on the last evening of Daniel's stay.

"Ya man, it's been a few years now," was the response. He seemed tired and irritable sitting with his hands supporting his head.

Aubrey probed a little more, "where do you guys fly to?"

"Ah well," Richard could sense his interrogation would not be over until he showed a bit of interest. "We do the jungle bash, through Kalakelae and then onto Vila Gamito once a week."

Richard had just finished this cycle of three round trips, having taken two of the strategic management staff up to the cobalt mines in the East. He was not looking his freshest, and Aubrey decided to give him a break.

"Oh, sounds dangerous! Who would you like another drink?" Aubrey realized he was not going to get too much out of him tonight, unless he loosened his tongue.

The rigorous regulations permitted the drinking of alcohol only in between flying stints into the interior. This was dangerous territory, and the short jungle strips made for some interesting approaches, and even more radical take-offs. Richard accepted the drink.

"What is the most interesting experience you've had?" Aubrey plied him for more information. Luckily for him bush pilots liked to talk about their escapades and brushes with death. Aubrey became captivated by the pure ballsiness of this guy and some of the near-death risks he had been prepared to take. Aubrey admired his spirit.

Aubrey had known an ex-chopper pilot in Zimbabwe, who had once set an Alouette chopper down on a tiny outcrop of rock on the side of a mountain in the Chimanimani Highlands. When the rotor blades had shut down, he and his three-man crew had been dragged to the edge of oblivion, as the chopper's blades had slowed. Centrifugal forces had propelled the relatively light French Alouette to the edge of the rocky outcrop, as the blades slowed. Aubrey had seen the pictures and the crew lived to count their blessings.

"Tell him what the approach to Vila Gamito is like." Martinus, a mine engineer, had a twinkle in his eye, and clearly enjoyed this story.

Richard perked up.

"We put down on the side of a hill with a twenty-eight-degree upward slope, which veers to the right on a negative camber." He smiled broadly at his accomplishment.

"Mind you," he quickly added, "we do fly the Caravan into that strip, and the bitch can put down on my dick if I wanted her to."

'Oom Piet' roared with laughter. This motley bunch had clearly got some history. Aubrey grinned. He was going to feel at home here.

"Nothing like a short dip into a two-hundred-meter strip, with the airbrakes full on and the engine pitched to zero, to get you hard!" Explained Richard.

'Oom Piet' guffawed once more, and then sat chuckling under his immense grey beard. He clearly could remember his time on the 'Hill' as they called it.

"Vila Gamito is not just a hill but a mountain in the eastern Congo, one of the wildest places on earth," Martinus quipped.

"The only thing riskier than putting down onto that strip, is the chance that one of those rebel Sam 7 missiles might hit you up the arse on the approach." He was now into his stride.

"All the mines are subject to the occasional snipping by rag tag outfits, which have chosen to continue the war on the side of the Burundian rebels."

Martinus explained. They had been passed over by the Kabila government and had a bone to pick with just about anyone. In particular, the multinational companies who were now walking off with all the mineral wealth in the east.

"Having fought a war against the invading Congolese forces of SeSe Seko for years, and now Kabila; they are not in the mood to tolerate an invading army of capitalists from across the oceans." Daniel was more commiserate.

"Unfortunately, these dictators are always too eager to sell off their resources if the price of the bribe is right. Since the Chinese have been far more willing to bribe than the western world, the multinationals are finding themselves increasingly hard-pressed to keep up their end of the deal. This is a battle for resource-ownership," he continued.

There was corruption and intrigue in abundance it seemed to Aubrey. "It's not surprising that the western world are loathed by African leaders?"

"Until they want free health care and UN Aid." Martinus added.

"Maybe they have a point! Now that the Chinese are starting to gain the upper hand in Africa, it's only going to worse. World War Three was not going to be fought with large atomic weapons, but rather for the resources needed to sustain those governments, and it's going to be ugly." Martinus had no loyalties.

"Bribery and corruption amongst these governments, is the only way anything gets done in Africa." Engineers, it seemed, had such pratical opinions on economics and politics.

"They have to curry favour with the two-bit dictatorships that sit on the resources; they couldn't unlock it themselves." Martinus continued.

Aubrey found himself drifting away again; the iniquities and inequities of this world were no more apparent than here in Africa. He did not hear Richard asking him a question.

"Hey man, did you hear what I said," He looked perplexed.
"Sorry. What was that?" Aubrey felt the blood rush to his neck. He was caught up in his own thoughts.

"I asked, if you had ever flown in one of these birds, into a war zone." He repeated. He was enjoying the attention now.

on

"No, I have led a comparatively boring life," he allowed just a modicum of sarcasm to take the edge off his embarrassment.

"Only time I have been on a small plane was up at Kinyambi on the Zambezi! We paddled from Mana Pools for four days to the border with Mozambique. But they had to fly us out of there."

"Ah yes," replied Dick, trying to sound a little interested. "I have flown some tourists into that strip. There is a game lodge there on the river, that has the most awesome wildlife. Not a human in sight for hundreds of miles. The Tsetse fly has seen to that!"

"And AIDS." Rebuffed 'Oom Piet'. It was the first comment he had made whilst having sat listening to them talking.

"Yes. And AIDS." Remarked Richard. "Do you know, I can fly from here to Kalakelae, a distance of 800 kilometres, and I won't see a single inhabited village?"

"Jeez," replied Aubrey. "Is that all to do with AIDS? Or is that the war?"

"Well, there has been mass urbanization because of the war, but nobody can tell for sure what impact AIDS is truly having." Richard conceded.

"They're fucking themselves to death!" 'Oom Piet' smirked.

Aubrey watched him, as he returned his attention to his drink. He wondered if the comment had come from the years of disappointment, which a life of mining had inflicted on him; or if it was maybe a deeper-seated resentment!

"AIDS started here in the Congo," Dick returned to the conversation.

"They have traced the origins of AIDS to the rubber industry in the 1930's. Scientists think it had something to do with human interaction with Chimps."

"Oh nonsense! I have heard that theory," Martinus interjected. "The fact that a disease can jump from a Chimpanzee to humans, does not mean they were having sex with them!"

"Naa, sies man!" 'Oom Piet' was horrified at the thought.

"No, I think it was simply by interaction. I mean that someone perhaps was bitten by a Chimp and the virus mutated into HIV." Aubrey was more judicious. He felt a pang of regret, rise in his gut; then it was gone.

"Ya, well. If the bird flu can mutate from chickens; why not Chimps? We are more closely related." Martinus agreed.

Aubrey watched as Oom Piet was about to say something more, but then resisted. He, at least knew when he was out of his conversational depth.

"There are swathes of previously cultivated areas on the river banks for hundreds of kilos' that have been abandoned." Richard was back on track.

"Imagine if that land was to be farmed correctly. They would be able to solve the food shortage in one good crop season." Aubrey was conciliatory.

"Yes, but there would be no one to farm it!" Martinus offered. "The infection rate is over forty percent in some countries and here there are already one million known cases; that's in the cities where the population can be tested."

"Africa has only fifteen percent of the world's population; but eighty-eight percent of AIDS victims."

"Really?" Aubrey was interested. "Maybe Africa needs to be re-colonised?"

"Don't worry, it will be soon enough," Martinus looked down at his drink.

"What, the Chinese?" There was a sudden lull, as they each reflected on their own thoughts.

"Not a bad idea actually! Maybe that's what is needed! I had some arsehole on board once. A cartographer, on his way up to Kalakelae to survey the area for a township! He was sitting up front with me. But after we took off my GPS went haywire. I had to fly in along the rivers." They happily turned the conversation away from death.

"We were behind schedule already, but thankfully I had flown the trip twenty times! It turns out he had left his magnetron on. It was with his survey equipment in a duffle bag he was carrying with him. We flew at five hundred feet all the way to try and locate the town, and I can tell you there was not a soul to be seen."

Aubrey sat up. "The GPS went haywire?"

"Yes," replied Richard. "The system relies on a satellite transmission to guide you, but this magnetron interfered with the signal. It threw the GPS into a spin. Anyway, we managed to get there, but no thanks to that moron."

Aubrey nodded. If he had it right, he had just solved his problem in the easiest way possible. That is, if he understood the working of a magnetron correctly.

"So the GPS was affected by magnetic wavelengths?"

'Ya man, I would have ditched that oke in the river, had I known."

After the discussion had dried up, Aubrey and the others retired to their digs.

Aubrey knew that he needed to get up early. Tomorrow would be the test day and then the system was due to go online. He knew almost everything he needed to know about the system. But he still had one or two final questions he wanted clarified before Daniel left.

He got up before the others; that is except for 'Oom Piet', who would be up at five regardless, as he always was. Aubrey needed to get down to the fabricating shop where he had seen the exact device he needed for the job. No one would be any the wiser, provided he was careful. If by achieving the element of surprise, he could get the jump on his colleagues, he would be able to run his project undetected for as long as he needed to. If as he suspected, it worked, he would create his own Robin Hood coup d'état. He could apply the theory and implement the actions, but he would need to be extremely aware of the consequences.

As he dressed, a knot of anxiety formed in his stomach. He had felt this before, as the Elephant herds had approached them on the Chobe. But he steadied it by taking three deep breaths, expelling all the air from his lungs, and sucking in the 'Gi'. This was his spirit; his life force.

Dropping in at the office on his way down to the plant, Oom Piet was at his desk, a large mug of Koffiehuis steaming on the desk.

"More meneer," Aubrey greeted him, nonchalant and self-assured. Oom Piet looked up from his paperwork, a glint in his eye. Despite the previous night's exploits, this man was tough as nails. His liver probably looked like an old deflated, leather rugby ball, but that certainly didn't seem to stop him.

"More". He smiled broadly.

"If he was expecting to see Aubrey a little under the weather, there was certainly no sign of the ill effects to be found on Aubrey's countenance either.

"Up early," commented Oom Piet.

"Yes," replied Aubrey. "Going to get a head start on Daniel. See you at breakfast." And he slipped out the side door, and through the security zone, his rucksack over his shoulder. He carried his operational folders with him for good measure, as he would need an excuse for the rucksack if asked. He met the kitchen staff as they arrived having trekked the two miles from their one roomed rondavel facilities, built on the outskirts of the mine property. They had to undergo rigorous security checks as they came on to and off the property. Since mine management and senior personnel weren't required to be checked, Aubrey had kept a mental note of who was and was not checked at security.

Aubrey worked his way down the perimeter fence and into the fabricating shop, entering the cavernous wrought iron shed. He made his way to the tooling area. The air clung to his skin.

The lathes sat on either side of a large crane which hoisted the steel shafts used for the gearing mechanisms, and he immediately saw what he had come for. The shaft lay on the floor awaiting the machinist, who was to skim the ends for the re-fitment process. Aubrey surveyed the shed. No one.
He shuddered involuntarily. In the distance the shaft siren began its morning- shift wail. He caught his breath once more.

Reaching down, his right-hand shook. He clenched his fist; then unclenched it. Repeating the exercise several times. 'Grasp; don't grasp!' His mind raced. This was the ultimate test. If he made this move, there was no turning back.

He released his fist; the sinew on his knuckles stretched, the skin white; blue veins showing through his African tan. His hand stopped shaking. Grabbing the end of the semi-circular metal object, he lifted it in his right hand, took a grease cloth from the table and brushed away the iron filings, before slipping the object into his rucksack. He placed it in-between the cover of an empty hard cover Croxley file. Not visible from the top of the rucksack, he lifted the folder containing his notes, and the operating manual, and placed them above the Croxley. Assured he could not see the file below, he shouldered the bag, and headed for the processing office.

The test would be to see how close to the machine he would leave the bag. Aubrey entered the office, but the security guard hardly raised an eyebrow. For good measure, Aubrey, opened the bag, just enough so that he would notice the file. The guy looked dismissively at Aubrey, made no effort to consider the bag, and Aubrey smiled and greeted him.

'Morning Bwana', he greeted Aubrey in return.

Aubrey entered the room with its' air-conditioned unit. He placed the rucksack against the desk leg and ensuring the flap was secured. Taking a step back, Aubrey noted that the bag looked harmless enough against the leg of the computer table. It certainly did not look completely out of place. For good measure, he picked up a black marker pen from the white board behind him and wrote in capital letters on the rucksack, "AUBREY PENNINGTON". He was now ready to take ownership of this project.

The possibility of spending a week, or a lifetime in a Congolese jail was not a terribly exciting thought, given the stories he had been told by some guy at the Falls. Geoff was his name. He was a con artist. A merchant banker, turned entrepreneur, who was ready and willing to do anything for a buck. He had spent the better part of a week in a Congo cell, awaiting his court appearance on attempted Cobalt smuggling. But as he said, he had been set up by his business partner, who knew he was walking straight into a trap.
As Aubrey saw it, Geoff had managed to wiggle his way out of that hole with a bribe. But for Aubrey, this was worth the risk.

Good God, if the son of a Lady Thatcher could get away with an attempted coup d'état, surely, he would have a chance! If his project was ever uncovered, that is. He checked the computer for any tell-tale signs of signal interference.

'Nothing!'

Into internet explorer, right-mouse click on the program. Internet properties; delete history and close the program. Switching off the computer he picked up the rucksack, headed for the security gate, proffering his open bag towards the guard, who gave it a cursory look, and waved him through. Breakfast was on the cards.

Daniel had not even missed him, and they were chatting animatedly about the planned trial run over breakfast. He was a stickler for detail, and Aubrey had to run and re-run the steps several times before he was happy. They had also practiced shutting down the system in the event of a technical problem, or any other possible catastrophic break down. Daniel was insistent. He did not want to see the stone processed unless the system was one hundred percent effective. Aubrey to, did not want to see a breakdown and particularly not a technical one.

They finished a leisurely breakfast, and headed down to the mine office. From there they would check the systems again for a dry run, and then, at twelve midday, one of the big shots was due to arrive for the system to go live.

Provided he never took the bag into the high security-sorting zone, they would never have any reason to search the bag. If security never gave it more than a cursory look at the office door, he would have no reason to worry.

"Don't worry," Aubrey remarked, "If I have a problem I will consult the manual," he proffered, the rucksack, patting the files of notes, on his shoulder.

Daniel relieved, smiled and thanked Aubrey. His pay check was waiting for him in Johannesburg.

"No!" exclaimed Aubrey. "Thank you for this opportunity." They both smiled broadly.

At twelve the big shot arrived at the mine having flown in from Kinshasa to view the trial run of the new system. With Daniel fretting more than a mother duck over her eggs, Aubrey managed to create the ultimate deception tactic, completely without knowing it. Aubrey watched as the mine owner, eyed Daniel with a suspicious regard over the rims of his half-moon spectacles, hooked conveniently on the end of a prominently sharp nose. Daniel was a perfect foil for his gambit, and Aubrey made the most of it by contradicting Daniel on the one occasion he had the opportunity to. This solicited a nod of acknowledgement from the man standing behind the console, and a comment to Oom Piet, which left Aubrey in no doubt there was a perceptible sense of faith in him.

He had placed the rucksack behind the control panel about six feet from the machine. The computers wound up, and before long the system came on line. The icons flashed, the windows operating system opened and the video feed from the plant came into view. They watched, as the cameras in turn flicked between the various views of the conveyor system, and the drop slide, through which the stones would fall.

Daniel explained, "the camera can be focused on a specific part of the slide using a remote-control toggle bar." The slide came into view and Aubrey moved the camera left and then right, up and then down. It was working flawlessly. There was no interference, and the openings on the slide could be seen clearly from the video camera. They would not be as visible once the shale was moving at a pace of two tons per minute along the slide, and any degree of variance would result in the wrong stone being sent into the catchments trays. There was no way Aubrey could tell if the theory would work until the system was operational, but so far so good.

Aubrey looked down at the bottom right hand screen and to the icon which showed up as a little compass. He clicked on the icon and a screen opened. It showed the position of the metal slide as a series of coordinates, in degrees, minutes and seconds. The screen did not flicker, so there was clearly no interference with the operating system. The test would come when the first stats started rolling in. That would be only after Daniel had already left to head back to Johannesburg and his next assignment.

Aubrey paused before pushing the key to activate the conveyor system, and as he did so, he looked over his shoulder to acknowledge that they were ready. A solicitous nod of approval was given by the big shot. Aubrey turned, and deliberately raised his hand for good measure, and with a not so subtle display of theatrics, he plunged his hand down onto the keyboard and hit F8. The irony was palpable; his future, and those of thousands of villagers, was in the hand of fate. The sound of the conveyor rose above the near silent air-conditioning unit, but other than a distant drone, there was no drama. Just a visual vibration on the video feed.

The CCTV cameras picked up the rolling stone as it fed into the shoot, and dropped into the cavernous waste buckets below. Time dragged on, a minute, which seemed forever. Then, like a bullwhip, the distinctive sound of a shot of air rose above all the other peripheral noises. Wwwheeewww. It sliced through the stagnant air, and was clearly visible, as the compressed air was degrees cooler than the ambient air in the chute. The effect was like a potassium catalyst in a chemistry experiment.

First, Daniel, then Oom Piet and then the big shot all jumped to their feet. Aubrey at the control panel was silent, intent on reading the return on the monitor. A stone of roughly magnitude point five carats had been ejected through the sluice gate and into the sorting tables below. They cheered from their vantage point behind the control panel. Aubrey read out the result, then smiled at them. They cheered again. Aubrey was pre-occupied with the monitor and the video feed. The stones rolled on and within a minute there was another loud whiz of pressurized air.

The team behind him, still standing, cheered again, and Aubrey smiled, this time to himself. The reading was point seven three, approximately, and the video feed flipped to the sorting tables where the stone lay, wrapped in its' carbonaceous coating. The stone was about the size or magnitude of the expected output; but the notes had said that the smaller stones, point one, through four, would be picked up quicker as the shale contained mostly industrial size diamonds. This report had been done based on the previous two years output.

However, this shale had been brought in especially, from a crystalline rich vent that Oom Piet knew would give good results. It had not disappointed. Within a twenty-minute period, fifteen stones all roughly point three up to one carat had been deposited on the sorting tables. The big shot was ecstatic. He would be able to report back to the Board, that their one-million-dollar machine was already producing fruit. This was going to be a grand success.

As they got up to leave the room, their next stop being the sorting tables, Daniel remained behind with Aubrey. Daniel looked perplexed.

"Wow," exclaimed Aubrey, ready to throw off any hint of a problem.

He looked at Daniel, puzzled by what he was seeing.

"What's up?" Aubrey was starting to get a little nervous.

Daniel shook his head. "Naa, just a bit unsure why the stones are all so big?"

Then he remembered 'Oom Piet's' comment in the bar the previous night. The sly devil had really put on a show for the big guys in Kinshasa, by using a crystalline rich vent.
Daniel turned, looked at Aubrey, shook his hand and said. "It's your baby now. Look after her."

"Oh, I will," responded Aubrey, smiling broadly, and giving Daniel a slap on the back. "I will!"

Chapter 19

An Elixir

Monday arrived, all too soon, that Aubrey was unprepared for the journey up to London.

"How are you feeling today?" Natasha wanted some confirmation that the procedure at the Ozone Clinic, was helping.

"No different from yesterday." He was staring out the window at the Oaks. There was a richness in their auburn splashes, a perfect match for her wild beauty. Aubrey had found his energy levels sinking with the onset of Fall. There was every reason for Natasha to be concerned.

"Let's get going. I would like to have a look around the clinic. The research shows that the tolerance levels for utilizing ozone, intravenously, are very a very narrow band on the haemoglobin curve." She was all doctor.

"It seems peculiar," Aubrey was stretched out on the large bed. Shorts, a sweat stained T-shirt.

"What does?" Natasha leaned in, instinctively placing her hand on his forehead.

"It's just that I felt more energetic on Friday. Now I am drained."

"The proteins in your blood have been depleted. But that is because your body is fighting the toxins. The blood test on Friday, and the tests we do today will verify this."

He considered the speckled green irises that appeared inches away from him. They reminded him of his mother. Butterfly kisses; and happy cuddles.

"What does the ozone then do?" He was confused. In his mind, it was supposed to turbo-charge his blood.

"It will require at least five sessions before we can be certain that the toxins are being purged. Perhaps, we should stay up in London?" The journey was a two-hour trek.

Aubrey smiled. "Yes. Let's get a suite for a week."

Alternative medicine was a far better option as far as Aubrey was concerned, and in Natasha, he had a medical student who did not need any arm-twisting. She had spent the last three years learning everything there was to know about medicine, but remained convinced that traditional holistic medicine held many of the answers.

Her face lit up. This was her passion; her elixir. So much of what she had learned was through her grandmother. Angeline, had been her care giver whilst growing up on the outskirts of Newbury. Natasha had started experimenting with alternative forms of medicinal healing from a young age, from ancient herbal remedies, to the new forms of naturopathy and even Chinese acupuncture. She was certain that these age-old practices that pre-dated the wonder cures touted by today's' pharmaceutical companies by thousands of years, were often equally, if not more, effective.

She believed that humans, from our ancient ancestors, living in caves, and wondering the vast deserts of the Namib, had taken herbal remedies, and perfected their use over thousands of years. These treatments, handed down from one generation to the next, provided better results than the expensive pharmacology of today.

"You know my feelings about modern medicine?" Natasha was passionate.

"Yes, I think I do now." He would not argue with a woman, whose eyes reminded him of a lost soul. How long ago had mom died; this thought crossed his mind. Would it be possible for a reincarnation? The idea was peculiar, if not somewhat oedipaeic!

"Phenology! It is the study of natural cycles, like the migratory habits of birds, and the seasonal flowering of plants", this was another keen interest of Natasha's. The three were sitting at her Grandmother's cottage on a small holding deep in the English countryside, rich with undergrowth.

They had returned to Newbury, a week after their London visit. Her Grandmother had insisted on meeting Aubrey, but despite their obvious age difference, she would approve of this liaison.

"Is that like permaculture?" Aubrey asked.

"Well, yes, but it also involves the natural cycle of the growth of these plants, unlike the mass-produced crops that are genetically engineered."

She had observed the way herbs grow in the summer season, and determined to find the best natural solutions to optimal health and diet, as Angelina had always maintained her own herb garden. They watched as these aromatic plants had grown in the spring and died in the winter, to recycle once again. Learning ways of re-using and recycling which meant that they never had to replant anything, or use pesticides or foreign substances. Nature had her own self-defence shields against disease, and Natasha was learning to use these natural remedies very effectively. Neither had seen a doctor, or set foot in a hospital, in her twenty-four years.

"We grow all our own vegetables and never have to buy anything from the stores." Aubrey squeezed her hand as she showed him around.

"The use of permaculture is the most efficient way of growing vegetables and herbs." Angelina's self-taught, traditional organic methods were very impressive.

"The chickens are free range, and the eggs are delicious. They only eat what they scavenge from the ground. Insects and natural grains."

"Well, we try to be as self-sufficient as we can, but I fear not everything is as pure as Natasha would like!" Angelina was a kind, gentle soul. Eager to please, and careful to encourage.

"Well, I suppose if you consider the thought of the rain water we collect may be tainted by chemicals in the atmosphere, there is a chance of contaminants. But we do filter all the water we use, and try as we might; the chances are, there is not ever going to be a one hundred percent natural cycle." Natasha was studious in all her deliberations.

Well, at least those illnesses, which with the correct nutrition and health regime can be healed by ourselves!" Angelina was busy showing Aubrey their shelves of homemade potions.

"What is this one?" Aubrey was pointing at a dark brown bottle that reminded him of the chemistry laboratory at Eton.

"That is an elixir. A concoction of anti-oxidants that will keep you young and vigorous for ever," she smiled bashfully, her attempt at a play on words, a veiled enticement of the evening to come.

"Oh, don't go getting him all roused up," Angelina was quick to pick up on the innuendo and pushed them both forward, rounding on Aubrey, her attention focused on the next shelf down.

"This is what you want for any liver complaints!" She knew enough to know his liver was the problem. Natasha had mentioned nothing, but their trip uptown had piqued her interest.

Aubrey looked from Natasha to Angelina. He had requested her to say nothing.

"Oh, don't be so bashful. I'm an iridologist too. Those eyes of yours gave you away!"

Aubrey smiled. Knowingness of his frailty and of the power that lay within the human spirit, gave pause to his concern. If only we like Angelina, had the time to recognize those qualities!

"If you are able to see that in my eyes," Aubrey was intrigued, "what else can you see?"

"I can see a desire that is driving you to return!" Angelina was gazing into his eyes. She had positioned herself between the two of them instinctively, shutting Natasha out for a moment. Natasha disregarded her Nan's impropriety, and continued nonchalantly along the shelved wall, looking for a tonic she had formulated the weekend they had returned from Amsterdam.

"To where must I return?" Aubrey was intrigued. He had recognized his own discomfort. It was not so much that he felt out of place in this world, but a hankering to his spiritual home which called to him through those gentle, evolved creatures. The Elephants beckoned.

"To your home! The spirits have sent their winged angels to guide you on your journey." Angelina was talking of his guide.

"Nan!" Howled Natasha in dismay. "Aubrey does not need to have an introduction to your ghosts!"

"Sweet pea," Angelina responded. "For a progressive healer, you have to learn to be more holistic. The souls of those departed, are our guides through life, to death. It is they that guide us in our life on earth, and if you listen very intently, they will answer your questions."

Natasha stood for a moment, staring at her Nan. Aubrey felt uncomfortable. He thought that this was maybe a bad idea, especially so soon after meeting Natasha. He was about to interject, the air in the room was getting heated.

"You are quite right," acknowledged Natasha. "I have so many questions, and so little time, it seems!"

He turned to look at Natasha. So young, he thought. He would ask her about that comment.

"Yes! The problem with youngsters today," remarked Angelina, turning again to Aubrey, "is they want to rush headlong into everything, and take no time to stop, catch their breath and listen to their guides." Aubrey wondered if Angelina was including him, in her conversation because she knew something. He had no argument with her practice of listening to her 'ghosts'. He knew he was being guided.

"Men or women would never stop to smell the scent of a beautiful rose, if at once their journey was fraught with demands, and distractions. How can mankind ever cease their endless search for materiality, if not at one with nature?" Angelina spoke passionately.

"Think of the simplicity of a four-leafed clover, to the visual complexity of a multi-layered rose. Each has such beauty, conformity, yet they are so different, but equally prized. The world was ultimately visceral, but will never be appreciated if mankind could not contain its religion of entitlement." Angelina spoke to truth. He liked her passion.

"The entire splendour of our planet on which generations of demands have been placed on our fragile ecology, is borne of a sad and undisclosed authorship, which has given dominion over all of nature." Was she referring to the Bible? Aubrey considered her eyes. They were alive.

"In a decree, which has single-handedly wrought destruction on the world we have inherited, mankind has been given dominion over animals, plants and all living things; but has not earned that entitlement." Uuhmm, he knew it was a reference to Genesis.

"But like this world we have been graced to control, mankind has also been given protector-ship. To challenge those words of such infinite wisdom was tantamount to sacreligion. But to fail to understand the real meaning behind those words was to misinterpret the meaning of our existence." Angelina smiled apologetically.

Aubrey knew that Mankind could not by his authority over all the "fish, the birds, the animals, small and large, domestic and wild," hope to live in peace on this earth, if a sense of entitlement gave the poachers, the crime syndicates and the international conglomerates, carte blanche to do as they pleased.

"You are being called to take back your family!" Angelina broke his wondering thoughts. She was talking of his Eles! Were the Elephants' talking to her through her spiritual guides.

Aubrey gazed into Angelina's eyes and he saw Natasha's spirit there. These were two formidable women. One consciously complex, the other with a complex conscience! Both equally at one with the natural world. He at once understood why he had met them. His journey would not have been complete, if not for their intervention. There was a force within them that had attracted him, and to them he had been drawn. Aubrey was putty in their hands. To be remoulded into the man he had aspired to, and his spirit guides would lead him forth.

Natasha returned from her foray on the far side of the room, returning with her bottle.

"This is a tonic for your liver," she announced proudly. "It will definitely help!" Aubrey took the bottle, without question and read the label, "Liver Tonic". Nothing more, nothing less. He was certain the tonic would help, and with no more than a grateful smile to Natasha, he opened it and unceremoniously took a slug. He felt better already.

"I learnt that formula during my last summer vacations. I always knew it would come in handy."

"Physical health starts with what you eat." Natasha slipped her arm around his waist.

"We need to get you onto a good diet of vegetables and a balance of naturally reared foods. None of that beef and chicken pumped out in animal factories, fed on steroids."

"If I had my way, I would be closing those chicken batteries and slaughter-houses down."

What a conundrum!

"The fast food industry isn't going to go away because of lobbyists ensuring that they remain" Natasha was eloquent.

"The consumption of highly processed starches, rich in sugars and with few nutrients, is causing more obesity in the U.K. It's the biggest cause of heart and cardio vascular disease. As well as sugar diabetes in young children!" She reminded them. No wonder the schools have so many problems with ADHD and other learning disorders.

"We didn't have those problems when I was at school!" She took a breath.

"It all stems from the fact that parents have effectively ceded the responsibility of their children's health to a government which has lost track of why it was elected. The blind, leading the blind." Angelina interjected.

"Maybe the NHS needs to revise its assessment on the billions of taxpayers' funds spent on non-essential salaries. Rather put that money towards training and educating kids in schools, on the importance of exercise and proper eating habits!" This was Natasha at her most vocal.

"The problem, is easy to address, it just requires a united nation which realises the importance of this fact."

"Yes, but people are lemmings," Natasha added. She was right about that. They bought into mass media advertising and consumerism.

"Ahh yes. That is the power of the devil. He hooks you into that world of desire, and want." Angelina made it sound as though the advertising industry was the devil incarnate.

Aubrey was quite happy to listen. He had no opinion on health food. He was the last person that could be held up as an example of a healthy lifestyle.

"Why does a dog with bowel problems eat the leaves on the ground whilst walking through the park?" The answer was quite simple, said Natasha.

"They instinctively know what to eat to settle their stomach." Therein lay the natural intelligence of nature, he knew the Elephant had a heightened sense of the natural world.

"We all have the ability to recognize these natural symptoms, but we have been so conditioned that we no longer recognize our own ability to rely on our natural intuition!"

"Humans will be completely dependent on pharmaceutical companies before very long; and they will be able to control human destiny, with prescription drugs!" She continued.

Natasha was going to be a force to be reckoned with. Aubrey certainly knew that. He could see her in a political career as Health Minister, helping a nation take back its health, from the avarice-driven fast food, and pharmaceutical monopolies.

"Do you know?" It was a rhetorical question it seemed. "There is one company that has their hamburger buns especially baked with higher sugar contents than their competitors, to ensure that they lure more children to eat their product." This may not have been illegal yet, but was categorically unethical in Natasha's eyes."

It was not that far removed from the tobacco companies that have advertised to younger and younger people, as the health concerns of smoking became more perverse. As older, more educated consumers were forced to realise the failings of governments to restrict the sale of tobacco, the big cigarette manufacturing companies simply began appealing to the younger, more rebellious generation. They knew the youngsters would not conform to authority. Once they tried one cigarette, they were hooked. Aubrey knew this all too well.

"If the food industry gets away with their attempts to control our eating habits, as pervasively as the tobacco industry could with cigarettes, we will be in serious trouble!"

"Yes, but if the establishment try to control it, it will just become another way that they are seen to dictate what we can and cannot do. The fast food industry will play on that idea to win sympathy; and customers."

It was everywhere you looked. CCTV cameras on every corner; road signs at every turn, and bloody Government Ministers on the television, telling people what to do every minute of every day.

Aubrey squeezed her hand, consoling her. Natasha relaxed, her shoulders slumping momentarily. She was a fighter, and they would do well to recognize her strengths. Aubrey loved her unconditionally.

"Yes. We have to take back our power from the State!" Angelina was no radical, but this seemed a typical refrain on many people's lips.

"I agree, but first we have to get you healthy." Natasha was returning his caress, her open palm following the contour of his rugged jaw-line. Angelina smiled on, grateful for his intercession.

As he passed Angelina, she slipped a hand into his and passed a bottled tonic that had stood upon the shelf. She winked. Aubrey could not tell, but slipped the brown bottle into his jacket pocket, and smiled back. An angel had been in the room, no doubt!

The trip to the clinic had gone extremely well. Aubrey had started with a session of five minutes for his lungs to get used to the additional intake of oxygen, and then had increased that by five minutes on each subsequent visit. There was no doubt, he could feel that he had more energy, and that his lung capacity was increasing. Natasha had put him onto a strict exercise routine and diet at the same time. Aubrey was already a good swimmer and had then been spending a lot of time at the local gym in their indoor pool. He had increased his lengths from twenty to thirty, and then to fifty, in a twenty-five-meter pool. He was now looking at improving his speeds over this distance. He could feel his general fitness levels were improving too, because he would swim a length under water and within a short time he could complete a length easily without over stressing his body.

"I would not worry too much about the lungs," Michael had said at a consultation after his fourth appointment. "The lungs have a remarkable ability to recover from damage, especially with the application of ozone treatment."

"How does the additional oxygen help?" Aubrey had asked.

"Quite simply in fact," replied Sean, "the ozone is created by charging ordinary air, containing oxygen with two molecules, the 'O2', with ultraviolet radiation. This happens naturally in our atmosphere at about thirty to fifty kilometres above the earth, when air is hit by ultraviolet solar rays. When they are bombarded by this effect, it is called ozonisation. Well this is the same process we use. By doing this, some of the 'O2' is broken down to a single molecule of oxygen which attaches itself to an 'O2' molecule, becoming 'O3'. This process forms a very effective sterilizing agent which is used in hospitals to help prevent the spread of disease."

"That is why hospitals smell so clinical?" asked Aubrey with a growing interest in the subject. The gas gave off a slightly pungent smell in its pure form. This was a factor of the ultraviolet process. It appeared bluish as it was electrically charged by the catalytic conversion to 'O3'.

"Yes, but not all hospitals utilize this practice. If they did, there would be a lot less spread of disease and fewer incidences of these super bugs that kill relatively healthy patients with secondary infections. It is this contagion that my machine can eradicate! You must remember hospitals, especially private clinics, make their money out of healing people with diseases. If they cured everyone they would be out of business!" Aubrey nodded politely.

He knew the relative ease with which disease spread. He had seen it first hand in Kinshasa, but was a little sceptical about the NHS.

"If I had to tell you some of the highly irregular medical practices I have seen in my time!"

Natasha sat up. She had been sitting beside Aubrey as the intravenous gas, worked its magic.

"I once had to call on a gynaecologist working at a private Clinic. This was when I was a medical rep. He told me categorically that he no longer attended to any natural births, as they were all done C-section or Caesarean – ensuring a greater cost-to-effort ratio for the doctors."

"Seriously?" That fighting spirit was again in evidence.

"When I challenged him, this doctor explained to me that by committing all his patients to Caesarean section, he could attend to the birth at a predetermined time; and then still make time for his round of golf in the afternoon!"

"He dismissed me by saying, 'women gave up the right to natural child birth when they climbed down from the trees, and started walking upright.' He meant to say that a woman's pelvis is no longer designed for easy childbirth, so we just assist in making it easier."

"I walked out of that meeting with the resolve to take on those hypocrites at their own game."

Aubrey now understood why he carried all this baggage. Michael was looking for some form of affirmation!

Aubrey's treatments had gone well, and Natasha was elated. She was eager to share her newfound knowledge, with the kitchen staff at Finsbury. They responded brilliantly, and were only too happy to have something knew to learn and constructive to do. It was a year now since the late Lord Pennington had taken seriously ill and the dinner parties had stopped. Being unable to get from his bed, he was always locked up in his room, with the only person able to see him in his state of illness being his personal confident, Highpot.

Now Natasha was breathing new life, literally, back into the household. There was an air of anticipation, and a new sense of direction. It was on one such trip that Aubrey, Natasha and the Professor had been joined by Margaret, as they sat around a large round wooden table in the kitchen.

"I often wonder what it is all about," the conversation had turned to the unlikely subject of religion. The Professor was silent.

"That's where you are so wrong sweet pie." Margaret flashed a crooked smile. Teeth, rotten as the world's economies.

"I know; I know. Nan always tells me to be less serious." Natasha was stroking Margaret's hand. The veins snaked alongside sinewy tracks, blueish-grey, belying stamina.

"How do you think I got to be so old?" She chirped. There was nothing frail about those hands.

"What is your secret M's" Natasha had a natural empathic bedside manner.

"Who, me? Nothing to it. I just learnt to laugh at myself, and everything except death." She grinned. "The good old doctor told me, 'M's, you're going to live to your nineties', God forbid."

"So, you believe in God?" Natasha was intrigued.

"Maybe God, but not religion!" She objected. "I told mum, when I was seven, that I was not going to mass on Sundays." Margaret stopped for good effect.

"Why?" Precociousness was not a characteristic that Natasha would have associated with dear old Margaret.

"I told her, 'They expect me to eat Jesus's flesh, and drink his blood.' I said 'no fear'."

"Yes, religion has had a hard time of it of late." The Professor, mild as he was, had never subscribed to organised religion.

"I think Richard Hooker said it best when he presupposed that… what was that he said?" The Professor was trying to remember the line.

"He basically said, 'human nature is so corrupt that people are no longer capable of living together without strife and envy, and it is this deplorable condition that makes the existence of government necessary'."

"My mother was a hooker," remarked Margaret to the guffaws of the table.

Aubrey and Natasha could not help but smile at her. This lively, somewhat wizened old lady had a penchant for the dramatic, but she was purposely trying to lighten the mood.

"Yes. My father was Willam. T Hooker. He was actually related to Richard Hooker." Her claim to fame now established.

The Professor gave himself over to the moment having heard this story before. He allowed Margaret to lap up the moment. She had always been his favourite patron, and was now an infinite part of their world.

"Yes. It is true!" added the Professor. "Margaret's great grandfather nine times removed; was Richard Hooker. He wrote 'Of the laws of ecclesiastical polity', a fabulous work which requires to be resurrected."

Aubrey recalled having been given a volume of a Folger Library edition of his work, to study for one semester. It was intense, but a fascinating reflection on society which had not changed in five hundred years.

"And yet, it is that selfsame selflessness which has spurred humanity onto greater heights of achievement than ever before, with such feats as space travel, the world-wide-web, and the development of infrastructure to be shared by many, for the benefit for many. Yes, you could argue that there is always a profit or power motive to be found in even these deeds." The Professor continued.

"So how do you achieve that?" Aubrey was tentative.

"Simply, the basis on which an individual would rise from the lower end of the pyramid to the top is by achievement and hard work. Now, most wealthy individuals obtained their wealth through inheritance and long term family wealth. Only a few rise to the top of that pyramid, on their own. Mostly, it is through family ties and networking. It then stands to reason; that a society that embarks on a systematic improvement of the class system, by allowing the benefiting of wealthy individuals, to become wealthier by default, would simply not be an equitable arrangement."

"Bronwyn's father had lost his entire fortune in Nyasaland, which then became Malawi, during the reign of Kamuzu Banda." Aubrey felt strange talking of Bronwyn in front of Natasha, but she was not fazed.

"That is a very African tradition. Old Banda was a right royal bastard, from what I understand. Many post-liberation countries in Africa have done the same to their minority populations!"

"Yes. The old guard, who had plundered the colonial coffers after Independence in 1965, also chased all the wealthy businessmen out of the country, and now, look where they are?"

"That country has the highest AIDS statistics in the world. The country is virtually bereft of a viable working adult population. Half of their population is under the age of fifteen." Natasha had studied the pandemic.

"Those who have looked at the ebb and flow of wealth throughout the ages have always seen one common denominator and that is wealth begets wealth. Yes, it is possible to make fortunes with a grand idea, and with luck and timing, but inevitably the banks want a percentage, and the purveyors of finance capital want a profit share, so the success of these ventures ends up in the hands of the few." The Professor was back on track.

"If by rights, the wealthy are getting wealthier, and the world's poor are getting poorer, then this process had to be reversed." Aubrey agreed. Handouts and charity were not helping to eradicate the poverty of nations as they could not be monitored and implemented properly.

"Most funding from donor countries ends up in the hands of the elite. We need a system that allows the help to get directly to the poor." Aubrey was the first to admit, it felt good to give back to the poor.

"We also do not want to create One World Order to try to deal with these issues, because as history has told us, absolute power, corrupts absolutely." The Professor added.

"But then we still need to tackle the root cause of why poverty still exists in countries where there are significant natural resources." Aubrey felt a pang of regret for leaving the Congo.

"When a society has too many 'fat cats' at the feeding bowl, you need to take the feeding bowl away, before you will get a response from those in power." The Professor was talking about an ideal democracy.

"True democracy does not exist in Africa. Every politician can be bought."

"Yes. But it takes time to develop true democracy." Rightly, or wrongly, the Professor felt they must, by rights be given the benefit of the doubt.

"What? Even the good old U.S of A has such powerful lobbyists, they can buy politicians." Fair play was very British. Natasha was un-apologetic.

"Education is the only way to an equitable society. But we are not being taught these things at school, are we?" The Professor turned to Natasha.

"No. But it is only possible to uplift a society from poverty through effective education. And I'm referring to practical hands-on education, not disempowering education, taught in mainstream schools."

"This is not possible if the only source of this education is being driven by economic interests."

"The clear majority of township kids in Africa don't need hip-hop music and gangster rap music videos. This is not going to provide them with a balanced view on how society develops, and what their role in society is." Aubrey volunteered.

"No, but it is a symptom of the pervasiveness of media." The Professor leaned back in his chair; his back was giving him jip.

"The big music companies and the record labels need to understand that this does nothing for their education, and very little for their self-esteem."

"All it will do, is reinforce the notion that they are downtrodden; a bunch of misfits, ensuring that they remain uneducated and trapped on the streets." Natasha argued.

"Yet Zimbabwe's education system is still the best in Africa. Their biggest export to South Africa, in fact!"

"But why is that?" The Professor wanted to be able to understand how a country, marginalised by corruption at the top, could achieve this.

"Because the GCSE system was inherited by Mugabe's government, and they have maintained a good level of education ever since."

"I must say in is one of those strange enigmas in societies around the world."

"Yes," Natasha understood his point. "Like the health system in Cuba. Despite sanctions against Fidel Castro, the country has defied the odds and exports their doctors."

"Ahhh! But I think this has more to do with the collective power of the conscious mind; and less to do with a systematic implementation of education." The Professor straightened up, arching his back.

"This is Maslow's hierarchy of needs, working through the conscious choices people make."

"They know that to get to the top, they have no choice, other than to work hard." The governments had to provide the infrastructure, and human ingenuity claimed the rest.

"So why is South Africa such a poor example of education based empowerment? They have only recently become achieved democracy!" Aubrey narrowed his eyes. The two countries; Zimbabwe and South Africa shared a common border.

"Because of a sense of entitlement." The Professor was victorious in his assertion. Aubrey looked unconvinced.

"The masses who win, will always feel entitled to the lion share of the country's wealth." Aubrey was aware of the promises Mugabe made in his 1980 election campaign. 'A Mercedes Benz, and a farm'. It took the government twenty years to deliver; but the masses never benefited.
"So, therefore, the youngsters who are told that they must determine the future of a wealthy country, like South Africa, will expect that the government they elected will provide them with what they want." This was despite the experience of Zimbabwe.

"Yes, but it is a psychological truth, that the richer a person becomes, the less empathy they will have for the poor." Natasha injected her philosophy.

"Yes, and this only further leads to a dis-connect, between the authorities and the youth. They become rebellious to a point." Aubrey had seen this on the streets of Port Elizabeth and in Kinshasa, a world away from the quiet streets of Finsbury. Or was it?

"This sense of entitlement, eventually leads to the expectation, that the government must provide everything they require, to the point that they don't feel inclined to have to work."

"When the government does not deliver, then they take to the streets and cause chaos. It is not dissimilar to the protest marches in the States during the sixties." The Professor, himself had been a hippie.

"I've seen these kids in the townships as far as Lubumbashi and even in the settlements around the mines. As soon as they are old enough, they only have one desire. To have a cell phone with an MP3 download capability, so that they can listen to the Americanized gangster rap."

"You cannot deny the cause and effect in all of this, but you have to start right at the base of the problem." The Professor was getting to the meat of his argument.

"There is only one way to solve the problems of an emerging middle class in Africa. The answer is an education of balanced proportions with a highly practical emphasis cultivating their long-term employability and stability."

"In English, that means what?" Aubrey grinned.

"Technical schools!"

"Well those governments are clearly not interested in getting people educated." The effect that twenty years of Mugabe's rule had achieved those results in Zimbabwe, was truly remarkable.

"Despite Mugabe's interference after independence, the private schools have remained the backbone of their education system."

"Yes. He has only himself to blame for the collapse of Zimbabwe. He created socialist cooperatives with the help of the North Koreans, but that did not last long. He single handed removed the one mechanism which could have assisted in creating a far more prosperous nation. He refused to invest into tertiary education, even though he was given that opportunity by the very people he had subsequently railed against." Aubrey must have known half a dozen highly qualified Zimbabweans working in the Congo.

"He probably did all of this purposely!" Natasha had a point. By controlling the intelligencia of Zimbabwe, the clear majority remained uneducated and poverty stricken. So, he could manipulate them with greater ease.

"Because education is needed, why have the churches and society organizations been so quiet of late?" Aubrey had seen little evidence in the past five years of 'on the ground' education.

"Exactly! You have hit the nail on the head!" The Professor was reaching a climax in his debate.

"So we need more education from the church and other social welfare societies?" Natasha was unclear on why.

"God forbid. No!" The Professor had understood one thing in all his years as a philosophy professor.

"You cannot educate people by forcing religion down their throats. The early settlers brought their Christian missionaries with them in the eighteenth century and evangelized the local tribes. This proved of no value to democracy and higher standards of living. Then after the war, the American Peace Corp arrived and continued on the same path of trying to convert Africans to Christianity"

"If we have learned anything from colonialism, it is that we cannot hope to control people through giving them what we think they need!"

"Richard Hooker said it best when he used this example," he quoted, 'Lawes politique, ordeined for externall order and regiment amongst men, are never framed as they should be, unless presuming the will of man to be inwardly obstinate, rebellious, and averse from all obedience unto the sacred laws of his nature; in a word, unless presuming man to be in regard to his depraved minde little better than a wild beast...'."

"You see, the problem is a fundamental one. To educate, you need to interest the locals into being educated."

This cannot be done either at the barrel of a gun, or by herding largely uneducated people into a makeshift church and ramming Christianity down their throats."

"What Hooker was saying five hundred years ago, is still relevant in Africa today. Human nature is inherently corrupt, and people living together cannot do so without 'strife and envy', unless there is a strong Government in place."

"But that point is only valid if the Government leads from the front with example. If a Kleptocracy is in place, the system will fail its citizens, and the process of education becomes ill-founded."

"Then what can be done?" Aubrey understood from his travels that he was certain to have made a small difference with the local Africans he had come in touch with.

"You should know better than anyone!" The Professor was sure Aubrey would understand his next point.

"By teaching through example! That's how you educate the masses. One person at a time! By making a difference in one person's life you are able to make them a disciple to your values. Providing they are willing to understand why they need to learn these skills! Otherwise the system fails, because they revert to their cultural understanding. The risk is that 'their' cultural beliefs will have taught them to respect and listen to their ancestors."

"Ancestor worship is still today a vital part of their culture." The common man or woman, will go home to their ancestral land, high in the mountains of Lesotho, or in the rolling hills of Kwa Zulu Natal and would beseech their ancestors through the medium of a Sangoma, or spiritual guide. Aubrey had known this from his visits to Hwange and Wellington, his Elephant guide.

"Yes, so there is a dis-connect with our culture, because the average black African is attempting through their understanding of Christianity, and their ancient customs, to come to terms with the divide."
"Why do you call them black Africans? I thought all Africans were black?" Natasha was confused.

"No there are 'Whafricans' or white Africans who have lived on the continent for generations. Just as America has African Americans, we are all becoming one large integrated society. Timothy is a Whafrican! His family are third or fourth generation Zimbabweans!" Aubrey had heard this term used before. Was he a Whafrican by default; dislocated and devoid of his inheritance?

"Now you come along, and tell them they must listen to your God." Natasha added.

"The reason they had Pagan beliefs, is that they did not have the luxury of two millennia of Christian education." Aubrey had seen first-hand the psychology of treating an animal as a source of food and nothing more.

"So if a cow must be slaughtered, they simply cut its throat. If a dog becomes a nuisance and raids the local goat herd, you whack it over the head. These values are ingrained and you are not going to change that overnight."

"No! If you want to educate people, it must be one person at a time. Rather evangelize that person in the values of compassionate and caring human ideals, and allow them the opportunity to do likewise with their families." Ubuntu was a thousand-year-old social mechanism, that allowed communities to survive droughts and pestilence.

"Cultivate good values by example?" Natasha quizzed.

"That would take forever." Aubrey could see the problem.

"Yes, precisely. There is no quick fix here.

"Every company in the 'West' must be forced through petitions, to provide education to the communities that they are doing business with. Free education, at the cost of the shareholders, but which becomes an asset in time as that sustainability allows the very people who need it most to be uplifted."

"How are they going to achieve that and does such a system exist?" Aubrey had seen the effects of plundering on the local populations.
"Demand!" The Professor was breathless. "Demand drives everything my dear Aubrey. But to create the demand for the 'value-adding' disciplines is a tricky business – as all business is driven by money – it's a simple economic principle!"

"The very customers, who buy these products from companies doing business in the third world, should have to provide an education for all their employees and the local communities. By getting school leavers in America for example, to go out, leave their Christian ideals behind, and just bring themselves, as a testament to what a good education, and a valued lifestyle can do for themselves."

"Yes, but that is already being done," volunteerism was a massive force in Africa.

"It has to be done, but in large numbers. Not just the trickle of 'near-do-well' social workers." The Professor was animated.

"You mean like a vocation thing." Natasha thought that a great idea.

"Yes, but more than that! It needs to be an orchestrated effort. If the States, for example wants to truly democratize the world with its Great American Dream, then they need to lead by good example. Undo the damage of the grossly avaricious corporate greed." Taking back the moral high ground by allowing the world to know what it truly means to 'live' and 'share' in a healthy democracy, would bring more equity.

"Without force feeding religion." Margaret had her say.

"What is so wrong with the Christian values and ideals?" Natasha was confused. "Don't they teach moral values?"

"Ahh, yes, but at the cost of individuality. If religion is truly the opium of the masses, then the way to deprive a population of its individuality and to disenfranchise it effectively is to force religion down their throats! What is required is life skills education, and long term programs of upliftment for the population."

"The USA has a lot to offer, and they can do it with the help of the profit takers." Aubrey had an idea; "An appeal to the corporate world to make this a reality!" It sounded beyond the possibility of one person.

Aubrey sat quietly for a moment taking this all in. He, more than anyone in the room, knew what the Professor had meant. He had instinctively done exactly this for the last five years, but with one important difference, he had taken the profits illegally from the company, and distributed them for the benefit of the locals.

It was not without reason that the locals had come to call him 'Inweti', 'the giver.' Aubrey had single handed managed to provide education for two hundred kids, all of whom were doing outstandingly well when he had left over three months before. He wondered how they were doing now.

"Do you believe there is a good reason for corporate America to get involved in social upliftment on a grand scale?" Aubrey now understood what the Professor was getting at.

"Yes," replied the Professor. "Instead of doing military service, the kids of America could spend a year travelling to impoverished countries around the world, in an orchestrated attempt by big business, to broker true peace, greater education and democracy."

What better way to achieve lasting peace throughout the world than by giving it away for free and not in dollar values. What better way for the world to see the value of genuine democracy, than to have the youngsters, fresh from college, complete a three-month course in social skills, and take them to countries where there is abject poverty. Through their sponsors, they could build schools, water purifying tanks, homes and whatever else there is that can be built, but do it on a scale never seen before. This kind of scheme would make the Roman conquests and their subsequent building of aqueducts, sanitation and roads, not to mention the skills they imbued on the locals, pale into insignificance. He could imagine a world free of all the guns and ammunition that the USA spends billions of dollars a year on. He could imagine further still that all of this was converted to plough shears and water tanks.

"That would be a Utopian ideal." Natasha was mesmerized by the discussion.

"Yes, but think of the long term benefits this scheme would bring to the youngsters who would receive the benefit."

"Not to mention," injected Aubrey, "the benefit it would have on the American way of life. There would be no need for billions spent on border security, billions spent on homeland security, and not to mention the value it would have on a nation of kids who have had all they can have at the touch of a button, or in a drive-through."

"Show them abject poverty from the soles of their shoes, and not from a classroom projector. Teach them real life skills to deal with hunger and homelessness. Get them into a township where kids must make do with a rolled-up ball of newspaper for sporting recreation and show them the real America. Not through the barrel of a gun!" Aubrey was breathless.

"You've got my vote," quipped Natasha.

"Actually, we're going to do more than that." Natasha had not seen Aubrey so serious since the day she had met him. It was almost as though he had been waiting for a moment to prove his real self-worth. She had not seen him looking so sombre, yet motivated. Until now he had only been focused on one thing; to get better. Now she could see he was no longer just thinking about himself. This was a different Aubrey. A sanguine Aubrey, who looked well and had a renewed zest for life.

Aubrey was absolutely convinced this was the way to go. Take the game on, not in the back of the classroom, but in the field where it needed to be addressed. Make an example of the real benefits of first world living by being there and getting involved, not shirking in the background.

"Wouldn't it be great if we could come back in a hundred years and see all this for ourselves, because to be honest, that is how long it would take?" The Professor was very sober.

"Yes, but that does not mean it can't be done." replied Aubrey.

"Exactly, but what I am saying is I won't see it in my lifetime!" The Professor was despondent.

"Unless", Natasha remarked, "we freeze you and bring you back."

"Yes", chuckled the Professor, "like some cryonics man?"

Chapter 20

Building the future

"Unatoka wapi?" The young children in the streets shouted. They stood in groups, four of five, huddled together, faces alive with the excitement; clothes often soiled with excrement and the little ones, their broad upper lips, covered in the white mucous of winter. "Where are you from?" It was a term of respect to the big white boss.

When Aubrey answered, "England", they would nod and say, 'Ahh, Mkugenzi Stanley?" The little ones would repeat it, again and again. It was a form of entertainment, but also served to reinforce the language. They learnt from the older ones, and the they learnt to jive.

The jive, was a little dance they mimicked from the older ones. Shaking their hips, they threw their tiny bodies into a rhythmic sway, all the while laughing outrageously. It was infectious, catching on from one group to the next. But Aubrey loved it. He always brought candy. When the mines Toyota Cruiser stopped outside a house; they flocked. He was the Pied Piper.

Angelo had become his right-hand man. He was Aubrey's shift supervisor, He was very capable, and accompanied Aubrey on his many visits to the township. The streets, still mired in thick sludge from the summer rainfall, were dark with stagnant pools of slime, where the mosquitos swarmed. The shacks built from cinder blocks, were uniform. Each apportioned to a square piece of land, side-by-side; grey and slapped together. No plaster, no paint; just ragged walls, and dark, soulless interiors.

Aubrey had earmarked for a very important job.

Angelo's father had named him after the great Michelangelo statue he had seen in a book, whilst studying at the Kinshasa University. It was during the early transition of Colonial power to Mabuso Sese Seko. The image of this majestic sculpture had so moved him, that he had named his first born in honour of that marble rendering. The caption had said 'Michelangelo's David'. He had shortened his name to Angelo, because the Michael was always tricky to spell. The mines always insisted on a name, which would fit into the column of a shift log. Saint Michael would have approved; the Archangel had always been with him, from birth, and was with him in the early days at the treacherous rock face. Angelo worked his way to shift leader, and then supervisor.

The Congo had soon deteriorated into anarchy, and peace was a distant companion. The current leaders fed off the chaos and the proceeds of the mining industry filtered into the hands of the greedy; whilst the people lived in squalor. Angelo had been sent away to be educated in Zimbabwe, but as the tide of political circumstances changed, he returned to take over responsibility of the family. Angelo's father had died at the hands of political foes. His educated outbursts, over the plunder of the countries ore reserves, had been seen as a threat to their tenure. It was in this political upheaval that Angelo was to become the family's sole bread winner, as all his other siblings were too young.

He was slightly built, unlike the marble masterpiece that had been his father's inspiration, but despite this Angelo was a pillar of strength in his determination and desire to uplift his own people. More like the diminutive child David, he gained his strength from an intellect. A mind, sharpened by adversity and keen.

His enthusiasm was way beyond proportion to his stature, but with that, came the disrespect borne of a nation where physical strength was a precursor to power. But it was just this determination that had garnered Aubrey's attention.

"What would you say, if I was able to provide the cash we need to build a new school house?" They were outside a ramshackle structure, with just one window and no electricity. He was purposely vague.

"That would be fantastic, but where will you get it? Have you found a sponsor?" The enthusiasm oozed.

"Let's just say that the sponsor is to be the mine itself!" Cryptic, Aubrey needed a co-conspirator.

"What! I thought you said that the mine bosses would not assist with the funding?"

"No, they won't, but they will be funding it indirectly." Aubrey smiled.

"I don't understand!" Angelo looked for a glimmer. Some hint of where Aubrey was leading him.

"Let's just say that they don't, or won't know that they are paying for it."

"That is provided you can keep a secret." Aubrey needed to know he had a collaborator.

"You mean that they will pay for it, but they won't see the money being spent?" Aubrey was an enigma, despite having worked with him for six months; Angelo still could not fully read him.

He knew the mine ran a tight ship financially, and that the auditors were always there to do an audit. He did not fancy being caught.

"Yes, but it won't be coming out of the company accounts." Aubrey hinted.

"How will you get money from the mine without them seeing the funds being taken? You would have to steal the diamonds to do that?" Quizzically he had his answer. It was a non-committal look from Aubrey. Angelo caught his breath.

"What! No way. Do you know what the authorities would do if they found you stealing diamonds? No Aubrey that would be foolish!"

"Nobody said they would be stealing them." Aubrey laced his response with an air of confidence. Angelo's jaw dropped.

"The diamonds are being disposed of as we speak, onto the playing field where we are to build the school." So confident in the new technology was Oom Piet, that he had authorised the screed deposits to be used as landfill for the saturated ground outside the mine security fence.

Angelo was dumbfounded. He considered Aubrey's eyes to be assured that he was not spinning a yarn. Aubrey remained impassive, just watching his reaction. There was a hint of amusement behind the blue irises.

"But how? Why would they throw away diamonds? Surely they will find out their mistake?" He was incredulous.

"No. It is pretty fool proof Angelo." There was self-assured twist to the corner of his mouth.

"Those playing fields are currently littered with diamonds, just waiting to be picked up." Aubrey allowed himself another wry grin.

"Incredible Aubrey! How did you manage that? Then again maybe it is better that I do not know!"

"Yes. Leave that angle to me and I want you to go ahead and choose a team to pick up whatever is available. We can manually level the field, taking the stones from the pulverized shale as we need it." Aubrey had waited patiently for Oom Piet to approve the building of a field. Aubrey had been hinting for months, that the mineworkers required some recreation.

Angelo looked sceptical, but was overawed by Aubrey's determination. He would go this Sunday to the screed dump and check for himself.

"Are you certain? This is not just a ruse to get my hopes up?" He considered Aubrey's eyes, but what he saw sent a shiver up his spine. 'This was the ultimate game. What a playing field!'

"Whatever we can salvage you will need to find a market for. I don't want to know the 'who' or the 'wherefores' Angelo, just get them to Kinshasa and the black-market." Aubrey knew enough in the time he had been there; to know that there was a lucrative black market.

Within those six months of arriving in the Democratic Republic of the Congo, Aubrey found himself working day and late into the night, to ensure the safe deposit of that shale. Aware of the divide in that mining community, Aubrey grew restless. The facilities that were available, intrinsically to the white, skilled mine employees, were a far cry from the township digs. That rift in the basic amenities had fuelled his sense of altruism. Aubrey recognised that someone like Angelo, with greater skills than himself within the mine, would have to live outside that compound.

It was here, in the remote north of the Congo, that Aubrey had found himself; in that period of relative calm between the mass slaughter of the Rwandan Genocide and a push by the big mining companies lead by the Chinese, to enlarge their foothold in the DRC. It was the 'naughties' and Aubrey had been away from home, nearly fifteen years. The mine, which had been the subject of a takeover bid by current owners in Belgium, was the only commercial mine operating in the north-eastern part of the country. Kabila was busy negotiating mining rights to some of the larger diamond mining conglomerates, but the prospecting rights certificate required an immense financial commitment and to some mining houses, the risk was still too high. The war still raged in the far eastern sector, with warlords employing child labour to ensure maximum profit for themselves. It was a hodgepodge of mining speculators, who used raw manual labour. But the produce from these mines were the subject of investigation by the International Crimes Tribunal, and were considered 'blood diamonds'.

Decisions to summarily award the mining concessions to other select groups, was always politically motivated. The change of government had led to a new political and economic dispensation. This had meant there was a change of power brokers at the table. This was the inevitable truth about the resource-based industry in Africa. For now, the mining rights for Kabinda Mine, were owned by a historically connected group in Belgium. It was for this reason that the mine was fitted with the latest technology, to create maximum returns in the minimum time, on their investment, at the expense of basic living conditions. The huge multinational ANARTO Group had been prospecting for diamonds and because their influence spread from the Canadian hinterland to the Australian outback, they were well placed to step in.

Aubrey knew these forms of oligarchies were only in business by edict of the current Kabila government, but that could change at a moment's notice. If the political power base changed, the mines could summarily be handed over to another mining consortium. It was because of this, that Laurent Kabila had invited Mugabe to the D.R.C. in the late eighties, and why the military required a vice-like grip on the country. Mugabe had utilised his Fifth Brigade with varying degrees of success, but the rebels in the east would not simply back down. They were being financed through the Sudanese and indirectly by the Chinese. The area was a war zone, and security came at a cost. Despite this the mine had produced two million carats during the previous year. But their profits were being reduced by lower yields, so they had introduced the latest technology.

Mabuto's death in 1997, opened the door for a second this War of Africa. They had seen Uganda, Burundi and Rwanda side with Kabila to get rid of the Mabuto regime; but it was his son Joseph, who rather Biblically took over when his father was shot by his own guards. Such was the all-pervasive iniquity of it all, that now that Joseph was in power, he had to rely on the Army Generals of Zimbabwe, Angola and any rough-neck band of mercenary willing to be on the payroll. Joseph Kabila, who like his father, had never been democratically elected, was now firmly entrenched by powers beyond the DRC's borders. They were intent on protecting their mining interests. In this environment of tyranny, the country had become the stomping ground for every potential profiteer. The system was no different to the colonial era of the past centuries in Africa; but no one would recognize the sheer lunacy of it all!

How to generate lasting economic wealth for the very populations that had lived on that land for centuries, was now Aubrey's fundamental quest.

The company manifesto talked about social upliftment and responsibly sustainable mining practices; but in reality, the change over from the old to the new, in that region had almost pulled the Congo apart with tribal war. In that environment, these were very pretty semantics. No business person in their right mind would have had to deal with the real issue of housing, development of the region, and education for the young. Glossy company Annual Reports mentioned yearly, how they were building schools and road infrastructure, and all the fabulous things shareholders in Europe wanted to hear. But these were simply printed to pacify consciences. None of this was happening, apart from token representations for the humanitarian minded. It was now up to Aubrey to make a difference where he could.

"Mkugenzi", the workers called him. He was the manager, due to his ability to solve problems. Even seemingly petty disputes between the miners, which he would facilitate with a laugh and an agreement from all involved.

The word Mkugenzi could also be used to refer to someone who came from outside the region. The dialect was so limited that its relatively new five-hundred-year history had not yet become blessed with all the nuances of other languages. Aubrey quickly learned to speak Swahili, and the workers began to trust him. So, when they spoke of Stanley and Livingstone, there was respect and an ancestral deference in their eyes. These great white adventurers still held a degree of awe amongst the relatively simple people of the Congo.

They were pioneers, but were not considered as one of the ancestors, who were above mortal men Their travels had been etched into the folklore of these people, and they still commanded respect over a hundred and fifty years later. Their expeditions into the Congo interior, had been seen as a vital step in the expansion of the known geography, and culture of the area, but he was not, "Mkuu Stanley", which would have earned their reverence.

The colonial past was all but forgotten in this land of opportunity, but it was a mark of the man who would forge those bridges of common humanity, that a meal would be taken with the families of these mineworkers.

"'Oom Piet' has provided the earth moving equipment to level the ground for the school field." He explained, whilst Angelo translated the word for earth-moving. "Unugutu". Literally meaning 'the earth shakes'.

'Oom Piet' may be a bit of a cynic, and his belief in the eventual upliftment of the black man in Africa may have been jaded by decades of working with menial labourers on mines across the continent. But this was not going to stop Aubrey from accepting this help.

Aubrey was now working his plan to get the diamonds from the screed dump, and into the open ground beyond the mine. They went door to door, like ass-kissing politicians, but were welcomed in, with great reverence and humility by the families. Angelo had identified community leaders who would hold their tongues, and work hard to see the field levelled.

"On Sunday, I want you to take a team out and begin crushing the rocks on the surface of the playing fields." He explained to Solomon. He was the rock-face drill operator.

"You need to incentivise the team. When they pick up any diamonds, they are to turn them over to you straight away, in return for a commission." Angelo translated.

"Each member of the team must be hand chosen by you. You must be able to trust them. Each member must have family, a child of school going age, and must be trustworthy." Solomon nodded solemnly.

"The risk is if they have loose tongues and talk to anyone, the mine boss's will eventually find out. I don't want any drinkers, they are to be quiet guys, and they are to spend their commission on their families."

"How do you intend to smuggle these diamonds into Kinshasa?" Angelo asked, as they left the rudimentary home, a meal of cassava and goats meat stew, warming his gut.

Aubrey had been giving this some thought over the past few weeks. The mine had operated pretty much untouched by all the civil strife around it, but most trouble was in the form of lawless bandits, eking out a living off the only means of income available. Contraband was the fastest moving easily disposable merchandise in the country, so every street corner in Kinshasa had a trader hawking goods, innocuously.

The key to wealth in the underground was the ability of a merchant to flog any goods from illegal DVD copies of 'Titanic' to uncut diamonds. The value of the informal sector as it had become, meant that a new stolen cell phone would trade for a commission, as much as a stolen car because of the demand. There was no way the cell phones could be traced. The car however, would have to be transported beyond the borders to another territory, which required far more effort, lest the thieves be found driving the stolen goods, and the vehicle impounded.

No! The real trade was in stolen cell phones, so in a country with poor infrastructure and very little communications, there was a ready market for cell phones which could be flogged easily. The cell phone market was booming, because there were less than 4500 fixed landlines available, amongst a population, that if the World Health Organisation could determine numbers, would exceed fifty million. Roughly one landline phone for every ten thousand.

This figure meant an alternative solution had to be found. No attempt had been made by the government to rebuild the infrastructure, left devoid of any assets, after forty years of upheaval. It was uneconomical, and besides the locals would just steal the underground cables for the copper value it would fetch on the black market, destined for China. So, as the cell phone operators moved in and began erecting their masts, the expansion of the industry blossomed.

"Cell phones are available everywhere. The business is rife, and cell phones can easily be disabled." Aubrey had begun to estimate the cost of providing a cellphone to each worker.

"What do you want to do with cellphones?" Angelo asked as the climbed into the Toyota cab. The canvas seat covers clammy and stained.

"The cellphone operators want as many units as they can. There is no way the government can control the market." Aubrey suggested. In effect, it was business as usual for them. The corruption seeped into the ground swell of the African Diaspora, and it was the post-independence euphoria of South Africa, that contributed the bulk of these stolen units. The big business enterprises that had spawned the primary mining rights of yore, now invested millions into the communications industries. In a secondary and tertiary driven economy, intent on evolution. It was a Darwinian delinquency, and the marketing gurus knew how to milk it for all it was worth.

"Each team member will be issued with a cell phone. We will take out the batteries, and they will place the diamonds into the phones immediately which they then hand back to you at the end of the day." Aubrey had wanted a pretence which would appear entirely plausible.

"Everyone has cellphones now."

"The phones I want in a suitcase, and they will be sent to Kinshasa and flogged for whatever we can get." The plan needed refining, but he would leave that to Angelo's ingenuity.

Aubrey had thought almost everything through, but still had a nagging doubt about the logistics.

"What if the 'tsotsies' steal the suitcase on its way to Kinshasa?" Angelo was now thinking for Aubrey.

"Yes. I thought about that. What if we ensure that the phones are all, old and have no real value to the bandits? We will glue the battery cover shut so they can't open it." Aubrey knew that the bandits along the road to Kinshasa would not steal something that they could not immediately sell, or use.

"Yes." Angelo was keen. "We must bribe them nonetheless. They will think they are being well done by, if they get paid to turn a blind eye to someone else's scheme."

"What do you think they will expect.....; let's say if there are twenty cell phones in the suitcase?" Aubrey needed to make the cash available. Fortunately, they were paid in US dollars and this was good hard currency for any bandit.

"I reckon only ten dollars a time." This was the standard fee for rite of passage through the roadblocks. There would always be some greedy commandant who would expect more.

"Yes, don't pay them any more otherwise they might get suspicious." Aubrey was pleased that Angelo had thought up this bit of reverse psychology.

"Okay. Then I must find enough cellphones before Sunday. That will cost about, let's see, probably four hundred dollars for twenty." This was the going rate for a second-hand cell phone. The older models went even cheaper. He would find it easy to purchase these in the shops of the informal shanty-town.

"Okay, I will get you the cash in the morning, and you organize the rest." Aubrey knew he had chosen well. Angelo would be reliable and invaluable. He could tell already. But mostly, he was certain that the thought of providing a decent education to his four children would be his greatest motivation. He had been provided an education through his father's recognition that this was the only way to success. Short-term goals were never enough on their own; it was a lasting education that would make the difference.

The Mining groups were the scourge of Africa, and Aubrey had every intention of playing the veritable Robin Hood on them, with his plan. With no hint of any seasonal climate change to allow the dank humidity of a Congolese autumn, fused seamlessly into the soldering heat of its winter, he began his work. The screed dump was inside the perimeter fence, and from the statistics rolling off the computer, Aubrey had a hint that they were to provide a veritable bounty of diamonds from it. The processing plant was working very efficiently at recognising the bigger stones; but with the magnet doing its job to throw out the GPS on the pneumatic selector, the smaller stones were getting through.

Content that the bosses were seeing a significant return on their investment, Oom Piet began to lighten up, agreeing to Aubrey's request for the building material to lay a permanent soccer field. This was all Aubrey could do, to level the proverbial playing field. Labour was plentiful, and Angelo had no problem to incentivize enough of the rock-face drillers and manual labourers to help with breaking up the rock into smaller pieces.

The work was arduous, but was made easier by the enthusiasm of the locals, who were helping hand over fist. The bonsella of being paid a commission was enough incentive, to motivate the guys, every weekend. The front-end loaders brought out the rock, and the workers set about smashing it to pieces. It was hard work, but behind every raised mallet, was an eager hand.

The foundation for the playing field laid, the next requirement was for the top soil, and before long, they had a soccer field. With the loads arriving every week, the rock was now being crushed for building material. This was used to build the school rooms, and before long, the roof trusses were on. In this climate of subterfuge and cautious optimism, Aubrey began his attempt to educate and empower the local population.

"How many cellphones do you have?" Aubrey needed to establish a secondary supply route and a market to which the diamonds could be flogged.

"Twenty-five so far." Angelo had begun storing them in the ceiling boards of the school house. Ironically it was with a middleman in Kinshasa who had agreed to meet with Angelo, but who was a front for a Zimbabwean based business.

"What do you expect to get for them?" Aubrey was going to join Angelo on his next foray to Kinshasa.

"About five thousand dollars," Angelo knew the weight and quality of their stones. The Zimbabweans had their fingers in every pie across the continent, and it was Mugabe who along with his Fifth Brigade had set up shop here. These troops had protected key mining interests for Kabila and Mugabe. The diamond mines, cobalt deposits and zinc and copper mines in the east, were ripe for the picking, and it had been the old liberation comrades who had then embarked on an active process of self-enrichment.

"Okay, I want to meet our guy in Kinshasa." Angelo looked up from his coffee.

"Do you think that is wise," Angelo shifted uneasily.

"If we are dealing with a new client, I want the middleman to know we are good for delivery." Aubrey was working on a schedule.

"We need this shipment for the books." He pushed the notepad towards Angelo. The order was for two hundred books, at twenty dollars each, there was still funding for some writing material.

Angelo looked up. Aubrey's eyes had turned steel-grey.

"The risk is that someone may recognise you!" Angelo looked perplexed.

"That is not my worry." Aubrey's mind was set. "They must know that we are doing this for more than our own profit."

Angelo was aware that the word on the streets of the township was, Mkugenzi, was building schools and providing houses next. It would not be long before word reached Kinshasa.

"Mugabe met his first wife Sally, a Ghanaian by birth, while he was working as a teacher in Ghana, years before the liberation struggle," Angelo told Aubrey. She had been very influential and the two had fallen in love.

Aubrey met his eyes, with interest and speculation.

"Sally had been able to challenge him and helped formulate his thinking. That was before his megalomaniacal descent on the African continent."

"Had Sally survived her bout of Cancer, Mugabe may have been a different leader. Alas, with her death, and the emergence of his second wife Grace, this all changed," he continued.

"Yes, I had heard the stories in Zim."

"There was speculation as to why, but it all stemmed from greed and power lust, at the end of the day." The new liberation comrades were as thick as thieves, and the DRC was a rich picking ground for the likes of Mugabe and Dos Santos from Angola.

"This is what set up the Second African War, which resulted in the deaths of five million Africans." The world had stood by, idly whilst they fought for the mineral riches of Central Africa.

"Okay. But Africa is and always has been a treacherous place." Aubrey, was unbowed.

Aubrey had been told that before Mugabe had been arrested by the Smith regime and sent to prison, he had fathered a son with Sally before this internment. He never saw his son again as the child died at a young age, and he was never able to have children afterwards. There was a lot of speculation as to why, but it stemmed from an incident that occurred whilst he was in custody under the Smith government. According to some, he had been given electric shock treatment on his genitalia. However, records show he was treated with great respect and never given such treatment. It was this speculation and Sally's Cancer that had been the reason he supposedly had no more children.

"When Sally died of her cancer, the basis for which Mugabe had previously been unable to have children was conveniently removed." Angelo was extremely opposed to his government's affiliations with "The Hitler of Africa".

"But to blame Sally for his incapacity to provide another child and heir, had a detrimental effect on his personal wealth!" Aubrey listened intently whilst they sat in the mess hall. He had been having an affair behind the scenes with his then secretary Grace, who was greedy and obsessed by wealth and power. She was later referred to, un-affectionately, as 'Gucci Grace'.

"Prior to this, Mugabe had amassed a king's ransom in his tenure, first as Prime Minister under the Lancaster House Agreement. This had subdued his megalomania somewhat; and then later as State President in the nineties. But he lost it all when Sally connived to have this fortune kept away from Grace." Aubrey knew of this.

"Mugabe had understandably concocted to have his assets, ill-gotten in the first instance, kept in Sally's maiden name, under some fiduciary arrangement, so as not to arouse suspicion of his activities. Sally then subsequently left it all in her final will and testament to her own family in Ghana." This incensed Mugabe to the point of inconsolable grief; not from her death, but from the loss of that fortune, which supposedly included a Scottish Castle in the Highlands. With Mugabe unable to hold onto his fortune, he descended into anarchical mischief. Aubrey had heard the rumours before.

Understandably, the British government who had bankrolled Mugabe after the connivances of Lancaster House were unwilling to interfere with the Testamentary settlement because they felt somewhat aggrieved that the money had come from their own state funds and the British tax payer. It was Claire Short, the then Foreign Secretary for Britain who had sent a letter to Mugabe, cancelling the Land Repatriation arrangement agreed to by Lord Soames in the Lancaster House agreement, and so began the litany of abuses. The British government had begun a strategy of wait and see, which has now culminated in Mugabe embarking on a public vendetta and strategy of land grabs, which was resulting in the land invasions of white owned commercial farms. This was his retribution towards a system that had disrespected him, and now he would use all the political savvy he had to orchestrate a reason to finally rid Zimbabwe of the English.

"This in truth was just a smoke screen for his activities here in the DRC." Angelo continued. "If he is astute enough, he will hang onto power until he dies." Mugabe had now achieved notoriety. He was a wicked dictator who used any means to procure a political dispensation which favoured his Zanu Patriotic Front government.

Angelo paused.

"What I am trying to say, is that these guys are devious! Do you honestly think they care about your school?" Angelo grabbed Aubrey's arm. The sinew flexed; then relaxed. Aubrey knew he was right.

"On a lighter note, do you know what they call the Zanu PF guys? 'Pamberi ne jongwe', which literally translated from native Shona means, 'Up with the cock'." They both howled, raising a few heads in the kitchen.

"Unfortunate as it is, the reality of Mugabe's government is it is now a total 'cock up'!" Angelo looked across at Aubrey, smiling: they both roared with laughter once more.

It was in a humid, treacherous country defined by Kleptocracy and on the brink of achieving statehood, where the climate was rife for the flogging of these diamonds. There was, however, an ultimate irony. Whilst most blood diamonds had found their way to New York and the illicit diamond dealers on Forty-Seventh Street; these diamonds had not seen the carnage of the Liberian and other central African countries around them. They were truly cleaved from the 'rock of salvation', but would always be considered otherwise. The fact that the diamonds, mostly gem quality, were worth millions meant little and the purchasers would only pay thousands. But given Aubrey's other needs, he never felt it worthwhile to argue it again. At least the funds, as insignificant as they were, would make someone else infinitely wealthier by access to a better life through education. These stones were the rocks on which they would build their school.

In November, the rains came with a vengeance. The mud created from the rain soaked into the newly laid earth works, and became several feet thick at times. This proved a real challenge to the team who had to sift through the muddied shale for the diamonds they needed to bolster their building fund. The rain would fall sometimes two to three inches in a day. Despite this laborious process, the rain performed a beneficial function. As the rain descended into the crevasses of the rock field, it took with it the top soil, which had covered the rock. This created the effect of sifting the unwanted soil to the bottom of the shale and was advantageous when the sun finally returned.

But as the rock pile rose above the rich red earth, the stones left bare on top which had been crushed by the team, gave rise to the diamond bearing rock. The process of sifting through the rock and crushing it manually with a ten-pound mallet.

This was their largest consignment yet. To ensure the safe passage of these stones to market, Aubrey arranged a leave of absence for the team who had worked so hard on the fields, and they each took their cell phones and headed for Kinshasa. This was a very easy job as it turned out, because their commissions were paid to them immediately on arrival as they handed over their cell phones. They each headed to the local stores to procure the supplies their families so badly needed.

Angelo took to the streets of the old Centre Ville on the outskirts of the old golf course, searching for an old-school friend he had kept in contact with. In the seedy red-light district, he found his good friend Claude. He had been educated at the Ecole Belge Secondary. But Claude had seen the effect of the political turmoil, and chosen the path of least resistance. For several years after leaving his once well paid job as an office clerk, he settles for the greener pastures of the black-market. As it turned out Claude had traded anything he could.

"I need a buyer for some diamonds," Angelo explained as they sat taking a coffee at a side-walk bistro.

"How many," Claude's keen interest piqued.

"Three hundred!" Angelo awaited his reaction.

"Three hundred? Claude responded, lowering his voice to a whisper.

"Yes, three hundred." He fished into his pocket pulling one of the old Nokias which had been built the size of a brick. He prized open the battery cover and handed the phone carefully to Claude.

Leaning back nonchalantly, he raised the phone with his hands clasped and casually lifted the battery cover. His eyes bulged, but quickly returned the phone to Angelo.

"Okay give me a day. I told you on the phone, I have a Zimbabwean guy called George. He is living at d' Hotel Supérieur."

They sat, taking in the sights of the cesspit, which had become home to the local prostitutes. Claude, it seemed, knew them all.

"Can I arrange a lady for you whilst you are waiting?" It seemed their friendship transcended the lively nocturnal activities of the red-light district.

"Non! Merci." Angelo had never allowed his altruism to be tainted by the temptations of the big city. Their friendship was strong, but somehow, he distrusted Claude.

"Ah! A principled man. It seems you are in the wrong trade?" Claude was fishing. Angelo, had shrewdly, never given Claude a hint of where they had sourced the diamonds. Angelo was playing his cards very close to his chest.

"You find the buyer, and we do the business." Angelo replied.

Claude watched him for a clue. There was not a flicker. Angelo would have made a gamesman at the poker table.

It was not more than two hours, before they took a taxi and headed down the Main Avenue, past the Stade Des Martyrs. Here was a briefcase full of cellphone's, laden with uncut stones, driving past the most famous landmark in Kinshasa, sponsored by the biggest cell phone operator on the continent, headed for the Hotel Supérieur.

The lunchtime traffic hummed with a swarming frenetic expectation. Everywhere, everyone was rushing to make their next dollar. The taxis honked, the tuk-tuks buzzed. The buses coughed out and the lorries belched, black soot. The humidity dripped off Claude's brow, and he mopped away with a somewhat dank handkerchief. Angelo sat, relaxed.

Along the Avenue du Revolution dans le 24 Novembre, with its street signs, festooned across the road, catching the eye, and the occasional bus window. The traffic danced around them, in a Parisian pantomime. Swooping north, then west, the taxi carved a path through the midday morass. The roads, wide and awash with momentum. They scythed here and there. The taxis had rite of passage, or so it seemed. There was a pecking order, and the loud reprimands, barked out through open windows, placed their purpose and presence, ahead of all else.

As the taxi, with its congenial driver, announced the hotel, Angelo looked up to see a large obelix shaped monument, and the old hotel. Brightly bedecked, with a fresh coat of white paint; its large balconies heralded the opulence of a bye-gone era. Angelo could almost see the rubber plantation dons, ghostly images, feted by swooning tribes of white sashaying temptresses. The old palms stood sentinel amongst the backdrop of the wide Congo River. Muddied by sediment and hundreds of years of progress. It swept past them to the north, carving out a wide arc seething with a plethora of craft.

Angelo disembarked, as the old French station wagon ground to a halt. The door, hinged bravely with signs of recent welding marks, opened with a loud groan. It seemed everything protested the humidity. The traffic fumes, thankfully whisked away on the water beyond, and the front entrance of this colonial relic, opened before him.

Palms greased, and a suitably dressed usher, in attendance, they were marshalled through to the lobby. Claude, dripping with perspiration, and the prospect of a successful deal, lead Angelo through to a lounge, heaving with humanity. They found themselves a two seater and a small round table, pock-marked with fallen cigarette burns. Claude quickly spoke with the usher. Hands were extended and in a clumsy attempt to curry favour, dollar bills passed.

The room was cool, with high ceilings arching pristinely into cupola domes. Angelo was thankful for a fan, that wafted the cool air. They sat. Claude hovered on the edge of the sofa. The room, hubbed with conversations. Every language was spoken, scattered like the four winds. It reminded him of Paul's description of the visitation of the Holy Spirit, in the Upper-room.

Angelo watched, reading expressions, eavesdropping on one, then another conversation. He turned to Claude.

"This won't do! We will need a private room." Claude looked in anguish. The two chairs, high-backed dining chairs arrived with faultless timing.

"What do mean? This is perfect. No one is interested in us. They are too busy with their own business!" His furrowed brow seemed to gnarl his wide forehead into a pumpkin crease.

"No, we need to be somewhere quieter. How am I going to show them the merchandise?" He held the briefcase close, but not too much so.

"We can go to the room." Claude offered.

"No. Somewhere private, but not too remote." Angelo had a sense of déjà vu.

"Where would you recommend?" Claude looked deflated.

Claude looked around desperately. The dark patches under the armpits of his linen shirt grew.

"There!" Angelo pointed to the dining hall. Sparsely pocketed with lunchtime diners, Angelo, suddenly felt hungry.

Claude swung round, expecting, what; Angelo could not tell. But he followed Angelo's direction.

"Yes, yes. Much better. He quickly gathered his cellphone and man-bag, and rushed headlong to the dining hall.

They settled into a table on the far side of the room, with a window behind them and a view of the river. The table was large enough for eight diners, and private enough, that Angelo could place the briefcase on the chair beside him. With a flat bottom, and a wrought-iron frame, it sat perfectly, the open side to chair-back, and the table shielding its contents from any casual observer.

They had just settled in, when Claude's cellphone rang. He jumped up, answering it. The Zimbabwean spoke; Claude listened. Then Claude spoke.

"Yes, yes, we are here. In the dining room...downstairs, yes next to the lounge. Of course, yes, you know it...okay see you now." Angelo listened for any hint of subterfuge.

"They are on their way." Claude stated the obvious. He was perched, like a falcon, ready for flight. Angelo recognised all the signs.

The two men, dressed in African lounge suits, grey, drab, and unassuming, stepped into the dining hall. They looked, a quick survey of the area, then advanced.

Claude was up. They arrived to meet each other halfway. A brief question, then a smile. The taller man kept surveying the room, as the shorter, stout man was about to accept Claude's outstretched hand; then he did something peculiar. He clenched his fist, and kept it clenched, offering it as a power greeting. Angelo immediately recognised the symptoms.

Claude, confused initially, then clenched his fist and they butted fists together.

Effused with some sense of camaraderie, Claude lead the men across to the table. Angelo only stood as they arrived.

"This is Angelo, my good friend from school." Angelo waited, the man appraised him, then stretched out his hand. The handshake was firm, not supine like some, who try to ingratiate themselves.

"Mr. Murandera." Claude introduced the man. The taller man stood his distance. He did not make eye contact with Angelo. There would be no introduction.

"Sit, sit... please." Claude offered. May I get you a drink. Something to eat."

Murandera raised his hand, palm towards Claude. Definitive. Angelo was now very hungry. A waiter hovered.

"Yes. I will have the buffet." Angelo made it very clear, he was relaxed. He spoke English.

"Ahh, yes good." Claude was clearly a good eater. He had stacked a good few pounds since Angelo had known him.

"Are you sure you won't join us?" Claude pleaded.

"No. Thank you, we are meeting the General for a lunch later." Murandera spoke. The taller man looked furtively towards the buffet table.

"Let us talk some business," he continued. There was no rush; just a seasoned professionalism in his manner.

"Yes, yes…" Claude lowered his voice, in a hushed tone.

Angelo gestured to the chair on the other side of the briefcase. Murandera, circled, then spotting the briefcase on the chair, sat comfortably, sandwiching it, Angelo sat placing a hand for measure on the leather exterior.

"This is what I am told it is?" Murandera asked, smiling.

"Yes. 300 stones, all good gem quality." Angelo returned his gaze.

"If the quality is as you say, then I may be very interested." The smile never left his lips.

Angelo's hand went to the brass locks, "Kkkllip, Kkkllip."

He withdrew his hand. The briefcase teased, a warm leather hide, holding a king's ransom.

"Ahh… I am also a keen entrepreneur." Angelo watched as he surreptiously handled the clips.

Murandera reached into the briefcase, without raising the lid to far, and withdrew a cellphone. Angelo handed him a table knife.

The knife slipped between the battery case cover, and levered it lose. Holding the cellphone below the table top, Murandera pulled it away from the black casing. He paused.

"How many cellphones?" His hand had a imperceptible shake, but he quickly covered it, by placing his palm face down over the exposed diamonds; cementing it to his thigh. He then, placed it between his thighs, looking up.

"Twenty, and all the same." Angelo watched.

Murandera reached into the case once more. Rummaged for a few seconds, then lifted a second unit out. Again, he levered the battery cover. This time he nodded approval.

He beckoned to the taller man, who stood sentry. Speaking casually into his ear as he leaned in, "ino i murume tine nga kutsvaga."

Spoken in Shona, Angelo translated, "This is the supplier we have been looking for!"

Angelo said nothing. His price had just been raised.

"How much do you expect?" Murandera couched his offer, with a phrase that Angelo found as peculiar as his power fist.

"How much do I want?" Angelo smiled. "I want twenty thousand, but I fully expect ten! U.S. currency of course?"

Murandera laughed. A quick, guttural, laugh. It rose from his belly, and was quickly snuffed.

"Yes, I like you." He smiled. Leaning back to the tall man, he whispered.

The man nodded his head, and disappeared.

"I will have a coke." The demand was thrown at Claude. Quickly, he ushered the waiter.

"You are from where?" Murandera asked.

"Nowhere in particular." Angelo offered.

"Yes, yes…..I understand; but you have an accent." Murandera picked up the nuance in his voice.

"Well, I was educated at Saint George's." Angelo dropped the name.

"Saint George's? I am not familiar with the schools here." Murandera dismissed him.

"No! Not Saint George's, Kinshasa. Saint George's, Harare!" Angelo smiled.

Murandera's eyes widened. He now recognised the accent. "Ahh… yes of course. Private education. You obviously speak Shona." His smile returned.

Angelo nodded.

This was how business was done in a frontier society, with little regard for the western laws that dictated other less fortunate countries to the south; but without which, it was ultimately doomed to perpetual poverty. With Claude's' fee of twenty percent, Angelo had closed an exceptional deal. Murandera was clearly the client, and Angelo had managed to sidestep the middlemen, in one easy deal.

The tall man arrived back with a closed leather satchel. Not unlike the ones he had seen his classmates at school carry. He had never had such a luxury, carrying books under his arm, whilst stomping the hallowed halls of Saint Georges. But the smell of the leather was unmistakeable. He had now finally graduated.

Back at the mine Aubrey had received a clandestine 'SMS' from Angelo to say everything was going well. The short cryptic message on his cell phone read, "HMWR", or "have money will return".

This was their pre-arranged message to say that the transaction had gone well and Angelo was returning. The mine continued effortlessly throughout their absence, and nobody was any the wiser. With three thousand in the bank, Aubrey could now make some progress with the school buildings, and so they began, buying bricks and cement; the foundations went in, and the first classroom was on its way up. This progress was swift, given that the mineworkers were building it themselves. After work and on the weekends in between crushing stone, they toiled over a seven-day week, and in no time the first school rooms were complete.

Angelo returned the following day to the mine, having deposited eight thousand dollars into a Trust fund for the mines school. To ensure no paper trail, he arranged for the cash to be deposited into one bank, at which he had his own account, and a bank cheque made out by his contact there, for the full amount. If push came to shove, and the mine officials got wind of any illicit diamond deals, the audit trail could never be traced back to any cash deposits. This was how they would conduct their business, and with the bank contact taking his five percent, the bank taking its' deposit fee, and The Trust fund being the beneficiary, everyone was happy.

To inaugurate the opening of the building, they held a small ceremony on the field, with the school children dressed in their new school uniforms, parading up and down the track, still covered in a layer of slowly hardening mud. It was at this ceremony that Aubrey truly recognized the humanity in Oom Piet. This great oaf of a man, with all his six foot something and broad shoulders, lifted the kids onto his back and carried them around the field in salutation of their new school. When he was finished, elated as he was and proud of his workers, he made a pact with Aubrey.

"Boet", he smiled at Aubrey, his crooked front teeth making a comical gesture of supplication, "I did not think you could do it, but I was wrong."

"Thank you," acknowledged Aubrey, "all it took was some incentive."

"Ya, I see that," 'Oom Piet' was impressed. "These guys have never done anything for themselves 'till now."

"Yes," Aubrey knew where he was coming from, "but every man has his pride." He was a little cryptic, acknowledging 'Oom Piet' himself who had arranged the earth moving machines. If he had truly not believed that Aubrey could get this done, why did he lend them to Aubrey in the first place? So it was that 'Oom Piet' had made his own pact of sorts, and shown his faith in the whole affair.

"Aubrey, I have a budget to spend for this year, which is in my income statement to be spent on the mines upkeep and gardens. Seeing that we do not have any maintenance work to do, and seeing that the year end is December, I am going to allocate those funds to planting grass on this field for the children."

"Thank you 'Oom Piet'", he said. "That is very generous. The workers and their families will truly appreciate it, and we in return, will name the soccer team after you."

"What, nee dankie!" 'Oom Piet' had his limits as any man might. But to name the team after him was a little too much for his blood. Recognition was the last of his concerns.

"Yes of course, I insist," added Aubrey. "We will call them 'Piet's Pirates' it has a somewhat catchy ring to it."

'Oom Piet smiled. Aubrey thought he caught a glistening in the corner of his eyes. Then 'Oom Piet', turned a roared. "Come on you Bliksims, let's have a game."

The kids charged him, and lifted them three to an arm, and charged back across the field.

Aubrey knew that this way, 'Oom Piet' would have a vested interest in the team, and he may have a further willingness to get involved in the school's management and upkeep.

It was time to think ahead. This would present a fantastic opportunity to have the team travel to soccer matches in Kinshasa, and other towns, obviating the need for subterfuge, and maybe he could even organize the mine bus to transport them. The obvious advantages were that they might even get through the checkpoints and avoid having to pay those gate keepers the bribes.

'No, they would be called 'Piet's Pirates'. That way no 'tsotsie' in his right mind would dare stop them on their way to their soccer matches, and the deliveries would go undetected.' It was fool proof! Little did Aubrey know that he was right on the money, but in a way, he would, or could not have imagined.

Aubrey went about his days with gusto, getting up early to be in the office before everyone else, except Oom Piet of course. The two of them shared a mutual respect and worked with a high work ethic. They worked side by side through those early days, with Oom Piet imparting valuable knowledge about the mine's operating schedules, and the 'Fail Safe' systems that would allow the mine to shut down if there was any chance of an underground explosion or similar catastrophe. The mine's record of safety was a badge of excellence that the owners wore with pride, but it was more to do with the strictness and excellent hands-on management of Oom Piet, than it was to do with any safety systems in place.

The mine had gone unsullied by accidents for almost six hundred and forty days. This involved a rigorous morning and evening briefing of the underground shift bosses, who were instructed regarding their roles, duties and accident and crisis procedures, which 'Oom Piet' diligently reiterated every day. Every mine had their systems in place, but Oom Piet had his procedure manual; this approach was his Bible for 'zero accident' success.

"If you fail to plan," he reminded Aubrey; "you plan to fail."

Aubrey made this his mantra, and adopted a work ethic to rival the best.

The operation of recovering the discarded diamonds was going better than Aubrey could ever have imagined, but now it had its own problems due to the sheer size of the haul. The discarded stone was usually shipped out to an old disused quarry, but due to the nature of the cost of transporting it, the mine had jumped at the opportunity to dump the stone closer by.

'Oom Piet' shared a problem with Aubrey, one afternoon, whilst watching a game of soccer against a visiting team.

"Meneer, we have a problem with production, and the okes from head office want to do a site visit." 'Oom Piet' looked grave.

Aubrey had been too aggressive in his deceptive approach and may now have to pay the price.

"What are they looking for?" Aubrey continued watching the game in progress, from the side-lines.

"They say our industrial size recovery is down and they want this machine looked at so they can estimate if the settings on the laser equipment are incorrect."

Aubrey continued nonchalantly watching the game. The Pirates were one goal up and the clock was ticking and Aubrey could sense the game was almost 'up'.

"Have they arranged for Daniel to look at the settings?" Was ultimately what Aubrey would have done straight out.

"Ya, but they are going to be here to check on what he does, and what settings he uses." 'Oom Piet' critically eyed him.

They, certainly didn't suspect Aubrey. But 'Oom Piet' had a sixth-sense. However, he could not negate the potential of the whole scheme blowing up in his face.

"What day will they be here?" Aubrey was concerned that their visit might be imminent.

"Next week Wednesday." Aubrey pursed his lips imperceptibly, allowing a slow exhalation of breath, to calm his jaded nerves. When 'Oom Piet' looked at someone, as he was doing now; it could only mean trouble.

Aubrey's mind whirled. As best he could, the slow out-breath clenched his stomach muscles. He steadied his nerves.

Because the hours Aubrey worked always coincided with the main production run, he decided that by leaving his satchel in his room for the next ten days; it might create an unforeseen opportunity.

If he could arrange a higher volume of screed for the auditors to be presented with, this might create the slight smoke screen he required.

"Why don't we work two shifts from now until they arrive, and give them a pile of rock so big that they will only want to check a small portion of it?"

Aubrey was thinking on his feet. When the plant was operating at its full capacity, it usually produced six tones per minute through the conveyor and out onto the screed dump.

'Oom Piet', was still watching him. He could appreciate where Aubrey was going with this, as he had often had to contend with these auditors, and they were a pain in the ass.

He thought for a minute.

"Ya, but then I have another idea," he looked quite jovial.

His long beard and craggy profile hinted at a rebelliousness Aubrey had not seen before. It reminded him of the Boer, who had given the might of the British army, the run-around; they invented guerrilla warfare.

If 'Oom Piet' was scheming, that meant that Aubrey's cover-up would be less difficult.

"What do you have in mind?" Aubrey was amused by the look in his eyes. He could not help but smile.

'Oom Piet' just shrugged his shoulders.
"So, come on! What are you thinking?" Aubrey was intrigued.

"Well, suppose we take the screed we dumped last week, work it back into the production run and give them a little reason for coming." He looked sideways mischievously.

"Yes, that will mean that the stone which has already been dumped will have to be resorted." Aubrey could immediately see a problem, it would pick up the stones destined for his school.

"Ya, but when it goes through the system, it will turn up even less stones, and they will walk away taking the previous production as a Godsend." He winked at Aubrey.

"Can I make another suggestion," Aubrey had his smoke screen.

"Ya, if you have any suggestions, sure."

"There is that quarry stone when we dug the new shaft." The exploration of a new mine shaft had recently been completed. The plug, or vertical vent, had an anomaly, which had caused the pipe to fragment.

"Ya! Okay, I can have the stone shipped back to the shale pile." 'Oom Piet' readily agreed.

"I have a feeling that fissure will have very rich pickings." Aubrey was confident.

"Let's work around the clock on that sector, so we can provide some really big stones." He had previous carat tonnage data to work from, but had assumed Daniel's figures would be slightly inflated, because the Australian company he represented would want the efficiency of the system to look better on paper.

"If we can give them a good reason for coming, they will go away feeling really chuffed."

'Oom Piet' glanced at Aubrey for a moment. A surprised look on his face! Then it was gone.

"Sure, that would be a good idea; maybe the auditors might even have a celebration when they return, thanking themselves for having been so thorough!" He chuckled.

He would have them sort through all the rock that didn't have any potential and get that shipped back into the shale piles for resorting for the following week.

Aubrey smiled at 'Oom Piet', and they allowed themselves a little chuckle, under their clenched teeth.

The day of the Auditor's visit Aubrey had a pile of stone mixed in with the shale, and now they were ready for the big show.

"Okay, I am starting up the conveyor belt." Aubrey leaned across the console, finger on the large red button. Daniel nodded. He had been summoned, along with the team.

The auditors were seated around the table, clip boards and multi-coloured pens. The medium sized stones continued filtering through just as they had planned. Aubrey's stones were nowhere to be found, as his guys had already done the sorting of the slag pile, and only that which had already been processed was being reprocessed.

"Point zero five two", he read off the screen as the first stone had been ejected onto the sorting table.

Aubrey had carried his bag and his files with him, as he always did, leaving it against the leg of his chair. Creating absolutely no suspicion, and leaving the large shaft magnet in the shed.

"Point eight three," the pneumatic whizz sounded. The auditors glued to the screen.

The day continued much the same. Just around lunchtime, a sudden noise, made Aubrey sit bolt upright. It was not the sound of the shot of air, but a distinctive clunk.

The microphone on the ejector belt had picked up the sound of a stone hitting the sorting table.

"Twenty-five point five," Aubrey shouted.

There was shouts, howls and applause, as the auditors jumped to their feet. Aubrey looked at the video feed. A stone, glistening with a devilish radiance, lay on the table. The spotlights refracted off the many facets, were reflected at them through the security camera. Aubrey jumped to his feet.

"There she is," he shouted. "I have been waiting for you my beauty."

The pandemonium was infectious. 'Oom Piet' leapt to his feet, barrelling his huge frame through the security door, and down two flights of steel tread plate stairs, clattering like a freight train.

Through the outer door to the sorting tables, security tag in hand, he charged, until Aubrey picked him up on the camera.

He picked up the stone and raised it to the light. It was a fist full. His hollering clearly audible. The auditors all standing, had suddenly lost track of their purpose, caught up in the infectious celebrations.

Chapter 21

Going home at last

The Roller swept through the Cornwall country lanes, Aubrey revelling in how the beautiful old girl, swept through the tight narrow corners. Swooping like a falcon in flight, diving into the corners and effortlessly whooshing back into the next. She felt heavy and floated a little too freely as the hit the hardest turns; but the old girl felt alive. They had the clean Atlantic air in their faces and the rush of the wind over their extended arms as they both delighted at the puerility of their new-found freedom.

Aubrey was a teenager all at once; care-free and uninhibited. A renewed vigour had also re-asserted his lost libido. Rushing headlong through the tight turns with Natasha, Aubrey felt a stirring in his loins. She was a natural aphrodisiac, and not too unhappy about these events. They stopped the car. A grand cliff overlooked the vast Atlantic, jutting out into the cooling dusk of a Cornish evening, and they clambered over the substantial leather front seats, falling disgracefully with an urgency, onto the backseat of the Roller. A pair of rampantly agitated teens, with no regard to the occasional vehicle that rumbled past behind them, they made love on that vast backseat. The red leather upholstery exuded a timeless fragrance of dubbin, lovingly tended.

They steamed up the windows and aroused no curiosity. The world let them be. Natasha lay exhausted in his arms as they watched the last remnants of a late November cold front, whisk the remains of an emerging bank of stratocumulus clouds away to the east, exposing a scarlet sunset, vital and brazen. Turning decidedly chilly all at once, the condensation formed rivulets, seeking a path across the icy glass. The sweet surrender of the moment alluring and evocative, Aubrey cradled her in his arms. They basked in the combined body heat of post-coital bliss.

Reaching behind them, with one arm extended to the floor, he secured a basket of French Champagne and a sealed white porcelain container of foie gras and smearing the lusty spread over a savoury wafer, he fed Natasha with one hand, pouring a glass of the champagne with the other. He had never felt so vibrant, and certainly never as sexually charged. He could have made love again, but instead, cuddled together and with the last of their desire ebbing into a soulful slumber, they dozed off, it seemed.

The cool air exposed naked flesh and their internal self-survival thermometers woke them. They discarded the picnic, rolling about laughing as they awkwardly put their clothing back in place.

Aubrey slipped back over the front seat just in time to see the head lights of a patrol car from the local constabulary, pulling into the all but vacant parking area.

With a flash of his blue lights, ensuring their presence was confirmed, Natasha slipped back into her jeans, her legs in the air and they were briefly silhouetted. Aubrey with his belt buckle and flies still open switched on the ignition and lowered the window just in time to see the patrol car pull up beside him. Waving a greeting and an impish smile, Aubrey engaged reverse, and slowly reversed towards the road and freedom. Extricated from the gawking patrol officers, with Natasha cheerfully waving from the rear window, he allowed the scrunching white wall tyres of the Roller to lead them back onto the tarred road and a welcome escape.

They drove the last of the forty kilometres to their hotel and unpacking their overnight bag and the remainder of the picnic basket, headed straight for the bedroom. Politely ignoring the quaint little bespectacled reception lady's pleas, they had no concern for the dining room, about to close for the night.

They made love again with even more reckless abandon, Aubrey carrying Natasha from the bed after having forsaken their traditional missionary style, they opted for the back of the plump couch, with its myriad of scatter cushions. Aubrey lifted her gently onto the fat, sumptuously upholstered couch, resting her buttocks on the rear cushions, and proceeded to engage every position in the Kama sutra conceivable. Physically drained and ravenous, they slipped the remaining foie gras from the hamper, and seated cross legged on the Axminster carpet, they finished it, washing it down with several glasses of the Champagne. Climbing into the old four poster bed, and pulling the crisp white sheets and duvet over them, they settled into the voluminous pillows and drifted off to sleep, curled into each other's embrace; the fresh Atlantic breeze filtered through the open window, and the distant cries of seagulls faintly echoed through their dreams.

They woke early the next morning, with a dazzling late autumn sun rising through the open windows, and Aubrey dressed in naught but his birthday suit, skipped to the bay window, and lowering the sunshade, but leaving the curtains open, jumped enthusiastically back into bed and the open arms of his love.

Aubrey dozed, as finely fingered slits of sunshine filtered through the shade's side panels. They probed into the room at an acute angle and made a magical dance across the bed sheets. Throwing shadows in intricate patterns over the rumpled duvet, the autumn breeze probed; toying his imagination.

He lay awake for an infinite period it seemed, watching this celestial display and marvelling at just how entertaining such a simple natural phenomenon could be. He had never been this satiated in the complete love of a woman.

Turning his thoughts from such inward satisfaction, he reflected. He was not quite the sceptic he had once imagined himself to be. Living for Natasha, he knew this happiness had no finite conclusion. They roused themselves by midday and headed down to the reception. The proprietor glared through half-moon spectacles perched on the end of her nose.

"Mr Pennington, breakfast is served until ten o'clock." Her arm extended and a Cruellaesque finger hooked to the face of a simple wrist watch.

"No worry," remarked Aubrey. "We will go and get lunch at the bistro on the quayside."

"But Mr. Pennington," she protested, "breakfast is included in your package."

"No concern," he waved as they walked through the lobby, and out into the welcome sunshine.

There may have been a time when he would have schmoozed her and given her the time of day, but now was not that time. He shepherded Natasha out through the door and into the brisk North-Wester. They walked down the very narrow Victorian terrace lined street with its steep decline towards the sea. The old town was a tourist Mecca during the summer, but now it was quiet. They kept to the side walk as they skipped down the slightly uneven cobblestone and ensuring they did not slip, Aubrey kept Natasha close and held her as they descended the last twenty meters to the main road that made a T-junction with the harbour road.

Continuing, they perused the local antique stores and old war memorabilia of the specialty store on the corner. Walking briskly, they reached the wide-open square. Wearing wind breakers, they turned from their window shopping into the open, were they were hit by the growing breeze. They clutched each other harder, and headed for the bistro on the far side of the square which had umbrellas out, but no takers. They approached the front door, and a tall wispy man, slightly bent, wearing a white chef's tunic, welcomed them at the door.

"Good morning Lord Pennington," he smiled.

"Jacques, you old rogue," Aubrey countered, "you still skinning those poor tourists with your crab curry dishes?"

Jacques laughed. Natasha smiled. It was a smile of acceptance; of intimacy shared. Aubrey grasped Jacques in a fond embrace. The signs of familiarity renewed.

"It is good to see you Jacques," Aubrey slapped Jacque on the back and they held each other again warmly.

"How long has it been?" Aubrey shook his head. "Twenty years?" He knew the answer; they had not seen each other since Aubrey left the country to pursue his dream.

"At least twenty years; I recognized you immediately."

"And you," replied Aubrey rather dishonestly, "have not changed a bit since our last drinking session."

"Yes, in Southampton, all those years ago." Jacques had been the last Englishman Aubrey had seen before boarding that freighter and sailed for Africa. He stopped, cognizant of Natasha and the cold south-westerly.

"Please come inside,"

"My apologies," Aubrey broke from their clasp. "Let me introduce you to Natasha."

"Pleased to make your acquaintance," Jacques made way for them to enter. "Excuse the reminiscing, but when we last saw each other, we were very drunk."

"Not at all," remarked Natasha. "I think it is wonderful that you guys can still get together and remember the good old days."

"Yes," Aubrey agreed, "but not too much of the old. We'll leave the 'when we where's' for the old Rhodesians!" Aubrey grinned.

Jacques raised an eyebrow. "What does that mean old boy?" He had a definite Old Etonian accent, softened with West Country lilt.

"Not much," Aubrey continued, "just when one meets an old Rhodesian anywhere, they all talk about 'when we were in Rhodesia'. It's a bit stale now."

"Ah," Jacques nodded. "I understand." Old school traditions were similar.

Aubrey caught the tell-tale sign of that long-lost passion, quickly snuffed out by grown-up decorum.

"Well let me show you through to our best seats in the house," Taking their jackets he hung them on a vacant peg inside the door. The room was warm and inviting. Jacques then guided them to a table at the window, with a view over the harbour.

"I will prepare you my chef's special. A lobster Thermidor and a bottle of Chablis! How does that sound?"

"Yes, delicious." Aubrey was famished; they had not eaten a proper meal since breakfast the previous morning. "As long as you join us to eat!"

"What! You don't trust my cooking," quipped Jacques. "You never complained before."

Aubrey's felt the flush of blood to his face. Jacques was intonating at an event he was not going to be drawn on.

"No quite." He added. "As I remember, you could always put together a spectacular flambé, using only an old battered frying pan and the most rudimentary of ingredients in the senior common room's kitchenette."

"Yes," agreed Jacques, "but in those days, I was a rebel. Today I try not to burn my food."

Their laughter echoed in the empty restaurant. Natasha joined with them. Jacques was infectious; she knew she would like him.

"How hungry are you?" Jacque was a keen judge of appetites.

"Famished," replied Aubrey.

"I'll get to it then." Turning and heading back to the kitchen Jacques made a looping stride all the way. They watched his stooped frame just short enough, so as to not hit his head on the low hanging lanterns, and Aubrey wondered how much of the stoop had been acquired from bending over the grills and stooping to extract his creations from the gas ovens. He could not remember Jacques so tall, but his wiry frame gave him a more exaggerated lankiness, that was not a good omen for his patrons.

"You guys were best friends at school?" Natasha watched Aubrey watch Jacques retreat to prepare their meal.

"Yes, you could say that, I suppose." Aubrey turning, smiled at Natasha. He was feeling a little nostalgic. His eyes glistened. There was a visible ache to his soul.

She immediately recognized the symptoms. Snuggling closer in the booth, she held his hand and they gazed out the window onto the boats, with masts bobbling like marionettes on some child-like stage.

When Jacques returned with a bottle of Chablis they sat for a while and pouring the vintage wine into three large crystal glasses, they chatted animatedly.

Jacques was desperate to hear about all his adventures. Natasha nodded approvingly, as Aubrey related his stories of the boat trip to Africa, and how he had met Bronwyn and they had decided to settle at the Falls; Jacques sat mesmerized by the story.

Suddenly he jumped up, and forgetting his companions for a moment, rushed back into the kitchen. He had been sitting for about fifteen minutes, and the preparations were well under way in the kitchen. Aubrey waited until he returned with six large lobsters, served on a traditional plate of basmati rice, lemons and Thermidor sauce oozing over the plump steaming fillets.

Apologising profusely, he motioned to the well-built assistant chef to approach the table, and introduced him as Trevor.

"This is Aubrey. A school chum; and Natasha!" Raising his voice an octave.

Trevor approached the table. He had clearly been briefed in the kitchen and stepping forward boldly he shook Aubrey's hand, taking a firm full grip, and tentatively holding Aubrey's gaze with a measured assuredness. Despite his large calloused hands, he was gentle; almost acquiescent. Interesting as it was, Aubrey noted the familiarity as they exchanged pleasantries.
Trevor smiling at Natasha had a warm demeanour and a charming smile. He made his apologies, then retired to the kitchen.

"I have been training Trevor since last year," announced Jacques, very proudly. "He is my protégé."

"Yes, I see that. You have trained him well," Aubrey addressed the sumptuous meal before him.

"Maybe you would like to invite Trevor to join us once he has finished up in the kitchen?" It was a remark from Natasha that got Aubrey's attention. He now acknowledged Trevor's true position in the restaurant. It was illuminating for Natasha who began to realize just how complex a nature was Aubrey's past.

Jacques smiled. "Okay, I will ask him in a moment. But first, let's eat. You must be ravenous."

They ate their fill. Aubrey lingered on the lavish feast, relishing the exquisite taste of the succulent meat that melted in his mouth. The afternoon morphed into evening, and by the time they had finished Jacques had been given the run down on Aubrey's expeditions.

Jacque too, had explained how he had left King's and headed into London to start at the culinary school, having always wanted to be a chef. Having had to placate his father by finishing his Batchelor of commerce degree, he was now able to pursue his dream. He had then been employed in several of the finest eating establishments in Piccadilly, and then in Shaftsbury Avenue. They had taught him all the skills he needed, but one major ambition eluded him. He wanted his own restaurant.

"I had hoped to get some funding from my father." Pausing for effect, he ran a forefinger across his throat. "But the old goat is hanging on with every fibre in his body and is well into his eighties," he chuckled. There had been no stipend and this meant Jacques would have to save up whilst learning his trade and awaiting his opportunity.

"I saw a newspaper article that mentioned how the Cornwall coast was fast becoming a popular tourist destination, and so I ventured down here to have a look." Penzance was a quiet little coastal place, where the summer months bustled with American tourists and equally ambitious English trade, exploring its hidden delights. It was a beautiful but isolated place.

"I fell in love with the place and decided there and then to make this my home."

"Potential sites for a restaurant were not easy, but them miraculously, this venue became available," Jacques swept his hand around him as a magician might announce their next trick.

"All the shops were boarded up through the winter months in those days." Here he had discovered a fisherman's home with this spectacular view of the harbour.

"I simply had to have it!"

"The place was derelict so I offered to pay the owner a rental which would subsidise his stay in a retirement home on the bluff." Aubrey was intrigued.

"With the old man Baragwanath on my side, it was easy to get help fixing the place. He had given me first option to buy."

"Who would have known," Aubrey chided.

"What do you mean?" Their banter was happy.

"Well, that you would have become a businessman, and negotiator." Aubrey smiled at his old friend.

"Well he had been a seafarer all his life, and his family for centuries before," the family had fished the coastal waters for decades, making a living from the Cod, Hake and Whiting which were once so plentiful.

"But as time had gone by, the large fishing trawlers with their factories on board had taken over and the decimation of the stocks had begun." Jacques lowered his voice for dramatic effect. There was no one to hear him.

"The Icelandic fishing fleets over-fished the Cod stocks, until eventually the EU had to put quotas in place." Jacques continued.

"They had ignored treaties and trade agreements, to supply their burgeoning populations. Many countries simply sent their fishing fleets further afield, but the local fishermen were devastated."

"But these Cod wars have been going on since the 'seventeen hundreds'," Aubrey commented.

"Yes, but then it was mostly the French and English who were fishing them. William Pitt was responsible for one of those treaties, going back two hundred and fifty years! But nothing's changed. Now it's the Taiwanese and Japanese who are the culprits." Jacques debated.

"But William Pitt was a commoner," Aubrey joked.

Yes, he reluctantly accepted a title despite his refusal to be considered a patsy to the English realm." Jacques countered.

"Ahh, but his father made his fortune as the Governor of Madras, by selling a diamond to the Duke of Orleans for what was then one hundred and thirty-five thousand pounds!" Aubrey sensed the story had an unsettling familiarity.

"So, these Cod wars have had a history that long?" Natasha was astounded.

"You could say that the founding of the American North-East was based on the establishment of Cod fishing off New Foundland." Nothing had changed.

"With the British and French at war for nearly a hundred years, this became just another catalyst to provoke another war!" Jacques agreed.

"But in those days, fishing was limited to demand and the demand was not that great." Aubrey offered.

"Sure, but consider the wars that will be fought over resources in years to come?" Jacques quipped.

"It's already happening in Africa," Aubrey stressed.

"The Chinese, the Indians, the U.S. and not to mention us and the rest of Europe! They will never be satisfied until they rape and pillage every last known resource from this Earth!"

Contemplating this, Aubrey was aware of just how iniquitous the world of corporate greed had become. It was simply a progression from State sponsored greed. The English had been the worst culprits.

"This entire island is founded on slavery, and enslavement of colonial populations. It is an historical necessity." Jacques commented.

"Yes, but that does not make it right," Natasha joined the fray.

"But to wish to change it, you would have to take on the large corporates with their vast array of attorneys and barristers." Aubrey reminded her.

"Isn't that the exciting part though?" Natasha was in a fiery mood.

"Taking on the big boys with their sanctimonious 'might is right' attitudes, and making them accountable." She laughed, throwing her head back, the auburn locks shimmered in the late afternoon light.

"Yes, take them on and embarrass the hell out of them," Jacques conceded. "The court of public opinion is far more powerful than any law court."

"I suppose that in time, we might even put a stop to the dolphin slaughter and whaling, if public opinion can be garnered." Aubrey offered.

"Yes, it is like these new social media websites that are becoming popular. If you can get a million people to follow your petition to stop whaling, the Japanese just might consider the loss of reputation and to save face, they could well be inclined to think twice about the bad publicity." Natasha knew that there was hope.

"Well, the only way to stop the Japanese is for the world to stop buying Japanese products. Put them out of business, through public pressure." Aubrey realised it would take more than platitudes and public opinion. The Japanese had been fishing whale and dolphin for centuries.

"But it can be done. Imagine having every consumer world-wide, stop buying Sony televisions, or cameras. Putting pressure on specific brands, would create the catalyst." Natasha was adamant.

"I agree," Jacques countered. "The corporates have too much to lose and would begin media campaigns to educate the Japanese people."

"Yes, but the same could be said for ivory poaching, but that has not stopped the Chinese triads from decimating Elephant populations." Aubrey pursed his lips. It was a sign of acquiescence.

"No, we can't just let them continue to do what they want, just because they have been doing it for centuries," Natasha lamented.

"Yes," agreed Jacques. "Public opinion is a powerful tool!"

"Indeed, but where has public opinion got Zimbabwe? It is the same old cronies holding onto the power and the purse strings." Aubrey was convinced that big business had a vested interest in Mugabe staying in power.

"We might not solve it over dinner, but if enough people keep up the pressure and talk about it, instead of acquiescing to the corporates because they control the purse strings; we can make a difference." Jacques was on her side.

"Yes, let's call it a Social Media Revolution." Natasha laughed again. She was feeling light-headed.

Jacques himself had revolted from corporate greed, by not joining his father's business. He had done what his conscience had directed him to do. Now the property owner, had really placed his roots in the West Country. No longer encumbered by concerns of his own father's reticence to help finance his business, he was now free to get on with his ambition, to turn the restaurant into the finest establishment west of the City.

Early dusk in late Autumn now rolled in from the east, and shrouded the old town; the street lights in their Victorian lamp posts brought an eerie quiet to the now empty square, as Natasha and Aubrey said their farewells,

With a promise to meet up the next morning for a drive up to the Monument at Lands' End, and a leisurely stroll along the paths in the nature reserve. Aubrey and Natasha wound their merry way back to the hotel.

He was now extremely tired, having really relaxed for the first time in a while, and with the fresh clean Atlantic air, he was asleep before his head hit the pillow. He slept for the entire night, while Natasha watched over him for several hours, before herself retiring to bed. She had sat on the Welsh chair, at the bay window watching him breath, the air rushing in through his nose silently, and exhaling back out with a rush and quiver.

Natasha knew there was that at a point in all life cycles, which can naturally occur between half a dozen of more times, that Cancer cells were triggered genetically. Had his immune system been high at that time, he would have naturally fought them off, and the cancer would not have had the chance to multiply. She needed to go back into his past, without causing him any unnecessary anxiety, and discover what could have set the Cancer on an unchecked growth spurt. Had he been fit and healthy, in mind, body and soul, his immune system would have dealt with it.

From a holistic healing process, it was evident what had caused his liver Cancer. Knowing the function of the liver was to excrete bile to aid the body in processing fats. The only cause of reduced liver function would have to be stress. In Medieval society, a man was referred to as feeling bilious, if his liver was not functioning properly; usually brought on by the excessive consumption of alcohol. It was fascinating to her that the drinking of alcohol itself, would cause irreparable damage to the liver.

It was the natural processing of bile, stimulated by the hydrocarbons of the hydroxyl group; which once excessively released into the blood made one feel bilious. If the bile, a yellowish green colour, were to be released excessively into one's blood. Then it stands to reason that the body would have a slightly greenish hue.

This was basic knowledge. But the fact that alcohol, in its' various forms was so readily available to the public, but was doing so much harm, made it necessary for further investigation. Smoking bans had helped reduce the amount of causal illnesses relating to lung and blood diseases, however, alcohol was equally harmful in excess, yet remained unchecked. Despite Government bans on underage drinking, as well as the restrictions on opening hours for drinking establishments, the binge drinking that was a common occurrence among the British youth, remained unchecked. Natasha resolved to investigate why?

She drifted off to sleep on a cloud of unchecked thoughts.

The next morning, they met Jacques and Trevor for a ramble in the country. Trevor wanted to take them to a pathway that led up along the craggy ridge on the northern part of the peninsular. It was a natural extension to the Ridgeway, the famous ridge that ran through the Devon countryside and into Cornwall. They drove up to the eastern boundary in the Roller, and then took the ramblers path through the country until they reached the edge of the ridge.

Heading onto the steeper inclines, Aubrey was upfront with Trevor, now allowed the others to reach him and overtake. He would take this section slowly and pace himself. The stunning countryside, and the sea breezes caught their breath as they climbed. The salt air and the higher concentrations of oxygen were exhilarating.

Slightly euphoric with a feeling of vitality, Aubrey was amazed at how easily he coped with the first section. They passed the morning skipping over rock and crevice until they were all at the edge of the ridge.

Looking down on the churning verdant sea below them crashing into the rocks, Aubrey realised that the waves, driven all the way from Iceland with the prevailing wind and current, would continue to do so for eternity. Long after he was gone, and the Elephant was no longer free to roam the Savannah of Africa, they would still be charging headlong into these cliffs with the same deafening alacrity.

Aubrey sensed the oxygen pumping through his veins, and was aware of how his body felt, as he drew deep gasps into his lungs. Not dissimilar to the Ozone treatment, he could sense the same burning in his lungs that he had felt while increasing his therapy to forty minutes, three times a week. It was obvious this was the reason for his health resurgence.

They sat on the precipice, and watched the mighty Atlantic Ocean smash into the rocks below, seemingly undeterred by this barrier. Relentless and determined, the ocean would eventually have its way, and in thousands of years that little outcrop would be gone, and someone else sometime in the unimaginable future might also be looking down onto this view, from a different angle. Catatonic, as a child might be captivated by the flickering of a fire, they were all held in the grip of this furry. Strengthened by his feelings towards Natasha, and despite what he knew he would have to do, Aubrey wanted to at least savour this moment if possible. This was food for the soul, and like every aspect of life, needed to be relished like the topping on a Crème Brule.

This was his way of coping, and it was thanks to Natasha, that he had come to realize this; thankfully, not too late. Aubrey would take Natasha with him to revisit that spiritual continent. They would take a trip back up the Zambezi, and witness the grandeur of those ancient ramparts. They would revisit his Elephants. Their soul was his, and he knew that they were beckoning him; but what were they saying? As far away as he was from them, Aubrey knew they were calling to him. Their message floated in on the Atlantic, stirring his heart, and making him feel homesick. It was that empty feeling he had when longing for the call of his mother; the sheer loss of kindred spirit. Guilt overcame him. Seated on that ledge, overlooking the voracious appetite of the Atlantic as its assault on the rocks, infinitesimally took the coastline back a hundredth of a millimetre at a time, Aubrey was reminded of the desolation of a maternal spirit, longing for her embrace; and he silently wept.

The wind provoked, self-flagellating; a curvaceous temptress.

But he was focused on how he had trained his Elephants every day, one step at a time. Coaching and rewarding, like the ebb and flow of this great ocean. It took the patience and determination of all his will power to coax them, and now they were calling him back for their reward. Somehow Aubrey sensed they wanted; no, deserved their freedom!

They returned to the hotel, Aubrey had a chance to thank Jacques alone as they dropped the guys off at small bed sit above the restaurant.

"When I get back from Zimbabwe, I want you two to come up to Finsbury and stay for a few days." Aubrey had not had any guests stay since he became the Lord.

"Yes, we would love that," Jacques returned.

"Until then!" He gave Jacques a hug, lingering in their embrace for just that moment of gratitude.

"See you then at Finsbury." It was Jacques' way of making this a definite plan.

Aubrey spun the power steering of the Roller, away from the curb-side. Then with Natasha leaning back over the passenger front seat to wave goodbye, they zoomed off up the road.

Their trip, organized within a week, Natasha, due to take her winter vacation from the University, was only too happy to be getting away. With flights into O.R. Tambo airport in Johannesburg and a connecting flight to Victoria Falls on the local carrier for British airways arranged, they decided to keep the tickets open. Accommodation was booked with short notice, at the splendid Victoria Falls hotel. They decided on the honeymoon suite, so as they might have the best view of the bridge and the 'Falls' beyond.

They said farewell to the staff again, and with Sean whisking them down the driveway, and Natasha leaning out the window shouting, 'Merry Christmas' to all the staff assembled on the stairs; they were off.

Chapter 22

A rude awakening

"The cartels that run 'blood diamonds' from Sierra Leone, under Charles Taylor find their way into Europe and the US." Angelo told Aubrey.

"The more the authorities try to stop them, the more sophisticated the syndicates become." They were sitting in Angelo's kitchen. Maria was preparing a simple dish of lamb stew with sweet potatoes. It was Aubrey's favourite.

"Yes, but the scientific process of determining the origins of diamonds will render them illegal before long," Aubrey countered.

"Do you really believe those guys from Le Winters?" Angelo cocked his head theatrically. "You do know that the buying and selling of diamonds is controlled by them!" The question posed, left no stone unturned, as to Angelo's belief, or lack thereof in the Kimberley Process.

"The entire process is set up to prevent nasty little illicit diamond deals, becoming an expose in the international media." The war in Sierra Leone was waged for the diamond fields of the north.

"Ultimately, those war lords will be brought to justice, but unfortunately that is not the case with Mugabe."

"Ahh, but there in lays the irony!" Aubrey reminded. Their success hung on the premise that without Mugabe, they would not be building the school.

"He escapes all the interests of the West's legal mechanisms because he has managed to cover his tracks so well," Angelo leant over, refilling Aubrey's glass. His eyes were stone-cold. Aubrey felt a shiver.

"So, you are saying, Mugabe should be brought to justice?" The question floated momentarily as Angelo replaced the ice which had melted, in the sweltering heat. The Congo was experiencing a vile summer with temperatures in the forties; Celsius.

"Of course, he should." Angelo sat.

"Okay, but what about our diamonds?" Aubrey would not countenance any changes that might prevent them completing their task.

"When Mugabe is gone; whether he dies in office, or whether he is brought to justice, he will simply be replaced by another dictator."

"Yes, I suppose you are right," Aubrey saw his logic.

"The question we should be asking, is; who is keeping Mugabe in power?" Angelo watched Aubrey for a glimmer of acknowledgment.

"Well clearly there are people who have a vested interest in his continued tenure as president." Aubrey had never really given it much thought.

"Mugabe has squandered a fantastic opportunity to turn Zimbabwe into the jewel of Africa. Instead he has successfully managed to bring the country to its knees, in less than a third of the time that the colonialists had taken to build it."

"At least the Roman Empire took four hundred years to dismantle; whereas Mugabe had worked so effectively that it has taken less than thirty years to destroy an entire economic success story in Africa." Aubrey concurred.

"Well, the question we should be asking is, 'What is 'Oom Piet' doing with his diamonds?" Maria looked over her shoulder from the stove. It worried her, that Angelo and Aubrey were intent on finding this out.

Aubrey would have to be very careful and not draw attention to himself, but would listen more intently to conversations in the office. But now that he knew he had an ally in the office, he would feel less exposed to the attentions of Head Office.

"You are so wound up about 'Oom Piet'," Angelo scolded.

It was true; he was getting knots in his stomach every time someone checked his bag, or went too close to the computers. Fortunately for Aubrey, the mine was not running the sorting rooms at night, but stock piling the shale dumps from the mine during the evening and then feeding the sorting process during the day. This had aided and abetted their cause.

Aubrey was sitting at his desk several days later, caught up the production of the new vent. The haul was so effective, that the stash of large, gem quality stones was creating an ideal cover. The phone rang.

"Aubrey," the caller was out of breath. It was Angelo.

"Yes. What's wrong?" The tone of his voice, unmistakable. There had never been arrangements for a code, in the event of a potential problem; they had been duped into believing their cause was worthy.

"It's Oom Piet, he's poking around on the shale-heaps outside the mine fences."

"Do you think he suspects something?" Angelo continued. Aubrey flicked his monitor to the security camera on the external fence.

"Yes"

Aubrey was immediately alerted to the look of surprise on 'Oom Piet's face, the week before. In no way had Aubrey let onto their scheme, but he had shown a surprised look nonetheless.

"I will be down to your office in a sec." Aubrey hung up, and taking his bag with him headed for the stairs.

He arrived at the pre-fabricated office within twenty seconds, and motioning to him, led Angelo through to the security office on the ground floor. Entering an antechamber, with a heavy corrugated tin roof, they cornered the duty officer behind rows of TV monitors. They reflected the various cameras dotted all around the mine. Several cameras positioned on tall poles screening the perimeter of the mine made it possible to zoom in from from several angles. Mounted on a moveable dolly, they were manoeuvred from this control panel.

The two partners in crime, made a casual perusal of the camera posts and surveyed the monitors. The shale-heaps came into view, and then the unmistakable frame of 'Oom Piet'. He was scouting the edge of the heap, and sifting through a pile of stones. 'Oom Piet' was gesticulating to the man on his left to have some stones removed. It was a dismissive gesture, his large sleeveless forearms bulged. He was intent on getting the heap of stones back into the shed, closest to the perimeter.

Despite Angelo's anxious look, Aubrey smiled to himself. He checked his watch. It was five after four. The shift change was at six. That would give Aubrey the entire night. Once the job of hauling those stones to the shed was done, he would set to work.

He turned to Angelo, a small bead of perspiration trickled down his forehead, leaving a residue of glistening skin, the colour of ebony.

Aubrey motioned to Angelo to follow him, and they set off back to the main office, Aubrey shouldering his satchel. When they were out of earshot of the others, he began to give David instructions.

Oom Piet was a dark horse, and Aubrey was going to have to do some serious investigating. If the diamonds he was siphoning off the mine himself were being flogged anywhere, someone in Kinshasa was sure to know. Aubrey assessed that, between the buyers at the Hotel Supérieur, and the back-street middlemen, someone was sure to have the information.

"So, Meneer Pennington," 'Oom Piet' pronounced the double 'n' with typical Afrikaans inflection on the letters. Seated at the long bar, the stench of rich brandy as he leaned towards Aubrey.

"Piet," Aubrey was so direct in his response, he wanted to make him stop in his tracks.

"I am going to take you to Kisangani next week to see our guys play against the local ANARTO mine out there," he deliberately changed the track of the conversation. The knowing was that this mine held the key to whatever was going down.

"Hhwwwhfff," Oom Piet stopped alright. Then went blood red. The brandy, burnt through his nostrils as he looked at Aubrey through alcohol infused eyes. Wiping his mouth and beard with the back of his great calloused hand; his beard glistening with specks of the brandy now mingled with saliva.

He cursed once. Sitting as erect on his bar stool, as that stoutly frame would allow. The wooden seat seemed to disappear up his generous backside, enveloped by the khaki shorts he wore and his large hairy thighs.

Oom Piet collected his thoughts, then turning back to Aubrey again, he smiled, nodded his head several times as if to suggest Aubrey had gotten one up on him. Somewhere out there in the jungle was the answer to the riddle; 'Where was 'Oom Piet' flogging his own stash of diamonds; and to whom?'

"That's a long way to take the guys," remarked 'Oom Piet', feigning disinterested.

"Yes, but we managed to get a charter flight in and we will stay the weekend!" Aubrey was pleased with the arrangements. They would use the airfield outside Kisangani.

"How are you paying for all this?" The question was direct.

He intuitively knew there was some way Aubrey was involved in a scheme.

Aubrey remained silent; whatever was to be said would be an indictment. They held an unspoken truce; for now.

Aubrey had a suspicion, the diamonds destined for his own buyers, were being sacrificed for Aubrey's benefit. This would irk him, so Aubrey would have to keep him close.

If his scheme had seriously impacted Oom Piet's', the quantity of lucrative diamonds finding their way through his own illicit network of diamond dealers would be causing some ruction. This was going to prove an interesting trip….

Kisangani, the capital of the central province, lay on the broad Congo river, at the crossroads of the great African highways. This was the focal point of so much mining and agricultural activity, that the city had now become the heart of the country; and the nerve centre for every entrepreneur and opportunist. It was the Witwatersrand of the early 1900's and every man, minus his dog was there.

"No, I am serious," Angelo had been filling Aubrey in on some of the intricacies of the city; and what they should avoid.

"That is just a saying," Aubrey reminded him.

"This is the centre of the dog-baiting industry in Africa." Angelo was looking out of the window of the Cessna, as they touched down.

"Dog-baiting?" Aubrey looked horrified. "That is a sport which died out with rabies!"

"Not so my friend," Angelo's frown, furrowed his wide forehead, giving Aubrey every reason to take him seriously.

"When you say centre, do you mean like an institutional sport?"

"Every year, tens of thousands of dogs, bred in hell-holes in the Cape and various townships in South Africa, are exported illegally to the Congo; and most of them end up here." Angelo looked back at Aubrey.

"Why here?" Aubrey felt the collective guilt, of all those under-handed deals.

"Because large transient populations, always become depraved once money becomes readily available." The guilt was shared.

"You see what happens when greed becomes the focus of man's inhumanity!" Aubrey felt the Cessna shudder as it breached the tarmac, and hit the dirt apron.

The dust cloud enveloped them, with the twin engines throttling back and reverse thrust was engaged. They had come this far; was the damage irreparable?

The team in their brand-new blue and white strip soccer outfits had won the game with the ANARTO mine, and their transaction had gone to plan. The local hotel on the banks of the Lualaba River; the main headstream of the mighty Congo, sat on the precipice of the Boyoma Falls. It had reminded him, in part of his time at Victoria Falls. Plunging sixty odd meters through the cataracts of the Kisangani region, it was not nearly as impressive. In the early days, it had been known as the Stanley Falls, named after the famous explorer and Christian evangelist missionary, Henry Morton Stanley.

"This is where Stanley made camp nearly a hundred and fifty years ago," remarked Aubrey as the pair wondered alongside the river bank.

Snaking through the city, the river churned liquid gold, as the sun set off their left flank. The river somehow seemed to countenance the city, looping northwards and tumbling through the numerous cataracts until it disappeared on its three thousand kilometre journey to the Atlantic Ocean.

"If you follow the river south," Angelo interrupted his conjuring thoughts.

"The river will eventually lead you another thousand miles to its source in the Rift Valley at Lake Tanganyika." The great geological formation defining the interior of Africa, had carved a great rift through her heart. She had hidden the source of the Nile River from those same intrepid explorers all those years before.

"Yes, and Ujiji!" Aubrey was drawn out of his reverie.

"That's where Stanley supposedly met David Livingston and uttered those famous words; 'Doctor Livingston, I presume?' Aubrey grinned.

"I suppose there may be some truth there. Stanley was known to have a wicked sense of humour!" Angelo jibbed.

"It does seem a little ludicrous, seeing as they were probably the only two whities within two thousand miles of Ujiji at the time!" Aubrey felt the warmth of their common experience.

"Ahh, I see your point. I think Stanley was very much misunderstood by his peers. The called him a slave trader and a racist; but I believe he has been unduly maligned," Angelo apologised.

"Yes, but he did have a reputation for flogging his porters to get them to venture into the Congo." Aubrey knew only too well how superstitious the early Africans were.

"Well he had to induce them to carry their supplies. But half of them mutinied."

"Their society was based on the worship of ancestors, and they found it very difficult to appease those ghosts when trespassing on sacred land." Angelo continued.

"The Congo has always been a dark and mysterious place to most outsiders! That is probably why there is still such savagery, a hundred and fifty years later."

The blazing sun appeared to expand with each passing minute bobbing on the horizon, like a bouncing ball as the light played tricks on their minds. That great celestial orb had derived such consternation amongst the tribal mystics and had griped them with the ancient stories that held them superstitiously in awe of her grandeur. Above the far river bank, the sky was indigo blue, slowly merging into the luminescent orange that finally ran blood red. She slid provocatively over the edge of the western horizon, teasing them as the great bulbous abdomen of the lethal button spider might attract the craven common crows, so prominent at the Falls in Zimbabwe. 'Latrodectus Rhodesiensis'. The brightly glowing protrusion a subtle reminder of the inherent dangers of Africa!

They watched, both mesmerized and thoughtful.

"We should get back to the hotel before dark," Angelo suggested as the sky began its afterglow of phosphorescence. It glowed with the energy of another brutal day on that unforgiving continent.

At the hotel, Aubrey and Angelo made their way to the bar. Sitting in the corner booth, taking in a myriad of mining traders and clandestine business relationships; Aubrey suddenly stopped talking mid-sentence. He was gazing over Angelo's left shoulder and motioned to be quiet. Watching intently, he then whispered:

"Oom Piet, just walked in with a bunch of European men."

Angelo resisted the urge to turn around. The group were ensconced at the bar and Aubrey could tell they were in the throes of a major negotiation.

Watching them silently for a few minutes, Aubrey suddenly rose. Indicating with his hand Angelo and he left the booth. Silently, the two slipped out through the side door.

"Oom Piet went to the toilet," Aubrey breathed once more.

"Who was he with?" Angelo was desperate to know.

"I could not tell, but they weren't locals for sure. They looked like they might be from the U.N. mission office!" Aubrey had seen their ruddy faces.

"Canailles!" Angelo spat the word out.

"What?" Aubrey was lost. His French not as strong as it had been in form six.

"Rogue traders," Angelo repeated the translation. They are here trading ivory for gold and diamonds and whatever else they can carry back to Europe."

"You're not serious?" The very mention raised his hackles.

"Very serious! I've heard rumours but never witnessed it myself." Angelo spat the word under his breath. "Canailles!"

"Where are they getting the ivory from?" Aubrey was now very interested.

"Up north. They are decimating the populations beyond the border with Sudan and into Uganda and Rwanda."

"WHO? Who is killing the Elephant?" Aubrey needed to know.

"The rebels hunt them down and then trade the ivory for diamonds and gold." The Chinese buy the Ivory and ship it through Sudan back to markets in the East."

"My God!" Aubrey felt like he had been sucker-punched. "I had no idea the trade extended this far north."

"Oh yes," Angelo nodded his head.

"How far is it from here?" Aubrey was gutted.

"North on the Bambili Road. About three hundred K's from here." Angelo responded.

"Come with me," Aubrey by-passed the bar and lead him out through the reception into the car park.

"We're going to have a look!" Aubrey stated matter-of-factly.

"You're joking?" Angelo stopped instinctively.

Aubrey paced across to the open-top Landy they had borrowed from the mine office at Tshakala. Hopping into the open driver's seat Aubrey started her up.

Angelo had run the remaining twenty yards, his eyes wild with expectation.

"No Aubrey! That road is extremely dangerous."

"Get in then," he shouted over the roaring engine. "I may need you to translate."

Angelo hesitated for a split second and before Aubrey could engage first gear, he leapt the four feet over the sill and landed on the passenger seat.

"You're crazy!" He watched Aubrey's face for a momentary hint of doubt.

The Landy lurched forward, Aubrey steeled his forearms against the manual steering, and wrenched the wheel sideways, and out onto the main road.

It was clear of any traffic and they charged north out of Kisangani's suburbs on the N4 and past the Central prison, as the lights of the city faded behind them. The road took them due north, flanking the Lindi River and out into the stillness of a cooling cloudless evening. At Buta they dog-legged to the east, taking the Bambili Road and heading into unknown territory.

It was eerily quiet, but the diesel engine beat counted down the miles with sustained monotony. Angelo kept quiet, his own remarks to Aubrey were to direct him as they raced through the sleeping town and back out onto the border road. Headed for the Garamba National Park on the border with Southern Sudan, Angelo directed each turn.

Aubrey kept his foot flat to the metal floor boards as they burned off half a tank of diesel. The Landy surged along the dark unlit roads south of the Park, undeterred.

"There is the gate," Angelo shouted as the approached a dimly lit signpost on the roadside.

Aubrey threw the Landy hard left and dipped across a cattle grid as they hit the ravine on the eastward leg.

"Grrrrrrrrrrrrrrrrr," the wheels grated across the steel grid, rattling everything including his teeth. The Landy bounced back onto the dusty road and entered some thickened brush.

"We can't get through at night, the gate will be closed," Angelo bellowed above the engine note.

"We'll take a short cut then," Aubrey shouted back, arms extended rigidly to the large steel three-spoke wheel.

"How far is the gate?"

"Twenty K's," he shouted back, a map open on his lap and the rising full moon the only source of light.

"Okay, we'll turn off the track before we get there," Aubrey resolute and uncompromising, peered fiercely through the insect be-speckled windscreen, his jaw clenched in a way Angelo would never have imagined.

As the light from a gate house appeared glinting in the distance, Aubrey killed the Landy's headlights and slewed to a halt. He looked once towards the bush on his left; engaged first and dived off the side of the road, taking care not to rev the engine as they weaved through the dense brush and into the forest. With the moonlight glowing silver, liquid mercury seeping through the branch canopy, brushed solicitously up against their flanks; each stab of light, leading them forward. Along a river bank that skirted the southern border of the park, the water shimmied in anticipation.

The gate house was now far enough away and the Landy's engine noise, muted by the thick brush, so Aubrey gunned the motor and roared through the shallow river and into the Park on the other bank.

"There is a road up ahead to the right," Angelo confirmed as they plunged through the thickening vegetation. Branches danced above their heads, swept aside by their haste.

They hit it running, the Landy breaching the side of the forest and charging up a slight incline before Aubrey slammed the brakes, turned the wheel and skidding to a halt, landed them broadside to the jungle.

"Where to from here," he turned for the first time to Angelo, looking a little unsure of what he intended next.

"North to Ukwa," Angelo pointed.

They were at the point of no return, and suddenly he knew exactly what was required. He had thought through just such a scenario in his mind, whilst alone with his ideals of retribution. The 'Canailles' were a blight on this land and he felt sure that a more caring world would have done something, if only they knew what was going on.

The 'Canailles' were modern day Crusaders, pillaging from the lands they were so-called intended to protect and deliver from servitude. It was human nature, but there was no end to the savagery they inflicted.

"We can approach the border from the east and they won't suspect us," Angelo shouted.

They were there to smite the infidels, once more, to atone for their sins; but in a quirky twist of fate, Angelo and Aubrey were the morally righteous. The infidel had brutalised the land and stood by idly as the women and children had been subjugated to slavery.

"It will take us half an hour; watch out for animals," Shouted Angelo.

The roaring engine drove any unsuspecting creature to cover, and soon they were through the last of the dense forest and out onto a plateau which was wider and more sparsely vegetated. Aubrey slowed, aware that the engine sound would carry further. Ghosted behind the lights of the Landy, they drove in complete silence. The world stood still for them and not an animal stirred. It was too quiet; too devoid of living creatures. Aubrey, concentrating on the road ahead appeared in tortuous profile, grimacing in the pale moonlight. Angelo, with only the whites of his eyes discernible, seemed tormented by the very thoughts that had gripped him so often and for so long.

On the outskirts of Ukwa, they found a small road that lead to the border post. Driving off-road once more and arriving at the summit of a hill on the eastern rim, they dismounted and crawled to the edge of the rocky outcrop. The trading post lay below them to the north. The border post, quiet with an assortment of shacks seemed derelict.

Somewhere beyond the furthest shack a dog howled. The moon was now high in the midnight sky. Sliding down the bank of the outcrop and making their way to the perimeter of the settlement, Angelo motioned to Aubrey to follow him. Settling into a crouching gait, they snuck through the adjoining buildings, making their way to a larger shed on the outskirts of the settlement.

Angelo signalled with his hand, below his hip, so as not to create an unnecessary silhouette.

The dog howled again, somewhere off to the left. They crouched on haunches; motionless.

The quietness returned; as they eased through a perimeter fence of barbed wire, hastily thrown around the building, gliding serenely on moonlit shadows, hunkered below them. To the side of the shed masked free from sight.

Angelo gripped the handle on a long steel door. It was on rails, but clearly locked. They slipped around the edge of the shed, exposed by the moonlight on its eastern wall.

There was a single door, unlatched and slightly ajar. Clearly, they had no concerns for theft this far north. Motioning again to Aubrey, he pulled the door; it creaked once then swung open.

Peering inside they allowed their eyes to adjust to the gloom. The shed was empty to their left, but stacked under tarpaulins to the right, Aubrey saw the tell-tale sign of tusks. The rank smell of the freshly cut ivory, still tinged with a residue of flesh was pungent.

Aubrey could sense a rage that wafted through that shed. He could almost hear the anguished bellows of those magnificent beasts. Circling to gauge how many there were, he could see the tusks piled as high as the rafters and as deep as half the shed. The strangled breath in his lungs screamed for release, but he held onto every gasp of air, tainted by the smell of death and channelled that anger.

Angelo was next to him now, having held back. He could sense the danger they were in, but said nothing. His blood boiled as they stood side by side; his soul, screaming for retribution.

Neither had cameras; neither could lay claim to the savagery of the spectacle before them. Chinese, Indian? It did not matter. Where these tusks were destined to be sold, Aubrey knew they would not care; not rage with the very indignation that he felt at that very moment.

There was only one way he could see their mission accomplished. It was risky, but he knew they had no choice. The shipment would be gone by morning, as the trucks laden with the wealth of a continent, would be gone; unwilling and unable to see the travesty of their plight, the army of rebels were only intent on one thing. They had to survive the purges and live to fight another day. Trading their ivory for ammunition and keeping the cycle turning in an endless proliferation of violence.

Unthinking and spurred by his rage, Angelo stepped forward. He gathered a bundle of packing box wood from the edge of the shed; broke some for kindling and raising a kerosene canister from a table. Surrounded by a rudimentary circle of chairs, a discarded pack of threadbare playing cards lay before him. He placed the canister amongst the kindling and turned it on its side. Retrieving a rusted knife from its resting place, beside an open tin can, Angelo pierced the container, allowing the liquid to flow into the can. Throwing the deck of cards into the mix for good measure, Aubrey watched, speechless.

They returned to the door, to confirm that they had not been seen entering the shed. Angelo again motioned to Aubrey.

"Head back to the Land Rover," he whispered, "and get her down to the eastern side of the hill." Then turning he pushed Aubrey into the stilted silence and pale moonlight, and stepped back inside.

Aubrey moved briskly to the edge of the perimeter and slipped out though the gap they had created in the fence. Ambling as quickly and as quietly as he could, he gained the summit of the hill, then turning to look over his shoulder. He could not see if Angelo was following. Looking again, he saw a flickering from within the shed. Visible only from where the gaps in the corrugated iron walls, allowed a brief glimpse of what raged inside.

Aubrey hesitated. He could not see Angelo returning across the open ground to the hill. Running as fast as he could to the Landy, he jumped into the driver's seat and turned the motor.

She caught once and then suddenly the engine note was drowned out, by the sound of sheer mayhem.

Angelo was running at full pace, his lithe athleticism carried him, a flurry of movement across the open stretch of ground. Reversing back and as he did so the Landy's natural turning circle had brought him off the lower incline of the hill, so he was in full view of the sprinting figure. Aubrey slammed the gear into first and the clutch protested, as the cogs fell into place, and he was racing perpendicular to the lonely figure.

The noise was deafening. There was an entire regiment of sound, as Aubrey's adrenalin surged within him. Blood turned to ice, as the desire to slam his foot on the accelerator pedal coursed through his soul. Angelo launched himself at full tilt, up and over the sill of the Landy, clutching at the windscreen.

The shots were coming thick and fast, interspersed by heavier explosions and it sounded like the entire Congolese army was in pursuit.

Aubrey raced the engine, aware that their escape was now entirely dependent on the speed they had, to get as much distance between them and their pursuers, whilst they still had the cover of the hill.

"What the hell happened?" shouted Aubrey his features harrowed and fraught.

"The shed was also filled with ammunition." Angelo seemed to be enjoying himself.

"Oh shit," Aubrey howled. "They are going to be pissed!"

He turned briefly to catch Angelo's reaction. He was holding onto the windscreen for dear life, as they cavorted across the remaining open field, the cover of the tree line teasingly ahead. The jungle was a dark morass, seemingly a mile away and closing fast; but behind them the sky was lit like the fourth of July. They grimaced as each furrow jolted them back to reality. Angelo seemingly allowed himself a nervous grin between each tooth rattling lurch to freedom.

Aubrey turned his full attention to the remaining distance they had to the edge of the field, but it seemed to be a void they would never breach. The Landy's engine screamed as the front wheels churned through the air and the chassis hit the lip of an undulating furrow and became airborne.

Travelling diagonally across the field at speed, the wheels bounced and broached each shallow trough as a mighty ship might plough through a raging sea.

Only as they hit the tree line and the brush scraped and scored the metal wings, did Aubrey hit the light switch to illuminate their retreat. Into the thickets on the edge of a road heading east, away from the carnage, Aubrey could see the eruption of the shed, brightly lit in his peripheral vision. The noise, a cacophony of loud blasts and interspersed ricochets still raging, highlighted the shed's roof had been blown right off. The intense blaze sent a beacon of light a mile into the crisp night sky.

"Keep going the way we came," Angelo shouted. "Then we will double back and head for the Mandoro road."

His voice on edge, but his eyes burning as brightly as the fire behind them.

Aubrey was galvanised by passion; or was it pure terror? The noise was slowly ebbing as the engine drowned out the remainder of explosions, but still loud enough to make Aubrey's heart jump with each intermittent bang.

"They will think it was the rebels from across the border with Rwanda," Angelo beamed.

"We just need to get to the Park fence on the western boundary and head straight for Mandoro." Aubrey looked over his shoulder; Angelo had no map, but was thankful nonetheless for his knowledge of the area.

"Keep going on this road and it will take us south."

"Why do you want to go west?" Aubrey shouted back, still expecting a hail of bullets to come flying their way.

"Because the rebels are to the south and east and we don't want to come across one of their road blocks; not at this time of night!" Angelo had worked through this plan in his mind.

"But why west?" The Congolese army were in that direction.

"The border police don't have jeeps or off-road vehicles, but they do have guns!" Yelled Angelo.

"Okay, so why are we running so fast," Aubrey felt the Landy slide each time he hit the corners and the large off-road tyres gripped the looser dirt.

"Because they will have radioed this in by now, and we don't want to be caught by an army brigade out on reconnaissance."

Angelo appeared to be calculating their route with precision.

Turning through a hundred and eighty degrees, they doubled back on their flight along the bush road, heading now perpendicular to the border post. Aubrey could not recall the last time he had felt such energy and complete satisfaction.

Within a half hour, they were at the Park fence. The road swept south and along the fence, which was a tangle of wire strands at best.

"The rebels cut through these fences to get to the wildlife," Angelo hollered.

"There will be an opening somewhere along the fence." He seemed too confident.

Aubrey took his eyes off the road for a moment to quiz Angelo, but as he did, Angelo yelled; a terrifying look washed over his face. Aubrey instinctively slammed on the breaks, and the Landy reacted by pulling violently to the left. In the instance that Aubrey reacted, he looked up and as large as any he had ever seen before; stood a bull Elephant directly in their path.

His tusks glistened like rapiers and the large ears flapped madly; but he was not going to move. He stood his ground, somewhat bemused by the commotion headed directly towards him.

The Landy slid inexorably to a dust choked stop right under his intimidating bulk.

"Reverse quickly," Angelo shouted. But it was too late. He was upon them, unthreatened and menacing. Through a cloud of dust, Aubrey could see the seepage of the tear ducts, now ominously smothered. Blinded, and unable to see, the bull would use the only mechanism it knew; its mighty bulk and tusks.

Those great broad feet and legs were planted like the trunks of trees. They swayed with a prosaic motion, perpetual and poised.

Instead of throwing the Landy into reverse, Aubrey jumped to his feet, leaping onto the bonnet and standing eye to eye with the huge Elephant, he waved his arms and shouted as loud as his croaking voice would allow. Looking up for just long enough to look him squarely in the eye, he shouted.

"Bayeti! Bayeti!" It was the ancient call of the wild, but it came as instinctively to him as though he had always known this moment would come.

Blinded by the bright lights and cloaked by the swirling dust, he raised his trunk, as one might wield a mace; then with the blood curdling cry resounding through his wildly flapping ears, he peered sideways at Aubrey. There was a knowing, almost sage glow of golden yellow, reflecting the light from the headlights. Aubrey looked straight into the soul of the grandfather of Batu, as he rocked back onto his haunches, swung around and retreated.

Those broad grey shoulders shuddered with the massive bulk of muscle rippling beneath. The ground below the Landy shook as this master of the wild stepped back, moving as nimbly as his five-ton frame would allow.

Just how he had survived the hunting that raged on his territory, God would only know. He was a survivor, but only because the years had taught him when to fight; and when to run. In that moment of realisation, the Landy lurched forward, unsteadying Aubrey and throwing him headlong into the load bay. A dark cloud settled over him.

The Landy was bumping over some rough terrain, as Aubrey raised himself from his crumpled foetal position. He had no idea how long he had lain there. Angelo was at the wheel, and the Landy was racing headlong through a heavily forested area, the canopy of stars no longer visible; only a dark greenery with intermittent splashes of silvery light, slashed through from overhead. As he regained consciousness, Aubrey realised that having leapt across the gearbox whilst Aubrey stood shoulder to shoulder with the Elephant, Angelo must have engaged first gear and sent him reeling into the back.

His head pounded.

"What? Oh, well done," he shouted across the space between them. He tumbled back into the front seat, just as Angelo catapulted through a small ravine and into the denser vegetation of a jungle path.

"How long, have I been out?" Aubrey questioned. The jungle surrounded them; dark and foreboding.

"A while," shouted Angelo. "Sorry!"

"No worry," Aubrey felt bruised with a hefty bump on his head, but no permanent damage.

"Where are we?" The jungle path was hampering their progress, but kept them from sight.

"South west of Wamba," Angelo wrestled the wheel. "But that is the least of our worries."

"What's up?" Aubrey scanned the path ahead. The headlights weaved a catatonic path between the dense vegetation of the jungle, and the quagmire that served as their track. The adrenalin kept his grogginess from overpowering.

"We've got company," David gestured over his shoulder. How he knew Aubrey could not tell. The old Elephant track through the jungle, ran alongside a river to their right flank. Aubrey could see the reflected headlights each time the path veered towards the river.

The old disused path had been used by the rebels for the last ten years.

He steadied himself as he looked up and Angelo for once, seemed unsure of himself. Aubrey immediately looked back over his shoulder searching for the source of alarm.

Then it happened.

"Kaakkakkkakakkkaakka," it was unmistakable sound of a Kalashnikov. The leaves above their heads splintered and splattered them in a deluge of greenery. The sound erupted again, this time closer and chillingly abrupt.

Angelo threw the Landy into another ravine, criss-crossing back to the eastern bank, across the breach of water with ease, but mired in think brown mud, which sprayed off the front wheels and coated them both. Darting from left to right, Angelo tried to catch the wheels in the firmer ground, but it was a sludge that dragged them back.

Another burst raked over their heads, and behind them, Aubrey could hear the voices of commands being barked out. It was a foreign dialect.

The Landy caught two wheels into the thicker quagmire on the edge of the path and then threw them both forward as the wheels lodged into the mud. They slammed into the metal dash, Aubrey catching himself in time to prevent severe injury, then they were through it and back out onto firmer ground.

Behind them the voices were yelling incoherently. One from the left, whilst it sounded like there were others trying to out flank them to the right. Angelo threw the Landy down a sharp decline and the front pitched at an alarming angle. Then the tyres gripped and she slewed irrevocably downwards towards the shallow trough at the base. They hit it running once more and the Landy lurched and pitched along the path as the voices echoed hauntingly behind and away to the left.

The path wound incessantly along the river bank, where each subsequent herd had carved its migratory route, avoiding the rocky outcrops of each twist of the river bed. The Elephant were ingenious engineers, avoiding the hard rock and fording the river with each lee-ward turn of the river. The Elephant had very cleverly cut the most direct route through the jungle, avoiding the cut-backs, and prospering from the natural levees created by the slower moving water. A million years of knowledge had honed their skills as road builders.

With each bumping grinding assault of the Landy jarring their bones, Aubrey and Angelo gained significant distance from the rebels. Intuitively, Aubrey clung to the dash, bracing with each sinew tearing drop; but the distance from their pursuers opened gratefully. On foot, they flailed through the heavy undergrowth, following the river course. The mud-soaked path, despite its treacherous drops, was vastly more direct. The path dropped into a lower flood plain, and the steep walls of the canyon gave way to a smoother ride.

The gun fire dissipated behind them, but it tormented them until they hit the Kisangani road to the east. One tortuous hour later they eased the scalding hot Landy into the parking area outside the hotel. The sun was rising with a fiery reminder in the east and Aubrey sat slumped in the passenger seat. Only as the engine spluttered to a halt and an eerily raucous call came from the crows in the trees above them, did Aubrey glance across the three feet that separated himself from Angelo.

He smiled, allowing himself a moment of introspection, then slapped him on the shoulder; clambering out, exhausted and haunted but elated. The euphoria kicked in; in the knowledge that justice had been served.

They awoke later that afternoon, having missed the flight out with the rest of the team. Battered, bruised, but non-the-worse off for their exploits Angelo was already up, and in the shower. Aubrey lay unable to move. He could feel his lower back, shoulders and arms screaming for succour.

The television beckoned and the remote lay next to his bed. He looked across at the rumpled, and soiled bedding across from him on Angelo's bed, reminded him of the gut-wrenching, mud track that they had escaped on. He poked the little green button on the remote, with a bruised index finger, still caked in rich, red mud. The television flickered, and came to life.

"In a disturbing trend of illicit trade, the company we see here has been operating with the direct assistance of the Government in Kinshasa. They have been mining for the rare and often inaccessible mineral 'Coltan'." The program was tuned to CNN.

"To many of our viewers who use their mobile phones on a daily basis, they would not understand the significance of this particular mineral, nor would they have heard of it." Aubrey listened intently. He certainly had not!

"The mineral has been smuggled and exported illegally from the Democratic Republic of the Congo for over a decade, and this little-known mineral which contains tantalum, is a prized resource from the DRC. It has been responsible for encouraging the perpetuation of the war here in the east of the country. Few of our viewers would appreciate that the battle to control the exportation of this mineral, has resulted in the deaths of millions of Congolese over the last few years. The Hutu and Tutsi factions, supported by countries and Governments in both the West and now by China itself, have been fighting for control of the mines and the routes through the jungle to get this mineral to market."

Angelo poked his head out of the bathroom door. Aubrey motioned to him to listen. As the story unfolded, they looked sideways, each searching for words. They remained silent.

"The Tantalum is a necessary component in every mobile phone ever manufactured. This mineral is purported to have been responsible for the deaths of over five and a half million Africans since its discovery in quantity in the Congo jungle."

"The coltan is mined in open caste mines, very close to the surface," the video footage showed a team of labourers sweating profusely in the humid jungle.

"It is then traded for diamonds, gold and ammunition to help finance the war, which is perpetuated by demand for this rare material." The anchor announced.

"Due to its rarity, the mineral which occurs in significant reserves in Brazil and the DRC, has been officially named Columbite-Tantalite and eighty percent," A large graphic appeared on the screen with "80% of the known reserves occur in the east of the DRC."

The irony was unmistakable. They had been indirectly aided in their pursuit of the dream of building the school, by the very object that had been responsible for the deaths of millions of their fellow countrymen and women. Angelo was about to say something, when Aubrey raised his hand to silence him. The reporter was continuing.

"Now in an expose of this sinister trade, we have tracked down the company responsible for buying up over half the reserves of coltan in its raw form. Trade in coltan is being funded by a further twist in the brutal saga of this country. Traders who have been buying the coltan have been paying the illicit miners in a currency that cannot be traced back to the company itself."

Aubrey was now sitting upright.

"We were able to infiltrate one of these trading sessions here in Kisangani, where an insider was able to secret one of our button cameras into the hotel room, in a downtown section of the mining community."

The camera followed a man with a duffel bag into a sleazy looking hotel room, and there in full view of the camera, from an angle below the level of his waist, but unmistakable; was a large Afrikaans speaking man, his face shadowed in the dim light of the curtained bedroom.

"These traders are now paying for the shipment of this coltan with another illicit mineral; uncut diamonds." The reporter continued.

"Oh my God! Aubrey was on the edge of the bed.

"The diamonds are then traded into the market place from the Congo, finding their way to the cutting rooms in India, China and Israel." The reporters' voice trailed off.

"All of this in return for enough tantalum to manufacture a thousand mobile phones. The miner would be lucky to find a buyer who would give him ten dollars a caret and the diamonds in return, once cut would fetch thousands on the markets in Europe. The coltan however, finds its way to the central buying floors in Chicago, and as a bone fide mineral, with no restrictions would generate a fortune for the seller." The reporter now back in frame concluded.

"Angelo, we have to get the hell out of here," Aubrey was on the floor, racing for the bathroom.

Chapter 23

Returning to the Elephants

Aubrey was woken by the intercom announcing their descent. The seatbelts light flashed above the vast first-class bed. They had slept through breakfast, and the Virgin cabin crew had tried to wake Aubrey, but Natasha had politely declined their offers. The cabin warning bell 'pinged' rather than chimed. It was without a doubt, the most irritating sound. Aubrey roused by the noise wondered why the airlines had never thought of an alternative idea. Why, could they not use light, rather than an irritating sound?

He looked up to his TV monitor which gave their satellite position. They were somewhere over the Zimbabwe. West Africa, and the bulge lay off to the north-west, and the Congo in-between. From the air, Africa was still the dark continent, divided by great lakes and nebulous borders; but it was the cities, burgeoning with vast populations that beckoned. Harare lay to their west, Johannesburg to the south and all around them cities that had not managed to become viable as destinations, to land a long-haul aircraft such as the Airbus in which they sat.

The Inter tropical convergence zone, they had encountered, was behind them, the severe weather over Equatorial Africa, was a distant memory. The rains of early December were at their zenith and even with the aircraft at thirty-three thousand feet, they were buffeted by those huge thermals. Africa was a continent of extremes, and the rising heat and moisture off that land mass, created massive vortex winds. Like the political winds that blew across this region, the ITCZ was a portent of the ill-will that beckoned.

Africa! What a contradiction of beauty and savagery! The splendour of it was only marred by its extreme opposites. Of its deserts, which while encroaching on the arable savannah plains of the central and southern African regions had destroyed more, much needed agricultural land; but the experience of that vast untapped, raw potential was what drew the adventurer back, again and again!

Somewhere down there, Aubrey surmised, was a peasant farmer slashing and burning another hectare of virgin forest, so that he can feed his family for the next winter. Africa relied very heavily on archaic farming practices, because until now, no one had really cared. But with the changing financial world, time would allow these countries to prosper.

The entire world would need to care, and those very mouths that needed sustenance now; would become the providers of food to the western world. The value of land in Africa was likely reach the typical values that European countries have demanded for centuries. Land was an untapped resource, and with correct farming methods this dark continent could become the cradle of civilization again, and its' bread basket.

If the Israeli's could fashion their great Kibbutz's out of the Sinai, Africans could also do the same for themselves? Africa needed visionaries; not political opportunists. This enigma which was Africa, was much maligned. Its politicians were a conglomeration of Kleptocrats; its people, a consortium in servitude, and their thinking, completely bankrupt. Nigeria, which albeit, through it's great oil wealth, had recognized the need for agriculture, and the need to feed it's growing middle class population, had embarked on the great commercial farming practices seen in Rhodesia before Mugabe; then why not the rest of Africa?

It needed the collective will of a new liberation of thinking, but unfortunately whilst old liberation politics were still being dragged out to serve the political desires of its dictators, the continent never stood a chance! Mugabe and the typical leaders who cried White supremacy! The very leaders', who kept their own populations in poverty to control them; were the leaders that needed to be removed from power.

The irony was that however hard one tried to get the masses to farm commercially, they could not see beyond the desire to feed themselves and their families. Zimbabwe after the land invasions was a classic example. Prime agricultural farms were standing empty, unused and derelict.

The paradox was re-investment. Into the farms in the African region, and into the people whose livelihoods had been decimated by that state sponsored madness. Commercial farms were unnecessary, but equity based sustainable organic farming techniques, were. These farms should be owned by real people; not just the politicians who had grabbed the land at the cost of its farm labourers, who had lived there for generations. Hard currency, and passion were the means of securing land tenure ship and the title deeds.

This would be the Pennington's legacy he decided. Once more to have some influence over the history of Zimbabwe, he could secure a vast amount of land back from the current owners, and call it Rhodesianna. Old Rhodes was a tragically maligned visionary. But it had been his minions, eager to win favour, who had named the territory Rhodesia. They had wreaked havoc on the general welfare of the Zimbabwean population, through their greed.

As the plane touched down in Johannesburg, the reality of his surroundings became evident. He had a knot in his stomach. He was thankful for the company of Natasha, but he was not entirely sure if he would be welcomed with the same level of fondness by the South African authorities. Aubrey had been careful not to book an overnight stay in Johannesburg as he had no desire to attract unnecessary attention.

Their onward flight to Victoria Falls, as tourists. This was to circumvent the process of having to disembark through South African customs. They were pointed in the direction of their connecting flight, and thankfully, having been ushered off the plane and through the devastation of a massive building construction site, they were quickly on route to Victoria Falls. As Aubrey entered the front door of the cabin, he was greeted by a familiar face. Seated in the front row, in business class, was none other than his friend Timothy.

"Greetings stranger," he smiled, "what a pleasant surprise." Timothy stood to greet him. With his quick charm, and an easy manner, Aubrey was immediately at ease.

"Hello Tim," their friendship remembered, as if it were just yesterday they had parted.

"You returning home?" Timothy spoke. His private school accent, honed from the colonial education afforded him by his wealthy father.

Timothy's gaze deflected off Aubrey. He quickly introduced Natasha.

"Let me introduce you to Natasha," they shook hands formally.

"Hello! Natasha. What a lovely name."

"Thank you." She smiled. "I see what you mean by, 'a real charmer'." Natasha spoke, hand held palm forward, as an aside.

Timothy laughed generously. His mirth titillated by this obvious reference to Aubrey's knowledge of their past. He looked on a little too salaciously, approving the splendid delivery from a lass as captivating as Natasha.

"He has always had a bit of a glad eye," Aubrey warned. Wanted to make sure Natasha was off limits. "How is that beautiful wife of yours?" He reinforced!

"Splendid, splendid!" Countered Timothy. "But come sit if you must, the lady is getting a little anxious," he remarked in clear reference to the senior cabin attendant who had ushered them into the aircraft.

"You have already held up the flight for long enough!"

Aubrey, finished storing their hand luggage and ushered Natasha into the seat by the window. Having done so sat in the aisle seat opposite Timothy. He would conveniently, be able to catch up on all the gossip.

"What has been happening in your life?" Timothy shucked his head in Natasha's direction as he said this.

Aubrey was happy. She clearly impressed.

"Oh, quite a bit." He smiled, knowing that the company of beautiful women always disarmed the married men.

"Just flown in from the UK, and we are spending some time at the Falls."

"Honeymoon?" Timothy would have been more astute in other circumstances, but the obvious lack of wedding bands on either of their fingers was a dead giveaway.

"No." Responded Aubrey. "Just a vacation. Natasha is on winter break, and I needed the sun."

"Really!" Timothy looked in Natasha's direction. She smiled.

"Studying? How interesting, I must quiz you sometime." Timothy interrogated.

The vaguely veiled innuendos, a private school heritage of his breeding.

"How is the business going?" remarked Aubrey, changing the subject.

"Splendid." This was Timothy's primed answer to almost everything. He was an eternal optimist, and very little got him down.

"I would ask you the same, but clearly 'Your Lordship' has been doing fine by the looks of it." Timothy was back on track.

"Jeez", Aubrey was stunned, "bad news certainly travels fast."

"What do you consider the possibility of a resolution to the economic situation?" Aubrey knew the answer.

Timothy shrugged his shoulders. It had been Timothy, who had advised him all those years before, "buy farm land. It's really cheap."

"Is there ever going to be a chance of an economic recovery?" Aubrey insisted.

"Fantastic," replied Timothy, "but I would not buy any farms anytime time soon!" Clearly the Mugabe regime were still hell-bent on destructing every potential farm to sell to the Chinese.

"But tell me about your news." Timothy was dismissive. He did not like talking about business, when there were more interesting titbits to be had.

"Well apart from sorting out the deceased estate, not much." Timothy would have to dig deeper if he wanted more.

"In fact, I have been in the DRC, and there have been a few health issues, but not much else." Aubrey was purposely vague.

"Yes, I heard about your trip to the DRC!" Aubrey turned his head, a little too quickly.

"Oh yeah," responded Aubrey trying to sound nonchalant. "Good or bad?" The African tribal drums have clearly been beating.

"So, it was true?" Aubrey's heart skipped a beat.

"A mate of mine was doing some business up in the Congo and said he thought he had seen you in Kinshasa!" he sounded intrigued.

On the back foot, Aubrey grinned. It would be interesting to hear what Timothy may have been told. "Do I know them?" Aubrey was enjoying the skull-duggery.

Timothy remained silent.

He leaned towards Aubrey. The aircraft was now full, and the doors closed. The air-conditioning units blasted a welcoming stream of cool air across their faces.

"No one you know, just a colleague of mine from Harare, who said he had seen the Elephant Man." It sounded grotesque. Like some circus act.

"Oh yes, what line of business is he in?" He was relieved that it was no one he knew. He had no secrets from Natasha.

"Wheeler-dealer of sorts." It was code for nefarious.

"That must have been about six months ago." Aubrey.

"Yes. Been back?" Timothy knew the answer.

"Since then I have been back in England," remarked Aubrey, changing the subject.

"Yes. Sorry for your loss." Jeremy was referring to the Funeral and the winding up of the estate.

"I would have preferred to have been somewhere else." He reminded himself, more than perhaps Timothy. He looked away, out of the window. Out of the window; at nothing.

Aubrey needed to know about Bronwyn, but now was not the time.

Then there was the elephant business; Aubrey's and Bronwyn's brainchild. Funnily enough, Timothy had purposely not mentioned her name once in the past ten minutes.

He was thankful in that regard; no doubt, he would have the opportunity to ask Tim.

Aubrey took that opportunity to take Natasha's hand, and squeeze it. She looked away from the window and smiled at him. She was charming to say the least. Looking into his eyes, her gaze was a quizzical look of concern.

She sensed his apprehension. She squeezed his hand back.

Returning home. This was the final leg of his journey. No turning back now! If ever he had been at home anywhere it was here. He was a Whafrican, and it was in his blood. No amount of money and privilege would change that. Aubrey had the spirit of Africa coursing in his blood. This was where he belonged.

Her journey was one of self-discovery too; to ground her belief in the eons old use of natural remedies in medicine. She could sense it. The medicine men of Zimbabwe beckoned. The witch-doctors, who had treated ailments for thousands of years. A shiver ran the length of her spine; or was it just the accelerating wheels of the aircraft on that ancient ground?

Faith was a leap between earth and heaven. Had those Angels beckoned in this way before. She may have not been able, or willing to recognise the call.

Natasha sensed the enormity of that flight into the unknown. Her Angels would lift them into the ether, and whisk them safely to their Spiritual Home.

Somehow, her journey was a flight of fancy, on their wings. The ramparts of an ancient civilisation was her destination. Zimbabwe. The mystics had appeared in her dreams; it was they who had provoked and cajoled. Natasha knew it was to be her nemesis she would face; but she was happy. Happy in the knowledge that they both shared the love of this man. She had no conflict with the destiny that awaited.

"What is in that powder you gave me last night," Aubrey had returned from the toilet.

"Why?" She looked up concerned.

"Because," he leaned in so no one, but she could hear. "My urine smells disgusting." The confinement of the cubicle had augmented the odorous repugnance.

"Oh good, it's working." She grinned.

"Well if that is good, I don't want to know what your bad treatment is!" He kissed her on the neck.

"Peewee." She feigned aversion.

"Extract of asparagus." She winked. "It detoxes your liver."

The two-hour trip to Victoria Falls, became a seamless series of questions. Natasha swopped seats with Aubrey, only returning to the window seat as they approached the falls. Excitement and apprehension, fuelled her banter. Timothy was smitten.

As they flew in over the Falls, Natasha's was a bird's eye view; the most magnificent natural wonder of the world. A sight to behold, she 'oohed' and' aaahed' as the plane dipped its wing on the approach to Victoria Falls airport.

The sight of 'Musi 'O Tunia', 'The smoke that thunders', was a sight worthy of its ancient spiritual name. It drew in one's breath. Appealing to the senses and inciting a veil which rose from the primeval ground. The souls of the dead rose to meet them. They buffeted the aircraft on its approach. An approach which brought them in over that ancient scar, slashed into mother earth. There were Angels all around. She felt their presence. They rose to meet their visitors; but Natasha could not recognise the myriad of faces. There were white, and black faces; young and old. She knew not who, but resolved to ask.

The vast Zambezi River rushed headlong into the cavernous gorge and dropped some one hundred and eleven meters over those granite walls. Hewn of a million years of continual erosion, the gorge, with its zigzag lattice work of oblique turns, traced its history.
The retreat of the original falls, was caste into the earth, some tightly at first and then stretching out like some vast kindergarten paper chain, the gorge disappeared.

Natasha counted one, two, three, four, and then five legs to the meandering gorge below the Falls; then the Songwe and finally the Batoka. Seven in all! Seven times that God had graced his omnipotent presence on that scorched dry earth; it was a good omen.

The river basin above the Falls was awash with a slick hazelwood torrent, having dragged river banks with it on its epic thousand-mile journey from the Southern Congo. The islands, resplendent in shimmering outcrops above the Falls, were now covered by an onslaught; a tumultuous deluge. Cascading over the rim of the first gorge, it created a magnificent plume of steaming foam, rising in swathes of mist. Oscillating across the face of the chasm. A cauldron, bewitched and effervescent, the steaming clouds colonized the tropical forest. Born from its humidity and gentle life sustaining moisture, the micro-ecosystem, drawn as a moustache across that gapping mouth.

Aubrey smiled to see her reaction. He turned back and was met by a similar self-satisfied grin from Timothy, who had obviously become immune to the sight. As a honeymoon couple, they would have been right at home; but to Timothy they represented a dark craven desire.

She leaned in, and almost unwittingly he sensuously bit her top lip. Feeding her essence into his mouth, Aubrey savoured her raw afrodisíaco. He had never been so satiated by a woman, and here he was returning to the very place he and Bronwyn had spent so much time together. The angst rose.

The airport building had not changed one bit since the visit by Queen Elizabeth all those years ago. Over a decade and a few ill-conceived ideas had set a country and its' dictator on the road to ruin. The visit of The Queen should have been Mugabe's crowning moment. The rise of Zimbabwe from its civil war and the change to a democracy envisioned as a 'one man one vote', system that would only have worked, had the very people it was intended for, been empowered. African politics was fraught with anomalies.

It was a country founded on a liberation struggle, invited back into the Commonwealth, whose very ideals were based on a sharing of ideas and resources. Greed had seen the founding fathers at Lancaster House falling out with one another.

A once wealthy country, self-sufficient in all but its petroleum requirements, had become a failed state. Land locked and prey to the whims of a tyrannical government hell bent on proving their point; Aubrey could empathise with the plight of the Diaspora. Founded on a positive education system, the educated had become its main detractors. No amount of philosophizing would make this once beautiful country work, until the leadership was prepared to allow those forced out; to come home. A return to its former glory, would only be possible once those languishing as economic refugees, could be allowed back; Zimbabwe's ruin had been precipitated by greed and stupidity.

It had the potential to become the bread basket of Africa once more. Property rights were sacrosanct and this would only be possible once Mugabe and his henchmen were gone.

Viable working farms, employing the so-called 'previously dispossessed' or farm labourers on whose shoulders these great farms had once been borne, would be the key. From the shifting cultivation techniques used for thousands of years, a return to a profitable business model on which they would provide wealth for everyone involved would only be possible with consultation and inclusivity. The project had to be conceived out of viable and sound business practices. This might work if they were based on a community of shareholders, working towards and benefiting from a common goal. He knew instinctively, that it was possible.

Timothy motioned to them to fast track through the same immigration booth. Tim had clearly got a familiar relationship with all the staff, and it was Themba, a big amiable Ndebele man, who now looked up and smiled.

Aubrey had once had a drink with Themba, whilst sitting at the Elephant Hills hotel. Aubrey returned his greeting.

"Hello shamwari," Aubrey grasped his hand. They exchanged a warm grip; each confident in their new-found positions.

Themba had been able to secure this position, thanks to Timothy's request to the Departmental head in Harare. Centralised government dictated even at the falls. Hard currency smoothed relationships and Timothy had managed to provide. This was how business was done and now he had a friendly customs official with whom he could get in and out of Zimbabwe carrying the hard currency on which his businesses depended.

It was no wonder he flew into Zimbabwe through the Falls, when the quickest and most direct route was into Harare! He was always able to wangle the business trips to Johannesburg, with a visit to the Victoria Falls on his return.

The occasional Vervet monkey gawked at them from the side of the road, then loped off into the underbrush when Natasha squealed for them to slow down and look. The little Vervet's; a nuisance among the campsites that doted the town square, were an amusing distraction. Timothy was patient enough to allow Natasha a good look as they trundled past. The Vervet's, not used to anyone paying attention to them, suspiciously surveyed Natasha, who in turn stared at them through the window of the double cab bakkie. She shrieked and cooed, the cute little faces with their disproportionately big round eyes, childlike with a habit of cocking their head from one side to the other, giving them a humorous and endearing quality.

Created for a purpose those eyes adapted for night vision were particularly good at spying night time predators. Leopard and snake, would seek out their lairs and it was a natural self-preservation tactic for potential threats that gave them such a charming quality. But woe betide one who got too close to that cherubic little face; that mouth possessed a pair of upper canines that would savage the hand offered in exchange for any titbit. Stitches and a Tetanus jab would be your reward. Wild they were, and they roamed their territories with impunity from local game rangers. Their natural habitat was being overtaken by humans; so, in a 'quid pro quo' of nature, they had now come to expect the free offerings of food in return for these loud and somewhat smelly outsiders.

Veering off to the right, the road that would take them to their hotel illuminated the spray from the falls. Natasha was up in her seat once again, and craning over his shoulder to get a look. Aubrey believed that this was the fundamental reason that Zimbabwe would return from the ruinous collapse of the last two decades, and emerge once again as the jewel of Africa.

No diamonds, or gold, silver or platinum could outshine the value of this seventh wonder of the world. Its spiritual significance as the seventh and last real natural wonder of the world was its saving grace. The allure of its beauty would be the catalyst that would secure the tourists and once again it would be the draw card that would bring an economic return of this magnificent country, back to its pre-independence days, and the return of sanity.

"Here you are," Timothy announced as they arrived at the front entrance of the hotel. With its driveway that swept down onto a colonial portico, white, with red tiled roof, and columns which announced a classical heritage dating back to the turn of the previous century.

It was just how Aubrey had remembered it. The blood-red washed concrete floors and a clean unsullied air that belied an even more impressive view that was designed to awe and seduce its' visitors. The Victoria Falls Hotel had been built during King Edward's reign, and was a testimony to the endurance of the adventurers and colonists who had gone before him. Those early settlers had brought a sanity to this land. They had tamed the malaria and tsetse fly; and brought the value of this spiritual land, to a legion of followers, likely to have embraced God. Timothy dropped them at the front door; porters scurrying to receive them and their luggage. Natasha dragged Aubrey, a wry smile on his face, through the reception area and out onto the veranda to view the magnificent sight that beheld them.

"It's stunning!" She stood breathless, engaging every sense.

The view down the gorge and into the narrow vista that framed the falls beyond was epic. A refreshing breeze, negated the stifling noon humidity. The sound of a distant roar, tumbled in on chariots, drawn by sphinx-like clouds. Wafting across the mile from the bridge spanning two inseparable lands, that great single-span of gigantic latticed metal accentuated the turmoil that emanated from the great rush of water beyond. The breeze conveyed with it the faint trace of Africa; it was difficult to pinpoint, but as

Aubrey flared his nostrils, he could almost taste the hint of acacia and the pungently sweet pods of the Amarula, interspersed with raw iron-rich soil, baked by a tropical sun. The breeze touched his bare forearms, eliciting a gentle reaction. It cooled the perspiration that oozed from his very core, sending a shiver along his shoulders, up his spine and raising the fine blond hairs that sprinkled the nape of his neck; climbing to his scalp and over his forehead.

Aubrey's essence had been stirred, and this physical reaction was a culmination of the anticipation of their journey, the wonder of the company, and the spectacle that embraced them. Standing on the wide veranda, gazing out onto that vista, he now understood what had inspired those early settlers to build this testament of colonial bravado. Surely this was a part of what made the mystery of this grand spectacle such an enduring legacy. No amount of recrimination for past injustices, could now underscore the achievement of those early Rhodesians.

They, as with all those that had gone after Livingstone, and up to and including Smith, were owed a debt of gratitude. No amount of subversion of history could wipe out their quest to tame and conquer this wonder of nature, for the generations that followed. It was and has been in their nature for millennia. It was part of their Saxon and Nordic blood that had brought the countless generations of Anglos to this part of the world; their mission to bring a sense of civility and order to a region almost devoid of it. By erasing the history of the early Pioneers; by changing street names; by stirring the masses to rediscover their ancestral heritage at the expense of Modernity; by the renaming of towns, cities and land marks, all that the Mugabe regime had achieved was to sully a significant portion of the country's achievements in favour of what? A failed state.

Aubrey had no time for the apologists who were intent on rewriting the history of Southern Africa. It was as it was. The revisionists who placate the ruling parties in a quest for some modicum of sensibility he could understand. But the apologists he considered lower than shark shit. They like the Taliban of Afghanistan had tried to wipe out an entire history on this continent, and no amount of apologizing would make it right. Why the hell, not just get on with life, embrace diversity, and take the strengths of a society that had so much to offer and forget about the differences. Sure, it was easy to say from a privileged position now, but Aubrey had not always had it so easy. He had worked his way up to a position where he had earned the respect of his work colleagues. They now had the luxury of witnessing the folly of those that wanted to tear down a system that had not in itself been the main protagonist for the failures of the system of colonialism to embrace all Africans.

By seizing the farms, destroying the infrastructure to serve his own devious political agenda, and leaving his own proletariat impoverished, Mugabe had inadvertently signed his own death warrant, and ironically subjected his own legacy to the trash can of history. Aubrey was reminded of the entertaining slogan he had once seen in the Explorers pub some years before. It had read, "Come to Rhodesia to see the Zimbabwe Ruins; Come to Zimbabwe to see Rhodesia ruined."

"This is breath-taking," Natasha announced, drawing Aubrey out of his inner thoughts and into the immediacy of their surroundings.

"It truly is!" replied Aubrey, as they stood shoulder to shoulder taking in that extraordinary vista. Aubrey placed his sweaty arm over her shoulder and remarked, "I love you Tash."

She turned looked into his glistening eyes, and smiled. This was the breakthrough she had dreamed of, and something she had always desired. The unequivocal love of a man. Of this man!

Aubrey took Natasha to the very edge; literally. They walked through the rain soaked humidity of the forest at the edge of the falls, gaping down into the huge Boiling Pot, and staring awestruck into the Devil's Cataract. These names summoned the visual images they possessed. The sheer magnificence of the spectacle a sight for sore eyes. Aubrey was drawn somehow spiritually to this place, and he was keen to see his Elephants.

Seated at the bar with Natasha, before dinner, they had arranged to meet with Timothy before he left to go back to Harare. Naturally gregarious, Natasha had struck up a conversation with a stranger at the bar. She began a light banter with a man dressed in khaki shirt and pants, a clean pair of veldskoens, and his felt brimmed hat, which lay on the bar next to his whisky. He was seated at the bar drinking on his own.

"Have you been at the Falls for long?" A question which seemed innocuous now.

"Yes, a while." The stranger had mustered.

"How long are you staying?" He politely replied, seeing the tourist imprint all over Natasha's demeanour.

"Oh, we are here for a few weeks. Or at least I am!" She added. "My boyfriend, Aubrey is originally from here." Glancing over her shoulder at Aubrey now deep in conversation with Timothy.

The stranger smiled as he looked up to see Aubrey, who paused as he heard his name mentioned. Aubrey politely smiled back, but immediately resumed the heated conversation he was having with Timothy.

Aubrey knew Natasha could keep her own in any dialogue, even with this craggy, sun blemished stranger, so he continued interrogating Timothy over some recent events. Before making their way to the table at the poolside, where they were to have dinner, Aubrey had managed to ascertain that there was ample opportunity for him to start purchasing land. Timothy had a contact within the deeds office. He would secure the appropriate data, regarding the state-owned farms, acquired under the Land Grab. These farms were now standing idle. Some of these, which were of no interest to the so-called war veterans, were available for purchase. These farms languished in the arable region in the Triangle area. There was no town close by with amenities and drinking establishments.

These could be purchased at a reasonable rate in hard currency. All Aubrey was interested in was getting enough land to start his communal farming venture. He would first take Timothy's bakkie, and with the drive through to the Lowveld a good day's drive, he would take Natasha with so she could see the country. As they stood to make their way to the table, Aubrey was introduced to the stranger.

"Gavin Lukan," he held his head at a jaunty angle to his broad shoulders. The crown of his head bore the scars of an interminably lengthy sojourn under the African sky.

"Aubrey, Aubrey Pennington." He replied. "A real pleasure to meet you sir."

The stranger held his grip, perhaps a little longer than was necessary. His grip manacle-like and the forearms ripped and gristled by time.

As they made their way through the scattered tables of diners' enjoying their summer evening supper, Aubrey was quizzed by Natasha as to how he knew Gavin. Aubrey did not, he confided.

"Well he seemed to know you," remarked Natasha.

No. Aubrey was sure. He had never met Gavin before. "Who was Tony?" asked Natasha.

"Oh, that would probably be Bronwyn's father," replied Aubrey.

"Well, he is Tony's brother!" The penny dropped.

Gavin was the Uncle, who lived up on the river near the town of Mlibizi. This was where the car ferry left, on its voyage up the Kariba Dam to the town of Kariba, nestled on the slopes of the Zambezi valley. Aubrey had never met him, but heard mention of his hermit lifestyle, fishing and hunting the Zambezi gorge, and never inviting guests to visit. This was, he recalled, despite Bronwyn's past attempts to crack an invite.

So, this was Gavin! Aubrey could now see the resemblance with Tony. He had not been introduced, but Bronwyn had mentioned Gavin, on the occasional visit he had made to Victoria Falls to stock up on much needed provisions, and several cases of whisky.
Aubrey had never met him as he had always been working with the elephants when Gavin had visited. Bronwyn would make mention of having had a visit, but it was always vague and never meant to be of significance. Now Aubrey understood the lingering gaze with those same piercing blue eyes. The thought stayed with him, until they finally retired to their vast Edwardian furnished suite.

"What did Gavin say to you when you guys were chatting," Aubrey inquisitive, now asked.

"Not much. He mainly spoke about fishing on the Zambezi and the problems they were having with poachers." Bronwyn was distracted by her task as she brushed her hair, head between her legs, doubled over and stroking her luxurious auburn mane. This was a nightly routine, and Aubrey now understood why she had such thick hair. When she finished and he had spat out the last of the tooth paste from his mouth, she stood up, flushed from the blood that had rushed to her head, and he smiled.

"What?" She asked, embarrassed by her obvious state. She always felt he could see through her soul.

"No. Stay exactly where you are", he stood behind her, and taking her in his arms. The vast expanse of mirror captured in an ornate carved Rhodesian Teak, framed her astonishing beauty.

The yellow hue of the bathroom light, reflected in the bluish tint of the mirror, exposed her eyes; caught beneath her naturally full eyebrows, framed in a deep set, wide almost Asian brow. She was flushed and alive with youth; made even more alluring by those pouting Angelinish lips. They were alive with possibilities. He stopped his thoughts right there and simply soaked in her raw essence. Making for good chemistry, Aubrey put aside any further thoughts of Gavin, and they made their way to the large linen draped bed.

There was a mysterious calm from the Boma as Natasha and Aubrey approached from the parking area. The big thatch reception area to the left, was abuzz with tourist chatter; but the elephants stood in a solemn group, gathered at the far end of the open stockade.

The Acacia trees scattered around the edge of the stockade reminded Aubrey of the Elephants staple diet. From those thorny branches, their supple trunks would pick, leaf and branch from the higher canopy, succulent and vital. The branches, poison to some antelope which over-grazed the succulent shoots, were a treat for the Elephant, whose tactile trunks were impervious to the thorn and toxic tannin.

As they approached on foot, one then another trunk rose to test the air, then a symphony of bellows emanated from the centre of the group. Then suddenly, a youngster broke away from the group like the star quarterback, despite the efforts of the Induna to stop him. It was Jimmy, charging out to greet them.

The group sensing some meteoric event, then lumbered around, and with an air of disdain, lifted their trunks in a dismissive wave, almost as though they were a group of women gossiping, but needing to acknowledge Aubrey, out of some sense of duty.

Jimmy was older, bigger than ever now, a young adult. But still enthused by his natural zest for life. Despite his size and the efforts of the Induna to stop him, he pressed his head against Aubrey, butting him, curling his trunk over his shoulders. Camaraderie poked at him, finger-like, demanding attention.

"The Elephant trunk has over a hundred and fifty thousand separate muscles." Aubrey smiled. Natasha had a biological measure of these majestic creatures.

"Yes, I can feel it," Aubrey laughed. Jimmy had him in a pythonian grip; but it was gentle and dextrose.

The Boma fence rattled as he roughed Aubrey, and Natasha instinctively held back. She was momentarily intimidated by Jimmy's obvious bulk and enthusiastic greeting. Stepping up to the wooden gum pole fencing, she stroked him on his handsome broad forehead. His trunk kept whipping up, catching Aubrey on the chest, probing his forearms, like the hand of a child, groping and needy. Once he was satisfied, he reached up to Natasha's face, and without warning, gave her the once over. Despite the protestation from the Induna, whom Aubrey placated. With Natasha now approved of, he returned his interest to Aubrey, and in an exchange which was surreal, the approval was registered. Jimmy was happy with Aubrey's new choice.

The group of females led by Lesidwa the matriarch, kept their distance. They were intent on their silent protest, now that they had recognized Aubrey. Their sense of disapproval was evident. When Aubrey rounded the side of the Boma, and got closer to the group. Lesidwa was gamefully ignoring him, and particularly Natasha, out of some innate sense of loyalty to Bronwyn, or so it appeared. She, being the matriarch, was the leader, and so the others also made little or no effort to greet Aubrey.

Sure, they knew who he was and had an immediate glint of recognition in their eyes. But when he spoke to them, those big black pools of liquid jellow, normally docile, and inanimate, seemed to well up more than usual, and the tear ducts, abnormally glistening. Aubrey knew too much about them to have them ignore him for too long.

"See how their Harderian gland is able to keep those eyes moist," Natasha made mention. Aubrey said nothing.

He coaxed each one, individually, moving through the group. They walled him in. To the left and right, the great bodies moved, hemming him into a corner of the stockade. Their great bodies, covered in a parchment skin, tactile and legible. He hovered amongst them, stroking those thick hides, sensitive as brail, until he had re-established himself once more as the alpha male.

Lesidwa, tried her best to move away, but approaching from the side, he placed his head against hers. She relented, allowing him to rub his open palm against her massive lobe, giving her a firm, but dominant rub, all the while coaxing her with a gentle conversation. His voice resonating with her so she began to calm her nervous sideways shuffling movement. Standing perfectly still while he held his hand behind her enormous tactile ears, and gently lifted and pulled them. She responded, brushing her head towards his outstretched hand and curling her long sturdy trunk around his forearm, sniffing him like a dog would greet its master.

The bond was resurrected. She seemed to forget why it was she had ignored him, but this changed as Natasha approached. Having remained perfectly still, while he worked the group watching him in amazement, Lesidwa, began her gently rocking again. From one foot to the other, it was a sign she was agitated, and the big ears began to move, slowly at first, and then flap in earnest. The forty-degree heat for which these huge radiators were designed not the only reason for her flapping.

Aubrey raised his hand motioning Natasha to stay still, and from a distance, Natasha asked.

"Is she nervous because of me?" The question directed at Aubrey, momentarily broke the now silent conversation he was having with Lesidwa.

Aubrey gesticulated with his free hand for Natasha to approach slowly. Domesticated, they were, but she was still a wild elephant and had never been broken like the elephants of India, whose spirits are snapped like a firm hand on a child might. No, these elephants were wild animals, and the luxury of time and gentle coaxing, had provided the source for their modest behaviour. But to push that understanding too far, would turn them rebellious, and the result could be catastrophic.

She approached from the front, where Lesidwa, could see her. As she did, even the poorest of eyesight, gave way to an inquisitive scenting. Aubrey stroked Lesidwa behind her ear and replied.

"The ears are used to cool the blood that rushes through these veins, so she remains cool. But this is too early in the morning for her to be hot."

Natasha from where she was standing replied.

"Do you think it is too soon?" An innate understanding between two Alpha females.

"No. It is good. I have told her you are not a threat to our relationship."

She took another step towards them.

"Now gently stretch out your hand from below your waist, and hold it out so that she can get your scent," Aubrey instructed her from where he was positioned against Lesidwa's shoulder.

Natasha did so, slowly raising her hand, so as not to alarm Lesidwa. As she held it momentarily in front of the beast, Lesidwa, ignored it choosing rather to scent Aubrey from his arm to his head and back again. All the while, Aubrey spoke to her in a calm deep voice that reassured. Then there was a moment when instinctively, Lesidwa, raised her trunk and slowly stretched it towards Natasha's outstretched hand.

She capitulated her natural distrust and within a few minutes was eating pellets from Natasha's outstretched hand. Aubrey knew that they would never leave this country again, and his spiritual journey had only just begun.

The moment with Lesidwa was lost as a group of tourists arrived. They made way for the tourists who gathered nervously alongside the Boma, and Aubrey and Natasha beat a hasty retreat, with Lesidwa raising her trunk and following them symbolically as they headed for the Reception and a familiar face.

A tall elegant woman with a traditional woven head dhuku stood behind the desk, and as she saw them approach, she smiled a broad flash of teeth. That distinctive and alluring smile, that only the local Matabele woman had. She stood with her head gear, at least six feet, and the tribal etching and motif around the top was intermingled with a display of elephant.

'This was new', Aubrey noted, but the thought was lost as he was greeted by Noomsa.

She appeared around the front of the desk arms extended in greeting, and as Aubrey shook her right hand, her left hand held the right wrist, in a common act of supplication. But her hand shake was firm. No limp-wrist greeting one receives from a person of lesser stature. Regal, from the tribe of Lobengula, she had been a member of the local politburo. She had left the youth league politics, when the opposition movement had been strangled in the early eighties. Her father had been a freedom fighter in the ZAPU Patriotic Front of Joshua Nkomo. She had chosen a life out of the political trench war which dominated African Tribal politics. Her name, chosen by none other than Nkomo himself, was her only link to politics. The life expectancy of a politically active member of any opposition to Mugabe in the eighties, was about one year. She had three grown children, but had lost her husband.

The extended family, a facet of normal tribal life in Africa, was no longer there to support her. Her father and mother killed at the hands of the brutal crackdown of the North Korean trained Fifth Brigade, had meant she was to fend for herself; so she had married at sixteen.

"Gukurahundi", a literal translation in the Shona language, was meant to signify the clearing out of any opposition to Mugabe. "The wind that scatters the chaff after the summer rains". An evocative statement about Zimbabwean politics.

The Matabele had opposed Mugabe's attempts to change the constitution and were re-arming as a resistance; so the Fifth Brigade had wiped them off the map. Two siblings had died of AIDS in the nineties, so she was left on her own, bringing up three children with no husband to assist her. Aubrey had chosen her well, and she had stood, literally head and shoulders above all the other candidates for the job.

"How are you, Mr Pennington?" Her eyes were sad, but the spirit still raged within.

She was a survivor, but those eyes were a reflection of her moral fibre.

"It is so good to see you again. Mr Creek had mentioned you would be here." Timothy was in the process of buying a canoe safari company. He would not join them at the Boma.

"Noomsa, it is so good to see you!" Followed by a warm hug.
Aubrey released her, overwhelmed by a normal constraint of intimacy. She was a fine-looking woman, and three children and a decade had not given way to the hefty hips and large posteriors that the local woman were prone to develop.

"This is Natasha!" Noomsa's beaming smile gave way to a warm hand shake, accompanied by a little curtsey. Warmth of sincerity flowed.

There were no divided loyalties, as Aubrey remembered Bronwyn's legacy.

She had held the group of women together during the early days, whilst Aubrey focused on the elephants.

Suddenly from behind the curtain which hid the food preparation area, a loud ululating began. "Uulllllluuuullruuuuuurru."

Natasha, swivelled alarmed by its intensity. Then the first of several women appeared, swaying rhythmically to the beat of a far-off drum.

The woman in single file came out, all dressed in similar fashion to Noomsa, and Natasha smiled and swayed with them. One by one they passed by, curtseying and shaking hands with both Aubrey and Natasha.

"Fantastic", Aubrey beamed. "They all look so well, and you have them groomed beautifully!"

"Yes, but I have to admit the dhuku would not have been my first choice!"

"Oh," replied Aubrey, "It quite becomes you!" A mischievous glint in his sideways glance.

"Let's just say it has its' a little too traditional." Modernistic yearnings, set aside for tourist dollars.

Aubrey felt the surge of a movement away from tribal heritage and ancient customs. The majority of Ndebele from Zimbabwe now wanted to become part of the twenty-first century. Dissipated across the southern region, they now formed a significant number of the Diaspora which numbered three million.

Lobengula would have wiped out the Shona, had his hands not been tied by the British colonialists. The Ndebele, a breakaway tribe from the south. Cousins of the Zulu, and borne of the Nguni tribe, had moved to the southern region of modern day Zimbabwe, to escape Shaka Zulu. Noomsa was a direct descendant of Mzilikazi.

It was the Zulu who had embarked on the Xenophobic attacks on these Zimbabweans, who having fled the oppressive regime of Mugabe, were now been targeted by their own kin. Driven from their homes in the townships around Johannesburg, and killed because of their willingness to perform a hard days labour.
"Yes, Timothy decided to change our outfits last year." Noomsa just smiled. It was unavoidable.

"Well, at least they look smart." Aubrey offered a momentary conciliatory comment. Noomsa just grinned.

"Where is Thabani and Goodman?" Aubrey asked as they sat to a lavish meal.

"AIDS," replied Noomsa, not looking up from her coffee.

The moment was left as a time of silence, in memory of them. He reflected on the plight of so many Zimbabweans, lost to the scourge of AIDS. Made even more poignant by the sheer neglect they had suffered at the hands of a government unwilling to be proactive. These young men and women, victims to a disease which despite being self-inflicted, was no longer a death sentence, with the right care, and the correct education.

The ruling party could have cared less, as long as they were not an encumbrance to Mugabe's political machinations. Ironically, even those who had fallen victim to AIDS would never be labelled as victims of the pandemic, due to deniability. If they officially died of AIDS, no one could be blamed. They all died from Tuberculosis or bronchitis, but never AIDS. It was and remains one of the simple truths of a society at war with itself. No leader would be prepared to stand up and claim their people were dying of neglect. Especially one founded on the premise that the liberation struggle was fought to provide all Zimbabweans with the opportunities and benefits of a previous system, supposedly reserved for a select few.

Despite almost three decades of leadership, Zimbabweans were, still fending for themselves. Only a few in privileged positions got to benefit from the real wealth of the country.

"That's why Britain pulled the plug on them," Aubrey could hear the Professor saying.
"The abuse of funding for the resettlement of the landless was being diverted to the bank accounts of a few ministerial members, and of course into the coffers of the Mugabe gravy train."

"When Claire Short became the Foreign Minister for New Labour, the first task she had was to tell Mugabe and his cronies to get lost."

They appropriately did so, but despite wondering around in international isolation ever since, Mugabe had somehow manoeuvred to retain his political legacy.

Aubrey sat and related his story to Noomsa. She listened intently, a sadness descending on her face as she took in the calamity of the circumstances, which had led to Bronwyn and him parting company.

She had not yet had the courage to tell him the saga that had transpired over the years since his absence. When he had finished telling her about the time he had spent in England, having met Natasha, she seemed to brighten up, but it was fleeting.

"Aubrey! Do you know that Bronwyn was here only a year ago?" It was a statement of fact. They both remained silent a moment. Noomsa was about to continue, when she looked up into Aubrey's face. She stopped.

"What? What is all this intrigue?" remarked Aubrey. "Noomsa. Natasha knows all about Bronwyn!"

The intrigue remained hanging. Aubrey looked at Noomsa and asked.

"Noomsa, enough with this! What do you want to tell me?"

Noomsa, looked over his shoulder at Natasha, and intuitively knew this was neither her place nor privilege. She stood abruptly.

"Natasha needs to talk to you." And with no further ado, she was gone, retreating, the kitchen curtain shrouding the mask of this enigma.

Natasha slipped onto the chair with him, sitting on the edge she held him by the hand, squeezing his palm.

"Aubrey. Last night while I was talking to Gavin, he mentioned something I meant to tell you; but we got side-tracked?" He just nodded; a numbness clouded his soul.

"Well", she continued, "when Gavin told me he was Bronwyn's Uncle I just assumed you would know him."

"However, when he told me why he was in Vic Falls, I never stopped to ask him more, fearing I might be imposing on him."
"However, what he did tell me did not sink in until just now and something Noomsa mentioned." He was waiting for the sucker blow.

"Gavin told me he was here for a memorial service for his grandnephew, I had no idea…." She paused, tears welling in her eyes.

Aubrey looked on; stunned incredulity began to seep through the fog.

He still was not able to put the pieces together; his mind was tripping over the possibilities.

Aubrey just was not able to string it all together. Natasha would have to tell him outright.

"Aubrey! Bronwyn was here as well." She tried desperately to steer him in the right direction.

"She had your child with her!" She stammered. He just looked on.

"His child!" What was she talking about?

"What then was the memorial….service?" He stopped his thought. Shattered by the deduction.

"Oh my God!" It now hit him like a steam train. The horror of it seeped in like a cold wind seeks out the weak. He could feel a chill in his bones like he had all those years ago, looking at that death pyre constructed of a thousand Elephant tusks.

Natasha kneeled before him hugging his legs and placing her head in his lap.

He let out a muffled sigh. The forest treeline was a cloak of verdant catacombs. There was no ending or beginning; one life paid forward.

She held him for a good while, until he leant down and kissed her on the nape. It was his signal that she could sit up, and she sought his eyes. There was a glistening, but little more outward emotion. He would try to be strong for them all. He would honour the memory of his unknown child by finishing what he had come to do.

The Elephants returned, and with them a spiritual blessing. Now he understood Lesidwa's eyes.

"You can tell me the detail later. Right now, I want to spend the rest of the day with my family."

He was up, and in a single stride was out the hall, and into the noon day sunshine, headed for his beloved Eles'. He wanted their emotional support. Throw himself into their tight-knit familiarity. Cherish the sustenance of his other family. Commune with nature, through the souls of these ancient beasts and they may open the portal to the soul of his unknown child.

A new baby Elephant, daughter to Andile; the second eldest of the herd, and son to Pondodo, the oldest male was soon to be joined with the family. The souls of the dear departed would live on forever in the guise of these beasts that would certainly outlive them; God willing and poachers' aside! The renewal of a time and place in the annals of their history would make this the place of choice for all who hungered for peace, and desired to avoid the animosity of a broken society. Willing themselves to heal that community and raise the spectre of a bright future. The holders of the covenant of truth, cherishers of a land which would forever have the Pennington name associated with them.

For in Zimbabwe, they would make their spiritual home, and as with all great societies, there had to be those that had gone before, and carved a place for themselves in the sun.

It stood to reason, that they would be those Pioneers; taking on the new challenges of a separate millennium, and in so doing, rebuilding a revolutionary new social order, founded on love, respect, and the fundamentals of human decency. They would put aside cultural indifference, on which any fledgling society would be bound to fail, and with their spiritual guides, they would find the balance of nature in the needs of the people; resorting to a time when, instead of greed, and self-interest, the community would come first. They need not look any further for this inspiration, than to the wondrous family that greeted them in their triumphant return. "The Elephants".

Printed in Great Britain
by Amazon

22867888R00253